I0716538

MONSTERS NIGHT
THEIR BLOOD
QUEEN
USA TODAY BESTSELLING AUTHOR
J. R. THORN

*You always see through their masks.*
*The men who wear suits and have pretty smiles.*
*But you know what they really are.*
*You don't just choose the bear.*
*You choose the **monster**.*

MONSTER
ISLAND
ELITE
ISLAND

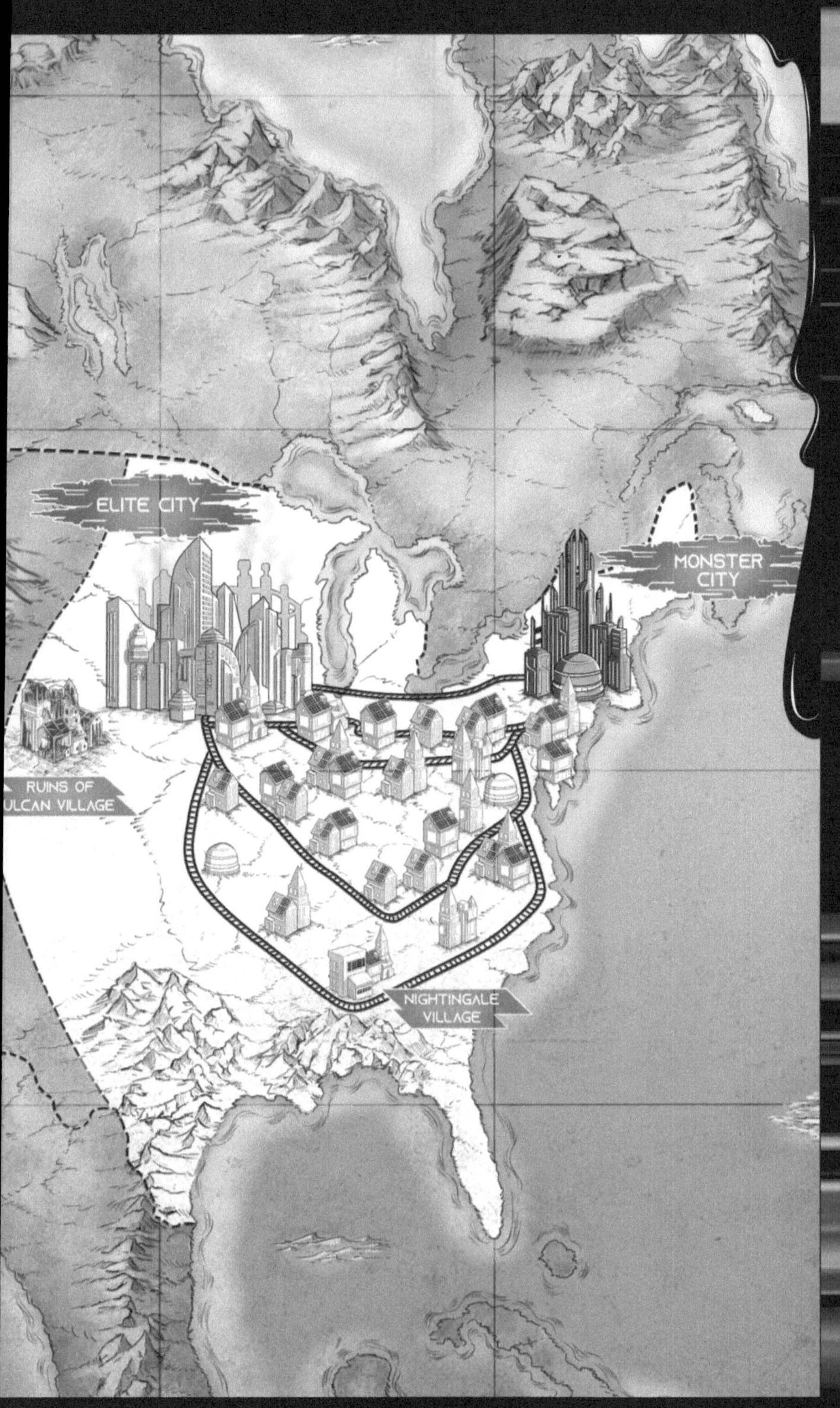

ELITE CITY
MONSTER CITY
RUINS OF
VULCAN VILLAGE
NIGHTINGALE VILLAGE

# Content Warning

Please note that reading these trigger warnings may contain significant spoilers.

There is an explicit dub-con/manipulative sex scene with cheating elements on the page that doesn't involve the FMC (Scarlett) but still may trigger some readers. There is no cheating within the harem. Her guys are all in.

If you would like to enjoy the story without reading this scene, please skip Chapter 21. I've written Chapters 22 and 23 to explain what happened in low detail for those who decide to skip that chapter so you can still follow along. It exists for necessary story context, not shock value.

There is also humiliation and sexual violation without consent in Chapter 32. This is not performed by any of the mates, but they sure are pissed off about it.

Don't worry, Scarlett and her monsters have their revenge.

This book contains disturbing scenes of sexual abuse (not from the harem), death, dismemberment, and graphic content. (Cain wants me to tell you the dismemberment was very much his idea.)

This book has a happy ending, but getting there is one hell of a ride.

—Jen

**Dark Techno:**

**Track 1: Rabbits**
**Track 2: Strigoi**
**Track 3: Sabbath**
**Track 4: Beyond**
**Track 5: Dream**

*Aim to Head Official — Copyright-free music for creators*

Check out J.R. Thorn's YouTube Channel to listen to "Their Blood Queen Mood Playlist" while reading.

**Three sexy vampires haunt my dreams, and they love to make me scream.**
***For all the right reasons.***

The nightmares started on Monsters Night. I figured my overactive libido was just tripping out because of all the monsters on the news. Some portal opened up, and they were terrorizing humans in particular.

But seriously, who hasn't thought about that monster under the bed in a sensual light? There's just something about danger, about fangs, about long tongues...

So, I let the dreams happen. I *invite them in.*

But one night, when I open my eyes and they're literally feasting on me... I realize it's no dream.

This is real.

## Welcome to the Elite City

In a world decimated by monsters, a privileged few remain. This is a story of the Elite City where Dukes and Duchesses rule.

Privilege comes at a price, and that price is to be paid on Monsters Night. Every year, portals open all over the world and monsters descend, ready to claim their new brides. But Monsters Night isn't what it was three hundred years ago. Humanity has dwindled and qualified candidates are sparse.

There are standards to be met.
There are debts to be paid.

Each Elite family owns a pool of humans. They can choose to divvy up their selections however they see fit as long as they remember their three tasks:
1. Maintain resources to feed the city.
2. Increase their human population.
3. Create the perfect mate.
The ultimate prize? Immortality.
Punishment for failure?
*Death.*

So play the game. This is a fight of words and wile. Be careful who you trust, or your family will be next to bleed.

# CHAPTER 1

## SCARLETT

I STARE at the cordial invitation in my grip. Correspondence isn't unusual. I get letters every day.

But this one is written in blood.

My fingers are so tense I'm surprised I don't rip the damn thing. The lighting offered by our new magical fixtures is pleasantly bright, much better than the tallow candles I had to use up until two years ago, allowing me to make out every word clearly. I read the first line three times because I just can't believe it.

*Please accept this formal invitation into the household of the Rinhold estate.*

It's a courtship proposal by the Earl Rinhold, a man I have never been formally introduced to, but know of by reputation.

And it's not a good one.

*I can't believe my father didn't tear this up the moment it came in.*

But there's a reason I was kept waiting in the drawing room while my brother and father spoke privately for hours.

So I keep reading.

The letters are styled in perfect penmanship, and every phrase is crafted with fluid, lyrical prose.

But I've learned to read between the lines. This is an invitation that will end my life as I know it.

My eyes track down the pleasantries and the subtle threats of blackmail I'd expect of a family with eyes everywhere, to the important bit I make sure to dedicate to memory.

*I, Earl of the Rinhold family, hereby offer my courtship terms for the hand of Scarlett Nightingale and the consequential alliance of the Rinhold and Nightingale families, henceforth and thereafter.*

*A bride price will be paid in full upon conclusion of an exclusive courtship at the Rinhold residence to take place in the span of thirty days, in willing agreement by both parties, in the sum of the following proposals:*

*Forty percent of Rinhold's resource village.*

*Eight-and-ten percent of Rinhold's treasury.*

*Three selections from the Rinhold Compound, no limits barred.*

*Should these terms be deemed acceptable, a signature in blood of the lovely Scarlett Nightingale is required. Henceforth, the blood timer of three days will be enacted for the intended to bring her affairs in order, to begin anew at thirty days for the duration of the courtship.*

*Which, as a member of the family with the top selections of last year's Monsters Night within the Magic Sector, I promise will be a lavish and enjoyable affair. I am eagerly awaiting your reply.*

*The terms of this contract expire at midnight.*

*May Cain's blessings be bestowed upon you and yours.*

*Sincerely,*

*Earl Rinhold*

My lower lip is quivering, and I sink my teeth into it before my father can reprimand me.

There was a reason he took me to the largest drawing room typically reserved for hosting and made me squirm while he and my brother decided my fate.

He wanted to remind me of what he's been working toward and the importance of this proposal.

All of our reserves had gone into this room, decorating it with three diamond chandeliers cast in gold, an appropriate arrangement of exquisitely lavish furniture, and two stories of portraits of my father's predecessors, as well as an obnoxiously large one of the monster in charge of our city.

As if Cain would actually ever pay us a visit.

But, just in case, my father had the painting commissioned after selling my mother's last jewels to pay for it.

I find myself staring up at the monstrosity, mostly because I hadn't seen it since it was installed, along with the broken mirror shards that make up its border. With all of the perfection of the room, the fractured shards add a refreshing touch.

Within them, a perfect male oversees the drawing room, and his depiction is not the creature one might expect of the Godlike ruler of the Elite City. It seems rude to paint him in his human form, but no one has ever seen his monster one.

*Maybe it only exists in dreams.*

That thought should give me the chills, but I find it an intriguing distraction from my current state of panic.

His human form is striking, of course. Most monsters are beautiful when they want to be. He has piercing blue eyes that are so light I toy with the idea that they might be mirrors, too. His hair is composed of sleek, midnight locks, and he has a sinfully beautiful face made of dreams.

There are different monster classifications, but Cain is

the ruler of our city for a reason. There aren't others like him that I have ever heard of. Most worship him, and those who have disappointed him, well, they don't live very long to talk about it.

But long enough for the entire city to give his monster side a name.

Cain is a Dream Eater.

*Dream Eater, huh? Maybe he can eat me before Earl Rinhold does.*

The absurd thought comes out of nowhere, and a nervous laugh bubbles in the back of my throat.

Because, for some reason, the idea of Cain *eating me* inspires very different images than the Earl.

"Scarlett," my father says, jolting me from my thoughts.

My father looks nothing like Cain's portrait. He's attractive for a man of his age, but he's growing older. Shadows sink under his eyes, and a new wrinkle has appeared across his forehead. His dark hair is usually styled, but tonight a curl just above his brow has become undone, probably because he's been sweeping his fingers through it. His prized pocket watch makes a circular outline in his vest, leaving a recently cleaned chain to loop down to a golden button on his tailored ensemble.

"Finished?" he asks, likely referring to the letter, not my gawking at Cain's portrait.

His tone isn't unkind, but it holds a warning, probably because I've been gripping the letter too hard and it looks like it's about to tear.

I catch my older brother staring at me from his lounged position behind my father. He looks irritated as he flips a coin over his fingers, but he's not saying anything.

However, I can read the truth under his mask all the same.

*Her pretty little red head probably has no idea what that*

*letter said. It doesn't matter. The only requirement was that she read it. Hopefully, she signs it and we can get on with this nonsense.*

I realize that it's entirely possible my father wouldn't have allowed me to read the letter had it not been a binding blood contract.

Which meant there was magic involved, requiring me to read it for the agreement to be legal.

Where there's magic... there are monsters.

My gaze briefly flicks to Cain's portrait, making me frown.

*Did his eyes just blink?*

Shaking my head, I give my father a small nod. He reaches over and tugs at the top until I will my fingers to release the parchment. It slides through my grip, leaving a sting when he plucks it from my grasp a little too quickly.

I curl my fingers into fists before any of my blood can get on the blasted letter.

*I am* not *signing that.*

*I don't care what they're offering.*

My father might have sold everything in our estate that wasn't nailed down to bring us this far, but he can't sell *me*.

Staring at him, I hope to see some sense. Instead, I see the desperate truth in my father's dark eyes, which have grown harder over the years. No matter how much I wish he wouldn't do this, I know he will. I've always been able to read others, and my father is no exception.

*I don't want to do this,* his eyes seem to say. *But you'll thank me when we make it to the Immorality Sector.*

*When I save your mother from this illness, every dark deed will be repaid in all the good I can do.*

What good will there be if my father loses his soul to this damn plight?

Will my mother even want to survive when she finds out I've been left behind with a family like the *Rinholds*?

The villages fear the monsters, and the Elites do, too.

But I fear men most of all.

Especially a man like Earl Rinhold.

I can't quite hear my father's thoughts, but his intentions are as clear to me as if I had.

The truth is outlined in every part of him.

The recently cleaned pocket watch.

The new golden cuff links to match.

He's not my father right now.

He's Duke Nightingale, who has just been given an offer he can't refuse. And with my wicked brother in his ear, he's beyond the point of reasoning with.

He must see the determination lining my face, because he plucks out his pocket watch and clicks his tongue.

"We have five-and-ten minutes until midnight, Scarlett. Whatever arguments you have, be quick about it."

My brother rises to his feet with a sigh and pockets his coin, one of the few valuables we have left that he refuses to part with. Usually, he stays in my father's shadow, but tonight Duke Nightingale seems to be wearing his mask.

And that means Earl Nightingale gets to teach me my place.

I'm not a Duchess. Both my father and my brother would have to die for me to take over on my own. Since they are both very alive and capable, I'm simply the daughter of an Elite, Lady Nightingale. That gives me certain privileges. But when it comes to the matter of alliances, dowries are taken very seriously.

And in my case, this is a reverse dowry.

A bride price.

And a substantial one at that. Even if I don't fully

comprehend all the terms, I can see the look on my father's face that it could change everything.

My lip starts quivering again, and I take a deep breath —at least, I try to. The corset I've been tied up in for tonight's events has me wishing I had been born with fewer ribs.

My brother doesn't have any problems breathing, mostly because he's wearing his traditional Earl apparel that includes a frilly undershirt tucked beneath a fitted— but not *tight*—embroidered vest. He dresses the part, topping off his look with long, polished boots with golden buttons that match my father's vest.

He kneels down on one knee, putting himself at eye level with me in my seated position. Every presentation of his posture and his expression demonstrates care and empathy, but I've always been able to see through the mask.

He's about to infuriate me.

"Aren't you excited, dear sister?" he asks with a charming smile that shows his stupid dimples.

Gently, I remove my teeth from my throbbing lip, ignoring the tang of blood that's on my tongue. "M-mother wouldn't approve of a Rinhold alliance, not when—" I begin, but the crack across my face shocks me into silence.

I stare at the floor for a moment, stunned, trying to process what just happened.

*Did Laurence just strike me?*

My brother has never laid a hand on me. My father wouldn't have allowed it, but when I glance up at him, I still see Duke Nightingale looking back at me.

He doesn't come to my rescue.

He doesn't correct my brother's crass behavior.

Instead, he smooths the contract out onto the table.

Then he pulls a short, delicate knife from his pocket and holds it out to me.

"I'm sorry, Scarlett," my father says, still gripping the tiny blade. "We have all had to sacrifice for this family. Your mother and I have tried to spare you, but we're out of options. It's time for you to pull your weight."

I don't know where I find the will, but I shakily rise to my feet and tilt up my chin, ignoring my brother, who is now towering over me.

Let him strike me again. Maybe I'll faint, either due to another slap to the face or from this blasted corset choking the life out of me.

They won't get their damn signature then.

My cheek stings as I clench my jaw, carefully weighing my words. My skin is pale, so I know the mark must be swelling on my face. Anywhere I go, I'm required to bring a parasol to protect my skin from the sun.

*"Wouldn't want you mistaken for a villager, now would we?"* my mother would always say. The sun has a tendency to bring out the freckles hidden underneath my skin.

My father can't be reasoned with, but he still needs me to willingly sign the document to get his way.

They can't force me.

*Right?*

He again glances at his pocket watch still in his grip, and I see the minute hand inch closer to midnight.

The lights flicker for a moment, making us all go silent. We've been in the Magic Sector for two years, but we've never had the lights go out.

When they stabilize, I take a shaky breath. Maybe I'm imagining things.

"Does Mother know about this?" I ask, mildly impressed that my voice doesn't hold the tremor I'm hiding underneath the boning of my corset.

"She went into a coma three days ago," my brother curtly informs me, earning my attention immediately. I jerk my chin up at him as my eyes go round with surprise.

"Why did no one tell me?" I demand.

But it explains why I haven't been allowed to see her. My father couldn't afford any *hysterics* during the past three days, not when he was hosting various families in an attempt to build alliances.

One of those visitors had been Duke Rinhold, and now I know it was no coincidence that I had been in his view. I'd been placed like a shiny new doll in a window, my position just outside of the drawing room in one of the smaller reading nooks.

With a new corset and dress that we couldn't afford, no less.

Hosting in the Magic Sector requires that all family members don a certain type of attire. For a Lady such as myself, that attire includes a suffocating corset that makes my boobs practically pop out. I hate that particular article of clothing, but the quiet time with a book almost makes up for it.

Almost.

"You've been *trying* to get a courtship proposal," I realize with a scathing accusation, now pointing my wrath toward my father.

His jaw flexes, betraying the truth once again.

*Yes, Scarlett.*

*You're more valuable than you could possibly know—but now... Now we have no choice.*

"Ten minutes," my father announces after checking his watch again. "I know this is a burden to place on your delicate shoulders, dear daughter. But your mother has taken an unfortunate turn. She won't last much longer past this Monsters Night."

The annual Monsters Night is mere days away.

A hiccup sticks in the back of my throat, and I shove it down.

"Do you know what that means?" my brother asks. His words are slimy and sickly sweet, as if he's coating them with poison just for me. "If we don't reach the Immortality Sector this year, it'll be too late. Don't be a whiny bitch, Scarlett. You'll become a Duchess of a family much more powerful than ours. You have nothing to complain about."

I flick my gaze to my father to see if he'll correct my brother's crude words, but he doesn't.

Because I know he feels that he can't. He loves his wife even more than he loves me.

And we both know I was adopted for a reason. She wanted a daughter, but her illness made her barren after my brother, so my father took me in when I was just a little girl.

I was a present for her, and even if he grew to love me, his wife has always come first.

We don't speak of my origins, but my bright red hair is a reminder for those who know the truth.

I'm not from here. No amount of voice training lessons or etiquette classes can change where I was born.

I'm from the *other side*.

I was always meant to be a sacrifice.

"She won't forgive you," I tell my father. My words are barely a whisper, but I can't hide the hurt that drips from them with my unshed tears.

Even if this works. Even if this saves her life and my family achieves immortality, my mother will never forgive him for this.

Or maybe he thinks that eventually she will. Eternity is a long time to try to earn back her trust.

The darkness in his eyes flickers, those chocolate

browns in his gaze briefly coming out as my adoptive father peeks through.

The one who loves me. The one who loves his family and wants nothing more than to dote on us and give us everything.

But he believes he's been cornered. He believes there's no choice.

*There's always a choice.*

"At least she'll be alive to hate me," he says as his dark mask slips back over his face.

I know it's going to stay there this time.

For now, my father is gone.

And Duke Nightingale is all that remains.

I find myself looking at Cain's portrait. I've never prayed to him, but the absurd desire to overcomes me, and I find myself whispering the words so quietly that it feels as if only my lips move.

*"Watch over me, Cain."*

I pause as a strange chill runs up my spine after uttering those words. I stare at the portrait, and it seems to expectantly stare back, so I continue.

*"If I do this, I'm going to do it for my mother. I don't want her to die. But please, please make it worth it. Watch over me and protect me."*

The air seems to ripple around the portrait, and shadows unfurl behind the mirrors, making my eyes go wide.

When I blink, the strange textures are gone.

I try to breathe again but struggle. I decide my corset is just too tight, and I'm starting to see black spots, so I continue my prayer before I pass out.

*"I'm going to need all the help I can get... if I'm going to be Earl Rinhold's bride."*

When I glance back at my brother and my father, I feel

like I'm outnumbered. A rumble passes through the room, making me peek at the walls to search for a storm that must be building overhead.

But there aren't any windows here, only portraits to make anyone under the Duke's gaze feel small and trapped and *watched*.

It doesn't much matter if there's a storm or not. I won't be going outside anytime soon to find out. My father looks like he's about to stab me with the dagger himself, but he can't.

I have to do this willingly.

"Is there no other way?" I ask, my chest deflating. Prayers to a monster are only going to get me so far.

My father's shoulders sink, and I realize there's more he's been hiding under his mask. "It's not just about your mother, Scarlett. I've spent all our money on medicine. Every coin. If we fail to reach the Immortality Sector this year to wipe our slate clean, it's possible we will *all* be killed during the culling."

The blood drains from my face.

Every family is expected to pay a tribute to the collective pot once a year.

The culling makes an example of any of the families who fail in that endeavor.

Moving to the Magic Sector opened up opportunities, but I knew it increased expectations of our family, too.

There is a cost to run a city like this, one full of monsters and men.

I've come to learn that the men are the ones who devour everything.

"We don't have enough points for Monsters Night?" I finally ask.

My father's mask stays in place, but his eyes darken with grief he's desperately trying to hide. "There are some promising tributes from the village this year, but... they might not be enough for the quota expected of a family in the Magic Sector. No."

My brother scoffs. "You mean we ran out of bribes to keep our quota threshold down because you spent them all on *medicine*." His jaw flexes as if he's debating the words coming out of his mouth next, but he says them anyway. "I've told you before, I could steal it from—"

"Careful," my father interrupts, giving my brother a stern look. "Stealing is a grave offense."

"Even from rival families?" my brother grumbles.

"Even from rival families," my father confirms. "We don't steal. Period. It's against the rules."

We don't question the rules.

And we certainly don't break them.

Breaking the rules comes with a price.

That price is death.

Now I understand the true level of my father's desperation. If we don't even have enough points to survive another Monsters Night, everything we've sacrificed won't matter. We'll be dead.

*What have you done, Father?*

With the new danger revealed, my brother's cordial kindness slips, and his cruel expression frightens me. His features seem sharper than usual, as if he might simply cut me with his brown-eyed gaze alone.

His eyes are even darker than my father's tonight.

He leans down and curls a lock of hair behind my ear, then presses his lips up against my cheek as he whispers a threat that has my heart going still.

"If you don't do this, Scarlett, I'm going to make your life a living hell. The monsters might let us live another cycle, and if they do, I will wait for Mother to die, watch our father dwindle into a corpse, and then take my rightful place as Duke. After that, I'm going to sell you off to the highest bidder regardless. I might even let Earl Rinhold have a taste before I do. So be a good girl and *sign the fucking contract.*"

We all jump as a hiss comes from the painting.

I stare at it with wide eyes, now sure that the mirrored eyes are looking at me.

I don't know what compels me to grab the dagger from my father. I'm running on adrenaline as I stab it into my finger, then I sign my name on the contract and shudder when the icy spell drapes over me like a shroud.

*It's done.*

*I was always meant to be a sacrifice.*

Blood drips from my finger and collects on the floor, the sound the only one in the room.

We all stare at the contract as it sizzles into finality. My arm stings, and I don't have to look down at it to know three slashes are appearing on my skin.

One for each day I have left in the Nightingale residence.

Three days to say goodbye to my life.

Before the true nightmare begins.

# CHAPTER 2

## CAIN

*A few moments earlier...*

"Will you take a mate thisss year, Cain?" Helia asks, her *s* slipping on her tongue.

I don't answer right away. Instead, I sigh and evaluate how serious she is about the dangerous prospect of a monster like me attempting to take a mate.

Again.

Usually, it's a joke after what happened on the other failed attempts, but this year I sense she might mean it.

If she's concerned enough to risk the life of prized selections better suited to build alliances, then perhaps I should start to worry, too.

She's wearing her monster form, so that makes it more difficult to read her intentions. She has the freedom to show her true self whenever she likes, and I try not to indulge in the sense of envy her freedom gives me. It's a luxury I don't share, even though Helia's true nature is almost as terrifying and beautiful as mine.

A long, pointed tail curls over her thigh.

Horns twist through her silky hair.

And a third eyelid flashes at me as she waits for my answer.

I'm looking at her face-to-face, which is a feat, given how tall she is in this form. In my current human state, she would engulf me if she weren't lounging.

But if I were in my true form, I'd be even bigger than she is.

She's resting on an elegant chaise lounge, seemingly at ease despite the excitement of an approaching Monsters Night. The white velvet of the furniture makes her purple skin stand out as she curls her long nails through a male's hair. The tattoo on his cheek marks him as one of the slave servants in Monster City, but it's his behavior that betrays his training. Despite the terrifying creature stroking him, he's currently kneeling obediently on the floor.

Humans serve a different purpose in Monster City than they do here. But their reward is the same as what the winning Elite families achieve in mine, so I don't pity them. They willingly sold their mortal lives into slavery, fully knowing what they were signing up for, all because of the prize at the end of the journey.

Everyone wants immortality.

I find it overrated.

Perhaps because I've lived long enough to know that there are things worse than death.

Like starvation and the threat of insanity.

My monster growls inside my soul, snapping at me to demonstrate his impatience. After so many years of wearing my human form, my mind has begun to separate from him out of self-preservation.

Because he's always hungry now, voraciously so. The only thing keeping him sated are the prayers of the Elites and some villagers who know my name.

Prayers have suited me thus far, mostly because I can't track my prey in the Dream Realm. I can only feed on what's freely given to me. I need to be invited in. Perhaps there are loopholes for such an invitation, but I have managed to create a system in my city that's entirely voluntary.

Maybe that's why I've never met any others like me. What creature would willingly give themselves to a monster?

But I discovered that prayers do the trick, enabling me to survive a lot longer than I probably should have.

Playing the role of a God has served me well, but it's a tactic that only works if I'm feared and worshipped.

As another brief wave of prayers feeds my dark beast, I flutter my eyelids closed for a moment to give him a snack.

He needs to stay in the shadows.

Stay in the realm of prayers and dreams.

I don't allow my monster form to peek through outside of carefully controlled stipulations.

He can't have free rein. Not ever.

Because it's not just a matter of appearance for me. When I allow my dark side to play, I lose control.

The Dream Eater takes over.

That can never happen. Not in a city full of fragile humans.

I only let him out in a controlled fashion, sacrificing an Elite family every now and then who hasn't met the unreasonable point quota I'm forced to raise every year.

The last time I released him, though, my beast consumed an entire village. Not everyone in that village deserved their fate.

Most villages fear the monsters when they shouldn't.

Me? I should definitely be feared. I don't want an innocent to die, but when my true nature escapes, I'm dangerous.

No one is safe.

I can't let him out again if the delicate ecosystem we've developed here is going to survive.

I'm not the only powerful monster suffering.

That is why qualified mates are more valuable than fodder. Genetic manipulation and generations of selection have created unique humans that are much needed by our kind. A mate can stabilize a powerful monster, as can other monsters in tandem with the right anchor if their types complement one another.

I've never met a monster who suited mine, not in this world, at least.

And any human I've tried to mate hasn't survived. Whatever genetics a Dream Eater requires, I've yet to discover it.

The growling in my head rumbles. My beast snaps inside my soul, hungry for more, but there aren't any further prayers right now.

Prayers come during times of desperation.

Of suffering.

Perhaps, it's time to bring them out again.

"That depends," I tell Helia's reflection in my two-story window that overlooks the Elite City. She always asks me if I'm going to take a mate, and I always respond the same way. "Are you?"

I take a sip of my whiskey that rolls around like caramel on forever ice—a fabulous product created by the Magic Sector just five years ago.

Her plump lips stretch into a grin, revealing deadly teeth and a long tongue that flicks out to taste the air. "You know I prefer my playthings," she says, still petting the male bowing his head in submission. Her smile dims as she evaluates me. "You seem tired, Cain. Do you need me to send some gifts? I have a few pets to spare."

The male at her feet shivers but doesn't protest.

Any *gifts* for my beast won't survive a true feed.

"No gifts," I tell her, earning a scowl from the Queen of Monster City. She doesn't wear a crown, but her horns and glimmering hair that seems to float on an invisible wind are crown enough.

She rules by power alone, just like I do as the Elite City King.

She's a better ruler than I am. The city lights blink through her, my magic that allows me to speak to her working only through reflections, so I can't truly appreciate her form in its entirety.

Mirrors are portals to other worlds, as well as faraway places.

Like Monster City, the hub between the ever-increasing realms and dimensions, with new monsters appearing every year.

New opportunities.

New alliances.

New *hope*.

"What about me?" she whispers innocently, but the wickedness in her sharp, silvery gaze is anything but.

We were lovers, once.

It nearly destroyed this realm. Helia brings out the worst in me, and I in her.

And the fact that she brings it up now means she's definitely feeling off.

"You know what would happen," I casually inform her as I allow my gaze to shift through her and focus on the city instead. "Perhaps I do need a mate, though."

But does such a mate truly exist?

It's been centuries of cultivating the highest-quality

mates for even the most powerful monsters, but one has never been born for me.

None that has ever survived, anyway.

*Maybe not all monsters are worthy of one.*

I certainly have done unspeakable things. No matter what excuses I try to make, I am a monster through and through.

A soft hiss comes from the reflection, and I flick my focus back to Helia's dark form. A shimmer of scales ripples over her body. She rarely wears any clothes. Her naked appearance isn't very human in that her breasts are full and rounded with no nipples—any spawn she might create wouldn't feed on milk.

The dip between her thighs is solidified, and it only opens when aroused and ready to mate. It's not unusual for powerful female monsters to have bodies that naturally protect themselves against procreation with the wrong specimen.

If a male can't arouse her, he's not worthy.

Her nakedness doesn't bother me. It isn't lewd. Rather, it's attractive in a fascinating way. She looks as if she's wearing a tight suit made of silky amethyst and it's styled perfectly for her long frame.

However, some things about her have changed.

I frown at the unusual spikes that sprout along her forearms and the new armored scales that indent around her abdomen and chest—areas that cover vital organs.

Even Helia has a heart in there somewhere.

The male beneath her whimpers, her nails having gone to his nape in a punishing grip. Blood trickles from the slight punctures she has created.

"Helia?" I ask, because this isn't like her.

She's not *cruel* to her playthings.

And her monster form seems to be preparing for battle

and sex all at the same time, something I've never seen it do.

A tremor goes through her when I say her name, as if I've reminded her that we're still talking. She flicks out her tongue and gently releases the male. He scrunches in on himself as though trying to become small.

"Go, Jason. I've no further need of you," she says, and if I'm not mistaken, I swear I can hear a note of apology in her tone.

"Yes, Your Majesty," he whispers, then folds himself onto the floor in prostration before rising and exiting the room, never turning his back to her.

They train them well in Monster City.

But Helia doesn't seem to be her whimsical self, as much as she's trying to hide it.

Something's wrong.

"I've felt off these past few years," she admits with her gaze still watching the space where Jason had once been. "My playthings don't amuse me anymore. Perhaps I've outgrown them."

I don't mention the obvious.

Perhaps her mate has finally been born.

It's too cruel to tease her with the prospect that her suffering might be over, that her mate might be out there.

But I find myself feeling hopeful that at least one of us will make it through this Monsters Night alive.

I set my glass down and cross my arms. Out of sheer force of will, lights flicker out in the city so I can see her better. I frown, realizing some lights are going out inside Elite homes, so I keep those on.

I just need to see Helia better, not thrust my city into a state of panic.

Of course, I could transition our discussion to one of the

mirrors in my estate, but I prefer to keep a watchful eye on the city while we talk.

She's calmed the spikes from her forearms, lowering them to gentle nubs, but the armored scales on her body remain. She stands, forcing me to look up at her as she stretches to her full height.

I'm in awe of her beast.

And afraid that she's becoming just like me.

A monster with no control and no remorse.

"Perhaps you should adopt your human form for a while," I suggest. If there is a mate out there for her, he'll be less intimidated by her more forgiving human form—it's more forgiving in both behavior and appearance.

Her thin brow furrows as her tail flicks around her feet. "And become divided like you, Cain? You chain yourself up every Monsters Night to prevent yourself from losing control of your other half. We all deal with the struggle of our situation differently. You handle the hunger your way; I'll handle mine how I see fit."

I don't rebuke her, because she's not wrong.

There's a price to my method, one that's making me slowly go insane.

Neither of us says it, but we're both thinking it.

*We need to find ourselves mates.*

"Did you know there's a new world joining us for Monsters Night?" Helia asks, deflecting to the true purpose of our meeting.

I raise a brow, that piece of information grabbing my interest. "What kind of world?" I ask, finding it odd that she didn't call it a new realm. There are so many that we couldn't possibly have documented them all yet. My desk is full of biometric and cultural summaries of new monsters to help me guide the Elite City families in their genetic endeavors. With every new alliance Helia forms, thanks to the mates my humans provide, the closer we come to solving an age-old problem for our kind.

Stability.

Safety.

Peace.

My beast growls inside my soul, snapping at the asinine idea that we'll ever find peace.

*Eat,* he seems to say. *Fuck. Devour. Live to see another blood-spotted day.*

Helia grins while she settles onto her chaise lounge, this time sitting as she crosses her legs. Her tail drapes over her knee, providing some modesty.

Not that Helia is modest, but she doesn't want to provoke my hungry beast.

Despite her flirtations and her teasing, she knows better than I do what kind of destruction we would cause together. She maintains full lucidity when in her monster form because she hasn't "divided" herself like I have, as she puts it.

Meaning she has to live with the horrors in all their brutal vibrancy. At least my memories of my monster's form are hazy and dreamlike.

If I try to grab on to them, they seem to slip away.

But there's a lilt of hope in her voice again, because she must have sensed the new energies and that excites her. "A powerful one full of possibilities," she marvels.

Well, that certainly is interesting.

A new realm with new monsters might join us this year.

And new monsters bring new energies. I've already noticed the stir in the magical currents that run through the Elite's strategically placed villages. I should have attributed that to whatever it is Helia has sensed.

But I don't have her power. My magic rests in the realm of dreams.

She runs Monster City, which strategically sits at the hub of the largest influx of exchanging energies from the other realms we have built alliances with, and the train tracks link that energy to the villages.

It's a system that has successfully created biologically and magically compatible humans over the course of many generations.

And careful selections as well. That's where human discernment and ambition come into play.

Pitting the Elites against one another to create perfectly compatible specimens was a brilliant idea—Helia's, in fact.

The Elites thought their proposal had been a human invention, but Helia had been the one to cultivate this world.

In hopes of helping monsters like herself, like me.

Oh, she has helped so many monsters.

But not *us*.

And time seems to be running out.

"There's a hide-and-peek portal that keeps popping up," she continues. "Every time it does…"

My eyes widen. "You feel a new realm?"

"New dimension, I think," she corrects me.

We've run into new worlds quite often, but a new dimension is something we've rarely encountered.

Her tail flicks. "I've come to a decision. If they join us for Monsters Night, I won't intervene. I might even send them an offer, should things go well. Let's watch them and see if any of the selections take. Then we can build an alliance with this powerful dimension."

I nod, interested in the idea of new monsters coming to play.

Sometimes the transition can be tricky, but it gives my beast something different to focus on.

And then there's—

*"Watch over me, Cain."*

A feminine voice I've definitely never heard before slips into the Dream Realm and shoots through me like an arrow, making my entire body shift as my beast reacts with violent hunger.

He eats up those four words immediately, not even stopping to appreciate how sweet they taste.

My tongue swells in my mouth, and the decadent flavor of a new prayer makes me shudder when I take a breath.

*Who the fuck is that?*

# CHAPTER 3

# CAIN

*HER PRAYER TASTES... delicious.*

I lick my lips as my jaw aches, long canines poking through when my beast chooses to feed on a little blood with his dreams.

Before I can rein him in, the new worshipper continues as if completely unaware of the danger she's put herself in.

Because my beast *wants* her.

Not just to feast... but to fuck.

*"If I do this, I'm going to do it for my mother. I don't want her to die. But please, please make it worth it."*

"Cain?" Helia says with a sharp note of worry in her voice, but I'm not looking at her reflection anymore.

My vision has fluctuated as my beast's form crawls over my skin, making me grow in size.

I'm slipping into the Dream Realm. I'm powerless against the siren call that draws my beast like a moth to a flame.

There's a mirror in the room where she's praying, and my essence settles into it.

I can't see her, not yet. I'm fighting the frenzy threatening to descend on my beast if she continues to pray.

"*Watch over me and protect me,*" she says, making my monstrous cock go rock-hard.

Fuck yes.

My beast consumes this part of her prayer, but more slowly than before, finally savoring the incredible taste of sun-kissed peaches mixed in wine.

With enough prayers to strengthen my beast, bolstered by her willing trust for me to *protect her*, a blurry view of the room she's occupying comes through. The clarity reveals two dark figures and a female bathed in red.

Is she on fire?

No, that's the color of her hair and her dress.

*Beautiful,* I think as she continues praying, allowing me to see the detail of her delicate frame and pushed-up breasts.

She's a Lady of one of the Elite families, but I've definitely never seen her before.

Because she's never prayed to me.

*Not a believer?* I wonder with amusement.

I like her already.

But I'm intrigued by what has her desperate enough to call for me. She mentioned something about her mother, but what is it she's going to *do*?

"*I'm going to need all the help I can get...*" she continues.

Each word intended for my ears gives my beast more power to work with. Prayers are similar to dreams, and I've never tasted a dream as satisfying as this.

I'm in an almost drug-like state, content to listen to her speak until she finishes her sentence.

"*... if I'm going to be Earl Rinhold's bride.*"

Glass shatters, and I realize I've destroyed the window

in my suite overlooking the city. A powerful wind rushes into the room, sweeping my hair back from my face.

A roar rips from my throat as I'm cut off from the female who has decided to end her prayer. I'm taller now, fully extended in my eight-foot-nine frame.

"Cain!" Helia shouts in my face, startling me.

She's somehow here, having traveled from Monster City to my suite.

*She formed a portal.*

She shouldn't have done that. It's a unique power that I had almost forgotten Helia even possessed. She's one of the few powerful enough to have the ability in the first place, but it still severely drains her to use it.

It's why we have trains.

It's why we conserve resources and utilize reflections and mirrors.

"Helia, I'm sorry," I say as I curl my fingers into fists. My claws dig into my skin, drawing dark blood.

My vision wavers as my beast clings to the mirror he found in that room.

He doesn't want to leave her, but I know who she is now.

Because I created the blood contract that has made her desperate enough to pray to me for the first time.

And penning it might have been the biggest mistake of my life.

Because the blood on it is mine.

Binding me to its terms just as much as her.

"Who is Earl Rinhold?" Helia asks as she rests a hand on my shoulder. I'm slightly taller than her now.

It's a miracle my teeth haven't ripped into her throat to get her out of the way so I can scour the city for the female.

But I'm keeping a handle on my beast. He wasn't supposed to come out, and he only slipped for a moment.

I pull him back in, inch by inch, while he's distracted. Helia's portal ripped open magic energies, giving me a wave to ride.

*Thank you,* I think at her, even though I know she can't hear my words.

She doesn't feed on prayers.

My monster doesn't seem to notice as I slowly shrink in size.

And now he's listening to the female with rapt attention as he slowly sinks into the back of my mind where Helia's question rattles around like a bad omen.

*"Who is Earl Rinhold?"*

"A dead man," I growl, even though I know I can't kill him.

Not if this female whose prayers taste like peaches signs the contract.

It protects him for the duration of the courtship. And if she chooses to agree to the proposal after thirty days, the union will be permanently binding.

I can't have her.

She's not mine.

*"Sign the fucking contract,"* a male voice says, making my beast snarl with unfiltered rage.

He wants to kill the owner of that voice.

Badly.

Whereas I want to kill Earl Rinhold.

No one should be able to hear my beast from the Dream Realm, but the occupants in the room all shift their attention to the mirror he is hiding in.

*What the fuck is going on?*

Before I have time to process this apparent new ability to cross realms, pain slices through my heart when the female stabs her finger. Her name scrawls out in front of my vision in perfect clarity written in her own blood.

*Scarlett Nightingale.*

I struggle to retain my human form before my beast takes over completely and does something that could kill us both.

*She's not ours,* I tell my Dream Eater half.

*It's too late.*

He growls in return, not caring about rules or contracts.

But I do.

If I lay a hand on Earl Rinhold, it will force the contract to prematurely end.

And anyone who interferes with a blood contract will die.

"Cain, I need you to talk to me," Helia says as she gently squeezes my shoulder.

She towers over me now, and I look up at her monstrous form, which is rippling with spent energy. "I'm in control," I assure her.

I'm definitely not in control, but at least I'm keeping my beast tucked away in the Dream Realm instead of trans-forming my body again.

Or maybe he's staying there willingly, waiting for the delectable female to pray to us again.

Helia grimaces and drops her hand, then she does something she very rarely decides to do.

Or is rarely forced to do. Her monster is a difficult one to tame, but Helia has always rationed her energy reserves carefully.

Now, it melts into her skin as if trying to take over. Helia growls in response.

Her body shimmers and shifts as she shrinks, trans-forming into her human figure. It's one I've only seen on a handful of occasions when she overextended herself.

She'd rather give up her monster than be controlled by it. In that regard, we are the same.

Purple shadows mist over her as she changes. She flutters her long eyelashes as she exhales, pushing away her natural form. Nipples develop on her breasts, and her horns recede as her long, luxurious hair grows even longer, draping over her shoulders. Her skin is lusciously dark but shimmers with purple hues in the right light.

The powerful wind through the broken window rips over her, making her hair fling over her body.

Normally, I'd be interested in this form of hers.

But all I can see is the redhead lingering in my dreams.

She glances at me and doesn't seem to like what she sees in my eyes. "You're not in control. The Dream Eater is," she says as she snatches up a blanket from one of my couches. It's large enough to wrap around her now small frame. "I suggest you focus on finding yourself a mate before it's too late, Cain. And since you just forced me to accelerate my timeline, I'm going to have to find mine."

She marches to one of the guest rooms that no female has visited in quite a long time, but she remembers where I keep the wardrobes for guests.

Or gifts.

She emerges after a few minutes with a skin-tight dress, a stringed corset I have no idea how she got into by herself, and a feathered hat with a long, fluffy black feather to match.

She pulls on black lace gloves that go all the way to her elbow while her silvery eyes narrow on me. It's the only part of her that gives her away.

"When does the train leave?" she asks.

"Three days," I say, knowing from memory that's how much time my mate has until she must begin her courtship.

*Not mine,* I remind myself.

Some trains will leave in less than two days, but the one

Helia needs to promptly return to Monster City is still waiting on new cargo.

New *selections*.

Helia gives me a subtle nod as the wind threatens to rip the hat off her head. She grips the end to prevent it from flying away. "Then I'll spend the night to recharge and portal myself back in the morning. If you need me, you know where to find me." She raises a dark, elegant brow. "I suggest you pay a visit to this Earl Rinhold before your Dream Eater does, Cain."

I swallow back my beast's growl.

"A visit," I repeat, wondering how I'm going to manage that without ripping into the male's throat.

Perhaps a visit to the female would be safer. It might subdue my other half enough to make that possible.

One-on-one with the female sounds much more appealing anyway. But I can't meet her in reality. I'd be too tempted to take what isn't mine.

I could meet her in her dreams, though. It wouldn't violate the blood contract because any acts performed in the Dream Realm wouldn't be real.

But they would *feel* real.

As long as she prays to me again, I'll have access to her mind.

She's done it once. The act can be addictive, so I'm certain she'll pray to me again.

*See you soon, little star.*

*In your dreams, at least.*

*You're mine.*

*For now.*

# CHAPTER 4

# SCARLETT

My cheek is still stinging when I return to my chambers. My face is flushed, and rage is making my jaw hurt.

I stab my heels into the soft rug along this corridor, hopelessly annoyed that my march to my room is a quiet one.

I want to scream and tear the paint off the wall. I want to find my brother and claw my nails down his stupid face.

I want to go *feral*.

That would be a great way to sign my death warrant, so, like the properly trained Lady I am, I stuff every single violent urge into a little box and mentally swallow the key —because I *cannot* let those feelings out. Not if I want to survive.

Unfortunately, bottled-up feelings festering inside my soul are only fodder for my nightmares.

I pause, wondering if I should turn around and curl up in my favorite reading nook until morning. The last thing I want to do is go to bed where my unresolved darkness will be waiting for me in full force.

I've always had rough dreams. Sometimes they aren't so bad.

Other times they are paralyzing.

And I can feel the itch of a night terror episode about to roll over me, taunting me from the recesses of my mind.

Pushing myself onward, I decide my room will be the safest place for me if I have a bad episode. At least where I'm located on my side of the wing, no one can hear me scream. I don't think too long or too hard about why I have a whole wing to myself.

Knowing my father doesn't want to deal with my *hysterics* doesn't make me feel any better. He can't fully fix me, not when he has to focus on my mother, who has invariably been his priority anyway.

I've always been a broken doll stitched back together. I've just been very good at pretending until I fall asleep.

My march now feels more like retreating, so I curl back my shoulders and straighten my spine.

"I'm not broken," I say to both myself and the darkness that feels like it's creeping in.

The hallway is dimly lit by magical globes floating near the ceiling. I used to enjoy their soft, purplish ambience, but tonight all I see is shadows leering at me from every corner. A strange draft I don't remember noticing before circles through the hall, making me hug myself.

Are our finances so pitiful that my father can't even afford to fix any drafty windows? I get that I'm in one of the more unused wings of our mansion, but it's still poor form to let it fall into disrepair.

I pause at my door and glance at the reflective handle. Normally, it's silver.

Tonight, it's black.

Somehow I feel like my nightmare has already started. The only problem is that I'm still wide awake.

Unfurling my arms, I let the chill in, hoping it'll ground me in reality. I run my finger over the handle, finding the surface colder and more unforgiving than I remember it to be.

"I'm going insane," I whisper to myself as I withdraw and make a fist. My nails bite into my palm, but the pain doesn't seem to change what I'm seeing.

Even my words seem to echo in the hall, giving me the strange sense they're being carried on an invisible wind.

But who's listening?

Surely not Cain.

*Perhaps praying to him was a bad idea.*

He might not be a God, but he *is* a monster. And monsters tend to have various gifts.

But everyone knows the Elite City King's power lies in dreams. Praying to him is just a vehicle for him to spread his influence through the city, to remind his followers to think of him so that he can fill their minds.

I've never dreamed of him, and I won't start tonight.

*Right?*

For some reason, having prayed to Cain for the first time gives me an uneasy feeling, as if I've unlocked a new danger around every corner, but maybe I'm just exhausted.

And *of course* I'm uneasy. I just signed a blood contract with a dangerous Earl. Blood contracts are expensive, and the terms were no less costly.

Men like Earl Rinhold want to flaunt their wealth just to show they can own anyone or anything.

And my father had been the one to orchestrate the whole ordeal in the first place.

*I hate men,* I growl in my head as I rest my fingers on the door handle and force myself to adjust to the cold sensation.

I squeeze.

*Tighter,* a voice taunts in my mind, sounding far too much like my brother, making me frown.

It's not unusual that I hear voices in my nightmares.

But this time, I'm not sleeping.

Leave it to my brother to make my night terrors evolve into something new entirely.

*Yep. I definitely hate men.*

Cain's portrait flashes through my mind.

*He's no man,* I decide. *He's a monster. One who hasn't the faintest idea that I exist.*

I know one thing for certain. Cain is no God, no matter how much he pretends to be. He might have the other Elites fooled, but not me.

"Why am I even wasting my time on you?" I ponder aloud, then inch open the door to my bedroom. The icy chill in the hall seems to follow me, flinging my hair over my shoulder with a wind I definitely am not imagining.

"Lady Scarlett?" a bleary-eyed maidservant asks, stumbling from my writing desk she has clearly been sleeping on.

I immediately deflate because I hate that she's been waiting for me. "Sorry, Rosie. I didn't mean to wake you."

There's enough light from the magicked fixtures for me to see Rosie blanch. Her brown curls have flattened on one side, but her green eyes are still as bright as ever even in the low light. Her concern seems to chase away the cold sensation of my impending episode, making me grateful for her presence.

"Oh, no!" she says as she fluffs her hair. "Don't apologize! I shouldn't have fallen asleep." She immediately swings the door open the rest of the way and hides behind it, only peeking enough to make sure I'm going to come inside. "Please, Lady Scarlett. I'll draw you another bath if you like. I made one, but it's cold now and—"

"No bath," I insist, even though I feel like I could use one. My brother's slimy words still seem to cling to me, and the blood contract makes me feel itchy just under my skin. I want nothing more than to scrub myself raw.

But a bath means being naked. And right now, I can't shake the sensation that I'm being watched.

*An asinine idea. No one is watching me.*

Then why does it feel that way?

I shake my head, rationalizing instead that I will have to be up in a few short hours for my duties as Lady of the house and I'm just exhausted. It's making everything worse, including my penchant for night terrors.

No one cares what time I retire or how bad my nightmares get. The morning will come after a few short blinks, demanding that I play host for a scheduled breakfast.

A breakfast with none other than Duchess Rinhold herself.

Now I know why my father set up the meeting for me with a Duchess—and why she agreed to it.

*She already knew I would have no choice but to sign my name on her son's contract.*

*In blood.*

She's probably coming to gloat. That, or lord over me with not-so-subtle reminders of my place, even if I do marry her son.

The wife of an Earl doesn't have much more power than the daughter of a Duke.

The only difference is I'll be a trophy, not an asset.

Won at auction...

Rosie's gaze drops to the slashes on my arm as I enter the room. She scampers to the nightlights and grabs one, then brings it to me. "Is that...?"

"Yes," I tell her as shock settles on her features. "My courtship begins in three days."

Instead of looking as upset as I feel, Rosie's eyes light up and she covers her mouth, which has tilted into a smile. "Courtship! Oh, my lady! Which family is it?" She immediately waves her question away. "Forget I asked. That was rude of me. I'm just so terribly excited for you after you've turned down so many suitors and—"

"It's Earl Rinhold," I say, interrupting her.

I know that Rosie thinks marrying an Earl is the epitome of a Lady's existence, but it's really not.

"Oh," she says in a strained sound of distress.

*Oh* indeed.

"I never had any intention to marry," I confide in her, pitching my voice low as if someone might be pressing their ear to the door right now.

She nibbles on her pinkie, then thrusts her fingers through her hair before clasping them at her front. She has a nervous habit of biting her nails. It doesn't really bother me, but that bad habit can earn her strikes against the monthly servant quota.

Our entire society runs on a point system. Villages decide their selections based on points. Elite families are ranked by points, living and dying by them.

And servants are expected to maintain a nearly flawless record, or else they'll be downgraded to stations less attractive than working for an Elite family.

"But you've had so many suitors," she whispers. "You could have any man you want." She opens her mouth as if to continue.

As if to say, *So why would you agree to a courtship with Earl Rinhold, of all people?*

But she remains wisely silent and glances around as though she has slipped into my building nightmare.

She must notice the slight shiver I'm trying to hide, because she violates another rule by curling her fingers around my wrist. "Are you okay, Lady Scarlett? You're shivering."

*A night terror is coming,* I think, but I don't say that aloud.

No one can help me when the night terrors come.

"I'll be fine," I lie. "I just... I had hoped the additional earnings in the past couple of years would have gone toward a new settlement." I don't voice why that was my hope. Rosie knew that my brother would take on Nightingale Village, and if I was left unwed, I would have the opportunity to start my own settlement. I could have become a new Duchess and taken a husband if and when I felt like it. I sigh. "Instead..." My words drift off as pain squeezes my chest even harder than my corset does.

I don't tell Rosie that my mother has been in a coma for three days. She doesn't need the additional stress.

If anything happens to my mother, we're going to have to severely slim down. My father might even try to sell Rosie.

*Over my dead body,* I think.

A hideous voice rumbles in the back of my head, laughing at my thoughts. *I can help with that,* it says.

I bite my tongue hard enough to draw blood. Pain grounds me in lucidity, but it still doesn't feel like enough to keep my impending night terror from taking over.

But now that my ambitions are crumbling before my eyes, my nightmares have a foothold in my weakened psyche.

That's when they like to strike.

My father's words roll back over in my mind in haunting memory.

*"I've spent all our money on medicine."*

*"Every coin."*

It takes all of my willpower not to let the sting in my

eyes progress into tears. I can't even entertain the idea that my mother won't improve. And, selfishly, I'm upset for myself most of all. Whatever future I had planned for myself is nothing more than a fantasy now.

And my dreams are nothing more than a prayer to a fake God in a corrupt city.

*I won't be praying to you again,* I decide.

There's a strange wave of grief that rolls through my chest, but it's gone before I can analyze it, so I focus on Rosie's little sound of distress instead.

"What are you going to do?" she asks.

I clench my jaw before I answer. "I'm going to let him court me."

That's all I signed up for.

I don't know what I can possibly do when the thirty days are up, but I'm going to have to take this one step at a time.

Rosie's throat works on a swallow. "Will you have a chaperone?" she asks. There's a little tremor of worry in her voice.

It seems that even the servants of the Elite City know of the Earl's reputation. One that I'm going to have to prepare myself to navigate if I'm going to survive the next few weeks.

Without a chaperone, there's not much to keep a handsy Earl from overstepping.

"O-of course," I sputter, even though I'm honestly not sure. That would be the proper thing, but then again, it wasn't in the contract.

Typically, a female relative would chaperone. Outside of my mother, there aren't any other remaining females in the Nightingale line.

Deflecting my gaze from Rosie's pitying look, I glower at the desk instead. Now would be the time to review every note I have on the allies and enemies of the Rinhold household.

Of course, the item that has all my secrets isn't on my desk. Something of such priceless value is safely tucked away in one of my room's many hidden compartments.

For some reason, I don't feel comfortable retrieving it myself, not when I'm feeling *watched*.

"Can you get my black book, please?" I ask as I snatch up my letter opener, then step into my closet, which is large enough for ten people.

Normally, it feels spacious. But right now, the walls feel like they're crowding in on me, and I'm itching to get out of my suffocating corset as a result.

Rosie nervously steps in and out of the entryway, clearly debating if she should help me undress or follow my instruction. She knows the location of my black book. She earned my trust years ago.

I don't need help undoing the laces. At least, not in my current mood.

I take the letter opener and shove it through the bars of my corset, smiling when it breaks and snaps open, finally allowing me to take a deep breath.

Rosie blinks at me, stunned, because I expect she knows how expensive the tailored piece was.

It doesn't matter, though. I'm about to become a Lady of the Rinhold residence. No matter how the courtship ends, I'm now his to dress like a doll he's just purchased, even if it's just for thirty days. I have no doubt there will be a whole new wardrobe of silky chains for me to wear.

"Rosie?" I press as I poise the knife over another taut row of laces. "My book?"

Her mouth bobs open and closed a few times before she answers. "O-of course," she stammers, finally composing herself and giving me a smile.

Her eyes crinkle, and I realize she's impressed. Rosie has always looked up to me, even though I don't feel like a great example for a servant who aspires to be nothing more than the perfect Elite family cog.

Because that's all we are. Cogs in a machine run by monsters and men.

Men can be the worst monsters of all.

I've long speculated why that is, and I find myself contemplating it now as I peel away the uniform of a Lady and slip into one of the few garments I'm allowed to choose for myself.

Since I don't have a husband, no one cares what I wear to bed. Maybe it's rebellious of me to dress outside of my station, but by now, it's become a habit I can't break.

That sensation of being watched makes the hairs on the back of my neck stand on end, but I ignore it.

I can't exactly sleep in my tattered corset.

Slipping into a perfectly white, gauzy nightdress, I appreciate the sheer fabric embroidered with pristine floral designs. My skin pebbles as the chilly night air prickles across my skin, making me feel alive.

It's my version of a wedding dress, one that's reserved for a sacrifice to be given on Monsters Night.

From the broadcasts, I know that the Offerings typically wear more robust gowns. Attractive, yes, but not necessarily revealing to the point of scandal.

I like to pretend I'm one of them, sometimes, just before I go to sleep. If I were to ever be a sacrifice on Monsters Night, it would have to happen in my room, in my bed, in my *dreams*.

Because I'm a Lady bound by duty to the Elite City. A life gifted to monsters simply isn't for me.

*It should have been,* I think to myself, the thought a rebellious, bitter one.

The last thing I want is to be Earl Rinhold's bride. I can pretend I'll belong to a monster instead. Preferably one who has a penchant for devouring Earls.

*Like a Dream Eater?* I muse.

I know Cain is no God, so maybe praying to him can be my fantasy. One where he saves me from my predicament and whisks me away into a realm of dreams and nightmares.

Except, I know it doesn't typically work that way. If Cain did take a candidate, he likely wouldn't be alone. Monsters tend to mate in groups, as far as I'm aware. I've never heard of a Dream Eater besides Cain, so there probably isn't a compatible monster who could handle him in a group setting.

*Perhaps that's why you've never taken a mate,* I wonder as I undo my hair from its many pins and curls, taking away the silver chains to allow it to unfurl over my shoulders.

*There's no one who can stand to be around you.*

I swear there's a growl that comes from the full-length mirror in my closet, making me raise a brow at it.

Rosie scampers in with my black book plastered against her chest, her eyes wide as she fumbles with it and then holds the leatherbound diary out to me.

Because it's more of a diary than a real book.

It's where I've written all my observations and emotions that flutter around inside my chest when I read someone. Those feelings tend to slip away after a few hours, so I write them down.

"Thank you. That'll be all, Rosie," I say as I take the book from her.

She lingers in the doorway and pulls at her fingernails, then curls her fingers into fists to stem the bad habit. "Are you sure you're going to be okay, my lady? I could stay." She eyes the doorway. It wouldn't be the first time she slept on the floor on a makeshift nest.

Because of my episodes. My mother's illness gave her other things to worry about, so I stopped going to her early on.

I sweep her into a hug, surprising both her and myself.

I'm not supposed to become attached to the servants, but really, I don't have any friends.

I don't have anyone.

Rosie has been a part of my life for over five years, riding the wave with me through the sectors and my mother's illness.

Without her, I would probably have already gone mad.

"I don't deserve you, Rosie," I whisper against her ear as I give her a squeeze.

Once the shock has worn off, she tentatively hugs me back. "You deserve everything. You've been nothing but good to me, my lady." She pulls away and runs her thumb down my arm, avoiding the fresh cuts. "And now they do this to you. It's not proper."

The wounds don't bleed out, but they're red and angry. The mark will stay as a reminder of what's coming.

A reminder of what I've agreed to.

But what choice is there? Allow my mother to die and possibly my whole family to be killed all because of pride?

Bowing to any man is a severe hit to that pride. I'm painfully aware it's my weakness, but it's also my strength.

It's why I would have made an excellent Duchess of a new village of my making.

One where women rule—not men.

Now that plan is nothing more than a dream to be sacrificed along with all the selections from my father's village.

No... Duke Nightingale's village.

I know what happens to every male or female chosen

for Monsters Night. They're put on a train and thrust onto the streets of Monster City, and we watch and wait.

We hope.

We *pray*. Or at least, the rest of my family has always prayed.

Not me. I know that our fate is one of our own making.

The past years have been good for my family. Many candidates are selected by compatible monsters, proving that my father's tactics in genetic manipulation, mental conditioning, and environmental factors can work well.

And they've also given us enough points to survive.

"Bribes," I mutter to myself as I unravel the ribbon securing my book, then open it as I sink into my writing chair. I curl a fluffy robe around my shoulders as I settle in to write.

Flipping past sketches of monsters and men along with their written impressions I've made, I ignore images of various family alliances and enemies—honestly, there isn't much difference between the two—and skip to a blank page.

I've never written an entry on my brother or my father.

"That changes tonight," I say as I accept the sinking feeling that my own family has now entered enemy territory.

They aren't my friends.

They're yet another political pawn to be watched.

*The game has begun.*

*And if I'm forced to play... I'm going to win.*

# CHAPTER 5

## CAIN

Those fierce, quiet words clothe me with the sanctity of a prayer as I allow myself to fall asleep inside my chambers. The broken window lets the chill night air in, but I'm no longer in my physical body.

I let my beast out. I let him *hunt*.

The Dream Realm is a hauntingly beautiful place. A low rumble creaks across the broken ground, sending vibrations into my large form that I easily read.

Each new dream, each new shift and change, sends a shiver through me, and I catalog every single one.

And rivers of blood freely flow. I can't drink from them, despite many efforts of trying. They run with powerful undercurrents, threading through various territories like the veins of a living creature bigger than even me.

I respect the Dream Realm, and in return, it nourishes me.

My view is limited to those who have given their minds freely to me. After this many years and the growth of my influence, much of the Dream Realm is open to me.

The sky is dark and cracked like dusty glass tossed in volcanic ash. It snows a soft black residue that melts into my skin, giving me little tastes of the dreams running in motion around me.

I follow the path I've made over the years, a solid obsidian road of hardened glass that grows with each new dream I encounter.

*Cain, bless this family.*

*Cain, my lord, my king, honor us with your oversight and guidance to harvest a worthy crop this year.*

Prayers make my mouth water, and my beast sucks them in, but he's not distracted by the tasty morsels.

He's on the hunt for the first true meal he's had in years.

I prowl across vast distances of the ethereal land in search of Scarlett Nightingale. Parallel worlds curl up into the sky and form hills. I can see various buildings, villages, and landscapes created by each individual dreamer.

But there's a new one I'm looking for tonight.

*Where are you, little star?*

My tongue flicks out, tasting the air and catching the faint whiff of wine-soaked peaches.

*There you are.*

I follow the scent until I'm led off my carved path and deeper into broken territory.

*What is this?* I wonder, marveling at the untouched, spliced, glassy ground that shouldn't be hospitable to any dreamer.

It's too dark and isolated.

Too painful.

Concern makes my nostrils flare as I soak in a heavier dose of Scarlett's aroma, only to find a metallic one accompanying it.

There's another soul-scent marking Scarlett's trail, and

I follow it, finding the blood-like taste tainting the shadows that lick around my face.

I delve into the darkness, unafraid of what I might find.

*I'm the Elite City King.*

*I'm a Dream Eater.*

But something else challenges my presence and makes me wade through the inky shadows.

Scarlett Nightingale hasn't been directly conferring with me since her first prayer, but she's been talking to some *other* entity in the Dream Realm.

And apparently, she's been linked to this other presence for a very long time. It is far too immersed in her territory not to have had time to take root like this.

*Who else is here?* I wonder as I pause on the fringes of Scarlett's territory. I don't know of any other dream-focused monsters, at least not in my world.

And I've never seen anything like this. I'm intimately familiar with the Dream Realm, but I've never been here.

There are still recesses I have not yet explored, and that excites me more than I care to admit.

Every living creature capable of sentient, complex thought is automatically awarded land in this realm. When I blink and send my body skyward, I hover over the fog that has settled onto her land.

It's massive.

Scarlett's plot stretches out with a vast, incredible space, one that is much larger than I'm accustomed to for a single soul, but it fluctuates with feathery shadows I often associate with nightmares born of bad memories.

It makes them tangible because their source comes from the real world.

It also makes them delicious. There are few energies more powerful than those born of terror.

As I descend, the dark tendrils lick across my skin, and I

can't help but thread my fingers through them, enticing them to dance with me.

Nightmares like me. I feast on them, giving them a vault to call home.

And my monster side can feed.

One curls across my chest, then hovers above my mouth, allowing me to lick.

I'm in my Dream Eater form in this world, so all I have to do is part my mouth and flick out my tongue.

The shadows are sucked in, my body acting as a void that consumes everything in this realm, if it dares to linger within my reach.

Ancient anger, grief, and sorrow stir in my soul. That's what these shadows are born from.

The memories are too old to belong to a human, so that means they belong to someone else.

Or something else.

Whatever type of entity they belong to has shed its terror and left it here.

*It's a wonder this female hasn't gone mad.*

I sense her farther in, resting in her territory beyond my reach. I can faintly hear her, the link between us having opened the moment she uttered her first prayer.

But she hasn't prayed again. She's been talking to someone else. There's no fear in her tone, and it seems to be helping her mental state. The shadows have calmed, whereas previously they had been vibrating.

So I wait.

And feast.

I give the shadows of sorrow a place, a *purpose*.

*You are mine now,* I tell those wisps that have curled inside my soul.

A light flares at that statement, one that I inexplicably know belongs to the female.

I tilt my head, curious, as the shadows part, revealing a world of broken mirror shards floating through the air.

*She's letting me in.*

In each shard, a different memory, dream, or fabrication glints back.

*A child running in a sea of flames.*

*A mother crying.*

*A room of three surrounding a contract written in blood.*

The last depiction is one I know well, because I was there, too.

In spirit, anyway.

*Or in beast.*

The shards float away from me as I step through. My heavy weight makes me sink into the ground that crunches under my steps.

Like Helia, my beastly body doesn't wear clothes or boots, mostly because I have no need for them in this form. Still, the broken, glassy ground seems to make my feet sting.

It's an unusual sensation in the Dream Realm.

*What have you been up to, little star, to make your territory so rife with pain?* I wonder.

*Who have you let in, other than me?*

Physical movement doesn't work the same in the Dream Realm as it does in the real world. Only three steps take me straight to the owner of this territory.

I was invited by her prayer, but it doesn't mean I can stay.

When I find her blurry form cozied in a chair and huddled with a book and gold pen, I realize she's still awake.

But just barely.

Those intrusive wisps are tugging at her arms, her legs, and plucking at her hair in an effort to drag her under.

To drown her in the dream world.

They don't seem to have good intentions, either.

"Get out," I say, forcing my words with my beast's growly sounds.

They flicker as if I've hit them with a forceful wind but then settle against the female again.

I frown, not accustomed to nightmares disobeying me in this realm—but this isn't my territory.

It's hers.

And whether she recognizes it or not, she has welcomed the darkness in. Even humans have a certain amount of control over their dreams. It might not feel that way to them, but they have more power than they could possibly realize.

It's why I tread carefully and can only access a mind where I've been invited. Even then, it works best if the human allowing me in is compliant and willing.

This female seems to be neither of those things. She's not praying to me, but I'm still lingering in the back of her mind, or else I wouldn't have access to her dreams.

*What are you up to, little one?* I wonder as I draw closer. I don't want to make her aware of my presence, but I can't resist the pull this delicate creature has over me. When glass crunches under my step, she pauses what she's writing and looks up but doesn't seem to see me.

I'm struck silent by the sight of her eyes. It's as if she holds molten silver inside her soul and it glitters through her fractured irises.

*Stunning.*

She only graces my space with a glance before her feathered eyelashes lower, hiding the incredible sight from me.

Now the nickname I've settled on for her fits. It's as if my soul knew what she was, even if I didn't.

I still don't have tangible answers, but now I'm even more curious. That in and of itself is a thrill, one I've rarely been awarded in my very long existence.

This brilliant little mystery has me captive as I dare to peer closer to see what she's writing.

The contents of her notebook seem to contain a diary of delicate penmanship of the highest quality that I would expect of a Lady. But it's her artistic skill that surprises me.

The creative arts are seen as frivolous by most humans when, in truth, expression in any form is a type of magic.

Art is an expression of what resides in one's soul.

And in this case, my star is drawing the reflection she sees of others through those broken little mirrors she has for eyes.

*Fascinating.*

My beast rumbles a thunderous growl inside my chest when I see her sketching the faces of two men, one I recognize, and the other being the one who struck her.

The urge to murder that insufferable speck of a human nearly makes me exit her territory in search of his.

He must not pray to me, either, because I've never seen him before. Just the older one.

*Duke Nightingale.*

I hadn't even paid attention to the fact that he had adult children. The affairs of families are inconsequential to me. All I care about is that quotas are met and contracts honored.

And rules obeyed.

I know who this female is now. She had been hiding just underneath my shadow all this time. It's rare that a family earns enough points to upgrade into a new sector. And even then, their quotas are exponentially increased in response, making any family who tries to overcome their station challenged to the point where many choose to stay put.

Because failure means death in my city.

Harsh rules, but necessary in this world teetering on the edge of survival. The human population plummeted those first few decades when monsters and men mingled.

It wasn't anyone's fault. Both creatures have dark natures that must be carefully navigated.

Predator and prey have learned to coexist, and I have never felt that more sharply than now.

Because this delectable female most certainly feels like prey—but I want to protect her from the predators.

My beast, surprisingly, feels the same.

*Has she already won you over?* I think at him as I step around her, then kneel so I can better look at her face.

Her eyelashes lower even farther, covering those mirror-shard eyes once again.

It doesn't escape my notice that this female has the same type of eyes that my beast does. It's the type of eyes the humans use in my portraits when trying to depict my form.

The only humans who have seen my Dream Eater side in person haven't lived to talk about it—but many have seen me in *this* realm. Even if a person doesn't fully remember my beast feeding on their nightmares and dreams, their subconscious does.

*You're compatible,* I marvel as I resist the urge to reach out to her.

She has eyes like mine because she's a match made just for me.

I've never met a human who's compatible with my Dream Eater.

This isn't just a human my beast is fascinated with. This is a potential mate—the first I have ever come across in all my many years.

Which makes the blood contract she signed tonight extremely unfortunate.

*We'll find a way around it,* I assure my beast.

We have to. There's no way I can give up this perfect creature to a human who doesn't understand her worth.

Or maybe he does. Earl Rinhold brokered a blood contract with me just a few nights ago for a reason. The Rinhold family is not one to do anything lightly.

They are wealthy, yes, and they could have elevated into the Immortality Sector years ago.

So why did they spend their wealth on a bride price instead?

I'd asked that very question when the young male had come to me.

*"You realize this is enough to elevate your family to the Immortality Sector, yes?"* I had asked Earl Rinhold, who'd been accompanied by the Duke and Duchess of his family.

But they had allowed their son to broker the contract with me. The bride price was a substantial one, but the price for my blood to make the contract binding was even more.

Normally, the families manage their own courtships. But if they want my blessing—and nonnegotiable terms— they handle agreements through me.

*"We wish to* rise *in the Immortality Sector, Lord Cain, not simply survive,"* he had said with a lowered head, keeping all respectful mannerisms intact. *"This will allow us to offer something unique to set us apart once we make the move."*

It had been a wise response, one I had respected and understood to be true. A smart family knows that the goal isn't simply to rise into the next sector, but to be prepared for the new challenges that will await them there if they wish to survive, much less thrive.

I spend the majority of my time in the Immortality

Sector. The Elite families there are held to near-impossible standards.

Immortality means those humans will be spared from the slow death of aging or illness—there is no promise they will survive *me.*

*"And this girl, who is she?"* I had asked. *"What does she offer that will be so unique you're risking an entire elevation fee for it?"*

His answer had satisfied me then, but now I realize it had meant so much more.

*"She is the key, my lord. The Nightingale family adopted her in secret, but we know she's from one of the lost villages that had been on the verge of a breakthrough. Her fresh genetics combined with a Lady's proper training makes her a perfect candidate for our new breeding program."* He had dared to raise his gaze to me for his final statement, allowing me to see the glint of excitement in his blue eyes. *"I am offering you my firstborn, my lord, for a future Monsters Night."*

That was an attractive offer, but this human was proposing something in uncharted territory.

*"And if it doesn't take?"* I had asked, referring to any offspring the union might produce. An Elite family that was not immortal would need heirs to continue its line.

This female the Rinhold line was so interested in was a risk. There had once been an Elite family who'd attempted to create a new breed of humans. It had resulted in many casualties and a poor selection pool, ultimately pitching the family below quota requirements.

It had not ended well for them.

This, though, was a new take on a failed concept. By bringing in one of the surviving villagers into an Elite family fold, only their own line would be manipulated.

*"Then we will accept a bastard child to continue our line,"*

Earl Rinhold had said. *"Regardless, our village's selections will still proceed as planned with no interruptions."*

It was a smart reply. There was no risk from my side of things. I had been intrigued by the idea of a family wishing to offer up those of its own line as candidates for Monsters Night. It was certainly one way to stand out once they rose to the rank of Immortals.

Whomever Earl Rinhold selected for his bride would become immortal, too, so if he wished to breed her intentionally, he had to choose carefully.

A female originally from a village rather than a born Elite explained her compatibility with me. That meant she was one of the humans genetically modified to be compatible with monsters.

*"She is the key."*

Did Earl Rinhold know how true that statement was?

She is the key to everything.

*I can't lose you,* I think as I reach out to her. I simply want to curl a lock of her gorgeous red hair behind her ear, but she flinches when my claws part through the shadows twining around her.

My hand is twice the size of her head. I'm not sure what I was thinking in trying to touch her, even in this realm, but I seem to have disturbed her territory enough for her to finally notice me.

She looks me dead in the face.

Then opens her mouth.

And screams.

# CHAPTER 6

## SABRE

The delicious sound has me frozen, completely thrusting out any of the thoughts I'd just been having and replacing them with *hunger*.

The sound is faint, though, as if I might have imagined it. And when I peer beyond the veil that exists between this world and the world of dreams, I catch something that shouldn't be there.

A shimmer swirls through the room, elusive, weak, but interesting. It travels through the objects surrounding me as if it can't interact with them.

*Red velvet furniture.*

*Gaudy diamond chandeliers.*

*A bar I probably utilize far too much—and is unfortunately stocked with booze instead of blood.*

The air is heavy, and the colors are muted as I skillfully shift my perception and try to track the disturbance, a talent that's more seamless for those in the royal line of Strigoi. I'm a dreamwalker, a vampire who feasts on dreams.

My medium? Blood. The elixir of life holds the code of a being's past, present, and future, if one knows where to look.

And it seems that I'm the one dreaming now, because the enticing shimmer that's vibrating through the air can't be real.

*I'm going mad.*

Whenever I dreamwalk, my surroundings take on an otherworldly distortion. The half-empty glass on the counter turns black, making the beverage look like shiny shards of coal. Blood runs down the walls. Given I'm peering into the dream plane, that's likely a reflection of my own debilitating hunger, as is the strange shimmer that's taunting me.

My hunger has grown over the years, even before the famine started. It's entirely my family's fault. My father can't maintain the needs of our kingdom, so the drain has already fallen to me. I have the burden of the throne with none of the perks. It's rumored that Morpheus, our God, gave us power over dreams, enabling us to better locate our prey.

It's a gift we have abused, because whenever we find a human with a powerful dream, they become a sacrifice to the blood fields that rest just outside my window.

The fields that require magic to tend to, to keep the mind buried in the soil alive.

Magic that my father, as King, should provide. Instead, he has grown weak, and he has been drawing power from the closest in his family line to keep the blood fields from withering entirely.

Namely, me.

And it's been going on for quite some time. My fangs are larger than any Strigoi's, and no human seems to satisfy me. Hunger is my constant companion. I can always feel the subtle draw of the throne to feed the fields.

*If I could just leave this Godsforsaken realm for twenty-four hours, I'd feel so much better.*

Alas, I can't leave. I'd just be tracked down and dragged back home. My blood is linked to this place. My scent is easily traceable. Unless I find an entirely different dimension where no one can follow me, I'll never find the reprieve I desperately desire.

I'm grateful for Cage. I watch him as he stares out the window, his long blond hair in gentle waves around his shoulders. He's not human, but his blood at least tastes good to me. Without him, I probably would have gone mad years ago.

But my hunger has ripened to new heights after hearing that sound. It came to me like a punch in the chest, making me weak for the satisfaction it promises.

The scream must have been my imagination, because there's nothing out of sorts. My hunger has turned so ravenous that I'm now creating echoes in the dream plane.

The effect of my delusion is likely amplified since I'm in the Strigoi Palace, which resides in the Morpheus Kingdom, one of many kingdoms in the Hell Fae Realm, and ours is a place where dreamwalking requires the least amount of energy.

The veil is thin here. That's why the Strigoi made it our home. But sometimes it backfires when I desire something too strongly.

My room looks like it always does when I'm peering through the veil. The ridiculously expensive furniture crowds a bookshelf. I added it when I discovered Cage had an affinity for human fiction.

The books are glassy and cracked in the dream plane, but that is normal. Books are broken-off pieces of the souls, which sit outside a person's body, a trait that's visible in the Dream Realm.

*Nothing is out of place.*

*No one is here.*

My observation doesn't explain why my body has reacted, though. Imagined or not, the sound of such a delicious meal has my fangs growing thick in my mouth and my cock swelling even though I just had sex.

"Did you hear that?" Cage asks from his favorite brooding window. His long fingers pause in buttoning his white silk shirt as he stares outside.

Except, he's not gazing over the blood fields that are pitifully sparse for the season. The famine has been going on for far too long, placing a burden on my shoulders that I'd rather not deal with.

Even though I'm the Strigoi Prince, it's a burden I must bear.

I'd much rather run away, forgetting my duties and the reason Cage and I can never publicly be together. I'm a Prince. He's the son of a rival line, one that is on the verge of war with mine for the throne.

Ironically, because I haven't found a mate.

Cage hasn't, either. But his family seems to think that if he had the blessing of the Strigoi throne, then he would magically find a female and produce an heir—and magic— to keep up with the demands of our kingdom.

We're a perfect match made in Hell.

Neither of us is in a hurry to find a mate. If we did, that would ensure we'd be trapped here forever. No more outings. No more liaisons when we can sneak away. We'd be locked down for good.

Cage helps me deal with my hunger, and I help him forget all the blood on his hands while we occasionally escape to the mortal realm for the rare escapade. While there are human females in the palace, they're untouched virgins my father hides away in an attempt to breed a new Queen. It doesn't work that way, but my father believes in old legends enough to try. I haven't even told Cage about them because I don't need more reasons for him to judge me. It's a problem I'll inherit when I'm King.

And when I'm King, I hope I can do something about that, and the many other flaws in this kingdom. I'm not hopeful, though. I have a feeling the throne will corrupt me.

I'm not as strong as Cage, even if I'd never admit that to him.

My future is a bleak nightmare waiting to consume me. Escaping it just for a little while is an indulgence I allow. One where I find a willing human female and then ask Cage to join us. We share her blood and her dreams, as well as her body. It's enjoyable enough, at least for a few nights.

But when her dreams turn sour, we always have to return home. We give her our blood, wipe her mind clean, and send her on her way.

Last time, we were almost caught. Last time, we almost killed our toy.

I'm too hungry.

Cage is too frustrated.

We shouldn't leave again.

But the famine has stretched on, and we have kept to our posts, leaving us both hungry for a proper meal.

Cage shouldn't have even come tonight, but the kingdom is distracted, so he took the risk.

Because he's just as hungry as I am.

Maybe that's why we're hearing things that don't exist, like a soul calling us from the dream plane even though that shouldn't be possible.

Souls don't call us.

We call *them*.

But a soul that sounded that delicious would be wonderfully distracting. I find myself working my jaw as my fangs ache for a bite. I've never had a female's blood that tasted *right*. There was always something wrong, like a sour note, or a strange aftertaste.

Because to a Strigoi, only a compatible mate's blood is perfect. I've always imagined what she might taste like.

Sugary, sweet caramel?

Or maybe more reserved, like a fragrant tea.

*Or peaches,* my hunger supplies.

Cage tastes like dark chocolate steeped in whiskey, not peaches.

Overpowering, but intoxicating.

The closest I've ever come to truly enjoying my food is biting Cage—but he's not human. He and I are both dreamwalkers who feed on blood laced with dreams, so exchanging our blood with each other leaves us hungry and dissatisfied.

*I'm just starving for a proper meal. That's all.*

Yet, Cage is searching the horizon for the source of that sound—even though I know it can't be real. He's been perfectly still in a way only an assassin of the Van Drakken bloodline can be.

His eyes are bright red, reflecting so brightly in the window that I can't deny we both heard the same thing. He's peering into the dream plane, too, or else I'd be seeing his pretty blues reflecting back at me.

*If that scream wasn't real, then why did he hear the scream, too? Am I really so hungry that I manifested the sound?*

*That I manifested a* mate?

Because that scream hinted at a soul worth devouring. One I would thoroughly enjoy for eternity.

My stomach twists with renewed hunger, but I don't want Cage to be slighted. We *just* had sex, and this is how I respond? Admitting I heard the scream would require telling him my theory.

I'm dreaming of a mate.

I *need* a mate.

Meaning he and I can never be together again once that happens. Not if I stay here. Our families would rather kill each other than unite.

We would have to run away, but there's nowhere else for "abominations" like us to go. That's why the Hell Fae Realm exists in the first place.

That's why I should be grateful to Morpheus for his gifts, to Lucifer for this kingdom, but I feel sour toward them both.

Morpheus is my God.

Lucifer is my King. All the kingdoms report to him, including that of my father, King Nos—who Lucifer actually calls his lieutenant. It's a reminder of our hierarchy.

Lucifer made his Hell Fae Bride Trials because he cares for his subjects. I should be happy with his efforts.

*But none of his* brides *appeal to me.*

And admitting that out loud would be both blasphemous and ungrateful.

"I didn't hear anything," I lie, then turn back to the portfolio I was flipping through a few moments ago.

Lucifer had sent one to each of us, hoping to entice us to select potential Hell Fae Brides for ourselves. All of the Hell kingdoms are celebrating, and I feel like I should be, too.

This is my chance to stop the starvation. Stop the famine.

Stop the fighting.

Lucifer listened. He's trying to fix the problems. He's a good ruler, and if I told him it wasn't good enough, I'd be the ungrateful asshole that half the Strigoi paint me out to be.

Between the famine, the rising animosity among rival bloodlines, and the hunger that has been consuming me, a mate would be a welcome solution. I could relieve my withered father from the throne and start a new generation. The magic of a new Strigoi child royal would rejuvenate our lands.

Which is precisely the reason war is on our doorstep. I haven't taken a mate yet.

Mostly because none appeal to me. I can't mate with just any female. It has to be a true soul connection down to the compatibility of our blood and our dreams, or else my body will reject her if I continue to feed.

This isn't something I can fake.

It has to be real.

I scan the portfolio again, hoping that one of the candidates will stand out to me. Many of the females are half-human, though not all of them are. That is my only requirement, as far as I'm aware.

I scan the genetic labels next to each pretty face's name.

*Human–Hell Fae hybrid.*

*Human–Fortune Fae–Elemental Fae mix.*

*Lunar Fae–Midnight Fae–human mix.*

I mentally cross the last one out. She's not only lacking mortal blood, being just one-third human, but the Midnight Fae are true vampires, unlike our dreamwalking hybrid version of them. I'm not looking for another mouth to feed when it comes to the blood fields.

Lucifer is just being thorough, so he had all potential candidates included. And he knows the Strigoi have special needs, like all hybrids do, so a small blood sample has been placed on each page next to the names. I'm not sure if I want to know how he obtained those.

But none of the samples call to me. I gently press my tongue to the spot of one red splotch, then make a face.

If I want a bride that tastes like overripe fruit, then that's the one.

Cage has silently moved to my side of the bed and yanks the portfolio out of my hands. "Sabre." He says my name like a curse. "What the fuck are you doing? You're going to tell me you didn't hear that? That you didn't *see* it? It's gone now, but there was something weird in the dream plane. Everything was... off, for a minute."

"There was nothing," I insist as I fling off the bedsheets, then immediately regret it.

We both stare down at my throbbing cock. The unique glands around the head and base are vibrating, and I shove my pillow onto it.

That only happens when I'm *really* turned on. Not all Strigoi have them. The vibrating bulbs are a Sanguinis family trait—or so my father tells me.

Proudly.

And from my experience with human females, they quite enjoy it.

Cage grins so wide I can see the glint of his own fangs coming out. "If you lie to me one more time, I'm going to fuck the truth out of you, and not in a good way. You won't like it."

Cage knows how to punish. That's his thing.

And I like that about him, normally. He feels like the living and breathing consequence of my failures, and in a fucked-up way, that makes me feel better about myself.

Not that I'd ever admit that to him.

What I lack in speed that Cage has inherited from the Van Drakken line, I have in *strength*.

Shooting to my feet, I crest his height by a few inches and snarl at him.

I let the pillow fall as I shove him away. "You're going to make me say it? Fine, Cage. I'm fucking starving. I need a real meal if my family is going to keep taking every scrap of energy I've gathered. I'm so hungry that I'm manifesting a fucking feast in the dream plane."

My temper flares, and I know I'm going to regret my next words, but I don't stop them from forming in my mind. I let Cage see why he should run far, far away and never look back.

I shove him again, this time against the wall, splitting the solid marble in a straight line by the force of the blow. He grunts as rubble cascades around his feet. His eyes are still bright red as he glares at me from underneath the curtain of his golden hair.

Slamming my fists on either side of his face, I snarl, letting my fangs come out to their full, horrible length. My body has half transformed into my monster form as I let my true nature peek through.

Cage annoyingly stays in control, silently judging me as he waits for me to land my final blow.

Not a physical one, but one with words. One that'll cut deeper than my fangs ever could.

"Say it, Sabre," he growls at me with a rumbling, ethereal sound that's the only sign he's fighting his monster. "Fucking say it."

My lengthy tongue runs along his cheek. He tastes so sweet, but it's still not right.

Not how a true mate should taste.

"You're not doing it for me, Cage. You're. Not. *Enough.*"

His entire body ripples with rage, even though we both know it to be true.

"You didn't manifest that scream in the dream plane, Sabre," he says instead. "I heard it, too. I *saw* everything change for a minute, then it was gone. It was as if someone opened a window and let us see something that wasn't there." His jaw flexes with frustration, one I share, because he might be right. Or we've both just gone insane. "I don't know what it was, but it was real, and that tells me there's a soul out there worth having. Not just for you, but for me, too. Do you know what that means, my prince?"

He never calls me that, not unless he's trying to rile me up.

My monster is taking over, making it hard to talk, but I snarl a response anyway. "What does it mean, my assassin?" I slither out the *s*'s in the final word.

I return the favor of using his official title because that reminds him of how we met.

He tried to kill me. That was his job, the first and only hit he ever failed.

Because he fell for me and I for him, when we shouldn't have.

Cage bravely—or stupidly—rests a hand on my shoulder in a claiming gesture. "It means we share a mate, Sabre. And she's out there somewhere. Do you want to find her? Or do you want to waste your time with that fucking portfolio of brides not meant for us?"

Cage is delusional, but I can't judge on that front. If I'm manifesting a mate in the dream plane, then I'm delusional, too.

"If you find another world I'm not aware of where she's hiding from us, by all means, Cage. Fucking find it."

I can't look at his face anymore. I'm not sure if I'll bite into his throat and coat this room with his blood or fuck him until he can't walk.

Maybe both.

"I'll find a way to escape our families," he says instead, forcing me back to him. "Maybe you did manifest that sound, maybe not. But at the very least, we can *leave*."

Now he's speaking my language.

Leaving sounds attractive, even if it's impossible.

There's nowhere to go.

"I'm sick of watching you wither into darkness, my prince," Cage continues as he presses his forehead to mine. He's using the title reverently now, putting me above him in our ever-changing hierarchy. "I vow to you, this won't be our lives—miserable and on separate sides." His punishing grip squeezes harder. "This won't be our nightmare. We will make a dream of our own—just stay with me a little bit longer."

Escape.

That sounds impossible, almost like a dream. But it's more realistic than finding a mate.

Despite my skepticism, I reply, "Find it, Cage. Find a world no one knows about, and if you do, I promise you, we'll leave."

I'll abandon my withering throne.

I'll leave this damned kingdom to fight over the bloodied scraps that remain.

I'm done.

And whether or not that scream was real, I know one thing for certain.

It'll forever haunt my dreams.

# CHAPTER 7

# SCARLETT

"Scream again. I liked it," the creature in the shadows says.

My entire body is trembling and my teeth chatter—because I'm *freezing*. My nipples bead and scrape painfully against the gauzy nightdress that had felt supple and soft a moment before.

I take a few steps backward as I attempt to put distance between me and the creature that has appeared in my room. The backs of my legs hit the mattress, and I fall onto it.

That's when I detect a splash of white on my left. I glance at it, then my eyes widen when I see myself asleep in my chair. My notebook teeters dangerously from my fingertips but doesn't fall. The leather strap seems to be hooked on my thumb.

A throb I hadn't noticed before settles on the same digit, and I rub it, realizing that I'm actually asleep.

*Is this... a dream?*

Because I've never had a dream like this. Not one where I feel like I've floated right outside of my body.

A rumbling growl steals my attention as the blood drains from my face. I glance back at the creature who is still there.

Except now he's stalking toward me.

"Sssscarlett," he says, slithering out the *S* in my name as if he can taste it.

Another scream builds and sticks in my throat as he reveals more of his form to me. I shouldn't be looking between his legs, but there's a massive cock dripping with liquid silver.

I feel the insane urge to lick it.

*What's wrong with me?*

"Mmm, you're pleased by what you see?" the beast asks, making me flick my gaze up to him again.

My nightmares are never like this. I usually feel like I'm drowning, like a thousand horrible memories are dragging me down into the darkness until I can't breathe.

My lungs refuse to cooperate, so that sensation is similar, but it's for an entirely different reason.

The creature is intimidating, but he hasn't tried to hurt me. Instead of doing anything threatening in nature, he's paused just out of reach.

And he's watching me as if waiting for me to respond.

*And he knows my name.*

Realization dawns on me when I look at his face instead of his monstrous cock.

His eyes are made up of shards of glass, reflecting my own face back at me.

What's odd is that I have the same kind of eyes.

*This is definitely the strangest dream I've ever had.*

And I feel far too lucid to be dreaming, but maybe the stress of signing a blood contract to become Earl Rinhold's future wife has sent me careening off the deep end.

*Or maybe it's the magic from the blood contract doing this.*

I know how blood contracts work. Elite families who want an agreement to be magically binding use a monster's blood to do so.

And, apparently, that seems to be having an effect on me.

Swallowing the scream instead of releasing it, I unstick my tongue from the roof of my mouth and attempt a reply. "Um, it's... large," I say with an awkward smile. Because he'd just asked me if I liked what I saw—and I assumed he meant the very large cock I'd been staring at.

My answer makes him chuckle.

Even though I'd been staring, it's not because I haven't seen male genitalia before. Even if I am still technically a virgin, I know what *it* looks like.

Well, maybe not this figment's *particular* appendage, but in general.

What liaisons I've had in the past were brief and rushed. Like most Ladies, I'm often trailed by a chaperone if I venture out on an engagement of any sort.

And in my case, that chaperone has often been my brother.

He's never cared about my purity. In fact, he would use me to gain blackmail over other Earls and possible enemies.

Or even allies, with the intention of turning on them.

Even if I found someone I was interested in, the act could never go too far. It would ruin any potential marriage if I really lost my virginity. It had to go just far enough to be scandalous, then my brother would have blackmail over both the target and me.

*Whore.*

*Slut.*

*You would just give it up for anyone if I let you, wouldn't you?*

My cheeks burn with shame and anger as I recall those memories.

Because there were a few times I had found pleasure in those engagements. They weren't forced. I was a poor actress and incredibly bored.

*Spoiled brat.*

Teasing my beaux of the moment sounded like fun, at the time. But now I realize how young and stupid I had been to let my brother use me that way.

The beast is watching me, and a soft, rumbling growl has grown in his chest. The vibrations of it seem to disturb the shadows that usually accompany my nightmares, but it's making them shrivel and curl away instead of growing like they normally do.

His muscles bunch and flex, rippling in a fascinating way that betrays raw anger.

What I'd been thinking about had displeased him.

"Can you see my memories?" I ask the nightmare creature.

Of course he can. He's a figment of my imagination.

"Yes," he growls, then flexes his jaw. "Can you see mine?"

That makes me laugh, and I immediately cover my hand with my mouth.

"What memories might you have, figment?" I ask as I trail my fingers over my lips, because that's all he is.

He grins as if the name amuses him. "Figment, am I? Well, that's all I can be, isn't it?" His tongue flicks out as if to taste the air. I gasp at the sharpened teeth that look like they can tear right through flesh. "Would you like to know more about me?"

A strange question from a figment, but I discover that the answer is "Yes."

He waves his arms wide. "Ask me anything."

"Is this real?" I wonder.

"No," he confirms, both satisfying and disappointing me. "It can't be real."

No, it can't, can it? Which was possibly a good thing. Even if my courtship hasn't officially begun, I wouldn't risk the exclusive stipulation.

I'm not allowed to specifically have intercourse with anyone else, and neither is the Earl. The blood contract would automatically dissolve if that happened.

Not that I've ever had intercourse. I've never been in a position where that would have been possible. My brother kept me pure in that sense, probably hoping to save that virtue to sell to the highest bidder.

Now that I'm in a blood courtship, it gives me a sense of pleasure to know my brother won't get to take that commodity. It's mine to give, or not.

Just because I'm in a blood courtship doesn't completely tie my hands, though. Scandal has always run rampant of those in a blood courtship finding other creative ways to pass the time.

My gaze drops. *Not that I have to worry about intercourse, because there's no way* that *will fit.*

His eyes glitter when he adds, "But it can *feel* real." His broken gaze sweeps over me, seeming to appreciate what he sees. "Do I frighten you?"

"Yes," I admit. Even if he's a figment of my imagination, I'm well aware of what my nightmares are capable of.

But this? This is new.

*Maybe my mind is going to have some mercy on me.*

I take my time to inspect him now that I know all of this is my own doing.

He's frighteningly tall, and his head is bowed to avoid hitting the chandelier. His skin is dark, but mostly because it seems saturated by the same shadows I often see in my nightmares.

*Almost as if he's eaten them.*

His face is beautiful with those broken mirror–like eyes. His cheekbones are sharp, and the quality of them reminds me of Cain's portrait in the drawing room.

*My mind has a funny way of painting a nightmare.*

Cain was the last entity I tried to call out to for help. It makes sense that my mind would justify those feelings of needed security by fashioning this creature after him.

The massive thing between his legs, though, seems unusual.

As does the silver dripping from it. The urge to taste that substance has my heart stuttering in my chest.

*Maybe my brother is right about me.*

*I'm a—*

A blur of strength and danger silences my thought before I can finish it. The creature moves faster than I would have given him credit for, rushing over me until I'm flattened against the bed and he's above me. He's enormous, but his face is level with mine as his claws sink into the mattress on either side of my head. Just one palm could crush me if he wanted. "You are no whore, little star. You are *mine.*"

A whimper escapes me, but it's not one of fear.

It's one of *need.*

His claim awakens something inside of me. The figment seems to see the mixture of my desperation and my desire. The ache rolling through my body makes me squirm underneath him as I squeeze my eyes shut, then force them open again.

He watches me as if debating something. Then he leans in and sniffs my neck, and for some reason, the gesture seems strangely intimate.

He *growls.*

My thoughts become a jumbled mess when the beast takes one massive claw and scrapes it down my body, instantly shredding my nightdress and revealing me to him. He was careful enough not to scratch me, minus one stinging spot just above my navel.

He growls again, but this time it's a possessive sound. "You hunger, little one. Let me take care of you. Let me give you what you desire."

I don't know what he means, but it sounds right.

He watches me with those mirrorlike eyes until I finally nod.

"I need your verbal agreement," he insists. He lowers himself until his face is close enough to mine that I can feel his heated breath. His tongue flicks across my lower lip, branding me with his power.

*He certainly feels real, for a figment.*

I don't know what kind of magic has made my dreams so vivid, but I'm going to take full advantage of it.

Because this might be the only pleasure I'll ever find in my life. I highly doubt a successful union with Earl Rinhold will result in any sort of empowering desire. He seems like the type of male to take what he wants without caring for anyone else's needs.

"I want you to take care of me," I tell the beast.

My words seem to greatly please him, because his lips stretch into a wide, wicked grin.

It's a terrifying sight full of teeth and danger, and I'm probably insane for reaching out to touch his face.

He lets me explore his surprisingly soft skin. It's cool to the touch, but not unpleasant. I brush my fingers through his hair, finding that incredibly soft as well.

He nuzzles into my touch before he lowers, and his

tongue flicks over my chest, making me suck in a breath. He tastes my skin, taking his time rolling his tongue around one nipple, then attends to the next.

"God..." I breathe, only to earn a chuckle from the beast tasting me like a snack.

"Call me Cain," he says, flicking his mirrorlike gaze up to mine.

Of course my figment would call itself Cain. That's probably the most insane thing I could possibly imagine.

Sex with the King of the Elite City, a monster who pretends to be a God.

A beast who eats dreams.

*Could he be...?*

The question flings right out of my head when Figment-Cain dips his tongue into my belly button, lapping up the droplet of blood that had fallen into it.

Then he proceeds to taste me lower.

He's just above my throbbing core when he glances up once more.

I wonder if he's going to ask me for permission again, but he already has it.

Instead, he intentionally keeps my gaze as he buries his tongue in my folds, making me bow off the bed.

He takes one hand, which is bigger than my entire abdomen, and slams me back down.

"Stay," he says against my sex, making me tremble as I whimper something unintelligible.

Because I've never felt anything like this. I've been touched before, very briefly over layers of clothing, but this beast's thick tongue covers the entirety of my aching flesh.

He rolls his tongue over me, giving me wet, delicious friction as I find myself spreading my legs for him.

*Whore.*

*Slut.*

My brother's words snap at me like a whip, and I try to close my legs to prove him wrong, but the beast between them won't let me go.

Not now that he's tasted me.

He growls as if irritated that I'm not accepting his pleasure without shame. He removes his tongue and stands, towering over me.

Fear jolts through my body.

*Or is that pleasure?*

His massive cock is between my legs now, but his shaft is pressing against my throbbing core. More of that silver liquid seeps over the bulbous tip, dripping down until the icy sensation coats my intimate flesh.

"I won't take your virginity, not until you're ready," he assures me, but he's moving his hips, rubbing the silky hardness of himself against me.

*How does he know I'm a virgin?*

*Dream figment—right.*

His cock feels different than his tongue did, but the sensation is just as incredible.

"I am going to make you come regardless," he informs me as if that's nonnegotiable.

I whimper as he pushes one of his knees onto the bed, propping my leg up on his thigh. It exposes me more to him, spreading me wide open as he continues to gyrate his hips and graze his massive cock over my clit.

The sensation is deliciously overwhelming, and my eyes roll as pleasure blooms between my legs, forcing out any distracting memories of my brother.

"That's a good girl," my figment praises. "Let me take care of you."

I sink my fingers into the sheets and fist them as his cock slides over me, but that's just the base. The rest of it rolls over my abdomen, and the head reaches just beneath my breasts.

And he's smearing that silver fluid all over my body in the process.

He continues to thrust, and I find myself wondering if his cock would even fit inside me. The base of it is rubbing over my clit, leaving his balls to erotically slap against me, all of it pushing me toward an edge that might make me go mad.

I see why he's inched his leg under mine now. He curls me, forcing his shaft to ride higher as he cups my breasts and pushes his dick between them.

The sight of that silver liquid spilling over my breasts makes my body go hot.

*It's not just liquid.*

*It's his cum.*

I stick my tongue out, acting on instinct, which makes my figment curse.

"Don't tease, little one, or I'll—"

I inch down, which removes the delicious pressure from my clit but brings me close enough to run my tongue over his weeping slit.

The flavor of peaches and cream isn't what I expected as I taste this figment's cum—but it's my dream. Why can't cum taste like a dessert?

Hungry for more, I lick again, earning a warning growl from the beast.

An insane part of me likes to taunt him, to test these boundaries I've created in my mind.

Maybe he'll turn on me and devour me.

Maybe not.

All I know is that I want *more*.

I slip down and grab his cock with both hands, then try to fit it into my mouth.

It's almost too large, but I manage it. He groans as more of that delicious peaches-and-cream mixture spills down my throat. It keeps going until I can't swallow any more, and I cough on it, making it run down my cheeks and onto my chest.

"Wicked little nightmare," he says, but it sounds more like a compliment than an insult. "I should have made you come first, but now I'm going to make you come on my *face.*"

I yelp as he scoops an arm around my back, then yanks me up with him. He flips onto the bed, then easily uses both hands to lift me onto his face.

I reach out for something to hold on to and find the headboard. I grip it as he runs his tongue over my throbbing core.

"You taste like peaches soaked in wine," he says, which takes me out of the moment.

That's almost what he had tasted like to me—which makes sense. This is a dream. I'm just reflecting what I want in him.

Still, when he pushes his massive tongue just into my entrance, I suck in a breath.

He doesn't go further, even though I want him to.

He said he wasn't going to take my virginity.

*It's just a dream. What does that matter?*

I push my hips down, demanding more of the delicious sensations that make my entrance spread and burn, but he wraps his fingers around my hips and stops me.

He holds me still as I grapple against his fingers, but he doesn't give me a chance to protest. His tongue laves me, pushing at my entrance while simultaneously stimulating my clit.

It's enough to force me over the edge.

"Cain!" I scream, not sure why I use the name he gave me.

When I know this isn't real.

The climax that shatters through me doesn't care what's real and what's not. My entire body bends to the pleasure, my spine arching as I throw back my head and let the ecstasy rule.

A crash causes me to fall, and then everything shatters like glass. Pain shoots through me, making the pleasure seem like a distant dream as I slam back into my body.

Groaning, I find my body still fully clothed, and my thumb has turned blue where my notebook's leather rope had been hooked on it.

The notebook that is now on the ground, the impact of it falling having woken me up from my nightmare.

*If that was a nightmare, I want to fall back asleep right now.*

Carefully, I wobble out of my chair and wince at a sting of pain that makes my dress stick to my stomach. I pull up the hem, then stare at the blotch of blood just above my navel.

There's nothing that could have cut me. But the blood is there, and so is the stain on the inside of my nightgown. I fumble with the silk and stretch it out, staring at it as I blink a few times while trying to decide if this is real.

*It was just a dream,* I tell myself, even though I can't explain the cut.

Maybe it's a strange side effect of the blood contract.

I can't entertain the idea that it was something more—something real.

Because that would mean I've attracted the attention of a monster.

Of the King of the Elite City.

*Cain doesn't care about me.*

*No one does.*

I let my dress drape back over me as I shuffle into bed.

The sheets are fluffy and undisturbed, but I can't help feeling like I'm crawling into it for the second time tonight.

It doesn't much matter, because I'll be up in a few short hours, facing a real nightmare.

The one where I become a Lady of the Rinhold family.

And that's a nightmare I won't be able to wake up from.

# CHAPTER 8

# CAGE

*"Find a world no one knows about."*

Sabre's words ring in my head, refusing to go away. He knows it's an impossible task.

This is how he handles difficult situations. He makes the solution impossible so that he can just give up.

*I'm not fucking giving up on us, Sabre.*

I'm determined to tell him we don't need another world. We can do what my family has been training for all along.

Take out King Nos.

I watch the royal bastard himself from my hidden position in the shadows. Stealth is my skill, one that allows me within viewing distance of King Nos without detection.

My perch is a hallway balcony within the palace. There are many of them throughout the various floors, and they're a horrible security risk. If I took over the palace, the first thing I'd do is close those off or add in detection alarms, if there was power to spare.

King Nos appears wilted as he shuffles along. He grumbles to himself as his long black hair tangles around his dull crown.

I can't see much else of him because four massive Strigoi guards surround him at all times.

That's why I was trained to go after Sabre and my brother was trained to take out the four guards, and finally the King, with distance weapons.

I need to get close up to make a kill. There's no way I'd get through four guards in time to take the shot. Not without an ability like my brother's to help me stay out of harm's way.

The group pauses as the Queen exits. Queen Serena had once been a beautiful woman, but the strain of her marriage to a male like King Nos shows on her face, making her resemble more of a walking corpse than the powerful Strigoi she should be.

Her cheeks suck in with dark shadows, and the dull red glow of her eyes flickers like a candle about to go out. Her long nails are manicured and have a fabricated sheen to them. I imagine that, underneath, her nails are gray and brittle, just like her fangs she keeps hidden behind painted lips.

To her credit, she has lasted longer than the other Queens, but that's because King Nos likely doesn't want to entertain the idea of finding a new one. He's been draining Sabre instead, leaving just enough power to keep his Queen alive.

It wouldn't take much to push her over the edge, now that I think about it.

Crouching down, I decide to listen. There might be a clue here I'm missing.

"What do you want, Serena?" King Nos grinds out, sounding irritated.

The Queen narrows her eyes. She has no guards of her

own, which shows how little King Nos cares for her. "Another section of the blood fields has fallen," she informs him. "We need bodies to replace them."

He pushes past the first two guards so he can face her directly. Honestly, it's a stupid move on his part. At this point, his own Queen might try to kill him so the torch can pass to Sabre. I don't think she's aware that King Nos has been draining him, or she might have done it already. She favors Sabre, in her own way.

He sneers at her and displays large, threatening fangs. "Then hunt for them yourself."

She hisses back at him, displaying her petite fangs. I was wrong, they're not gray or brittle. They seem to be the only part of her she's held on to, her last line of defense. "Don't tempt me, husband. I might find a supple young male to sink my fangs into, and I'll never come home."

He chuckles as if that thought amuses him. "You'd be doing me a favor, Serena. Now, if you'd kindly get the fuck out of my way, I have a kingdom to feed."

The blood drains from my face.

*King Nos is heading to the throne room.*

Which means Sabre is about to go unconscious for a few hours and I won't get to talk to him at all, not unless I can find him in the dream plane before he's shut himself off.

He doesn't want me to see whatever happens in there when his father drains him.

I've never caught the exact moment when King Nos sits on the throne and begins the drain. I've yet to actually locate the throne room in my meanderings. Given that it's the center of power for the Strigoi Kingdom, it's well hidden.

The hum of voices dissipates behind me as I work my way silently through the shadows and head back to Sabre's room. I'm in an entirely different wing, and there are numerous Strigoi servants and guards I need to avoid. It'll take me time to get back to him.

I rarely pray to Morpheus, but I find myself doing so in my mind.

*Please don't let me be too late.*

WHEN I FINALLY REACH SABRE'S CHAMBERS, I FIND TWO GUARDS standing sentry outside.

*Fuck.*

King Nos sometimes guards his son. Not for any concern for his well-being, but because Sabre is his source of power to keep the kingdom alive. And based on what I've seen, it's holding everything up by a thread.

*Sorry, Sabre. I don't have a choice on this one.*

Skittering onto the ceiling, I draw on my reserves that keep me in my monster form. I use my claws to stay aloft as I dig them into the grooves and cling to the surface.

If the guards had been any other species, I could simply put them to sleep and trap them in their dreams. But they'll have abilities of their own, and I can't risk them fighting me or going back to King Nos to tell him that I was here.

A roar from inside Sabre's room sends a chill up my body, finalizing my decision.

He's in pain.

*Fuck this.*

Dropping from my position, I slice my claws straight down the spines of the guards. They don't even have time to cry out.

They split in half as dark blood pools around their mangled corpses.

I frown at them before I ram the door open and find Sabre with no shirt as he grips the bedsheets. Sweat drips down his neck as his eyes blaze with red.

He snaps his wild gaze onto me, then he snarls, showing off his terrifying fangs. They're twice the size of his father's.

Because he's twice the Strigoi King Nos will ever be.

"You shouldn't be here, Cage," he growls at me.

"Where else should I be?" I ask.

Sabre's chest heaves as he seems to fight the drain. "Anywhere else. I don't want you to see me like this. I—"

His words are cut off as he throws back his head with a roar of pain. Black veins snake up his neck, and blood rolls down his cheeks in place of tears.

I go to catch him when he falls, but the second I touch him, I'm drawn into the dream plane.

I'm drawn into a nightmare that Sabre has to live every day.

*I'm here, my prince.*

*And I'm not letting you go.*

## CHAPTER 9

## SABRE

No, dying must be more pleasant than this.

All of the energy I've carefully built up since the last time my father stole from me is ripped away. It doesn't matter how far I bury it down. The power of the Strigoi throne is merciless and obedient to the King.

A roar rips from my throat as invisible daggers tear me open, digging deep enough that the cut grazes my very soul.

Sometimes I wonder if the drain doesn't work as well on my father because he doesn't have a soul left. Maybe he made one too many deals with Lucifer. Maybe he's whittled himself away with greed and ambition, only to find himself in the deep end of madness.

"Sabre," a voice echoes.

Cage's voice.

*No...*

I don't want him to see me like this. I know what happens next, and it's humiliating.

My father drains me too often for me to have the

strength to stand up to him and the four pet Strigoi he keeps on a leash. He wouldn't kill me. Instead, he'd chain me up in a dark dungeon and keep me alive, and then the feeds would be even more brutal.

At least if I play along, I can be with Cage every now and then. I can pretend to rejuvenate my reserves when I hunt in the mortal realm.

What I really need is a true break to stop the constant drain and build up my strength enough to take out King Nos. I don't want the throne, so that poses another problem. As my father's killer, I'd be forced to take the crown. The throne itself would call to me and lure me until I played my part.

"Don't follow me here," I say as I keep my eyes closed. A headache throbs at my temples, and the world around me swirls, even in darkness.

I'm trapped in a forced dreamwalking episode, one where I'm taken into the core of the Strigoi Kingdom itself. It resides deep within the dream plane that can only be reached through the throne.

My father always sends me to a horrid, dark place where icy chains snake around my arms and legs and criss-cross over my chest.

Goose bumps spread across my skin as the sharp pain of frost sweeps over me. The chains slowly materialize. Blood runs down my arms and legs as tiny spikes thread their way into my flesh.

Cage must be stupid enough to try to stop them, because he curses in pain as I feel him grab the ones going for my chest. I fling my eyes open, not surprised to see him holding on despite the pain.

But he's not meant for the drain. It could kill him.

"Let go, Cage. Let it happen," I tell him.

He growls and shows his fangs, but he doesn't have

anyone to sink them into. My father isn't here. He's tucked away in his throne room with four powerful Strigoi guards who probably get the lion's share of the power he steals from me.

It's almost as if my father is biding his time, waiting for something or someone to bail him out.

Cage holds on like the stubborn, beautiful idiot he is. "I'm tired of this shit, Sabre. Don't just stand there and take this. Fight it!"

Pain lances through me as the chains stretch and move, digging deeper in response to Cage's interference.

"I have before," I admit. "The next drain was only worse because of it."

I've learned to get it over with. I store up the hatred and anger, saving it in place of the life force my father has stolen from me for the day I can unleash it all back.

Cage continues to struggle and grips one of the chains still attempting to wrap around my chest. He yanks it hard enough to tear my skin. I hiss in pain, but my stomach drops when the chain flinches and moves for Cage.

"Cage!" I heave against the restraints, ignoring how they tear at me as I try to grab the chain. "Get the fuck out of here!"

The Strigoi throne has sensed Cage's interference. Now it's going to feed on him, too.

My father doesn't know what he's doing. I've confirmed that on numerous occasions when he's failed to describe the actual process. He simply states that I "owe the family my due." He's aware the throne takes my power, but he doesn't know how it does it.

King Nos's mind has corrupted the throne. He's the reason the kingdom is slowly dying and falling apart.

But damn if I let him take Cage from me, too.

I roar as I grab the chains with both hands. A frantic urge inside of me burns in my soul, desperate to get out.

To my shock, the chains shatter. They splinter through the air like glass as a scream rends the air.

A feminine scream, one I've heard just once before.

Twisting around, the pain vanishes as Cage and I appear in a woman's bedroom.

It looks like a place out of the Regency Era, except the purple glow of magical orbs seems out of place.

A massive bed takes up much of the spacious room, but my attention is on the petite female sitting on it.

She's wearing a white, gauzy nightdress that leaves little to the imagination. The sight of her nipples beading against the fabric as she leans back has my cock going rigid.

"Tell me you're seeing this," Cage whispers.

"I am," I say. Although, I have no idea why the Strigoi throne would replace its standard torture with a treat on a platter.

I quickly realize we aren't alone when I take note of the beast the female is staring at.

"Cage," I say when I catch sight of a massive creature, one with horns, fangs, and red eyes, and a massive cock leaking silver cum onto the floor.

He seems like he's about to tear the poor female apart.

Except, as terrified as she appears with her pretty chest fluttering like a bird's, she licks her lips with interest.

*Holy fuck. Please say this is real.*

"Scream again. I liked it," the creature says. "Ssss-carlett."

That appears to be her name, because her cheeks flush with color, and her gaze drops to the monster's cock.

The scene freezes for a moment, giving me a chance to slowly peruse the scene.

"Are you doing this?" I ask Cage.

He shakes his head. "No. You?"

"No," I confirm as I approach the female.

She's perfect.

She also can't be real, because when I look at her, I see a future I have yearned for. One where I don't have to seek out a messy patricide followed by a worthless life on the Strigoi throne. I imagine the drain would feel about the same, except I'd be forced to do it to myself.

I wouldn't have my father to hate. In all reality, I suspect that's the strongest reason I haven't tried to kill him yet.

Cage whistles. "Damn, look at the junk on this guy," he says. "I seriously doubt that'll fit inside this female. Or any female, for that matter."

Glancing over my shoulder, I have to agree. But where there's a desire, there's a way.

A flicker of silver light trails in the air, catching my attention. I run my fingers over it and find the hairline thread. Lifting it, a trail glimmers between Cage and me, as well as the human and the monster.

"What do you think this is?" I ask Cage.

He finds one of the small threads and examines it. His eyes flash with red as his tongue flicks out to taste it. "You're not going to believe me."

"Try me."

He matches my gaze, and there's an intensity there I haven't seen before.

"I think these are mate ties, Sabre."

A humorless laugh rumbles from my chest. "Then I've definitely created this asinine dream."

Cage straightens. "What if this is real? What if that scream we heard before was a compatible mate meant for us, *waiting* for us."

I shake my head. Cage likely knows about the legend of

a Sigil, but if there was a Sigil out there for me, I would have found her by now.

I've searched all the realms. She's not out there.

"There was no scream," I say as I turn away from the enticing female.

Cage growls. "Stop denying it, Sabre. I know you heard it. Which means if you aren't dreamwalking us here, and I'm not either, then—"

A feminine moan interrupts him, and out of curiosity, I turn around.

My jaw drops at the sight. It's almost as if time has sped up and we missed whatever had happened from their first meeting to now, but I'm not sad about it.

The female named Scarlett is holding on to the headboard.

While she rides the monster's face.

"Cain!" she cries as her entire body spasms, and she throws back her head. Gorgeous red curls tumble down her back all the way to her ass as she gyrates her hips.

"Fuck," Cage says, panting at the sight. His cock is as hard as mine. "Look at that."

"I'm looking," I say breathlessly.

It would be impossible to look away.

But in the periphery of my vision, I spot another version of the same female fully clothed in a chair. A notebook is hanging from her thumb and falls, thumping to the floor.

The second it does, the vision shatters like glass, and Cage and I are thrown back home.

# CHAPTER 10

# SABRE

My cock aches as I stumble into Cage's back. He doesn't have far to go because the wall of my bedroom is right in front of him.

We're precisely where we began. We haven't moved at all.

*It was all a fucking dream.*

*She isn't real.*

*None of it is real.*

He slams his fists against the wall and heaves for breath. "What the fuck was that?" he asks, his voice husky with need.

"Desperation," I decide aloud as I undo my pants. I use my claws to rip his clothes, going too deep in my hurry and leaving bloody lines down his back as I peel away his cloak. I work on his pants next, shoving them down.

Because I need him. I don't care if I'm going insane. My mind is cracking under the pressure it takes to fuel the Strigoi Kingdom without a mate.

Without a Queen.

*Without her.*

I need Cage to help me stop thinking about it.

"Sabre," Cage says with a warning in his tone. "If anyone was desperate, it was our mate—for *us*. She just doesn't know it yet."

Cage has always been the dreamer. No one knows better than a Strigoi how fleeting dreams can really be.

I drag my palm down his back, gathering blood that I then sweep over my rigid cock. The bulbs at the base of my shaft vibrate under my rough touch as I coat myself with Cage's blood.

"If that's what gets you off, I'll play along," I tell him. I'll play games. I'll entertain fantasies.

But I won't believe something that isn't true.

It can't be true. If my mate existed, she wouldn't be a fleeting vision in the dream plane.

And she wouldn't be riding another monster's face. She'd be riding mine.

"Do you want my cock?" I ask him. As much as I want to pound into him, I always ask for permission.

*Always.*

The old habit comes in handy when I'm feeling particularly ravenous like I am right now. I don't know if it's the result of the drain or if my need for a mate is shining through. No one has done what my father is doing. We don't know the effects it might have on me.

My mind could be fracturing. My powers could be creating phantoms of what I desire. Of what I *need*.

"Fuck, of course I want your cock," Cage growls. "I'm rock-hard after seeing that. I'm about to explode. If you don't fuck me, I'll—"

That's all the permission I need. I slam into him from behind, and his muscles bulge from the impact. He braces himself against the wall as he curses, the sound a mixture of pain and pleasure.

I'm not going to be gentle. Not tonight.

Not when I hate myself for what I'm doing to Cage. I can see I'm not the only one acting out of desperation.

"You killed my guards," I guess. It's the only way he could have come here during one of my father's drains. I'm not to be disturbed, for obvious reasons. That's often the only warning I get that a drain is coming—the guards show up.

He grunts when I wrap my hand around his cock and pump him with my thrusts. Moisture beads around my fingers as I coat his shaft with his cum.

"I should have killed more," he growls and every muscle in his body coils like a snake about to strike.

He takes my thrusts like a punishment. He could easily get out of my hold.

I have strength.

But he has speed.

"How many would you kill for me?" I ask as I pant and fuck him harder. "A hundred?"

Claws extend from his fingertips and scrape lines down the wall that I'm going to have to repair. I can't have evidence left behind of what Cage and I do in private.

"Only four," he says with lethal intent.

I stop thrusting and stroke him, tip to base, as I feel a gush of his cum trickle over my fingers. His cock throbs as I edge him and deny him an orgasm. "You saw my father today," I guess.

He hisses when I slowly fuck him, and I twist my fingers over the swollen head of his cock. "He doesn't deserve to live," he growls.

"He doesn't," I agree. "But for now, he is King."

"And when he's dead?" Cage asks as he looks up. "What then?"

I press my lips to his shoulder. My fangs prevent me

from truly kissing him, so I lick the blood and sweat off his skin instead. "Then I'll die a slow death, too."

"It doesn't have to be that way," Cage says.

I don't want to hear his dreams, but the conviction in his soul makes my heart twist. "That's the only way it'll ever be," I say as anger brews in my chest.

I don't want to feel the pain, so I let the rage consume me.

Rage that I can't give Cage the life he deserves.

Rage that when I finally am rid of my father, I'm doomed to become him.

"You'll see," Cage says. "I don't know how, but you'll see."

"Are you going to keep dreaming?" I ask as I stroke him harder and squeeze the base of his cock. "Or are you going to come for me?"

His cock throbs in my hand as his ass tightens. "I'll come if we talk about Scarlett," he says.

I curse. Of course he wants to entertain the fantasy.

"What about her?" I press. I'll play along.

And I won't admit that just the sound of her name has me about to explode.

"I saw silver on her lips. That was the color of Cain's cum. We missed the part where she tasted him," he says as I softly stroke him.

My pace increases as I slap against his ass. "Do you think she liked it?" I ask. The question isn't meant to be genuine, but I find myself excited by the idea.

"Based on how hard those pink little nipples were, she was ready for anything," he says.

My breath is coming in short pants as I entertain the fantasy.

The woman in the dream plane was a fabrication, a

vision, nothing more. She didn't interact with us or notice us.

I don't know why I'd create a dream with another monster to share her. Perhaps I know, on some level, that a mate like that will never belong to me.

"If we ever locate her," I find myself saying, "then I want you to lick her while I take you into my mouth for her to watch."

He groans. "Fuck, yes. I'd like that."

"You'd come in my mouth," I press, feeling my entire body going taut, preparing for an explosion that'll leave me completely spent. "And she'll come in yours."

"Fuck, Sabre. Please, please bite me now."

I didn't realize I'd been grazing his neck with my fangs, leaving teasing little punctures while I talked.

I don't wait. I grin against his shoulder, then thrust hard as I sink my fangs into his flesh.

He groans as his blood burns down my throat. I lick up the nectar that is all Cage as I bury myself in him and fall into a powerful climax. I stroke his cock with each of my thrusts, and I'm rewarded when he explodes with me. His cum and his blood are everywhere, painting my room like a nightmare.

We're both panting as we come down from our high, and I finally release him.

Stumbling back onto the bed, all I can think about is that beautiful female arching her back, and the post-orgasm reality comes slamming into me with the knowledge that I'm never going to see her.

Cage pants from the floor where he's fallen to one knee. He glances up at me, and he must not like the expression on my face.

"You were faking that?" he asks.

I swipe my fingers through my hair and look at the ceiling. "Fuck, Cage. No. I wasn't faking one of the most powerful orgasms of my life."

"But you don't believe she's real," he presses.

I blow out a breath as my cock throbs, still twitching after the indulgent fantasy. "She's not real, Cage. I'm sorry."

Darkness sweeps over his eyes. He heads for the bathroom, no doubt to wash up before he storms off in one of his tantrums. "You're wrong," he growls. "And if you don't try to find her, then I will."

"Have at it, Cage," I growl in return.

He shows his teeth.

I show mine.

Mine are definitely bigger.

As predicted, he storms off into the bathroom. Normally, I'd join him and wash away any blood, help heal any wounds, but not when he's acting like this.

But I can't leave. There are two dead guards outside my door, and that won't go unnoticed for long.

I don't have to lie. I can say that the enemy tried to come after me. It explains all the blood in my room, anyway.

But I'm not sure how much longer my father will believe the story that an assassin got away.

*We can't keep living like this, Cage,* I think as I close my eyes.

I know I should open them again, because the instant my eyes are shut, all I see is Scarlett with her glimmering red hair tumbling down her back.

*I'm going insane,* I lament. *But if you truly are real, Scarlett, my dear, know that the moment I find you, I will covet you.*

*I will own you.*

*I will burn the fucking world for you.*

*So be a good girl and scream for me again.*

*I'll reward you with my tongue.*

# CHAPTER 11

# SCARLETT

The irritating *clink* of a spoon against delicate porcelain has me flinching in my seat.

"Have you been listening to a word I've said, Lady Scarlett?" my guest of today's morning tea barks.

Duchess Rinhold doesn't look amused that I haven't been paying attention. She tilts her head, sending a cascade of her loose curls tumbling over her shoulder. Her hair is done up in the latest style, threaded with dozens of pearls and gems that boast the wealth of the Rinhold family. My own hair is laced with silver, but I have none of the embellishments, making me feel plain next to her.

Her corset is stuffed over a skirt made with layers of muslin and silk that frill around her petite form as she perches on the edge of her chair. She must be around my mother's age, but she doesn't have a single wrinkle on her face. Her golden hair is a crown of ringlets that seem to burst from the style pinning them down, making her look elegant and youthful. She has pale blue eyes that are startling more than striking, giving her a wide-eyed, alert appearance.

Or maybe that's just the evidence of too much magic bleaching her irises. Women in the Magic Sector wear their magic just like they do perfumes or makeup—except this brand of indulgence seeps into the skin.

The biggest reason I've stayed away is that I'm aware of how addictive the expensive tonics can be.

I'm aware of the anti-aging properties of certain elixirs obtainable in the Magic Sector. It's not quite immortality, but a woman like Duchess Rinhold can surely afford a bottle or two—as well as the supply needed to keep up with any ensuing addiction.

She's watching me pensively, her perfectly shaped brows finally arching on one side when I don't answer her.

I want to, but it's difficult to focus every time my mind shifts back to the erotic dream I had last night.

I can't stop thinking about it.

My palm falls to the spot just above my navel. The tiny wound still stings beneath my corset, and even though I can't feel it through the boning, I can't stop resting a hand on my stomach.

The blood had vanished by morning, making me wonder if I hallucinated the wound and the accompanying stain—but it still *feels* like there's a cut on my skin.

Everything about the dream had felt real, leaving me aching in intimate places well into my waking hours.

I cross my legs to stem the throb that doesn't seem to have completely gone away.

I've decided that I've finally snapped after so much pressure. That, combined with the side effects from a courtship blood contract, and my brain is just trying to make sense of things.

"Apologies, Duchess," I eventually say with my smoothest, most elegant voice. My voice training comes in handy when I'm feeling flushed and laying on a thicker accent native to the city than I normally would. The dialect in the Magic Sector seems stronger on that front, anyway. "I'm afraid I'm feeling faint," I tell her, and I know I'm convincing because it's not a lie.

I do feel faint. I haven't slept. And despite the circular trays of finger sandwiches and silver bowls of fruit for today's breakfast, I haven't eaten. Attempting it might just suffocate me entirely because my backup hosting corset is even tighter than my others, given that it was fitted for me years ago.

Duchess Rinhold offers me an empathetic smile and pats my other hand, which is on the table. I had been reaching for my tea, but now I awkwardly flatten my palm against the surface as she makes a show of consoling me.

She thinks I'm overwhelmed by the honor of a courtship with her son. Her thoughts are written all over her face.

*Poor dear. She probably has no sexual experience at all. A courtship with such a sexually active man as the future Duke of the Rinhold family must be too much. Her father should have better prepared her. My Edward will be watched too closely to make use of his mistresses for at least the first year or two. She's going to have to step it up if she's to produce an heir.*

I can't hear her voice in my head, but I still somehow know what she's thinking.

Like the Earl of Rinhold's first name being Edward—a fact I've never come across before.

And the better-known detail that he's apparently a sexual deviant.

That, rumor can confirm.

It's a bit unnerving how she thinks of her son as some sort of prized stud and I'm a mare to be bred. But when it comes to my experiences, her thoughts couldn't be further from the truth.

I'm not naïve. And if anyone had prepared me for the realities of marriage, it was the creature in my dreams.

My cheeks heat as I wonder what she might say if she knew I was feeling faint due to reliving the most intense orgasm of my life, which had happened while I was asleep.

"Yes, of course you're feeling faint, my dear," she says with a gentle tone as her fingers skitter up my arm and trail around the three red scars still embedded in my skin. One will disappear tonight and has already started to fade. "You're still wearing the countdown marks, and I know they can take a toll," she adds, hinting that she, too, found her husband by means of a blood contract, "but you best get used to it. You'll wear more, each numbered for the days of courtship when the timer starts anew."

My eyes widen.

I did not know that.

"Where?" I blurt. The three slashes have already taken up my entire forearm. I'm not sure where I'd fit thirty.

She shrugs. "It varies. Rumor is that they'll appear on your erogenous zones, but they'll be less dramatic. Don't worry."

She doesn't confirm if her marks had been on *her* erogenous zones, not that I'd want to know either way.

A swallow sticks in my throat. "Erogenous zones?" I repeat.

*Dear Cain, does she not even know what the word means?* her narrowed eyes seem to say.

"I assume you don't know where *yours* are," she says aloud instead, thankfully not defining the word for me as she continues, "but it gives your suitor something to work with." She smiles at me as if that should inform me of the word's definition, then pats me again. "The Magic Sector has a lower fertility rate, but it doesn't mean you can't get started right away once you're wed." Her long lashes flutter as she sips her tea, giving me a moment to digest the news that I'm supposed to produce a child as soon as possible. She finally looks me right in the face. "Your family has done well to keep you pure, but a lack of experience might provide frustrations for a new couple. Wouldn't it be helpful if things could be... enjoyable? Hence the placement of the marks among your erogenous zones so that you don't have to say a word." She gives me a soft smile. "Perks of a blood contract, dear."

The Duchess's crude conversation doesn't faze me. I am fully aware of the expectations of a married woman in an Elite family.

My cheeks heat for an entirely different reason.

Am I to assume that Earl Rinhold cares so little of female anatomy that he needs a road map of how to make me orgasm? The figment in my dreams didn't need any guidance.

*Why do I keep comparing the two?*

My dreams aren't real. Earl Rinhold very much is.

"Did I hear something about erogenous zones?" a silky male voice asks as the most handsome man I've ever seen in my life walks through the doorway.

I blink up at the gorgeous specimen of a male, staring for a bit longer than I should, but I can't look away.

I had not expected Earl Rinhold to be *beautiful*.

Rumor had circulated of his attractive appearance—likely enhanced by magic at birth—but rumor can't always be believed. No one looks like the culmination of every woman's desire made into flesh.

In this case, though, the rumor seems to be accurate. That's exactly what he looks like.

His face is perfect. His blond hair has a note of his mother's curls, but it's charming on him as it frames his gentle eyes.

He's wearing the latest fashion of velvet and stripes that flared up two weeks ago. A royal blue embroidered vest is fitted to his muscular but lean form, betraying that it's tailored to perfection. The vest's design matches the blue stripes down his dark pants. Even the metal buttons on his polished boots have a blue tint.

My gaze doesn't know where to settle, so I find myself admiring his face again.

"Don't let my mother intimidate you," he says as he grips the back of her chair and leans in to plant a chaste kiss on her cheek. He lowers his voice as he chides her. "No frightening my future bride, please, dear mother." His marble-blue eyes flick up to meet mine.

The simple gesture has my stomach doing flips as he gives me the faintest of smiles.

Somehow, that smile makes him even more attractive. There's a kindness there that seems almost fabricated, too sweet to be real.

*No one is this perfect.*

He doesn't keep my gaze for long. Like a true gentleman, he breaks eye contact first to give me a sense of security.

To let me think I'm the one in control.

This isn't the terrifying, ruthless Earl Rinhold of rumor.

And, most interestingly of all, he doesn't seem to be hiding anything.

There's no secret agenda written in his features. There are no inner thoughts bleeding out through his eyes.

Which is a first. Every time I meet someone, I see the image they try to present, but I can also sense what they're really thinking, as if I'm looking through broken glass.

I can glimpse who they really are underneath the surface —but Earl Rinhold doesn't seem to have another layer to view.

*No. This can't be right. Everyone has a mask.*

It's a strange thing for someone with my affliction to meet another person who is exactly who they present themselves to be.

*Maybe it's confidence?* I wonder, trying to make sense of it.

Because I know not to doubt my abilities. My *affliction* is that I'm originally from a village, meaning I've been genetically modified and my bloodline is the result of generations of experimentation.

Something my brother likes to remind me of when I don't give in to his demands.

But it's the memory of my father that rises to the surface first, bobbing on an ocean of the past.

*"What do you see, Scarlett?"* he asked. I remember my father bringing me to a dark place with lots of people. I couldn't have been older than six or seven.

But he was testing me.

*"Never let them know what you can do,"* my mother had said in one of my earliest memories.

*"Just a bunch of men, Father."* I gave him the answer I'd been told to give.

Give them nothing.

He seemed relieved at the time, but I learned something about myself that day.

Because I *had* seen something in that room. Some men had been out of place, their eyes the wrong color and their thoughts terrifying enough to make me wary of men in general.

But the Elite City was made up of different kinds of men. One of them had been thinking about slitting my throat just to settle a debt with my father.

Mysteriously, he died not too long after that night. But I

imagined my father had various ways of settling his debts —ways that I hadn't been ready to accept until now.

The things I'd written about him in my notebook had broken my heart, but I wasn't lying to myself about my father anymore.

He's a man, just like the rest of them.

I tilt my head as I watch Earl Rinhold draw up a chair and strike up idle chatter with his mother. He's giving me a chance to observe him, one I take full advantage of.

He's not like the men I remember from that night.

Earl Rinhold is gentle and charming. The air around him seems lighter when he grins, and I can't help but watch him as my curiosity blooms.

He slips his fingers through silky blond hair that immediately bounces back into stubborn, wavy curls. His stormy blue eyes are mesmerizing, seeming to change color with the light like mine do. They were definitely marble blue earlier. He steals a glance, giving me one of those faint smiles again, before responding to something his mother had said.

No matter how hard I try, I can't read him at all. Normally, some sort of thought pops into my head, some flutter of emotion or hidden agenda.

There's just... nothing.

My ability is one that comes from my background, but it's a secret that only my mother knows about.

*A secret that she'll take to her grave.*

Grief swells in my chest before I push it down. I cover my emotion with a cough, and I dab my lips with my napkin before putting the cloth back onto my lap.

I need to visit her before I leave.

It might be the last time I see my mother ever again.

"She's overwhelmed, the poor dear. You'll have to ask her again, Edward," Duchess Rinhold says. Her tone has sharpened like a blade, drawing my attention enough for me to pull out of my own thoughts.

Earl Rinhold doesn't seem put off in the least. Instead, his eyes brighten when I finally look at him. "You're quite beautiful, Lady Scarlett. Is red hair a recessive gene in the Nightingale line?"

My eyebrow inches upward. Even though I'm unprepared for the personal question, I have an answer ready. It's not the first time my legitimacy as an Elite member has been questioned because of the unusual color of my hair. "Would you like to see my papers, Earl Rinhold?" I glide to my feet with trained elegance. "If you'd like to follow me to the study, they're—"

He stands and offers me his hand. I don't take it. "Please, Lady Scarlett. I was not questioning your origins. I wanted to know if..." An adorable blush warms his cheeks, making his eyes look brighter as he smiles, then he looks down. "Presumptuous of me, perhaps, to bring it up so early. I'm just asking about children." His gaze flicks up to mine, trapping them in the storm of his sapphire irises. "Perhaps they will have red hair like yours?"

I furtively blink at him, not sure if I should be offended or flattered.

*He is already thinking about children?*

Nothing about him gives away anything more than what he's said. The silence of him unnerves me and fascinates me all at the same time.

"Was that really your question, Earl Rinhold?" I ask as he finally pockets the hand he had been offering.

He hums before he answers. The sound does funny things to my insides that I try not to think about. "No, it seems I've fumbled my way off topic." He licks his lips, looking at me with boyish charm before he speaks again. "Would you like to go to a fête with me, Lady Scarlett?"

"A fête?" I dumbly repeat.

Why am I a broken record today?

His mother clears her throat as she rises and flicks her fan open, then seems to beat the air with it. "At the Rinhold residence, of course," she adds as her curls brush over her shoulder. "In three days' time."

"For me?" I squeak.

Duchess Rinhold trills with an irritating laugh that's one octave too high. "Dear me, no. The Choosing for the Rinhold Village is in three days, child. Doesn't your family hold celebrations, too? The Nightingale Village's Day of the Choosing should be…" She counts off on her fingers. "Right, a little under a week from now. I haven't seen an invitation, so I'm going to assume it's a quiet affair for the Nightingales." Her eyes glitter. She knows my family can't afford a party, and she just demonstrated that she already knows the ins and outs of my family's business down to the Day of the Choosing on the train schedule. "You'll get plenty of fêtes of your own if you pass the courtship," she adds.

My cheek stings in the same place where my brother had struck me, but it feels like Duchess Rinhold lashed out at me with words rather than her hand.

And the sting is sharper for it.

She acts as if the courtship is some sort of test, one that I'll have to pass if I'm to *earn my place* as her daughter.

Earl Rinhold seems to have noticed that the blood has completely drained from my face—making me feel faint again—as he reaches out to steady me.

But when his fingers brush my arm, ice shoots through my system, making me yelp.

*What was that?*

Shadows blink into existence through every reflective surface, making me swear I can hear a growl rumbling through the room.

It's gone in a second, and I force myself to take in a shaky breath.

*It's just like last night.*

*I'm losing my mind.*

Earl Rinhold flexes his fingers, frowning as though he isn't sure if he should touch me again, then gently grips my elbow. My world doesn't flip upside down this time, and we both relax.

"My mother seems to have been incredibly rude and embarrassed me in front of my delicate bride," he says, sending a cold glare to the woman still fanning herself. There's a brief spark of the icy sensation I sensed a moment before, but it's gone in a flash and he's guiding me out of the room.

"Please forgive my mother. This is a trying time for her—she feels like she's being replaced," he says conversationally as he guides me down the hall.

I don't know where he's taking me. The only things in this direction are more drawing rooms and a locked hall that leads to the rest of the woefully under-furnished manor and our living quarters.

"She has every right to feel threatened, Earl Rinhold," I automatically reply. I've been trained to say the right thing in the right tone and at the right time.

I know I've done all those things, but I'm still expecting some sort of backlash. The warm smile that Earl Rinhold gives me feels so different from the shock of ice a moment before, including the look he had given the Duchess.

"Please, call me Edward," he says with a conspiratorial whisper.

An unbidden blush heats my cheeks as I lower my eyelashes. "Edward," I say, sensing his pleasure as he squeezes my elbow.

Is this what flirting feels like?

He stops at the locked door to the rest of the manor and surprises me when he produces a key. "I bribed your lovely handmaiden for it," he says with a wink.

Of course Rosie would be susceptible to Earl Rinhold's charm. She was as afraid of him as I was, but now I know she's going to be waiting for me in my room to gossip well into the hours of the night.

I find myself looking forward to it. It's something a Lady would do and is also a pleasant distraction from my family's situation.

"Which one is your mother's?" he asks, making my skin prickle with warning.

It's not a secret that my mother is sick, but it wouldn't do for a member of the Rinhold family to see our weaknesses.

*My future husband,* I correct myself.

*Edward.*

"Third door on the right," I find myself telling him.

He gives me a nod, one that seems to show gratitude for my trust and not just the information.

When we arrive at my mother's door, he produces a small vial that glitters with silver.

My eyes widen.

"Place two drops on her tongue. It'll make her lucid enough for a conversation, but don't give her more, or else she'll become dependent. And I can't say I'll be able to procure more than this."

He presents the tonic, one that I was just thinking about earlier.

An anti-aging tonic, an elixir that is probably for cosmetic purposes, but it should work against illness, too.

Theoretically, anyway.

"Thank you, Earl Rinhold," I say as I take it and coddle the vial to my chest. It might be from lack of sleep, but the edges of my eyes sting, and I squeeze them shut to keep the tears in.

When I open them again, the attractive Earl is smiling at me. "Like I said, call me Edward, Lady Scarlett." He presents his hand, and I give him mine. He lifts my hand to press a small kiss against my skin.

My stomach flips, and I stay poised like that while his gaze lingers on mine.

*This is definitely what flirting feels like.*

Except, he's given me a tonic that's worth more than I care to think about.

If Earl Rinhold is trying to impress me, it's working.

"And you can thank me by accepting my gifts. I'll be sending a new dress for the fête, and it would please me greatly if you wore it," he says.

I hadn't agreed to go to the fête, but given that my courtship starts on the same day as the Choosing—an important event for families before Monsters Night, when selections are made that will determine our point earnings —I don't feel like I can rightly say no.

"I'll think about it, Edward," I say with a shy smile and just a touch of a proper Lady's dialect intertwined with my words.

But there's enough of me in the phrasing that I'm kicking myself.

I expect him to be vexed with me, but Earl Rinhold seems to like the display of my inner spirit.

"And I'll be thinking about *you*," he says as he retreats from my view.

My heart is pounding in my chest as I watch him leave. Only when I'm sure that he's gone do I enter my mother's room.

No matter what happens, I'm grateful for this moment.

I'm grateful for a chance to say goodbye.

# CHAPTER 12

## CAIN

Days in the Elite City normally fly by in a flurry of paperwork, meetings, and the prayers of my loyal citizens. Nighttime is when I get to walk the Dream Realm and look for a real meal.

I know I'm not eating tonight.

An incident has made the humans fearful, giving me more than enough nourishment, should my beast want it. I suspect Helia is to blame for that, and I'm glad she has likely already returned to Monster City. She tends to forget that the Elite City and her capital have distinct differences.

My citizens are more delicate and must be handled with care.

There's one particular citizen I'd very much like to tend to right now, but the woman who has captured my interest isn't giving me an opening. She's not praying to me, so that means I can't watch over her.

I might be able to find her when she falls asleep. But until then, I'm left in the dark.

My beast ignores a barrage of prayers he would

normally gobble up, but he's abstained from any prayer that didn't taste like peaches since last night.

Sadly, Scarlett Nightingale hasn't prayed to me again.

*Why isn't she praying?* I wonder with a frown as I rummage through endless paperwork.

I hate being the King of the Elite City some days, and loathe it during others. Namely because there is always a request, a form, or a letter that needs my attention in the ever-growing pile on my desk.

A faint knock at my door has me growling as my teeth thicken in my mouth.

My beast is just a hairsbreadth from the surface, and I don't seem to be able to gain a full handle on him.

My secretary, Bernard, is one of the few monsters on my staff in the city. My tower has more than enough guest rooms to accommodate monsters who might stay here, and Bernard has become a permanent fixture.

"Rough night, my king?" he asks as he tilts his head with a birdlike gesture.

He's a Raven, a creature that lurks in the shadows and is known for its stealth. His human form has fluffy, jet-black hair and eyes as dark as pitch, and his face has symmetrically sharp features. Helia has asked to borrow him multiple times, but I've always refused.

Bernard is not a *pet*. He's my friend.

Which is why he's comfortable enough to observe that I'm on edge.

"On the contrary. I had an eventful night that was quite enjoyable," I say as I lean back and grab my sweating drink. It has created a ring of moisture on the neglected paperwork it was sitting on. I have trouble caring about what it might have damaged. I take a swig, almost unaffected by the spike of alcohol that humans seem to enjoy, but this one has a fruity flavor I requested the kitchens to add.

Peaches.

I shouldn't be this obsessed... but after tasting the flavor between her legs, Scarlett Nightingale has become an all-consuming desire that haunts my waking hours, and if a Dream Eater can dream, she'll be mine.

*"She is the key."*

Those words roll over and over in my head in Edward Rinhold's voice.

The overconfident human seems to know a lot about her. Perhaps more than he should, which has drawn my attention.

"Then why do you look like you're about to eat another village?" Bernard asks, placing the stack of new envelopes in the incoming mail tray, which is already overflowing.

I glower at him. "Careful, Bernard. I'm in no mood."

He's a good friend. He's warning me that he can see my monster threatening to take control. The last time I let him out, too many people died.

I promised that wouldn't happen again.

Humans are a rare and precious commodity. Even if some might need to die to keep the entire train from careening off the tracks, a massacre wouldn't help anyone.

And contrary to popular belief, I am not evil. I regret that sort of bloodshed at my hands.

But no matter how hard I try to play nice, at the end of the night, I'm still a powerful monster without a mate or a mate-circle to keep me grounded.

I'm dangerous, and I need to do something about that.

Bernard sighs, then digs through the pile and slaps a blood-red envelope onto the desk. "Then maybe you should accept this invitation, my lord. I was going to suggest otherwise, but I think a fête might do you some good."

Arching an eyebrow, I take the envelope and slit one of my extended claws through it. My monster insists on bleeding through my body, so I don't even try to hide the fact that one of my hands has changed.

My eyes widen when I read the invitation. "A Choosing fête at the Rinhold residence?" I ask, then glance up at the Raven who has eyes everywhere. "You know exactly who's going to be there, don't you, Bernard?"

He grins, showing off sharp teeth. His black tongue flicks out when he talks. "I wouldn't be a very good Raven if I didn't pick up on the fact that you've found a compatible mate, my lord. She's going to be there."

"At her courtship entrance," I clarify. "Under a contract written in *my* blood."

Bernard shrugs one shoulder, betraying that he already knew all of that information. "I'm sure you'll find a way around those details. Plus, maybe you can solve a little riddle for me while you're there."

Now my Raven has my attention. "A riddle?"

He clicks his black tongue. "Yes, Sire. There's one thing I can't seem to figure out, and it has to do with this new red-haired bride everyone suddenly seems to be so interested in." His dark eyes glitter as I silently wait for him to continue. Bernard delights in dragging out the suspense. He's incredibly smart and, at the same time, infuriatingly calculating. "There's something different about her. I just can't place my feathers on what that *something* might be."

Indeed, I noticed that right away.

"She's from a village," I say, then add, "but you knew that already."

His head flicks to the other side in that distinctly bird-like gesture. "I did."

So he wasn't necessarily talking about her genetic makeup.

There was something *else* that made her special.

*"She is the key."*

But why?

Neatly folding up the invitation, I tuck it away in my vest pocket. "I suppose I'm going to a fête, then."

Bernard awards me with a bright smile. "Shall I go with you?"

I nod. "You'll be my eyes and ears. And if you find any shiny things to play with when you're done, that'll be your reward."

His dark eyes glitter with the prospect. Bernard loves shiny things—namely, Elite women who have a penchant for losing their chaperones.

A fête at the Rinhold residence will have a surplus of those. None of the eligible high-class ladies, of course, but there are plenty of second- and third-class Magic Sector citizen fodder who will likely attend.

And I'll be there to observe if Earl Rinhold disappears with any of them. Because if he does, he'll be violating the blood contract.

Then... Scarlett Nightingale will be mine.

A devious grin overtakes my face. "A fête sounds exactly like what I need right now."

My monster growls in the back of my mind as my claws recede.

"It seems your beast agrees," Bernard observes.

My Raven bows and takes his leave, not bothering with pleasantries as he gives me blessed solitude.

I pick up where I left off on the paperwork, approving train schedules and other activities for the various Choosing Day activities the Elite families have planned. They're not all on the same day, but they're all in preparation for Monsters Night, which is just around the corner.

The annual event where monsters find their mates and balance their powers has become a ritual, one that doesn't include me.

This year, though, I feel a stirring of hope.

For the first time since I can remember, a Dream Eater dares to have a dream of his own.

*I'll find a way to have you, Scarlett Nightingale.*

*Even if I have to burn everything I've built to the ground.*

*You.*

*Will.*

*Be.*

*Mine.*

## CHAPTER 13

# SCARLETT

It takes my eyes a moment to adjust to the dreary darkness of my mother's room.

My nose wrinkles as musty, foul air assaults my senses. I fumble with my dress and pluck out a sheer handkerchief, pressing it to my face in an attempt to stem the stench.

As I pass by the magicked lights, they flicker on, having been spelled to activate when they sense movement.

I spot the culprit of the horrid smell sitting on my mother's nightstand. A rotten peach festers, and flies buzz around it.

My mother doesn't look much better than the peach, but she's alive. I watch her for a moment, confirming the slow rise and fall of her chest before I move farther into the room.

I consider the silver bell next to her bed that will call the staff, but a sense of wrongness about the whole situation makes me feel like I need to take care of this myself.

Taking the vial, I pull out the dropper and squeeze the end to suck up the contents.

*Will two drops be enough for this?*

She's not just in a coma. She's been neglected.

My mother's lips are dry, and her hair is stuck to her face. Anger builds inside my chest, beating against my rib cage with no outlet, for this level of neglect.

Has no one tended to her since I last saw her four days ago?

She's alive, but her lips are cracked and her face is deathly pale. The shadows under her eyes and the cast over her sunken cheeks are new. Based on her shallow breathing, I fear how much time she really has left.

*How dare Father leave her in here, alone, to die of neglect next to a rotten peach.*

But something rubs me wrong about the whole thing. My father loves my mother more than anything else in this world. He'd never allow her to be left alone, uncared for, and suffering.

With that reassurance, I decide to summon him when I'm done here. He couldn't have known about this, and his anger will be far more respected and feared than mine.

I let two drops of the elixir fall onto my mother's lips. Her skin greedily swallows up the silver contents.

But she doesn't move. She doesn't lick up the moisture. Her body merely drinks it up.

The skin on her lips smooths out and a kiss of red returns, but everything else stays the same.

Indecision makes my hands tremble. Caution tells me not to do what instinct says is necessary.

*She needs more than two drops.*

Which means she could potentially become addicted, and then what? My family can't possibly afford anti-aging elixirs.

*But Edward can.*

I inwardly roll my eyes at myself. I'm already on a first-name basis with a man I hardly know?

*My betrothed.*

*My future husband, with whom I am bound to spend the next thirty days in a romantic courtship that will end in marriage.*

Earl Rinhold has made his intentions clear. He wants me.

He wants my children.

He wants a marriage, and in effect, that gives me certain assurances that should I need more of the elixir, I can get it.

*Maybe that's exactly what a man like Earl Rinhold wants,* I think as I bite my lip.

I'm giving him a means to control me. That's dangerous.

But I find my fingers overriding all the what-ifs and obeying instinct.

The reality is that if I don't do anything, my mother will die.

I wind up praying for the second time in my life after I have added two more drops to my mother's lips.

"Please, Cain. Let my mother live, and protect me against the Elite games I must play."

The room seems to tremble as I say the words, and shadows unfurl over every reflective surface.

The rotten peach on the nightstand vanishes.

I blink a few times, then drop the handkerchief I had been holding. It falls to the bed, and my mother's fingers twitch and pick it up.

"Scarlett?" she asks as her long eyelashes flutter, then her eyes open.

I resist the urge to throw myself at my mother and completely fall apart. I'm clearly suffering hallucinations from hunger and also dealing with sleep-deprivation effects.

The stench in the room had been my own manufacturing. So had the rotten peach.

*It's just a reflection of my worst fears, that my mother was withering away like a rotten piece of fruit.*

It was almost as if my nightmares were merging with my waking hours, giving me day terrors.

*Just what I need.*

"Mother. How are you feeling?" I ask, even if that's a stupid question.

She had just been at death's door. Although, I now see a glass of water by her bed and a clean basin with a damp towel. She had been recently tended to, not neglected. My nightmares had shown me what I was most afraid of seeing.

It was a good thing I hadn't summoned my father, or else he'd lock me away until I left for the Rinhold estate.

A smile lifts my mother's lips, and a silver glow seems to flash in her hazel eyes. Mine are silver or gray, depending on the light—or even my mood—but I've always been jealous of my mother's eyes. There are flecks of bronze throughout the exterior green on the bands, and she looks more like her stunning self as she glances up at me.

Even her hair seems to perk up as the sickly sheen fades from her face. "I'm... better. Why am I better?"

Wincing, I hold up the vial. "I'm afraid I cheated."

It's dangerous to cheat in our world.

But sometimes it's necessary.

Her features soften as she pats my hand. "Did you steal it?" she asks.

"No," I answer quietly. "It was a gift."

Her gaze rakes over me, taking in my appearance and the obvious three slashes up my arm.

She doesn't ask me who it is I've entered into a courtship with. I think she knows. There is only one family in the Magic Sector wealthy enough to have freely given me an anti-aging elixir.

"Thank you, Scarlett. You're so brave. I'm proud of you, you know that?"

I can't stop the tears from rolling down my cheeks. Swatting them away, I take her hand and squeeze it. She squeezes mine back with more strength than she's demonstrated in months.

Gratitude for Earl Rinhold dares to flutter in my stomach, replacing some of the anger that had been there, though I can't help but feel the reality of my situation.

I'm going to have to go through with the courtship now. Not that I wasn't going to, but I've taken away any remaining choice I might have had.

"You need at least two drops every day," I tell her, shoving the vial into her hand.

She parts her lips as if to protest, but I continue.

"Two drops, okay? And you send word when you're running low. If you need more, then take more. I will get another vial."

*I have to.*

She gives me an empathetic smile. "Don't worry about me, Scarlett. You're all the matters. I know this illness frightens you. It frightens me, too. But death comes for all of us in the end. We are not cut out for the Immortality Sector."

My mother is about to go on with her typical argument that death is normal. Immortality is the oddity that was never meant for humans.

I know there's merit to her words. Most families in the Immortality Sector are rumored to be vicious, soulless beings. Immortality has made everything less precious to them, and when nothing is precious, nothing is sacred, either.

*Does it really have to be that way?*

My usual arguments rest on the tip of my tongue, but I swallow them back down and instead let her talk.

Because it feels so *good* to hear my mother talk.

When one of her maidservants comes in with soup for lunch, her eyes widen to see my mother awake. "Duchess Nightingale!" she exclaims, then immediately goes into a curtsy. "I'll get something more robust for lunch right away."

My mother keeps her from running off with a wave of her hand. "Wait, Eliza. Please get something for Scarlett, too." She turns to me with a bright smile. "What would you like, dear?"

I laugh and gesture to my corset. "I don't think I can eat with this torture device, Mother. But watching you eat is fulfillment in and of itself."

My mother pinches my cheek. "Nonsense. When was the last time you ate?" She doesn't wait for me to respond, likely because she knows she won't like the answer. "You're too thin, sweetheart. Eliza?"

"Yes, Duchess?" the handmaiden asks, perking up.

"Can you please grab Rosie on your way back and have her bring something suitable for Scarlett to change into?"

"That's really not nec—" I begin, but Eliza is already gone.

When a Duchess makes an order, it is immediately obeyed.

But in my mother's case, it's not necessarily because she's feared.

It's because she's loved.

By the time the handmaiden returns, Rosie is with her. And she's brought a loose-fitting day dress for me to replace the corset. I give my mother a look, and she only smiles in response.

Sometimes the women in this household are insufferably supportive.

While Rosie helps me change behind the privacy screen, Eliza gives my mother a tray for her bed that's laden with a hearty meal and a frosted dessert.

Without saying a word, Rosie and Eliza ferry over a small table and chair for me to dine next to my mother.

Maybe it's becoming a bad habit now, but I find myself praying once more before I delve into the first real meal I've had in days.

"Thank you, Cain."

I look for those shadows that seem to follow prayers, but this time there aren't any.

I can swear I hear a rumble of thunder outside again, though.

My mother brightly smiles. "Since when do you pray to our Lord, Scarlett?" She's a devout believer, and despite her many lectures, I never followed her lead when it came to worship or prayer.

I shrug and stuff a garlic potato wedge into my mouth, moaning at the delicious oily taste. "I'm just trying something new."

She hums in thought before tasting another bite. She seems to be enjoying her food as much as I am, and with a pang of sadness, I realize she probably hasn't eaten in days.

Because she was in a coma.

"Promise me you'll take the drops," I suddenly say.

Rosie and Eliza have left us alone for our meal. Normally, they are included, but I'm not surprised they felt this occasion was a private matter.

"I will," my mother says. "But only if you promise me something, too, dear daughter."

I nod. "What is it?"

"Never regret who you are."

I blink at her a few times. I'm not even sure if I *know* who I am, other than Lady Scarlett of the Nightingale household.

But I have a feeling she is referencing my true origins. The ones that give me the kind of backbone that can land me in trouble.

Or win me a place as a Lady of the Rinhold family and save my mother's life.

"I will do my best," I tell her. If I don't know exactly who I am, then there's not much to regret. So as far as promises go, I've made worse.

Seeming satisfied, she takes the medicinal box from her nightstand and puts it onto her tray. She opens it, takes out one of the layers, and reveals a secret compartment where she places the anti-aging elixir.

She puts everything away without saying a word.

She knows what I'm willing to give up to keep her alive, but it also has to do with what she just said.

"Don't let the nightmares control you."

My eyes widen.

*Does she know about my nightmares?*

"What do you mean?"

She blows out a slow breath. "I just mean that everything you've gone through is enough to give anyone powerful nightmares. Don't let them make you doubt who you are."

Who am I? I am the child of a village designed for monsters.

I was always meant to be a sacrifice.

And I don't regret that one bit.

One of the marks on my arm starts to fade, and we both watch it as the visual countdown reminds me that my choice has already been made.

*No regrets, Scarlett,* I tell myself.

My nose twitches as the sour scent of rotten peaches flickers in my memory. Ignoring it, I begin to stack up my empty plates.

*I won't let the nightmares control me... No matter what.*

# CHAPTER 14

## CAIN

Hunger stirs in my stomach. Despite enjoying the most succulent prayers from Lady Scarlett Nightingale, I haven't had another taste of them in days.

So I indulge and slip into the Dream Realm to relive the moment. Sometimes the dream of a good meal is almost as fulfilling as the real thing.

Her prayers wash over me, or at least the memory of them does. My eyelashes flutter as I taste the faint echo of peaches as she says my name.

*"Please, Cain. Let my mother live, and protect me against the Elite games I must play."*

I might not be a true God, but prayers don't entirely land on deaf ears when I hear them. I'm a powerful monster, one with many talents, including the ability to make subtle changes in the Dream Realm.

Changes such as opening up Eveline Nightingale's mind to hope instead of death. She had succumbed to a coma days prior, one that had been just as much a battle of wills as it had been an illness.

I can't necessarily heal her, but I can possibly help.

The prayers have opened a portal between my mind and Scarlett's vicinity. I can see her mother through her eyes, as well as the sickness that clings to the Duchess. It's a memory of what I had seen, so everything is even fuzzier than it had been a few days ago.

Her sickness is strange and seems to cling to the Duchess with black tendrils that stretch over her eyes. I touch them but find them hard as iron. She's too far gone right now for me to assist very much.

I still feel powerless in this moment. Without physically being there, or understanding the strange sickness, all I can do is help the Duchess's body absorb the anti-aging tonic that Scarlett drops onto her lips. I don't know where my little star has acquired such an expensive elixir, but I could hazard a guess.

*Her new suitor is trying to win her over.*

Perhaps two can play at that game if gifts are the way to Scarlett's heart. I can offer more than a mere mortal can.

And even the elixir that mortal has provided doesn't seem to be enough. At least, not the two drops Scarlett has given.

*She needs another dose,* I realize with a strange shudder of panic as the Duchess's body sucks up the magic and seems to cry out for more. I don't want Scarlett to suffer more nightmares than she already does.

I encourage the panic that wafts over Scarlett's mind. She needs to understand the dire situation. She can save her mother. But *she* needs to do it. I can only assist, given the right medium.

Relief washes through me as she places two more drops on her mother's lips. I'm able to bleed away the rest of the black tendrils over her mother's eyes, and they finally open.

Scarlett rewards me with a prayer, not giving credit to the elixir at all.

*"Thank you, Cain."*

I slip out of the dream and settle back into the present. But I keep my eyes closed to appreciate the fleeting sensations.

There had been such desperation, then gratitude, that I had felt the fullness of satisfaction from a true meal for the first time in many years.

If ever.

She had talked with her mother after that, from what I gathered through the wisps I was able to overhear from the Dream Realm. And whatever her mother had said to her had set Scarlett against me.

Or against dreams in particular. Because she's completely shut me out since.

I open my eyes and find that my lunch appointment has arrived. Killian waits patiently in the doorway to one of my sunny meeting spaces designed for both dining and official work.

Killian is a friend, so it's a little bit of both today. Although, he'll be the one eating, and I'll be the one working.

Feeling moody and irritated, I tap my fingernails over a table while Killian takes his seat across from me. I've managed to keep my beast from peeking through these past few days, but he's painfully scratching underneath the surface, threatening to come out. Simply revisiting the memory of Scarlett's prayers isn't cutting it.

*We wait,* I tell him, because Scarlett needs her space right now. In fact, today is the day she will join the Rinhold residence for the first time.

I debate attending the fête now. I'm not entirely confident my beast won't claw his way right through my skin and devour anyone who even looks at her.

"You're not looking so good, Cain," Killian casually observes as he accepts a water from one of the human servants.

He makes a good show of seeming at ease, but I know he's indulging in the sensation of being on land for this long. It's all he'll indulge in, though, given his choice of beverage. He could have any of my aged wines or golden whiskeys, but he always sticks to water and foods native to his world. He's lived on a ship most of his life and came here in search of a mate, like most monsters do. That's his purpose, and he has a beautiful single-minded drive to fulfill it.

His dark hair shines with health, and his vibrant blue eyes catch the sunlight, revealing specks of gold. His true form is almost as frightening as mine, one of layered muscles, burning tribal scars, a forked tongue, and claws. He's as much a creature of nightmares as I am, in his own way, and that has earned my respect over the years.

He takes a sip of his water as he watches me, not looking away like other monsters might. He's arrogantly brave and always ready to challenge authority, but that's what I like about him.

It's why I asked for him today. I need someone who'll challenge my beast, not bow to it.

"Still just sticking to water?" I ask, nodding to his beverage. He shrugs, sending more of those dark locks tumbling over his shoulders. He's wearing a warrior's fitted garb that strains with his movements. A sash winds about his waist, and he flicks it over his hip as he leans back. "I shouldn't get used to the fancy stuff. Maybe I'll get lucky this Monsters Night and have cause to celebrate."

"Hmm," I reply, giving him a sound of agreement. "I wish you fortune this year, then, good friend."

*I could use some fortune myself,* I think but don't say aloud. I didn't bring Killian here to commiserate. Still, there's more than enough for me to handle before Monsters Night—and during as well. It's the busiest time of the year for all of us, and the most tumultuous. I have to set everything in motion to run smoothly for twelve hours without me while I chain myself to my tower.

A precaution that I imagine will be needed this year.

Even if this is when prayers are at their peak and I should be feasting on them right now, I can't trust myself to stay in control.

Not when all I can think about is Scarlett Nightingale.

"You'll be using the train, I assume?" I ask him. I'll have to secure his transit with the one direct train we have to Monster City. For security reasons, every passenger must be approved by both Helia and me.

He sighs. "Yes. Although, I'm going more to observe than to participate. They have better feeds there."

I don't take offense to that. The broadcast in Monster City is more comprehensive and designed for monsters. The broadcasts here focus on the competition between families.

I mark down a note on one of my transit papers to add Killian to the roster. "You're a powerful monster, Killian. It's rare to find a compatible mate for a higher-tier creature such as yourself."

He gives me an arched brow as he sets down his emptied glass. The servants begin filling our table with various plates, most of it being food native to his world, such as pastries called Moon Puffs and meat skewers that drip with green ooze. I know that's his preference. "Are you speaking from experience, Cain? Maybe you should attend this year, too."

I chuckle. "Wouldn't that be a sight? I'd wind up killing everyone if I let my beast out. That's definitely not an option." I take one of the beverages, and my tongue flicks over my lower lip. I sense a hint of peach, even though the wine I selected should have tasted bitter. "I've already found a compatible mate."

He straightens. "You have?" He glances around the empty room. "Then... why isn't she with you?"

I sigh. This is why I brought Killian here. The question about the train could have been completed by courier, but I want to hear his take. "She begins a courtship with Earl Rinhold today, one established via means of a blood contract." I match his gaze, taking in the flare of concern in his eyes. "Today is also the Rinholds' Choosing Day for their village, so I've been debating attending their fête tonight."

He chuckles. "Well, that's a predicament. I take it the blood contract was written in *your* blood?"

There are few monsters with blood that can make an agreement magically binding. I typically use mine for blood contracts so that I can monitor all agreements through the Dream Realm.

It's likely what has given me such free access to Scarlett's mind, but she still has to open the door to let me in.

Maybe if I attend the fête... she'll be inclined.

And maybe, if I keep visiting her, I'll find a way to untangle the binding agreement from the inside.

*Yes... I want to be inside her.*

My jaw aches as my teeth change, and I take a moment to push my beast back. Killian watches me closely as I bring him under control. "As you can see, I'm a bit... unstable."

"You need to go," he says.

I take another sip of my wine, this time indulging in the

fragrant peach flavor my dream powers seem to have added. "My compatible mate is spoken for, Killian."

His jaw flexes as if I've angered him. "At least your compatible mate is *alive*."

His response surprises me. I haven't intruded into Killian's quest for a mate. It can be a private matter, and I've given him space, but if he found a compatible mate, only for her to die... Well, yes. That would inspire some regret.

"I apologize for your loss, Killian. I will make sure that on this Monsters Night, you are given access to all of the surveillance documentation so that you can see every candidate who enters the city."

I don't ask how she died. Humans are fragile creatures, and I can only hope there's another human out there suitable for the warrior beast. If he found one here, maybe he'll find another.

"I appreciate that, Cain." He tilts his head as his emotions settle. His personality is like an ocean, fluctuating with the ebb and flow of the tide of his heart. "Can't you sit inside the head of humans and see through their eyes? What's she doing now?"

The temptation to intrude on what Scarlett is seeing is irresistible. It's possibly a good thing that I can't see through her eyes unless she has prayed to me.

But there's another who acts as my eyes and ears of this city, and he just so happens to have been watching over Scarlett for me.

I slip into Bernard's mind as a compromise. My Raven flutters about of his own accord, and while I ordered him to watch Scarlett, he hasn't had much luck. She's been trapped indoors and hidden away as she prepares for her relocation to the Rinhold estate.

The Dream Realm unfurls before me as Bernard senses me and immediately lets me in.

He's outside and in his animal form, allowing the vision to be sharper than I'm accustomed to. He flutters through a cracked window just large enough for his bird form to peek through, then he skitters into the shadows.

Because there are three people talking.

I immediately recognize Duchess Rinhold and her son, the Earl. Irritation makes my beast growl as we land our gaze on the obstacle between us and Scarlett, but he's engaged with his mother.

They're in a closed room—what looks to be the back of a shop. The rarest magic tonics I've seen in this sector line the walls, so this must be one of the exclusive areas.

A clerk offers her a silver-encased box and opens it. The interior contains various vials stuffed into velvet slots.

Anti-aging elixirs.

"I'll take three," she says, frowning when the clerk slides her a piece of paper that must tell her the price.

She flicks her gaze up at him. "That has tripled from the last time I was here."

"So has your order," he says with polite regard. But a shopkeeper of tonics in the Magic Sector knows how to handle the Elites, even one as powerful as Duchess Rinhold. It's her privilege that gives her the disadvantage here because he knows she can afford his price.

And, per the laws of my city, merchants must pay a quota on Monsters Night, too. Their annual tithe ensures they keep their stock attractive enough to afford business in my city. One stocking elixirs as desirable as the rare anti-aging tonic would have a high tithe indeed.

She glowers at her son as she closes the box. "We accept your price," she tells the clerk, "but be mindful that I expect prompt delivery."

The clerk gives her a low bow as he retrieves the box, no doubt to go into the back room to wrap it for her. A

Duchess wouldn't be expected to walk around with her purchases.

She waits until he leaves before she lays into her son.

"How many did you take, Edward?"

*Oh, so he didn't buy them himself? That's interesting.*

He gives her a raised brow. "Whatever do you mean, Mother?"

Shadows swirl around her in the Dream Realm, drawing my interest. I can hear Killian ordering another water. He's patiently waiting for me to finish my snooping. He knows I have a tendency to lose myself in dreams.

In this case, though, I'm inside my Raven's head while I linger in the Dream Realm. He's my anchor, but the Duchess with nightmares dripping from her curls doesn't seem natural.

*An effect of too many anti-aging doses?* I wonder. She looks far younger than her true age, and her eyes are unnaturally bleached—a telltale sign of magic addiction. Every human reacts to the magic differently, but I can't say I've seen this sort of effect before, which has bled into the Dream Realm.

It reminds me of the shadows clinging to Duchess Nightingale's eyes. Hers weren't bleached, but there was something wrong about them. Nightmares had clung to her, too.

I make a mental note to research for a new sickness that could be plaguing my people. I normally let them manage themselves, and illness is all but eradicated in the Immortality Sector, but not an unusual occurrence in the others.

A plague, though, would not do.

"Did you give one to your new bride?" the Duchess asks, not buying his lie for a second.

He shrugs. "If you insist on pressing the matter, Mother, yes and no."

"Yes and no?" she echoes with an edge of irritation in her voice.

He adjusts the cuff of his frilly shirt. "I gave it to her, but it wasn't for her."

She flicks her fan open and cools herself. My city can be warm during the day this time of year, hence the open window that let Bernard in. "Her mother's illness is what made them desperate enough to accept the proposal in the first place, Edward. Is it wise to take away that motivation?"

He gives her a calculated glower. "Are you suggesting we leave an ailing woman to die when we can do something about it?"

Duchess Rinhold scoffs, then pauses and narrows her eyes. "Are you being devious, Edward? If her mother becomes addicted to it, that'll require Lady Scarlett to procure more. It'll put her in your debt."

He seems irritated rather than pleased by her observation, making me question his motivations. "On the contrary, Mother. I told her the limit: no more than two drops per day. If she keeps to that, then she won't be indebted to anyone." He snatches up his sleeve and rolls it at his elbow. "Now, if you'll excuse me, I am late to escort my intended. I'll see you at the fête, *Mother*."

He leaves the room, and so does Bernard as he follows him.

I slip out of his mind and return to my lunch meeting with Killian. Although, I've lost my appetite.

It would be so much easier if Earl Rinhold was just like the rest of his family. Greedy, ambitious, and conniving.

He doesn't seem to be any of those things.

In fact, he seems to be a much more suitable mate for Scarlett than I could ever be.

"Well?" Killian asks, setting down his plate.

I sigh and stand. "Scarlett is about to be escorted by the Earl to her new residence. So I think I'll—"

He's on his feet, already challenging what I was about to say. "Fight for her, Cain. Trust me when I say there is no greater regret than letting a compatible mate slip through your fingers. Don't let that be the nightmare that haunts you for your very long life."

I know he's right.

But I also know what would be required if I took Scarlett for myself, even if I did find a way around the blood contract. She might not survive... not unless I managed to locate at least two other compatible monsters to share the burden. They'd have to be compatible with not only me but also her. And they'd need to earn my beast's approval. So far, I haven't been in a very sharing mood when it comes to Scarlett Nightingale.

I don't like Earl Rinhold, even if he seems like someone who would be good for her. It doesn't matter. He's still a *Rinhold*.

I've seen enough to know that the family she's about to get in bed with is a dangerous one.

It wouldn't hurt to make an appearance and set the record straight. Even if Earl Rinhold isn't a true threat to Scarlett, there's still Duke and Duchess Rinhold to worry about.

Scarlett Nightingale might not be mine.

But she is under my protection. And any who harm her will have to go directly through me.

"You're right, Killian," I say, earning a wry smile from the male. "I'll make preparations to attend. And you," I add, lowering my chin, "will get on a train to Monster City and take one of Helia's best suites."

Killian chuckles. "Sounds like a good deal. See you later,

then, Cain." He claps a hand on my shoulder. "Don't do anything I wouldn't do, yeah?"

My beast is the one who smiles back at him, all teeth and wicked intent. "Of course. I'll be on my best behavior."

I won't kill anyone.

But I don't make any promises that I won't visit Scarlett Nightingale tonight. Earl Rinhold can have her during the day.

Tonight, when she closes her eyes... she'll be all mine.

# CHAPTER 15

# SCARLETT

I try my best not to fidget in the smoothest carriage ride I have ever experienced. My countdown marks have all but faded now, leaving only one pink line down my arm.

In just a few moments, it'll be gone entirely.

*And then thirty more are going to take its place.*

I try not to let my nerves get the best of me about *where* they might show up on my body or how much it's going to hurt. After seeing my mother shuffle around her room and smile at me just before I left when she had been bedridden for months, I know this is something I have to do.

*It doesn't mean it has to be unenjoyable,* I surmise as I wait for my host to engage. He's not sore on the eyes; that's for sure. It's no burden to gaze at his naked forearms as I patiently watch him steal glances at me. He's rolled up his sleeves for his task, and I half wonder if it's just to show off his beautiful physique.

As pretty as he is, I am curious as to what he's preparing. He's currently occupied with opening up a bottle and pouring its contents into a glass. The carriage ride is so smooth that there's no risk of anything falling. He places the bottle into a magically chilled basin before swirling the glass.

Earl Rinhold smiles at me from across the enclosed space and offers me the fizzy drink. "Champagne?" he asks.

Blinking at him a few times, I try to catalog all the social beverages I've heard of and draw a blank. "I can't say I have had the pleasure of trying it," I admit. When encountering something unfamiliar, it's best not to reveal ignorance.

In this case, Earl Rinhold sees right through me. He wouldn't have chosen me as his potential bride without having substantially researched me. If I haven't heard of champagne, it's because it's either too rare or too expensive for me to have tried it.

I know why I'm valuable, and it's not old family wealth. The first thing he asked about was my red hair. Whether or not he knows I'm originally from a village doesn't truly matter. In fact, it might be why he was so interested in me in the first place.

The gene pool when it comes to Elite families has become... slim. The practical thing to do would be to dip into the cultivated selections from the villages. But it's frowned upon to take a bride from that sort of social status. It's not just because such a bride would be reserved for a potential monster match—it's the training.

I've spent the majority of my life learning how to sit exactly as I sit now. My back is slightly arched, my shoulders are rolled back, and I keep my eyelashes low as I size up the Earl.

I know how to speak.

I know how to dance—both literally and figuratively.

I know how to play the *game*.

His smile grows until his eyes sparkle. "I wouldn't imagine so, Lady Scarlett. Champagne is from the old world, but it's still made in one of the other Elite cities. Or perhaps one of their villages. I didn't ask the details the last time I spoke to my overseas contact."

"Oh," I say. Taking the glass, I inspect the contents just to give myself something to do.

Earl Rinhold just disclosed an entire lump of information I don't quite know what to do with.

While I know that other Elite cities exist, I've never had the opportunity to communicate with one. My family was originally from the Industrial Sector. We had no business with high trade such as working with another city.

But the Rinholds, *of course*, have contacts everywhere.

The *champagne* in my hand is just another indicator of Earl Rinhold's wealth and status. I know he's testing me, but I'm not sure what terms will allow me to win. If he's expecting me to be as cultured as he is, I've already lost.

But if he simply wanted a cultured bride, he would have chosen one of the many Ladies who would do anything to become his bride. The Rinholds are one of the families in line for the Immortality Sector any year now.

Deciding to trust my instincts, I place the edge of my glass on my lips. I match Earl Rinhold's gaze as I tip it far enough back to taste the contents.

I can't help it. My eyelashes flutter with appreciation as the fizzy liquid hits my tongue. A subtle splash of flavors lingers in my mouth as I indulge in the taste.

It's a mixture of sweet and bitter, ending with a distinct note of peach that feels slightly out of place. But I figure it's best not to comment on that.

The peach addition might not even be real.

I'm learning the subtle signs of when my night terrors are attempting to come out to play. I clamp them down as best I can because I absolutely cannot handle any night-mare nonsense today.

*"Don't let the nightmares control you."*

*I won't, Mother.*

"Delicious," I tell him honestly. I blush when I see his gaze has settled on my lips. He lingers there before glancing up at my eyes again.

"I'm sure it is," he says, giving me one of those too-charming grins again before he peeks out the window of the carriage.

*Is he flirting with me again?*

I don't know why I'm surprised by the idea of Earl Rinhold flirting with me. But it's more than that. He somehow makes me feel special and desirable.

*This feels more like a seduction.*

And so what if the most powerful eligible bachelor of the Magic Sector wants to seduce me? Maybe that's not a bad thing.

I'm not sure why the rumors portrayed him in such a horrible light. He doesn't seem at all like the cruel playboy he was painted out to be.

*Maybe they're just jealous of his status and ability to buy whatever he wants, like delicious champagne.*

*And he is very good-looking.*

I find myself admiring him as I appreciate his handsome features. He's a little too perfect, but I can spot the flaws that make him human if I search hard enough.

There's a small scar that curls around the edge of his jaw, and I feel the obscene urge to touch it.

I want to feel his humanness, to see that this is a man, not a monster.

Not like the figment haunting my dreams.

"We're here," he says, smirking at me when he catches me staring.

I don't shutter my gaze or look away. Instead, I return his smile with one of my own.

Because I'm excited by the prospect of entering into the Rinhold estate now.

His smile fades the instant I feel it.

Sheer agony.

A scream rips from my throat as invisible knives score down the length of my spine, making me feel like I'm a doll about to be pulled apart so that all the stuffing can fall out.

Another painful, cold slice nicks just above my belly button, making me grasp my stomach. I unfurl my palm, expecting blood to be pooling from my corset, but there's nothing. Only fine lace embroidered with tiny floral designs.

My hand is shaking as Earl Rinhold gently pulls me into his lap, shushing me. A sob catches in my throat as he wraps an arm around me and tugs me close. "I'm sorry. I thought that wouldn't hit until we were inside."

"Wh-what happened?" I ask as my teeth chatter against the echo of agony. It's fading now, but my mind feels like it's taking longer to catch up.

"We crossed the gate. We're within the Rinhold estate now."

My eyes widen. "That activated the contract prematurely?" I had signed the contract well after sundown, and my marks have been slowly vanishing after retiring for the night.

He nods. "Yes. But the terms to begin the courtship have more to do with when you arrive on the estate grounds rather than when the three-day period is up."

I blink at him a few times as I realize that horrible pain I felt was the appearance of my courtship marks. "They're on my spine," I blurt, then feel silly for announcing their location.

He instantly moves his hand away from my back, but

it's not necessary. They aren't hurting anymore, just tingling.

The one on my stomach still stings, though. I keep my hand there, and for some reason, I don't want to disclose to him that I have one placed just above my navel.

*Perhaps because a certain figment also marked me there?*

I trap my lip between my teeth to prevent myself from making a sound.

"Are you well?" he asks quietly. He doesn't move until I answer.

"Yes," I say honestly. "I'm fine." Then my gaze drops, and I notice the blood on his fingers. "Are you hurt?"

He turns over his palm, then chuckles as I gape at the *S* tattooed onto his skin. "Hmm, look at that. I get a mark, too."

I'm not sure how I feel about that. It isn't customary for the male in the courtship to earn a mark. But it makes it feel more exciting.

*Is this really happening?*

Earl Rinhold nods, then quietly eases open the door of our carriage, and a pleasant breeze rushes in. There's an entourage waiting for us, even if it's a smaller one than I expected. Today is the Choosing Day fête for the Rinhold residence, after all. My arrival seems to be secondary to that affair.

I notice that neither Duchess nor Duke Rinhold is in the group of servants waiting in a line to greet us. I spot a few handmaidens clutching boxes, as well as a butler holding a long staff horizontally with both hands.

"Welcome home, sir," the butler says as he presents Earl Rinhold with the gilded cane that's engraved with symbols and decorative designs.

Earl Rinhold cleans the blood from his new mark on a handkerchief, then accepts the cane with a polite dip of his chin. "Thank you, Davis." The skilled way he twirls the cane before turning to me has me pensive. I can't help but wonder if he has ever used it as a weapon rather than simply porting the scepter-like staff around as the status symbol that it is.

Giving me a bright smile, he holds out his hand, and something defiant in me prevents me from taking it. I struggle out of the carriage, but at least it's of my own accord.

I'm put off that his parents aren't here, but I don't want to admit as much until I know more.

"I'll escort you to your new quarters, where you can retire before the fête, Lady Scarlett," he finally says when he realizes I have no intention of moving closer to him.

I brush invisible dust from my corset before accepting a parasol from one of the handmaidens who I imagine will be following me around like my shadow. She doesn't match my gaze, making me frown. I befriended Rosie and any other handmaiden who was part of the staff. That's what my mother did, too. Everyone was treated like a human being no matter their station.

It doesn't seem like that's the norm here.

*If I'm to become a Duchess, then things will change in the Rinhold household.*

The parasol, though, is a bane I must endure. The sun is already setting, but Cain forbid a dusting of sunlight hits a Lady's face. My dialect already slipped a few times in the carriage, so it's best if I don't let all of my flaws as a village-born show.

"Will your parents not be greeting me as well?" I ask the Earl to inform him of the source of my displeasure.

A passing shadow darkens his eyes like clouds in a storm. "I'll speak to them later. I presume they are busy with preparations, but I did ask them to be here."

I force myself to calm my ruffled emotions. I can't rightly be vexed with the Earl for his family's actions, especially if he tried to make me feel welcome.

"Very well," I say, slipping my arm through his.

The tension in his jaw eases with my unsaid forgiveness. As long as he's trying, that's all I ask of my future husband.

*Future husband,* I muse.

Have I already accepted my role here?

The marks along my back tingle as the Earl strikes up casual conversation, easily making me feel like I belong at his side as his mansion devours me whole.

The interior wealth is astounding, as is the space. Massive halls span in all sorts of directions, sparking my curiosity when I notice more than one reading nook tucked into various corners between statues and finery.

Every now and then, I spot a depiction of Cain, our city's ruler. I can't help but feel like his eyes follow me.

A chill runs up my spine every time we pass one.

It's not a full tour, but the Earl finally leads me upstairs and pauses outside one of the larger bedrooms. I can see as much because the door is open, and the extravagant space inside could fit three of my living quarters at home. There even seem to be two attached rooms, I'm guessing a bathroom and a parlor, from what little I can see from my vantage point.

"My room is just down the hall," he says with a friendly smile, but that news puts me on edge.

"And my handmaiden?" I ask. "Where are her accommodations?"

The Earl seems confused for a moment, then his gaze drops as he smiles. "Ah, you're concerned about your virtue during the courtship." He flicks his blue eyes up to mine. There's a spark of interest there, but I somehow find it charming instead of predatory. "The staff is downstairs and can be summoned by bells. However, know that I will never ask anything of you that you're not comfortable with, Lady Scarlett. I simply meant to keep you close because, should you stay, this will become your permanent chamber." He shifts his cane into his other hand. "I suppose I hoped you would make yourself comfortable within it right away."

My eyes widen. "And at the conclusion of the courtship, should we choose to marry, I would not stay with you?"

His tongue flicks out to wet his lower lip. I can't help but let my gaze drop to follow it. "If you would like, but it's not customary. I should not presume you are interested in my advances, even if you were my wife. I can only come into your chambers upon invitation, you see. That prevents any miscommunication on my part."

While I have been educated on social etiquette and upper-society culture, this doesn't seem customary. At least, the houses in the Industrial Sector did not operate this way.

My mother does have her own room, now, but only after she fell ill and it made sense to separate her and my father. We weren't sure at the time if the illness was contagious. It became apparent that it wasn't. At least, no one else succumbed to the same symptoms.

But this has nothing to do with illness and everything to do with respect.

*Do they really respect women this much in the Magic Sector?*

Maybe they do, or maybe that treatment is only reserved for the upper class. Regardless, I've already revealed enough of my ignorance to my potential husband, and I have a fête to attend in a few short hours.

I'm already tired, but that's to be expected. I consider myself lucky that my marks don't pain me to tire me further. At least, most of them don't. My hand falls to my stomach because that's the only mark that stings.

*Or maybe I'm just imagining the sensation.*

"Thank you for the explanation, Earl Rinhold," I say as a means to let him know I'm ready to retire. There are two handmaidens just at the corner, keeping their distance, seeming to be waiting for a signal that they can approach. I give them a nod, and they look at each other, then hurry toward us.

"Edward," he corrects me, making me smile. "You are not my lesser, Lady Scarlett. You are my better in every way. It would honor me if you would use my first name."

A blush overtakes my cheeks, and I wonder where this suitor of mine has been hiding.

Had I known a courtship would be this pleasant, I would have agreed to one sooner.

"Edward," I concede, earning a bright smile from the male across from me.

He straightens and clears his throat. "Very well. I shall leave your handmaidens to attend to you," he says, dipping his chin at them as he retreats.

He keeps his eyes on me when he adds, "I do hope you'll wear the dress I had made for you. If it pleases you, Lady Scarlett. I will have the pleasure of our first dance when the music begins."

I try to read the meaning behind his words as he runs his finger over his new mark in an unconscious effort. It feels like there's a glimmer of a mask for the first time, one I should pay attention to, but the harder I look, the cordial and friendly Earl Rinhold is all I seem to be able to see.

The scratch above my navel twinges with pain, as if trying to tell me something.

Or maybe it's only my apprehensions getting in the way.

"See you soon, Edward," I say, enjoying how my stomach flips when he smiles at me again.

When he leaves and I retreat into my new room with two handmaidens I'm sure are hurrying to peel away my corset, they present to me the most beautiful dress I have ever seen.

Shadows threaten to close in on me as a now familiar rumble echoes throughout the room. Unlike my old accommodations, this one has many wide windows and a balcony that allows me to overlook a massive courtyard.

I glance at the sky, expecting to see storm clouds, but there are only bright bleeding reds of sunset scattered across the horizon.

Turning from the sight, I pick up the dress and smile at it.

*Why do I have to fear the nightmares?*
*Maybe, for once, I can live in a dream.*

# CHAPTER 16

## SCARLETT

"I'll take that, my lady," one of the older handmaidens who followed me into my room says, startling me.

I stare at her as she tugs the outfit from my fingers. She instructs me to step onto a platform against a large mirror while a younger handmaiden closes the door.

There are too many reflective surfaces in the room. I try to look outside, but shadows flicker through the glass panes and disappear the moment I blink my eyes.

"We'll get you dressed in no time," the older one assures me, likely mistaking my anxious expression for the fear of being late to the fête.

Rather, I have a fear of what insanity lingers in the back of my mind.

*It must be a side effect of the blood contract,* I decide.

Turning away from the windows, I obey more out of instinct than understanding.

*There's no privacy screen in this room,* I realize with a sinking sense of dread.

I feel strangely vulnerable as I take the step and stare at myself in a mirror bound by gilded designs. I'm not sure what to do with my hands, so I tuck them over one another on top of my stomach out of a habit born of ingrained training. "If you're going to undress me in the open, can we at least close the curtains?" I ask. My gaze goes up to the long velvet drapes that are attached to a curved rail.

The older one blinks up at me, then the younger one laughs. A look of horror crosses the older handmaiden's face as she shushes her.

"Julie! I'll have your hands raw on dish duty if you cannot behave in a Lady's presence," she threatens, making me frown.

"I don't know what the other Ladies are like in this house, Miss…" I trail off, then wave my fingers for her to fill in the blank.

"Beatrix," she says as she straightens her spine.

"Miss Beatrix," I continue. "You needn't hold your tongue around me. In fact, I do hope we can all become friends with occasions that contain more such laughter. I presume we'll be spending a significant amount of time together."

*And not to mention, my only friends at my own house were the staff.*

No amount of finery and etiquette training would ever make me feel like I fit in among high-class Elites. My memory from my village is broken and faded, but my body seems to remember things I cannot. There's a stress response I can't explain around other Ladies.

It probably has a lot to do with the masks they wear. Not literal masks, but ones where they hide who they really are in an effort to blend in—or stand out.

Beatrix has one, but it's for very different reasons. Underneath her professional and efficient mask, her eyes are kind and her soul is weighed down by troubles I can't name. I'm sure there are many that an aged handmaiden might have on her hands.

Julie, though, has a flimsy mask that flies back into place. She bows her head, and her hair hangs around her like a curtain.

Stepping off my stupid pedestal, I tuck my finger under her chin and force her to look at me.

Her brown eyes are as wide as saucers.

She's young, full of life, and hopeful. I'm glad to see a young lady working for the Rinholds having hope in her heart. That's something I can work with.

"Can you tell me what was funny, Julie?" I ask. Her mask threatens to slam back into place as she goes tense. "You're not in trouble," I assure her. "I'll admit, you probably know a lot more about how things work in this house than I do, Julie." I use her name again and with purpose. I want her to understand that she's a person with a name. She is no different from me, other than the fact that I was adopted by a Duke and she was not.

Julie's brown eyes flick to Beatrix, and the older woman must have given her the go-ahead because she turns back to me with a tentative smile.

No, not tentative.

*Hopeful.*

"The tonics dress you, my lady. It would be improper to be naked." She indicates a tray with various bottles on it. "Would you like to see them?"

I eye the tray, then roll back my shoulders. "Do you mean to say that I won't ever undress? Even for bathing?"

Julie's cheeks blush. "No, my lady. Not unless you enjoy baths for relaxation, that is. Tonics will keep you clean otherwise."

I'm not sure how to feel about that. On the one hand, I

never have to feel like someone is watching me undress again.

On the other... would I want to eliminate the sensation entirely?

The shadows flicker in the mirror through my peripheral vision, mocking my dark desires. My nightmares are so sensual because I wear the most prominent mask of all.

I'm a village girl pretending to be a Lady.

"I'll take that into consideration," I say as I take the pedestal again. "All right, why don't you explain to me how it works?" I ask, holding out my arms.

Beatrix approaches and matches my gaze in the mirror. Her smile is genuine, and the way her mask dissolves around her puts me at ease. "You're a gentle soul, Lady Scarlett. Those are rare among the Elite families these days, so I promise you I will do everything I can to explain how it *all* works."

I have a feeling she's not just talking about tonics.

Beatrix slips the cloth over my head. There must be magic in the fabric, because what I'm wearing completely melts away, and the new threads hug every curve of my body with perfect precision.

The corset is still tight, but not suffocating enough that I feel like I can't breathe. It wraps around my waist and my chest, sufficiently lifting my bosom better than any of my dresses have ever achieved.

I take the time to admire my reflection as my two new handmaidens quietly chatter. They spread ointments through my hair and seem to have accepted my decree that they should be themselves, so that gives me a moment to study them.

Beatrix is old enough to be my mother, and Julie is a cheerful little doll who does everything Beatrix tells her. I would have thought them mother and daughter had they not looked so different from one another.

Beatrix has dark hair wrapped up in a skull-tight bun, while Julie has wild blonde hair tucked back with pins around her face.

Beatrix rummages through a jewelry box as she directs her conversation to me. "Duchess Rinhold told us to make sure you were fashionably late for the fête, but that's because she doesn't want you to make a grand entrance," she informs me with a click of her tongue. "Can't have you stealing her husband's thunder with the selections he's made this year." She frowns at various pairs of earrings while she takes turns holding each pair to my head. "But Earl Rinhold told us to have you ready promptly." She gives me a wink. "I'll just pretend I didn't hear the Duchess. She refuses to give me any anti-aging elixirs, so my hearing could be going bad, hmm?"

"Does the Duchess not want me here?" I ask honestly.

If Beatrix is surprised by my frankness, she doesn't show it. "Of course she does. She's the one who pushed so hard for a blood contract in the first place. But your ultimate role here seems to be up for debate. I suspect the role Duchess Rinhold imagines for you is quite different from what the young master has planned."

"Young master?" I ask.

I glance at Julie, who adds, "Earl Rinhold, she means."

Beatrix sighs when she seems satisfied about her choice of earrings. She selected a dangling pair of rubies with silver chains that complements my complexion. As she loops them into place, she gives out instructions without looking up. "Julie, can you grab the flourish tonics, please? The red and black lace and jewels set. That'll go with this."

Julie hurries and collects the indicated potions. She

takes a dropper and covers me with it, hitting my shoulder, my hairline, and my arms.

Magic seeps into my skin and bright red locks, and gems appear out of thin air as they loop and twine through various parts of my outfit.

I might have lived in the Magic Sector for the past two years, but I have not actually partaken in the luxuries offered in this segment of the Elite City. As I touch the jewels in my perfectly styled hair, I hardly recognize the woman who stares back at me.

The tonics have taken away shadows I hadn't even realized were there. My eyes seem brighter and boast a new shade of silver. My cheeks, once pale and lackluster, now look as if I've pinched rosy hues back into them. Even my lips are plump and a shade of red that matches the rubies in my hair.

I don't look like Lady Nightingale anymore. The drab Lady of a dying house is gone and now replaced with someone new.

*Lady Rinhold,* I say in my mind as I test the name.

The mark above my navel spears me with cold pain, making me wince. I haven't been given a chance to see my skin to confirm anything is actually there, but I certainly feel it.

Just because something feels real doesn't mean it is.

"My lady?" Julie shyly asks. "Are you all right?"

"I'm fine," I say, giving her a forced smile. "Just tired."

The young girl rummages through what looks to be a medicinal box, then presents a bottle with a crystal top and smiles at me. "For energy," she offers.

My eyes widen when I recognize the tonic. It's not an anti-aging elixir, but it's nearly as expensive.

"No, thank you," I say.

She shrugs as if she hadn't just offered me something I could never afford and puts it back into the box.

I am fairly certain she just presented me with a dream inhibitor. For some reason, the idea of not needing sleep for the next four-and-twenty hours doesn't appeal to me.

And neither does the prospect of avoiding whatever might be lurking in my dreams.

*Slut.*

*Whore.*

My brother's words rush over me, and I straighten and stare at myself in the mirror as I push them out.

My figment had said I wasn't any of those things.

*He had also said I was his, which I'm not.*

*I can't be.*

Can I? Can I not have a little fun in a pretend world of dreams that isn't real?

Maybe I'm foolish. Maybe I just want something that belongs to no one else and only to me.

My hand falls to the place above my navel as it throbs in memory.

"What views do Earl Rinhold and Duchess Rinhold differ on when it comes to me, if I may ask?" Turning to Beatrix, I give her an encouraging smile.

She is holding a variety of trays and stops eyeing them to look up at me. Her brow crinkles, seeming to mess up her dark makeup that slashes onyx lines over her wilted eyelids. It rubs me the wrong way that Duchess Rinhold won't even give a few drops of anti-aging elixirs to her staff. "I watched the young master grow up from a mere babe. I've been here for a long time, and I'm a good judge of character, Lady Scarlett, so I will tell you this." She leans in as she lowers her voice. "Duchess Rinhold has never loved the Earl like she loves her daughter."

It's my turn to crinkle my brow. "Earl Rinhold has a sister?"

Julie and Beatrix share a look. If I was supposed to know that, I didn't.

I bite my lip. "She wants her son to produce an heir, but she doesn't want me to outshine her daughter," I surmise. "Because, technically, I could surpass the role of Duchess, leaving it to Earl Rinhold's sister, should I be deemed unfit for the role."

Beatrix gives me a wry smile. "Something like that, my lady. And given Lady Liliana's exposure to anti-aging elixirs during the Duchess's unexpected pregnancy..."

My eyes widen. "Edward's sister is barren?"

Beatrix places a finger to her lips. "We don't know for sure. Her mother has always used the elixirs, even when pregnant, we suspect. Which would have an impact on the child growing in her womb." She sighs. "We certainly don't gossip about it. But..." She lowers her hand and gives me a grave nod. "I know what kind of tonics a fertility test requires. I had administered them to Lady Liliana during a routine doctor visit when she came of age."

Irritation prickles my skin. Duchess Rinhold wants it all. She requires her son to produce an heir for the family because her daughter cannot. But she wants this Lady Liliana to inherit the Duchess role all the same.

*So where does that leave me?*

*I'm to be nothing more than a breeder...*

"Which fragrance would you like, my lady?" Julie asks while presenting a tray of labeled bottles.

The dismal thoughts fade away as I peruse the selections. The important thing for me to remember is that I have thirty days to secure my place. I never planned to become a Duchess. In my own family, I was preparing to take over a smaller settlement with the population created by offsetting inhabitants from Nightingale Village.

With all the extra selections, though, there won't be much of a population to offset anyway.

*So where does that leave me now?*

If I did return home, it would be to ruin.

But if I stayed... I refused to play a role determined for me.

*I'm Scarlett Nightingale and I make my own fate.*

*Nightmares won't control me... and Duchess Rinhold certainly won't, either.*

A thrill runs through me that I'm not accustomed to. I rarely play Elite games, but now that I've been thrust into the biggest one of my life, I'm determined to *win*.

For some reason, I feel that my selection of fragrance will determine the tone for tonight, so I judge each one carefully. I'm drawn to the bottle titled Peach Elegance in a scrawling script on a glittery label. "That one," I say with a pointed finger, then smile when she sprays it along my collarbone and a frosting of peach-colored glitter shimmers on my skin and pushed-up breasts.

"Would you like me to fetch the Earl?" Julie asks, her eyes bright with wonder as she gazes up at me. I can tell I'm everything she hopes to be.

That only makes me want to succeed so I don't let young girls like Julie down.

"No," I decide aloud as I rest my hand above my navel. "I'll make my entrance alone."

# CHAPTER 17

# SCARLETT

Beatrix and Julie escort me as far as the entrance hall. Once the harmony of wind instruments and deep, dreamlike notes of a cello thrums in my chest, they're gone.

So I endure the rest of my journey alone, venturing through a wide-open archway that lets the sounds of mirth and richness spill through.

My view as I step forward takes my breath away.

Hundreds of Elites are here, all in one place, dressed in their best finery for the occasion with a blood-red theme. I run my fingers over my lacy dress glimmering with reds and black-sapphire hues.

For once, I fit right in—had I been in the crowd. Now, peering over them from above, I feel like I sorely stand out.

They haven't noticed me yet as I stay a few steps just out of immediate view, so I take a moment to gather my scrambled thoughts.

*Is this my life now?* I wonder as I try not to gape at the oversized ballroom filled with the Magic Sector's most prominent and prestigious families.

Deciding to make my entrance alone now feels daunting—and possibly like a mistake.

*I have no idea what I'm doing.*

The ballroom spans out in a sea of extravagance and glittering jewels. My perch from the top of a gilded stairway lets me see just how many families want to impress the Rinholds. The Nightingale Village Day of the Choosing attracts perhaps four or five families to our meager ballroom. I doubt there will even be a fête this year without my mother being well enough to put it together.

My brother certainly won't be of any help. He often travels off-site for Cain knows what, and my father goes in person to oversee the selections himself at the village multiple train stops away.

But *Rinhold's* Choosing Day is quite the affair. I lose count after fifty as I take in the mingling crowd.

*There has to be half of the Magic Sector's upper echelon here tonight.*

I have never seen most of the faces in clumps of embroidered silks and sparkling jewels. That makes sense. Even if I've been in the Magic Sector for two years, I've spent the majority of it behind the walls of the Nightingale estate or the rare outings outside while I hid underneath a parasol.

I can't help but scan the crowd for my mother, even though I know she can't have possibly improved enough to attend. She would have enjoyed this.

She might have even been proud of me. While she had not prepared me to take a husband, she had told me that I could always choose my own fate.

*Is this what I choose for myself?*

It seems like a better alternative to taking our chances with the culling.

But that's next month's problem. Today is Rinhold's Choosing Day. Nightingale's will be coming up soon, meaning my own family has many tasks to attend to in preparation.

Such as my father departing on the train to Nightingale Village just this morning. He gave me a kiss on my forehead as he said goodbye.

I can't remember the last time my father had kissed me.

My brother had also disappeared, not onto a train but by carriage. He wouldn't tell me where he was going, but there was mention of the Nightingale Compound among the servants. I know even less about the compound than I do the village.

The fact that Rosie wouldn't tell me anything only made me more concerned.

*Maybe things will be different as a Lady of the Rinhold family,* I wonder.

Although, I feel incredibly unprepared for this courtship and all it might entail. Despite all of my training, my family only has so many connections here. Most families are incredibly private, so it can be difficult to obtain any documents with likenesses or information on those who wish to remain mysterious.

I have largely relied on rumor to navigate the new families I have encountered. But based on my interactions with Edward so far, I have reconsidered that method. Perhaps I need to reserve judgment based on my own experiences and not that of idle chatter likely born from a place of jealousy and disgruntled families unable to afford such extravagance.

Because this is no fête. This is positively *lavish*.

I no longer have the luxury of remaining frozen as trumpets sound. The blaring notes announce my appearance, and I instantly wish I were anywhere else.

Because the entire ballroom has fallen silent and all eyes turn to me.

"Announcing the arrival of the esteemed Lady Scarlett Nightingale, blood-betrothed to Earl Rinhold," says the announcer I hadn't seen emerge from his post. He's wearing a velvety red suit with frilly black under layers. He gives me a low bow after the damning introduction.

A wave of shocked gasps sweeps through the room as the music comes to an abrupt stop. My heart jumps into my throat, and it feels as if my corset has constricted, cutting off my air.

*Was our courtship not yet publicly announced?*

The only moving object through the crowd is my so-called blood-betrothed, a term I'm familiar with, so it doesn't surprise me. I dislike it immediately, though, because it makes the whole courtship period sound like a dispensable ceremony.

It isn't. I can still say no.

*Can't I?*

Earl Rinhold's eyes appear a fairer shade of blue in the bright ballroom. Every corner is gilded, and white marble reflects the cheerful light that catches in his blond curls, but he holds my focus.

Because he's wearing a black suit with frilly red cuffs and ruby cuff links encased in silver. It's an outfit that complements mine.

He smiles at me from the bottom of the staircase and gazes up as if I'm the most beautiful sight he's ever seen.

He doesn't move to retrieve me. Instead, he patiently waits, and I realize I'm supposed to do something.

*Right. Stairs.*

No one is here to escort me, which was my own choice. A rush of panic makes butterflies flutter in my stomach, but pride creeps up my blood-marked spine.

Resting my hand on the rail, I marvel that I successfully suppress a tremor and begin my descent. My elegant shoes clip along the marble, sending a heartbeat through the room as everyone watches me do exactly what Duchess Rinhold didn't want.

Make a grand entrance.

I spot her eyeing me from across the room. Her eyes are narrowed as she aggressively fans herself with a lacy contraption stuffed with silky black feathers.

Becoming enemies with my future mother-in-law wasn't what I had in mind tonight, but if it makes my purpose here clear, then that's how this will have to be.

If I fell now, I'd be under her shadow for the rest of my life. Which, if the Rinholds moved to the Immortality Sector, would possibly be forever.

"You're stunning, my lady," Edward says, pitching his voice low as I venture in range of his words. He holds out his hand, the one with the first letter of my name branded in blood on his skin. "It seems my sister's cosmetic tonics suit you, even though she didn't think they would."

*Sister's tonics?*

Conflicting emotions batter on the inside of my chest as I take his hand and he presses a kiss to my skin. A tingle runs up my arm, but I'm too caught up in what he just said to react.

My gaze flicks over him and to the crowd—they're still watching us. I don't have as good a vantage point to be able to see his mother anymore.

And I have no idea what his sister looks like.

"Will you introduce me to Lady Liliana?" I ask, then mentally kick myself when Edward gives me a raised brow.

If he's surprised I know her name, he doesn't comment on it. Instead, the hesitation melts away as he smiles and then gives me a low bow. "Of course. I'll be happy to introduce you after our dance."

My mouth pops open to question him, but he lets go of

my hand and slaps his palms together. "Music! Lady Scarlett and I will begin today's celebrations with the first dance."

He eyes the crowd as if waiting for a protest, but no one dares say a thing.

Then the music begins. It's too slow to dance to, so I wait.

My eyes go round when all of the walls morph and change in response to the tones. The once solid walls have now turned into massive screens displaying a place I've never seen before.

*No, that's not a city,* I realize when I spot the platform and a large device scrolling with numbers atop it. While my family has a different system to call forth selections, I understand the format.

This is Rinhold Village.

My family's village could be called quaint. It has farms on the mountainside, little to no technology for the natives, and simple homes. While I've never visited, I have seen it on my father's monitoring devices. He explained the importance of keeping their objectives focused on developing the community and cultivating selections. Genetics isn't the only thing that comes into play when creating a human compatible to mate with a monster. Part of it is environment and training, too.

Footage of Monsters Night when selections go to Monster City is publicly broadcast, but insider images of rival villages are kept private. We're all in competition with one another. I always knew that other families had different methods and styles for how they formed and ran their villages, but I never imagined anything like this.

Rinhold Village looks as if it's made of iron. There's not a single speck of greenery as I blink at the militaristic surroundings and massive structures.

The inhabitants wear protective leathers, and the men have swords strapped to their backs. Even the women seem like tiny warriors with their hair up in tight bands and braids, each of them wearing what I could only describe as armor.

Except for three beautiful figures in the center of them all, protected by the largest men with swords. Each woman wears a glittery dress made of diamonds that flows with their movements.

Three various walls zoom in on each of them as the music thrums to life.

The women stiffen at the noise as if they can hear it.

"They'll dance after we do," Edward whispers in my ear as his hand snakes around my waist.

My blood-marks sting as he swoops me into a practiced move that has my spine bending to his will.

I don't resist. My muscles move on instinct, obeying the years of training that have cultivated my body as an instrument to be played on the dance floor.

But no man has ever played my body like this.

A curious murmur of voices rolls through the crowd, but I don't care. My entire focus is on Edward's kind eyes, which have a hint of desire in them. He's not wearing a mask, but something seems to bleed through his skin as if he's done a good job of suppressing things I shouldn't be seeing.

He leads me into a swirling maneuver, making my dress fan out before I'm pressed against his chest. His nose brushes mine as he grins.

"Everyone is watching us," I whisper when he draws me into a dip, then strokes his fingers through my hair.

The movement is distinctly sensual, and my body zings with excitement.

The screens all around us darken, and I wonder if

they've lowered the broadcast, or perhaps the skies have gone cloudy wherever Rinhold Village is located.

"I don't care," Edward says, his breath hot on my ear, as he swirls me again.

He lets me go, and the notes of the music lift, making me rise up on my toes as I instinctively reach for the air.

That's when the shadows descend and the room goes dark, but there's still enough subtle light from all the reflective surfaces around us for me to see.

I try not to panic. My first thought is that this is part of the dance, but when screams rip through the discorded music, I realize something is terribly wrong.

When I come down from my lifted position, I find myself in the arms of someone new.

*Definitely not Edward.*

My breath catches in my throat as I stare up at a face that is foreign and familiar all at the same time.

Cain, the King of the Elite City, smiles at me as his grip tightens on my hips.

"Hello, Scarlett."

# CHAPTER 18

# SCARLETT

*The King of the Elite City knows my name...*

I dumbly realize that I previously prayed to Cain. Did that mean he had actually heard me?

"H-hello..." I manage as I allow his embrace to move me closer.

I have to tilt my head up to look at him. To anyone else, he's a beautiful man with bright blue eyes. I can see deeper, just as I always can. And I can see that he wears a mask, but it's unlike any mask I have ever seen.

There's something grand about Cain. A shadow seems to unfurl two feet taller than his current form, flashing in and out of existence as a low growl rumbles through my head.

The edge of my nightmares seems stronger in his gaze, but that's to be expected.

Cain is a Dream Eater.

What taste would he divine from my scandalous dreams of a figment who wears his face?

Except the figment is much larger and has sharp teeth and mirrorlike eyes.

And a monster cock between his legs.

My cheeks flush when he pulls me against him, and I definitely feel something large along my hip that suggests he knows where my thoughts are going.

I invited him in when I prayed. I can almost feel him in my head.

*I've made a grave mistake.*

The room is still cast in shadows, and the music has changed. Before, it was a festive tune of instruments. Now, a haunting melody has taken its place.

I realize it's coming from all directions, and Cain seems to be the logical culprit of the dreamlike music that drifts around us. "I wanted a moment to talk," he says, which I suppose is his way of explaining why everything in the room is cast in shadows.

Reflections splinter off from what seems to be broken shards of glass that float through dark gaps. I can't see any of the multitude of guests or even Earl Rinhold, but every now and then, I see their silhouettes in the broken reflections.

*This isn't my world,* I realize.

The King of the Elite City has brought us somewhere else.

A tingle of fear skitters up my spine, and the mark above my navel throbs.

Cain seems to react to my trepidation and puts distance between us while holding my hands. I have a feeling it would be a terrible idea to let go.

Without his body warmth shielding me, chill air wraps around my middle and makes it hard to breathe. I feel as if I've been immersed deep into the under layer of an ocean that hasn't seen sunlight in a thousand years. He's an anchor I need in this alternate world.

Without him, would I be lost forever?

"Does this have something to do with the blood contract?" I guess, trying not to let my teeth chatter. I can't rightly think of another reason that the King of the Elite City would personally make a visit just to see me or go through the trouble of slipping us into this strange in-between of worlds. I have witnessed magic before, and I know power when I see it.

This is a display of both in immeasurable quantities. As far as I can tell, I'm his only audience. Everyone else is hung in suspension on the outside.

*Is he really here for me?*

I mentally kick myself. Of course not. He's here for the Rinholds. *They're* on the verge of moving to the Immortality Sector, and that would justify the King's attention. It doesn't happen very often that a family ascends to the Immortality Sector.

If I'm to wed Earl Rinhold, I become implicated. Cain's scrutiny of those who might be worthy would also fall to me.

I hadn't considered my worthiness of the ultimate prize offered by the God of our city. With the constant threat of failure looming over my head, I've always been Lady Nightingale.

Hidden, insignificant, and unworthy of anything but my brother's wrath and my father's passing affection.

My mother's love is certainly something I don't deserve. I am a fleeting dream, a fantasy, of the daughter she wished she had. She has never treated me as such, but that is the truth regardless.

Cain seems to look right through me with his blue eyes that pierce the darkness. Just like in his painting, they seem to reflect an inner light that doesn't match the dullness of the ballroom.

"The blood on that contract was mine," he explains.

That knowledge makes my stomach flip.

*Edward managed to pen the contract with* Cain's *blood?*

That made the courtship itself incredibly powerful and binding.

It must have also been obscenely expensive. Maybe even enough for a family to buy their way into the Immortality Sector.

*Why would the Rinholds pay such a price just for me?*

An insane urge to curl into myself overcomes my senses. I release one of his hands so I can press my fingers to the throb on my stomach. It's almost as if I can feel the slice through my corset.

*His power is inside me.*

That explains why my nightmares have taken on their strange form. The magic woven by the King himself has taken root in me.

A tic of my jaw threatens to release the bubble of hysterical laughter from my mouth, so I clamp it down hard.

"I was given little choice in the matter, Lord Cain," I say. Even though a trained apology was lingering on my lips, a suicidal tirade of truth seems to be coming out instead. I straighten as I cling to one of his hands, knowing that if I let go, I could be lost to this dreamworld forever.

But I keep my other hand plastered to my stomach as if to keep myself from bleeding out. The mark throbs so badly now that my toes curl against the pain.

He raises a brow at my defiance but doesn't strike me down. Instead, he seems amused by my lack of self-preservation. "We always have a choice, Scarlett. I'm simply curious about what yours will be."

A flare of anger in my chest surprises me, but I don't

care for the notion that I'm a *curiosity* to the God of our city. My life isn't the subject of entertainment for others.

Yet, that's how Monsters Night always seems to go. Selections are called to become Offerings for the monsters who will come to this world in search of a mate. Many moments are documented throughout their travels to Monster City. Their wide eyes are put on big screens when the monsters hunt them down.

We all know they are the ones who have it easy. The objective of Monsters Night is for monsters to find their compatible mates. If successful, they will treasure their mates and protect them against any threat.

In a world like ours, that is a boon indeed.

The Offering always has an option to say no. Those pairings aren't mandatory, but I can't ever recall seeing a rejection. Resistance, perhaps. Fear, naturally.

But eventually, that sort of bond roots itself in incomparable love.

While I find myself growing fond of Earl Rinhold, I haven't seen any such sort of vicious protection in his eyes.

And now this monster looks at me like he wants to *devour* me.

Because I'm in a courtship with one of his citizens? Men always want what they can't have.

I would have thought monsters were above that petty tendency.

"I'm afraid I will only disappoint you, Lord Cain," I say, unable to hide the sneer in my voice. It doesn't matter how beautiful this monster is. How safe I might feel in his arms against the cold of the outside world.

He's the reason I'm here to begin with.

He's the reason I don't have a choice at all.

Something aggressive flares in his eyes. I'm not sure

how to name the surge of unexpected emotion that makes the shadow above him grow taller.

He pulls me in close so that I'm forced to lean on my toes as he presses his lips against my ear.

"The only one who is a disappointment here, dear Scarlett, is *me*."

# CHAPTER 19

## CAIN

I DON'T GIVE the delicious peach-flavored treat time to ask me what I might mean as I slip away from her.

Because I've already disappointed myself by my lack of control.

I shouldn't have gone anywhere near Scarlett, but the instant I saw her sparkling like a gem on the ballroom floor, I had no power over what happened next.

The Dream Realm descended the moment I spotted her.

I'm not a dreamwalker, if such a species even exists. I can only travel into the Dream Realm when I have an anchor to pull myself in.

Tonight, the Dream Realm sucked me into it along with Scarlett, and that wasn't on purpose.

Shadows skitter across my skin, enticing me with soft touches as I retreat. My power seems different when Scarlett is in the room. Everything is more effortless, and there's a pull to stay that makes it hard to fight.

Something about Scarlett Nightingale is endless and extraordinary.

She isn't entirely human. She can't be.

I watch her as she searches the room for me. Observing her is a luxury in which I indulge. I appreciate how her lacy black dress with red highlights accents her hips and her curves. Her lips are ruby red as if she has dipped them in blood. Her hair is a similar vibrant color, and it glitters with complementing jewels and silver chains.

Breathtaking.

The Dream Realm slowly sinks around me as I concentrate and force my beast back. He's satisfied to watch Scarlett and bask in her beauty, so he doesn't fight me.

Just as well, because I need a minute. My dick throbs from the memory of Scarlett pressed up against me. It would be preferable that all of my subjects didn't remember me with a raging hard-on.

There's enough dream essence that no one pays attention to me. I'm a passing memory. Dreams exist in various states. There's such a state when one is awake that is just out of reach, and I settle into that space while I gain my bearings.

Scarlett has unduly unsettled me. I have no doubt about her silent power as I watch her slide into the crowd that resumes socializing and exchanging fake pleasantries. My nightmare fog made them forget the last few moments where I had blanketed the entire room in darkness.

Scarlett seems unaffected by the memory-alteration magic. Her wide eyes scan the room with a bright spark of fear, but there's curiosity in them, too. I give her credit for not cowering in terror like most mortals would when in my unleashed presence.

That alone proves my theory. There's something hidden and buried deep inside of this female. I'm eager to carve my way to the pit of my little peach and find it.

It's clear she doesn't know she is something *other*. It

would take more than just genetic manipulation to create whatever it is she has inside her soul.

Something dark.

Something that has no end to it like the center of a black hole. I'm well versed in the workings of the universe, but never have I encountered a creature with the same pull as that celestial object.

What are you, little star?

A smile tugs at my lips as I ruminate over the nickname I had instinctually chosen for her.

She's a star indeed, one that is ready to implode and show the world her true power.

I have a feeling that if that happens, it might destroy her and everything about her that calls to me.

If she survives, I suspect that I could tap into that power, should she become my mate.

*I can't do it alone*, I grieve. *I would kill her before she has a chance to shine.*

Even if she survives the explosion of her awakening, the frenzy of my beast in the aftermath would ensure she didn't live very long. He would be drugged on such power.

My true nature would shred her to pieces. Not intentionally, of course, but there's something fragile about the mortal frame she wears. My beast would take over, and there'd be no holding him back.

I would need another compatible monster mate, or two, to even out the score. There are a few monsters quietly in attendance at the fête, likely by invitation, but none of them are even close to the kind of bond I require. Scarlett Nightingale is a Goddess inside a mortal frame, and if I broke her, it would mean an eternity of damnation for a monster like me.

Fuck.

"I see you decided to attend, Sire," Bernard murmurs from my side.

It says something that I hadn't sensed his approach. No matter how distracting my little star might be, no one is silent enough to sneak up on my Dream Eater.

I glance at the male wearing a sharp suit, fitting for the night's festivities, if not a smidge of Monster City's style rather than the Elite's. He is a monster, though. I don't pretend to keep up with Elite fashions, but I know Bernard cares little for them. He resembles a shadow in a room of peacocks.

I like that about him.

"Perhaps I shouldn't have come," I admit, turning back to the crowd.

Bernard neither agrees nor disagrees with me. He simply stands by my side, showing his silent support. Whatever opinion he might have, he keeps it to himself, as he often does.

The music starts up again, and the Earl finally finds his potential bride. He rests his fingers on her elbow to guide her in his steps.

I've already decided he won't get to keep her.

But in the end, it'll be Scarlett's choice. That's how it always works when it comes to mates.

I want her willing, or not at all.

*You're already willing,* I remember, indulging in the last time I encountered her in her dreams.

Her peach-like flavor tingles over my tongue as I recall her bowed off the bed, my Dream Eater's tongue deep in her delicious pussy.

And then my massive cock rubbing over her entire body, painting my beast's silver cum over her skin.

When she tasted it...

I shut the memory off before I do something stupid.

Like emerge from the nightmares and go on a bloodied rampage to claim her as mine in front of everyone's torn bodies.

Earl Rinhold's arm goes around Scarlett as I contemplate all the reasons I could justify flaying him open and painting the marble floor with his blood.

That would look pretty all over my little star.

I'll bathe you in the blood of your enemies.

Then I'll bathe you in my cum.

To my grave disappointment, she doesn't treat Earl Rinhold like her enemy. Instead of pushing him away like I expect she might, she leans closer to him as if she finds comfort in the vile human.

The growl that rumbles through my chest isn't just in the Dream Realm. It skitters along the walls and sends a nervous energy through the crowd.

Earl Rinhold seems oblivious to the very real threat of my beast desiring to rip off his head.

Perhaps he knows why I can't.

He's immune.

Killing him with just cause would be a viable option, but killing him to take his bride would breach the blood contract's terms. The magic would recognize the intent and backfire.

Fucking bastard.

Bernard doesn't make a sound at my side, but I sense his taut discomfort. He's watching to see if I lose control.

Because if that happens again, he must report it to Helia.

Flexing my jaw so hard I swear my molars crack, I manage to hold it together. The Monster City Queen and I have a strong alliance. But if I can't handle my role as King, I know she'll challenge me.

Too many would die in the fight that would ensue.

Perhaps Helia, even.

Or perhaps me. We are evenly matched in many ways. I'm honestly not sure who would win in a true fight between us.

And I am not interested in finding out.

*Bide your time, beast,* I instruct my Dream Eater.

He doesn't have a voice of his own. But I sense his reluctance to behave.

*We will see her again in her dreams,* I assure him.

Because I know we will. After my encounter with Scarlett, I can almost feel her inside her mind.

She's close to letting us back in.

And then... we will play. Tasting the peach nectar between her thighs holds no violation in the Dream Realm.

For the time being, my beast seems satisfied enough with that. We watch as the Earl guides Scarlett to various families and seems to show her off like a new bauble he's just purchased.

I suppose that's all she would be to him. A toy he intends to use and then throw away when he's finished. That's how most Elites function. I would expect no less of a member of the Rinhold family.

He makes a good show of being a gentleman, though. And, in truth, I know very little about him. I typically pay more attention to disobedient families or problem-makers. The Rinholds have always paid their quotas and then some. I've had little cause to investigate them.

Until now.

"What have you discovered of Duke and Duchess Rinhold?" I ask Bernard. I briefly flick my gaze to the older pair conversing with another wealthy family on the verge of ascension.

The Duke and Duchess in question don't appear old, of

course. Neither of them boasts a single wrinkle, despite their elevated ages, as far as humans go.

"Not much outside the information I've already shown you," he admits. "But I've been doing more than just tracking their comings and goings. I've also been taking an account of their assets against the history of their awarded points for successful monster-human matches."

"And?" I press when he goes silent.

He takes his time continuing, but I don't have the patience for his delay tactics tonight. I glare at him until he responds. "They have more wealth than the numbers say they should. We've missed something."

"Hmm," I agree. The Rinholds might have a large village population and excellent selections with many successful monster pairings, but their wealth doesn't add up if I take everything into consideration.

They didn't so much as bat an eye at paying my blood price for Scarlett's courtship contract. There's no lack of anti-aging tonics, even with merchants raising their prices. Sure, the Duchess protested when that happened, but she would just on principle.

The Rinholds act like they can no longer afford to upgrade to the Immortality Sector, but I wonder if that's really true. If they tried to pay it this year, I would run an audit of their finances.

Perhaps they don't want me to look too closely.

*What are you hiding from me?* I wonder.

The Duchess is wearing a black lace choker with an oversized blood diamond at her throat. Such jewels are only sold in Monster City, and importing them comes at a great cost. A secondary chain holds an even larger red gem that nestles above her ample cleavage. The fashion is more suited for a younger lady, but she pulls it off.

The bleached effect of her pale blue irises explains why.

She has probably used anti-aging tonics at high doses since she was a teen.

Duke Rinhold is a more mature version of his son. He greets his guests and slicks back his brown hair he prefers to keep bound by a silk bow at his nape. There's not a single hair out of place. He doesn't choose to display his wealth with frills like many of the other peacocks in the room, but I spot the matching blood diamonds sewn into the belt around his waist. His polished boots whisper with magic, too, that keeps his steps silent.

Why would a Duke need silent steps at a noisy fête?

I figure that out when he breaks from the Duchess and moves through the crowd. Like most Elites, he regularly prays to me, so I have some access to his mind. I'm able to catch snippets of the conversations around him. I'm not omniscient. I can only listen in if I'm intentionally doing so.

I'm listening now, Duke Rinhold.

He blends in as he eavesdrops on various conversations, only to swoop in at the right moment to control the narrative of his guests.

He wants them talking about the village selections, not about Scarlett. The families are taking bets on who will mate the highest-level monsters and, therefore, who will earn the Rinholds the most points. It's a competition between families. Some place bets on their own selections, and the Duke shakes hands more than a few times.

This might be a fraction of their wealth I'm missing. But how does he control who wins? What makes him so confident?

I pocket those questions for later. It's one piece of the puzzle I intend to figure out.

Moving on with my observations, I glance at the servants taking care of the guests. I make note of more than a few who were previously members of various villages. Some are stunningly beautiful or handsome, more so than is necessary to be simple servants of an oversized household.

Which might mean they're being held for trades, or for sex labor among Elites.

Elite families think I haven't noticed that they've kept the best for themselves. That seems to be a new trend the members of my city are doing, and they think they're getting away with it.

They're not. I'm just waiting to see if this works to my benefit. All I care about is that my city is successful. Leaving the humans to find new and creative ways to accomplish the ultimate goal has often surprised us.

Even if I hadn't been watching the Rinholds too heavily, I do know a thing or two about Duke Nightingale, Scarlett's father. His escalation across sectors is due to keeping additional selections for himself for bribes.

But that's what brought Scarlett to me in the first place. Without her desperate prayer, I wouldn't have had the pleasure of finding her.

I watch her as she goes through the motions, but I recognize trained reactions when I see them.

Her mind is elsewhere.

When she looks directly at me, I go still.

I'm not sure if she can see me. She shouldn't be able to, but she presses her hand to her stomach and looks away a moment later.

The Earl leans in and whispers something in her ear. I should be able to hear him, but Scarlett seems to have cut me off somehow. I can only guess what he might have said as he leaves her in the custody of Elite females of similar station. One of them must be a younger sister because she's a more petite version of her mother. Beautiful, but there's an innocence to her that Duchess Rinhold lost a long time ago.

Scarlett outshines them all and looks pleasant enough, but I suspect she wishes to be anywhere else.

My gaze tracks the Earl, though, as he continues his rounds without Scarlett. He smiles when eligible Ladies flirt with him, no doubt trying to win his affection. A courtship might be binding, but it isn't permanent. Not until it has reached a conclusion.

When a female whispers something in his ear, then slinks out of the room, I raise a brow. Earl Rinhold pretends not to have heard her, but he's gone completely stiff.

I know he's going to follow her.

This might be my chance.

"Would you like me to track him?" Bernard asks. He's watching the Earl just as intently as I am.

"No," I immediately decide aloud. The growl still rips through my voice as I utter the word, but I allow my beast that much. I share his anger. "Stay with Scarlett."

I cloak myself in nightmares as I follow the Earl, who predictably retreats from the ballroom and into a dark hallway.

Darkness is where I live.

And darkness is where you will die, Earl Rinhold, should you cross a line.

## CHAPTER 20

## CAGE

"There has to be something in here," I grumble as I swat away centuries' worth of cobwebs. Navigating the underground archives of the Sanguinis Palace is grueling work.

Dangerous, too, given the fact that I'm a sworn enemy of the royal family.

My family is no less royal, if I'm being fair. Royalty is determined by the blessings from our God. Whoever is the strongest takes the throne. When it comes to the Van Drakken and Sanguinis bloodlines, we both have different strengths that make us comparable.

I was always taught that Strigoi like Sabre are pompous weaklings not suited to the throne. But after trying to kill him and losing, only to be on the blade-end of his mercy, I have learned that strength is not always about physical prowess.

Sabre is smart. Incredibly smart. And passionate. That's why I fell for him and why I can't allow him to go through with the asinine plan our families have for each other.

He's stronger than my entire family put together. He's a

Prince, yet he's been the one giving enough power to the throne to keep the blood fields functioning.

*Fuck them all,* I growl inside my head.

No, my father is wrong about Sabre. He's wrong about everything. The Sanguinis family is no less powerful than we are.

But he doesn't see it that way. It's not black and white enough; therefore, he refuses to acknowledge it.

And therein lies the problem between Strigoi clans. It's always a fucking dick-measuring contest.

My mood improves as I imagine that playing out in the Strigoi throne room. Sabre might have vibrating bits that are immensely pleasurable, but when it comes to size, I'd win that contest hands down.

If my family had their way, his dick would be cut off, and not long after that, his head.

Returning home right now turns my stomach. The protocol Sabre and I established is what keeps us safe, but I'm not ready to leave yet. We only meet up in secret when our families are otherwise occupied. With all that's been going on in the Hell Fae Realm, it's been easier to find time to be together.

But my family is coming back from a hunt today. We don't have access to the Royal Blood Fields. So the Van Drakkens are forced to go to other worlds in search of food.

We are a hunted species in most worlds we venture into. This world is no better, where we all squabble over titles and resources.

I'm a sentinel for my household, meaning they expect me to protect the estate in their absence.

I've seen the blood fields. I know the Sanguinis family can't afford an attack right now.

As for my absence, infiltrating enemy territory is as good an excuse as any. So I keep an eye out for anything my father might find useful in theory, but wouldn't be truly damaging to my lover.

The sound of kicked rocks down the dark hall sends my instincts flaring. Like any Strigoi, I can see in pitch darkness, so I don't have a torch.

There's a light at the end of the hall that follows the sound, though, making me curious about whether they keep any mortal staff on hand. That wouldn't be uncommon, but most mortals are better suited to be blood bags in the ground. Strigoi feed on blood and dreams, and those marinate better when the intended target is kept in a permanent sleep.

Being in the Morpheus Kingdom, it's easier for me to slip into my true Strigoi form than if I had been on a hunt with my family in a mortal realm. I'm able to skitter up the wall and cling to the ceiling while I wait for the light to dim.

Instead, it grows brighter.

I go perfectly still as a petite female walks through the hall. Or rather, she's limping.

*What are the damn Sanguinis assholes up to now?* I wonder.

She nervously glances around, stopping just beneath me as if she can sense my presence.

If she sees me, she doesn't scream. So either she has nerves of steel, or she's coincidentally staring right at my exact location for no reason.

The female is young, too young. Her blue eyes are bright with fear and make her look like a ghost. We have those in this realm, even if they have a different name depending on their type.

Such as Banshees.

Or worse, the Kuntilanak Fae. Those are terrifying things.

And then there are various spirits with no known names.

I hear a rapid heartbeat, though, so that eliminates the latter possibility. And the scent of blood makes my mouth water.

As do her nightmares. Even though she's awake, I can sense them lingering in the back of her mind, waiting for me to taste them just as much as her blood.

Both of those things suggest she's human, or at least partially human. Banshee blood won't sustain a Strigoi.

And a Banshee would have screamed at me by now. Not stared up at me with fear in her eyes.

My hunger, though, makes my fangs ache. The pattering in her chest makes her sound like prey. It wants to tear into her flesh and drain her dry. Sabre fed me his blood, but that doesn't truly nourish me.

The nightmares dancing in her eyes promise a fulfilling meal.

I'm hungry. I need to go home and feed on whatever blood infused with dreams my family has brought back from their hunt.

*Or I could feed now.*

*No,* I decide as I swat the vicious hunger away like an irritating pest. I have more control than most of my kind, and I can go impressively long periods without feeding. That's what makes me a good assassin. Everything I do is with controlled measure, and I kill only when it's intentional. Sabre is the same way.

It's one of the reasons we've bonded.

"Hello?" the girl suddenly asks, making me nearly lose my grip on the ceiling and crash down right on top of her.

Wouldn't that be a sight?

Prized assassin. Startled into falling into a clump of claws onto a poor mortal girl.

She chews on her lip as if contemplating something, then drops to her knees and sets her torch next to the wall. It sizzles against the moisture of the underground tunnel. Ignoring it, she fumbles in her bag and pulls out a book.

It's old.

And magicked. I tense as the scent of its ancient power drifts to my position on the ceiling.

This girl could be a means to trap spies, so I don't reveal myself. Still, she's an odd sentinel to put in the archives.

Or the halls to the archives, if I could find them.

She leaves the book on the ground and snatches up her torch, then backs up a few paces. Her shoulders sink as if she's glad to be rid of the thing. "I know you're here," she whispers as she glances up. "I've lived in this palace all my life, creature. Long enough to know what you all smell like." Her nostrils flare as if to make a point. "So you can either keep hiding up there like a coward or come down here so you can find what you're looking for."

*Coward?* I muse as my lips stretch into a wicked grin. My fangs throb at the challenge, but I won't bite this interesting little mortal speck.

I do finally reveal myself, though. Curiosity might have gotten the better of me, but if I can't handle a small mortal girl, then I deserve to have my life cut short.

Dropping to the ground, the girl flinches as I stretch to my full height while still donning my monster form. She's an unknown, so I have no intention of relinquishing my armored skin, my fangs, or my claws.

Or my ability to walk in her dreams and see her truth, if I so desire.

Her torch is what keeps me from dreamwalking, though. The bright light makes her far too alert for me to gain a foothold in her mind.

I realize that is likely on purpose. She knows what she's doing.

*Smart girl.*

"And what do you think I'm looking for?" I ask her.

I see that she's not as young as I previously thought. She has a developed body, one that the Sanguinis line might abuse.

There's not a single mark on her, though. Her nails are clean and her complexion is fair. There aren't blisters or calluses on her fingers, betraying an easy life.

A slave would have worked in the fields. And if she had been used for her blood or her body, there would be evidence left behind.

I make a mental note to ask Sabre about untouched females in his palace, as it's truly an oddity.

She indicates the book on the ground with a jerk of her chin. "Hell if I know. The book told me to bring it to you, so I did."

My tongue flicks out to taste the air as I contemplate that strange statement. "A book told you to bring it sssome-where," I repeat, my *s* unintentionally slipping on my long tongue.

She leans onto her hip as if she's growing impatient with me, but her fingers tremble with fear she's obviously trying to hide. She's holding it together pretty well, so I believe her when she claims she's lived among the Strigoi all her life. "Yes. It's not uncommon for powerful beings to have a piece of their soul manifested into a book. Books always hold magic, given that they are something created out of nothing. Books defy nature. Especially this one, as it was written by the first Sigil."

My eyes blow wide as I digest a word I haven't heard in a very long time.

"Sigils are a myth," I say out of instinct, but the way the girl eyes me with defiance suggests that's not true.

And the evidence is at my feet. A Sigil is a creature of unlimited power. Rumor has it that the Strigoi were formed by three Kings who shared a Queen they named their Sigil. With her endless power, the blood fields were created and the land didn't even need living souls to function. The Sigil's memory of them had been power enough, and high-quality blood flowed freely in rivers filled to the brim with vibrant dreams.

The entire kingdom thrived, and there was no need to hunt, no need to squabble over territory or resources.

There had only been peace—until the Sigil was gone.

Then the three bloodlines went their separate ways. For many, the story ends there.

But as I examine the female before me, I notice her eyes aren't blue like I had assumed.

They're silver, and the irises are fractured like broken shards of glass.

"They aren't myths," she insists. "But a Sigil is rare enough that I can understand why you might think so. And one is born only during a time of great need. King Nos has been trying to awaken a Sigil for centuries by using any human lineage to the last Sigil, who just so happens to be my distant relative. That's why I live here. I'm one of his experiments."

Now I have more questions than answers. "Does King Nos have a habit of sharing all his plans with his experiments?" I don't slip my *s* as badly this time, having regressed my monster features in favor of my mortal ones.

This girl is no threat.

But she is interesting. I can guess why Sabre kept her kind a secret from me.

He was embarrassed by his father's desperate attempts.

And he didn't believe her story. Just like he didn't believe he had heard a compatible mate's scream rip through the dream plane just the other day.

The girl scoffs as she adjusts the torch to her other hand. The light no doubt reveals my nakedness. There's no point in wearing clothing when I'm in my true form, but she keeps her gaze on mine. She doesn't seem at all sexually attracted to me, which is just as well. I have no interest in playing with one of King Nos's experiments that Sabre also happened not to tell me about.

"He can't hide anything from us," she casually explains. "We might not be awakened Sigils, but we still have some of the innate power that comes from being potentials, especially with the training we've gone through. Such as seeing the truth behind a person's motives. And—"

"We?" I ask, cutting her off.

Her cheeks flush as if she hadn't intended to reveal that there are more like her under King Nos's thumb. "You're missing the point. Just pick up the book so I can go back to my wing." She eyes the cobwebs and wrinkles her nose. "I don't like the archives. The halls change every few minutes, and you'll be lost here forever until someone else finds you. So when you've read whatever it is you're supposed to read, I'll show you the way out. Only someone like me can, unless you have enough magic to find the exit yourself."

I flex my fingers, irritated that I didn't know about that safety mechanism when it came to the archives.

But it makes sense.

*Rescued by a girl. Sabre will never let me hear the end of this if he finds out about it.*

Kneeling, I pick up the book and open it. The pages are like papyrus dipped in liquid metal. I only see an obscure reflection of myself. The longer I stare at it, I notice that tiny cracks seem to form across the page.

Two other spots appear as the liquid metal moves and changes. Two silhouettes, one next to me that takes on the shape of a Strigoi with large fangs.

*Sabre?*

Then there's another male at the top, who seems to have two faces overlapping onto one another.

One looks like a pompously rich man.

There's a shadow that overlays his image, one that towers over him like a dark cloud with red eyes. Long horns emerge, making me wonder what kind of creature that could be and what it has to do with Sabre, me, or the lost soul of a Sigil who created this book.

Then a blood diamond appears in the middle of the page, connecting all three of us.

When I reach out to touch it, I flinch back at a sharp stab of pain. Blood pools on the tip of my finger even though I'm fairly certain I hadn't touched the page.

The book slams shut and then vanishes.

"Well, that was rude," I say, glancing up at the girl, who is watching me expectantly. "Any idea what the hell that meant?" I ask before popping my bloodied finger into my mouth.

She shrugs. "Whatever message she had for you is for you alone. Now, if you don't want to be stuck in here forever, I suggest you come with me," she says, then marches off down a hall I didn't remember seeing a moment before.

I frown but follow her.

It frustrates me that I've already decided to keep this from Sabre, but I have no doubt about it now.

That scream I heard had been real.

And it had come from more than just a compatible mate. I think it belonged to a Sigil.

*My* Sigil.

And whoever or wherever she is, she is the key.

The key to my problems.

The key to Sabre's broken heart.

The key to *everything*.

# CHAPTER 21

# EDWARD

*Tonight was supposed to be about Scarlett,* I think, frustrated to be blackmailed away from her when I want nothing more than to stay by her side.

She is going to be so much more than my mother had planned. Yes, she will bring new wealth and new status to our family by the fruit of our union. But an heir is the least that Scarlett can offer. She is special. She is an untapped source that even the monsters have let slip by under their noses.

My mother is too shortsighted.

I intended tonight to be my announcement, one of a public intention to show that Lady Scarlett will not be swept aside amidst the workings of our family. Nothing is more important than my future bride. Not even Selections Night.

She will be the star that makes us all shine brighter.

That's what I had intended to say tonight. Instead, Lady Eleanor thinks she can threaten me, which is why I'm forced to march through an empty corridor rather than entertaining my guests in the ballroom and calming Scarlett's nerves.

She's worse than I would have expected. I know she has a different background than most Elites, but she seemed truly rattled.

My sister will take good care of her. At least, long enough for me to deal with my little problem.

*Jealousy is an ugly beast.*

I can't blame the poor girl, though. Reaching out, I trail my fingers along the gilded walls that practically glimmer with gold. The hidden flecks catch on my nails as I turn the corner.

There are actually gold flakes inside the paint, making everything shimmer in a way that's just not replicated in other estates. Of course, the riches of my family are mostly earned off the books. My parents are brazen to flaunt it after I just took a large withdrawal to pay for Scarlett's blood contract. We should be broke until the accounting after Monsters Night.

We're not. In fact, I think we're richer now than ever before. My father had set up bets against Scarlett's family accepting our courtship, and that alone had won us some new servant staff and various treasures.

Including the new vial of anti-aging elixir that clinks against a key in my pocket. It's a vial that I will use as a bribe tonight, if needed.

One such vial that I took from my mother's stash has already served me in earning Scarlett's trust. Or maybe she doesn't trust me at all and was acting out of desperation. But that's just as well. The investment was worth it all the same.

There's no better position to be in than in someone's debt.

I hope this trade will be as fruitful, but I doubt it.

Once I turn one more corner, I spot Lady Eleanor practically preening from her perch on a chaise lounge large enough for two people, despite its petite size.

I would know, because I've fucked her on it before.

But not tonight.

Not ever again.

The old Edward is gone, and now I am a new creation in Cain's image. It's almost as if I can feel him here with me tonight, following me wherever I go.

*I'm going to make you proud,* I pray as I trace the blood mark on my hand, one that promises me to Scarlett.

A rumble echoes through the room as if I had imagined his response. I'm excited, nervous, and now rather irritated.

Because Lady Eleanor is a problem that needs to be dealt with, and one of her breasts has fallen out.

"Cover yourself," I command in a voice that would make any servant fall to their knees.

Lady Eleanor is no servant. She scowls at me as if I've told her there was piss in her wine.

She reclines along the chaise lounge and inches up her dress. "Why, Edward? Can't get it up anymore now that you're spanking yourself because the new girl won't do it for you?"

Growling, I set one foot on the furniture she's trespassing on. Leaning in, I yank my knife from the hidden compartment in my boot and point it at her. "Careful."

A wild gleam enters her bleached eyes. Eleanor isn't any older than I am, but she's used every magic tonic she can get her hands on to enhance herself to her tastes.

It's why she has plump, gorgeous breasts now on full display, because I realize she's slipped the other one out, too. She toys with one of her pink nipples that are too perfectly symmetrical to be natural.

"Or what? You're going to use that on me?" she asks.

She wants to call my bluff?

She wants to behave like a whore?

I'll treat her like one.

Gripping her corset, I pluck at one of the straps with my blade.

*Snap.*

Her eyes go wide when I do it again, and she realizes what I'm doing.

"Edward, I—"

*Snap.*

*Snap.*

She most likely doesn't have any magic tonics on her that'll give her a new dress. She's going to have to hope one of our servants takes pity on her or seek help from a stranger.

Or, if she really chooses to piss me off, I'll leave her for our monster guests.

When she's naked and used, and everyone can see what she really is.

An icy chill on the back of my neck makes me pause when I have my blade at her thigh, ready to cut off the layers of her dress. The slut isn't wearing any underwear.

She had hoped I would fuck her.

But I can't, not if I want Scarlett to be bound to me forever. I remember the terms of my blood contract.

*Exclusivity.*

Maybe when we've been married for a few centuries and have enjoyed the Immortality Sector for a time, Scarlett and I will grow bored of one another and expand our horizons. I have no intention of sticking with one woman for the rest of eternity. To pretend otherwise would be asinine.

The angry lust pressing against my pants doesn't seem to understand that having toys to play with will come in time. Right now, I am a new creation. I belong to Scarlett.

*I can't belong to her if I am held back by my past.*

A masterpiece isn't created overnight. I have a few weeks yet to work on becoming the perfect husband for Scarlett.

Until then, I need to make sure women like Lady Eleanor don't interfere. She won't be the last to try something like this.

"Did you think you could spread your legs and I'd forget my duty to Scarlett?" I ask her. My words drip with venom, and Eleanor tries to close her legs.

I hold them open, then flip my blade with a trained motion so that the hilt presses against her thigh. I drag it up her skin until I reach her pussy, then I hold it there, just at her entrance, and wait for her response.

Her eyes are wide when she responds. "Duty?" she asks. "Is... is that enough to make you forget me, Edward? Forget our love?"

"Love?" I all but snarl, then shove my hilt into her wet cunt. I clamp a hand over her mouth when she squeaks. "You don't love me, Eleanor. You love *this*." I move the hilt deeper until the wide handle bumps against her clit. Her hips move, betraying that she's sick enough to enjoy what I'm doing to her.

Which makes any remorse I might have had vanish.

Because I'm going to make her come all over my blade so that any monsters attending tonight will smell her lust. They'll come after her like a treat I've left out for them to feast on.

I decide to recall any servants from this side of the wing.

I don't need to take care of my Eleanor problem. She'll do it for me.

Pumping the hilt into her, I thrust harder and faster until she's a trembling and whimpering mess. I stop just before a climax overtakes her body, because I have a special sort of humiliation in mind for a manipulative slut like this.

I can't help but admit that my breath is coming in soft pants, that my cock is as hard as a rock and all I want to do is find Scarlett and claim her to release this need inside of me.

But the blade of my desire needs to be dulled first. Unlike Eleanor, Scarlett is untouched in that way. I know her brother teased her as a lure with other Earls and Lords, but she's still a virgin. She's still untainted.

She's sweet and witty and special.

This slut is nothing, which makes her the perfect outlet for my cruelty.

Scarlett won't ever be subjected to this dark side of me. It's best I get it out of the way, for her sake.

Scarlett will only get my sweetness.

My tenderness.

Everything in me that is gentle and caring. Her needs will come before my own.

*Which means my needs must never be wanting.*

I have to satisfy my darkness if I'm to protect Scarlett. I should thank Lady Eleanor for giving me an outlet I hadn't even realized was sorely needed.

Ripping the long hilt from the slut's wet cunt, I stab the blade into the sofa's material just between her legs so that the hilt sticks up.

"Ride it," I command her.

She blinks at me with incomprehension as I slide away the rest of her clothing, leaving her naked except for the ballroom-style hair that seems out of place now without her frills and lace. The silks I've removed puddle onto the floor, shredded and hopeless to ever be used as clothing again. There's not a single piece large enough for her to drape around herself, should she come to her senses when she realizes what my punishment is.

Humiliation.

"And if I don't?" she challenges. Her lower lip quivers, but she manages to look me in the eyes.

There's still some fight left in this whore that needs to be dealt with.

I lean in and lower my voice, enunciating my threat with dark promise. "Then I'll drag you into the ballroom just like this. I'll throw you on the floor and tell everyone that you took off all your clothes and tried to seduce me. You'll never find a husband after that."

Her fingers dig into the velvety material of the chaise lounge as she stares at me. "I'll tell them you did this to me."

Cocking my head to the side, I call her bluff. "Who do you think they'll believe, Eleanor? The slut with a wet cunt, or a fully clothed gentleman?"

I'd pass any monster-grade examination. I haven't fucked her. Sex generates energy. So does lust. Such a scan would detect I'm aroused, but I'm thinking about Scarlett. It would point the needle to my betrothed, vindicating me of any wrongdoing.

I followed Lady Eleanor to nip this sort of behavior in the bud. No one blackmails me and gets away with it.

"Ride it," I growl, giving her one last chance to obey me.

Or else I'll do exactly as I said. I will drag her right into that ballroom and let her see what humiliation really looks like.

Scarlett will be offended, no doubt. I'll have to explain, apologize, grovel, even. But at least I'll be a man of my word.

If nothing else, I have my honor.

Lady Eleanor steels her jaw, giving me a look of determination as she rises on her knees, then positions her hips. She holds on to the edge of the chaise lounge as she makes a show of sliding onto the hilt.

*Fuck.*

I watch as she slowly moves up and down, coating the hilt with her juices as she obeys me. It takes everything in me not to move, not to even breathe.

She's not moaning, though. I need her to play the whore she pretends to be.

"Touch yourself while you ride it," I add.

"*You* can touch," she offers seductively as she bats her eyelashes at me. She rolls her hips with an expert motion I've been on the receiving end of before, one that twists and makes me want to explode. "I won't tell anyone."

The stupid cunt is still trying to bait me. But it's exactly what I need to rein in my lust and make sure this ends my way.

"Touch *yourself*, Eleanor."

She bites her lip, then finally obeys me and rolls her fingers over her clit. A shudder of pleasure ripples through her, making her nipples harden as she finally loses herself to the moment.

She likes it when I'm cruel. She thinks that like all the other times, I'll pay her back in riches or favors out of guilt.

No, this time I have no regrets. No guilt.

She tried to blackmail me. Her threat was to tell Scarlett about the scar on my lower hip she had given me during similar blade play. If Scarlett knows about my dark tendencies, she might not agree to our pairing.

The truth is the scar could have been from anything, and the fact that Eleanor knows about it wouldn't be secret. I have regular doctor examinations with a public record of any scars. Had Lady Eleanor actually looked me up in the eligible bachelor records, she would have seen that the scar was part of a public health document anyone could read about. Scarlett herself probably already knows of it.

Eleanor's blackmail held no real threat to me. Maybe an inconvenience, but now I've worked it all out.

I'm going to show her what happens to those who find themselves on my bad side.

"Come for me, Eleanor," I say with a tender voice.

She falls for my fake charm and flutters her eyelashes closed as she rubs herself harder, sinking on the hilt as a spasm finally overtakes her body. She moans and leans back, drawing out her orgasm until she finally slides off of the hilt and her wetness drips down the blade to stain the couch.

"That's a good girl," I praise her as I fist her hair.

She opens her mouth to say something, but it turns into a scream when I yank and drag her onto the floor.

I'm going to need a scapegoat for the story already weaving in my head of Eleanor's humiliation. So I dig out the anti-aging tonic in my pocket and smash it onto the ground. The magic instantly dissipates, but the signature will be unmistakable.

It might be a waste of a valuable potion, but this is how I'll ruin her.

"Have fun being tonight's entertainment for our monster guests," I shout over my shoulder as I walk away.

The temperature in the air drops as I feel like I'm walking through a dark cloud of disapproval. Maybe a monster was already watching the show. It wouldn't be uncommon.

I still did nothing wrong. I served justice for an enemy of my house.

"I'm finished here. She's all yours," I say to the disembodied entity.

A growl rumbles in return. For some reason, I don't feel like this monster is going to take the bait.

*Fine. More for the others, then.*

# CHAPTER 22

## CAIN

"Don't believe the lies about her, my king," Duchess Amesbury begs as she once again rises from her seat. She goes so far as to press her head against the table. "Please, I beg of you, spare her from judgment!"

Her husband, Duke Amesbury and the father of the recently shunned Lady Eleanor, yanks her back into her seat with a glare. "Sit *down*. Our Lord has had enough hysterics to deal with lately. Let's not plague him with more than what Eleanor has already embarrassed this family with."

Steepling my fingers, I watch the exchange while I contemplate how to navigate the situation. If I had been less distracted, none of this would have become public scandal and the lies wouldn't have twisted everything out of proportion.

It took me two days to even realize what sort of rumors had been spread. By then, it was too late. So here I am, trying to pick up the pieces.

*It's my fault,* I lament. *I should have known why he broke an anti-aging tonic on the ground.*

It had left a magical signature, one that supported the rumor I know he started with unmistakable evidence.

Because no one in their right mind would discard a tonic of that value for no reason.

My beast remains silent. Not even a growl. He's displeased with me, not just because I've made matters worse. But because we haven't played in Scarlett's dreams as I had promised.

She hasn't let us back in. Not yet, but at least she's safe. For the moment, anyway.

My concern for her safety is why I am in this mess to begin with. I wrongly assumed that I had enough time to follow Earl Rinhold back to the ballroom and make sure he didn't do anything untoward to Scarlett before going back to rescue the poor girl he had humiliated. I should have trusted Bernard with that task, but I had let my emotions control me. After seeing the Earl's true colors, I needed to watch over her personally. That had been selfish.

I watched the whole thing unfold. She had lured him into isolation using blackmail and tried to seduce him, that part of the rumor was true. But the rest of it was a twisted version of what really happened.

He tore the clothing from her body, then he fucked her with the hilt of his dagger as if to prove some point.

He couldn't have just left it there. He stabbed it into the seat of a chaise lounge and made her ride it while she touched herself.

Then he dragged her onto the ground and broke an anti-aging tonic before abandoning her.

I'm the only one who knows what really happened. The public scandal story is that Lady Eleanor tried to throw herself at Earl Rinhold, who rejected her. But she had planned for it, according to the rumor, so that's why she had stolen his dagger and performed a black magic ritual to make him fall in love with her.

It made her sound manic and desperate.

It also allowed Earl Rinhold to weave a story very close to the truth, but in his favor. And after two days of circulation, the story had effectively ruined Lady Eleanor's reputation. It was an easy story to believe. Her jealousy over the fact that Earl Rinhold is betrothed to an unknown Elite recently risen in the Magic Sector ranks is real enough to make the story true.

I regret not putting a stop to it now. I'm a dream region monster, so I was able to sense her lust and enjoyment of the exchange, giving me no reason to interfere. If Earl Rinhold had engaged in true intercourse with her, it would have given me a justified means of ending his life. He would have broken the exclusivity clause in his contract with Scarlett, but he was too smart to violate that term.

My own selfish reasons put one of my citizens in danger. I regret that, even if I would have done the same thing all over again. Scarlett needs protection, and I chose to watch her in favor of Lady Eleanor.

When he left her there on the floor with no usable clothing and even announced to my presence to use her if I wished, I knew what kind of man Earl Rinhold really was.

*A dead man.*

But I will bide my time. Until then, I have to untangle this snarl he caused and I let happen on my watch.

Duke and Duchess Amesbury quietly bicker in front of my desk while I peer over their heads to the darkened city outside. I spot a Raven's silky black wings reflecting against the moonlight, so I know Bernard has finally returned.

*Just in time.*

This time he went all the way to Monster City to run an errand for me. Even if I can see through his eyes, I haven't as of late. There have been other things on my mind, so I trusted Bernard to get the job done.

Gladly, my Raven is worthy of my trust.

I see the evidence of his success in his beak. Two blood diamonds glimmer with ruby-red tones before he soars upward to the roof where he has an entry hole just large enough for a small Raven.

The purity of a blood diamond increases my effectiveness when scrying. And I intend to find a compatible breed of monster in this realm, or another world altogether if I must. I will find one, though, who can help me keep Scarlett alive when I take her as my mate.

That's next week's problem, though. I need to scry for such monsters when the portals open to hundreds of worlds in eight days' time. That'll only require one blood diamond. The other is for my current task.

Today, I need to work on cleaning up this mess and finding a way to show Scarlett what kind of man Earl Rinhold really is. Anything I do to impact her opinion of him could be considered a violation of the blood contract just as effectively as if I had killed him.

I have to tread carefully.

So I'll use Earl Rinhold's tactics of spreading rumors against him.

"Lady Eleanor is still recovering within the guest level of my tower," I explain. "She's welcome to stay as long as she requires."

They stop bickering as they glance back at me. "She's being kept here as a guest?" Duchess Amesbury asks hopefully. "Not a prisoner?"

I nod. "She was wounded, so I have a team of doctors tending to her injuries. She'll need a few more days, but she'll make a full recovery." I tilt my head. "I apologize that I wasn't aware of the rumors until now."

Bernard was in Monster City, so I had been deaf without him as my ears. Prayers don't often include rumors, only requests for help or blessings.

The monsters attending the fête only made matters worse. I am just as guilty as Earl Rinhold for abandoning her while she was naked and smelling like sex in an empty hall.

Conveying that information to Helia was one of Bernard's tasks. I've spent the majority of my time monitoring prayers and communications to ensure Scarlett's safety, as well as all the other tasks I must take care of during the busiest time of the year. While I've let the humans rule themselves even more than usual, I've almost forgotten that there are monsters to keep in line, too.

Monster justice is Helia's territory. Maintaining the humans of the Elite City is mine.

"What kind of injuries?" the Duke asks while he fiddles with the frill of his shirt. He pretends not to care about his daughter, but I know he does. The Amesbury Elites stick together. They are more of a middle- to lower-class family who scrape by on enough points to survive in the Magic Sector, which is no small feat in and of itself. Their daughter had simply found a currency that served her well in such circumstances, until now.

"That is still under investigation, but I can confirm that she suffered extreme blood loss," I say.

The Duchess's face blanches. I can tell she wants to confront me on why this information hadn't been disclosed sooner, but she doesn't.

I'm still their God. Whatever reasons I have for the way I do things are mine alone. I sent word to her parents that she had been taken into the tower, and they were the ones who had chosen not to respond until I sent an invitation.

To be fair, my first correspondence had been informative, not requiring a response.

"Was she violated in... other ways? By the monsters, I mean?" she asks instead. The tremor in her voice betrays the nightmares I can taste dancing around inside her mind.

She's always worried about her daughter attracting the wrong kind of attention. Luckily, most monsters aren't rapists. But taking a human's blood without permission is almost as unforgivable a crime. They will pay, once they are found. Hopefully, Bernard has good news for me. It was my assumption that the monsters we are looking for boarded the train for Monster City to prepare for Monsters Night.

It could be why they fed against the rules, too. Mortal blood is a coveted resource, but monsters must obtain it legally. That can take time, and with Monsters Night in just eight days, maybe they didn't want to wait.

There are many different types of vampiric species within Helia's city walls who seek her favor to earn time with a willing blood donor or be given a small supply to live off of for a while.

Feeding off of Elite citizens is frowned upon, to say the least.

If my followers don't have my protection, what good am I to them?

"No," I confirm. "At least, your daughter says they didn't do anything else to her but feed." I'll still explore their minds when they are found and discover the truth.

I decided against scrutinizing Eleanor's nightmares. What little I could see was darkness and screams. She wasn't recovering with such heavy nightmares tearing open her mind.

So I ate them.

"Can we see her?" Duchess Amesbury asks.

"What of the rumors?" her husband interjects, cutting

her off as he taps his fingers on the table. "No one will do trades with us, and merchants are refusing to sell us wares. They can't have their reputation damaged and risk other families boycotting them, you see. This can prove difficult just days before Monsters Night."

"Do you not have confidence in your selections?" I ask.

Amesbury Village isn't much to look at, but it's a pretty little place by the sea. I know of it because I've stopped there before to enjoy the scenery. With the infertile land, though, pretty is all it could really be.

The Duchess gives her husband a frightened look while he takes a deep breath. "I need to buy one from another family for us to reach our quota this year," he admits. His wife makes a strangled sound.

Shadows grow against the walls as irritation crawls up my spine. "I approve the sale of breeders and resources between villages. Not selections," I warn him. Even if I know the underhanded practice happens, I often pretend to not notice.

I let the Elites manage themselves, and it doesn't hurt to have a little blackmail over them now and again.

"I know," he says, bowing his head. "But it is how we've survived this long, King Cain. And I promise you, once we get through this rut, we will serve you well."

Bernard enters the room, pausing by the doorway as he taps his boots on the ground. He could be silent if he wanted to be, but he's trying not to startle my guests.

I wave him in.

"I sent my Raven to Monster City to pick up a gift for you," I inform Duke and Duchess Amesbury. They both glance up at me with wide eyes. "The fault lies with me. I am responsible for the magic tonics that are permitted within your sector, and their use should be properly divided. Therefore, I will officially pardon Lady Eleanor. She will remain here until I have found the monsters who fed on her, for her recovery, and in the meantime, I give you this."

I hold out my hand and wait for Bernard to retrieve the blood diamond. He drops it into my palm.

Presenting it to the Duchess and Duke, I place it on the table.

I lean back while they stare at the gem that sucks in the light around it. "If anyone refuses your trade, pray to me. I will hear you, and I will come."

"Th-thank you, King Cain," Duke Amesbury says as he picks up the treasure and examines it. Bernard had done well. The quality is impeccable.

The Duchess bites her lip, then looks down.

Darkness swirls around her, tormenting her, because I'm not entertaining the rumors she knows are lies.

I know they are lies, too. But it doesn't mean I can do anything about it.

This, though. This is what I can do for them.

This is how I clean up Earl Rinhold's mess.

After closing pleasantries and slightly lifted spirits, I send Duchess and Duke Amesbury on their way. I consider the matter closed after providing the servants with orders of Lady Eleanor's care, and I turn my attention back to Bernard.

"The other one?" I ask.

He nods and produces the second blood diamond. It's even more perfect than the first.

"Helia sends her regards with the finest blood diamond ever created, as well as her vote of confidence," he says as he hands it to me. "If there are monsters compatible with you out there, my king, you will find them."

I hold up the gem to the moonlight and examine its symmetrical facets.

"I hope you're right," I murmur.

Because if I fail, it won't matter what kind of man Earl Rinhold really is.

Scarlett would still be safer with him than with me.

*Eight days,* I promise myself.

*Then the nightmare really begins.*

# CHAPTER 23

# SCARLETT

It's been three days since the fête, but it feels like three years.

My betrothed has been doting on me, but today he's been out of the house, leaving me far too much time to think about things.

To *rethink* things. And then I found the letter on my desk, penned in my mother's writing.

I'm still sitting at my vanity just staring at it well after the sun has set. The correspondence should give me relief, considering it's the first letter I've received since my courtship began, but all I can do is read it over and over again, looking for something that isn't there.

*Dear Scarlett,*

*I'm so proud of you. I know it isn't easy to navigate the trepidations of a family like the Rinholds, but I have heard nothing but news of your grace, dignity, and elegance amidst the tides of scandal and intrigue.*

*This is what it means to be a Duchess, Scarlett. You aren't one yet, but it's as if you've slid right into the role most suited for you.*

*Maybe life looks foreign to you now. Especially since I know that you had planned on running a small settlement once the population of Nightingale Village had grown enough to support branching out, but I don't truly believe that was ever a realistic option. It was a dream I had hoped would come true for you. After my illness, I only brought this family down, and for that, I deeply mourn the cost of my life and the burden it has placed on your delicate shoulders.*

*Because you're the one holding this family up now, Scarlett. My beautiful, dear daughter.*

*As you know, the Nightingale Selection is tonight. Your father has high hopes that there is one selection in particular who will attract a powerful monster mate and earn our family direly needed points. I do hope you can watch the broadcast with me. I have already invited Earl Rinhold, and the Duke and Duchess as well.*

*Please don't forget to bring more of that fragrance you found for me. I've almost run out of mine.*

*In Cain's name,*

*Eveline Nightingale*

It's not uncommon for my mother to talk about fragrances or frivolous things at the end of her letter. But I know she's not talking about perfume.

She needs more anti-aging tonic.

*It's only been a matter of days. How could she be almost out already?* I wonder as I fold the letter and slide it into a drawer.

To go through it so quickly means she's most assuredly reliant on it. Not getting her more could even kill her if she's used so much.

*What am I going to do?*

Looking up, I stare at myself in the vanity mirror of my room. I half expect wrinkles to form on my face or gray hairs to sprout amidst the bright red strands.

I look perfect, unfortunately. The damned magic tonics in the Rinhold household work every time.

I'm a little over *tonics* right about now.

Reaching out, I press one of the tabs on the wall that'll summon Julie or Beatrix. I'm hoping for Julie, but the older woman appears at my door a moment later.

"You called, my lady?" she asks but doesn't hide her perusal that's accompanied by a frown. "You're far too tense, Lady Scarlett. Keep your spine like that and it's liable to snap."

She's right. Which is exactly why I called for her in the first place. "I need a bath, Beatrix."

Bracing myself for her protest, I'm surprised when she slides inside and shuts the door behind her. "Finally. I was wondering how long you were going to pretend to be so comfortable with all this frivolous use of magic tonics," she says as she marches toward the parlor. "I could buy dinner for the entire sector every night until I leave this dark world with the number of tonics used by some Elites."

I chuckle at her frankness. "So you're not a fan of them?" I hedge. She had previously admitted that Duchess Rinhold doesn't share her anti-aging tonics with her staff. So for the rumor to have circulated that a tonic had been used for such scandalous purposes inside her own house had definitely put a damper on this year's festivities.

But that was precisely the source of my stress, now with the addition of my mother's predicament.

My mother seems to think I've handled the scandal well. I saw Edward that night. He was shaken, but there wasn't evidence of a mask that one would wear when lying. He had to be telling me the truth.

Which means that the fires of jealousy I've ignited in this sector can cause very real danger. If one of my rivals was willing to go so far as to magically compel Edward into leaving me, what kind of enemies am I making just by being here?

Beatrix seems to like me, at least. She gives me a wry smile full of wrinkles as she gathers up towels and a robe. "I'm not a fan of magic when it makes everyone act insane."

I doubt that magic is really to blame when it comes to the games Elites play. Living this life and trying to stay ahead is enough to make anyone go mad.

I'm feeling a bit manic myself, so when Beatrix asks me how I want my bath, I breathe out an honest answer. "Hot. Steaming, piping hot so that I can steep in it until I emerge as a wrinkled prune."

She awards me with a bubbling laugh as she carries a bucket and begins filling up the claw-foot tub. I know there is a magic tonic that would fill it in the blink of an eye, but I quietly help by grabbing another bucket.

She doesn't try to stop me. Beatrix and I have fallen into an understanding of one another. I feel better when I can do something. I hate just sitting around.

In no time at all, the tub is filled with steaming water that looks positively sinful. My skin itches for me to remove my clothing and plunge into it.

I realize, though, that I have yet to examine my blood contract marks.

And after encountering Cain himself, I'm apprehensive of what sort of nightmares that might spur to life in my mind. His blood is infused in my skin, which explains my strange dreams.

I've avoided them for the past few nights, but it feels akin to putting a lid atop a boiling kettle.

I might just explode if I bottle everything up for much longer.

Which, honestly, was another reason I had in mind for a bath. I need a moment of solitude to... take care of things.

"Thank you, Beatrix," I say in lieu of a dismissal. When I give her a low nod, she drops the towel and the fluffy robe onto a stool.

"At least let me unbind your corset, dear," she says with a stern look.

I sigh, then turn my back to her.

She slowly undoes the threads, then leaves my corset open at my back. She lingers there for a while, then clears her throat. "Please ring for me if you need me for anything further, my lady."

I nod but don't turn around.

Because I'm embarrassed. I can't imagine what my marks must look like, or how someone like Beatrix might judge me for accepting this courtship.

*"We always have a choice, Scarlett."*

Those had been Cain's words that still rattle around in my mind. Why he had chosen to dance with me and pull me into his realm of nightmares on the Rinhold ballroom floor is lost on me.

He was probably trying to frighten me and make sure I understood the gravity of my situation.

*Pick on someone your own size, Cain,* I think as I peel away my clothes.

I stand up against a long mirror and run my finger over the mark just above my navel.

I hadn't imagined it.

Twisting, I try to see my remaining marks that run up my spine. Unable to see from that particular angle, I grab a hand mirror and peer at the reflection.

The sight makes my eyes go wide.

Slashes run all the way up my spine, but they aren't straight lines. They look like sets of jagged claw marks.

Like a hand had raked down my back multiple times.

Frowning, I put down the hand mirror and collect some

oils, then dump them into the tub. The scent of peaches marinates the room, making me relax.

Finally, I grab the sides of the tub and climb in. The sides are high, allowing the volume to be substantial enough to submerge me.

"Oh, yes," I breathe as I pinch my nose, then dunk my entire head underwater.

My world grows smaller as the roar of the water rushes over my ears. I stay there for a moment and look up through the water at the ceiling. My view is broken as I try to make out the designs on the ornate tiles.

Then things begin to change.

Smoky black tendrils snake over the swirling designs, and I squint to see if I'm imagining things.

Everything alters, and the shimmer of the water makes it look like I'm peering through a melting pane of glass.

*What is this?*

Unease winds through my stomach, and I decide I've been underwater long enough.

I try to get up.

*I can't.*

Panic strangles my chest as a strange sort of paralysis takes over. Ice frosts over the water as it slowly goes solid. My body freezes, and I can't move a single muscle.

My lungs scream.

I can't move.

*What... What's happening?*

I'm not sure how long I'm stuck that way, but just before I black out, hands dive into the water and grab hold of me, yanking me free of the ice that instantly vanishes.

A racking cough sputters in my throat as I wheeze in a lungful of blessed air.

The hands that saved me are gone, but a man is standing there now.

After handling a coughing fit, it takes me a moment to register that my savior is my suitor.

Who is now in my bath parlor.

Staring at my naked body.

I cover myself with my hands as best I can, but there's plenty of light for him to see everything. But he doesn't appear to be gawking at me. Rather, he's wearing a very concerned expression as his chest heaves. He's fully clothed, donning what had been a frilly dress shirt and pants with trendy blue stripes along the sides that are now wet and plastered to his muscular form.

"Are you okay?" he finally asks as he searches my face, although I'm not sure what he's looking for.

The last shred of my sanity, perhaps? Because there isn't any ice. There aren't any smoky tendrils rolling through the ceiling.

Whatever I just saw had been one of my night terrors, and I almost died because of it.

Sinking deeper into the water, I wish I had drowned so I didn't have to suffer this humiliation. "I'm fine, Edward. You can leave now." I glance at the quiet entryway. "Although, I'm not even sure why you're here." My gaze flicks back to him as I wait for an answer.

He told me he could only enter my room by invitation. I don't recall having invited him.

Even if he did save my life from whatever weird bath paralysis I had just suffered, he can't just expect to walk into my room whenever he feels like it.

He pulls a letter from his pocket, which is now hopelessly soaked, but I can barely discern my mother's handwriting on the outside.

*He came to ask me about my mother's invitation. Of course.*

Sighing, I thump my forehead on the edge of the tub.

"I'm sorry, Edward. I'm fine, really. And thoroughly humiliated, so if you please—"

I freeze when I hear the wet letter drop to the floor.
Then his fingers are brushing my nape, followed by his
palm. The raised mark of the *S* on his hand reminds me
what we are to each other.

The instant his mark hits one of mine, electricity shoots
straight through my body, settling between my legs. "I've
never seen courtship marks before," he murmurs with a
concerned tone. "Still, this doesn't look normal, Scarlett.
Does it hurt?"

No? Yes?

How do I explain to him that just touching me there has
desire surging through my body?

Heat builds between my thighs, and the flash of my
figment growling inside my head has me whimpering.

Edward must misread my reaction, because he hauls
me out of the bath and plasters my wet body against his.

"I'll call a doctor immediately," he begins, but I cling
to him.

"Don't go," I say into his wet shirt. I don't dare look
up or seal my humiliation with any further acts of
insanity.

But I also know he can't leave me like this. I'll fall into
my nightmares, and I might never come out.

*Maybe that's why I almost drowned.*

Whatever darkness lives inside of me has been gradu-
ally awakening ever since this mess began. I'm not ready for
it. I feel like I'm slowly losing myself and in danger of
imploding if I don't do something about it.

Tears sting my eyes as Edward pinches my chin and
makes me look up at him.

I don't see any nefarious intention there. He isn't the
man that Lady Eleanor told everyone he was. I'm sure

there's more to the story than the scandal I've heard, but I can't find a fracture in Edward's face to refute it.

He's a complete gentleman. If he weren't, I would be able to see his truth behind the mask.

He's not even wearing one, which makes me feel safer than I ever have before.

"What else is Cain's blood doing to you?" he asks, surprising me.

I knew it was Cain's blood in my contract only because Cain himself had told me. I hadn't expected Edward to admit its origins. Information is power, and men like Earl Rinhold aren't known for freely giving up their power.

But maybe he's not Earl Rinhold at all.

He's just... Edward. At least with me.

"Why did you use Cain's blood?" I ask, purposefully not answering his question.

Because the truth is that it's making me want to speed our courtship along.

It's making me want to do everything I probably shouldn't before I'm officially Lady Rinhold.

His gaze flicks to my lips, which I realize I've wet with my tongue.

"Because you deserve the best, Scarlett. My offer of courtship isn't in title only. I want to show you what you're worth to me. Nothing else would do. I just... I didn't know it could be overwhelming like this."

I know the rumors and the tradition of Elite pairings. A courtship bound by a blood contract is a statement of intention and wealth. And it enhances everything.

Desire. Romance.

Sex.

But I didn't expect it to feel like my insides are on fire and only my mate can stop me from burning alive.

*Is Edward my mate?*

"Why me?" I ask. My fingers have gone to his chest as I explore him.

There's something missing. Like his body doesn't quite fit mine, but I'm inexperienced. A man's body simply feels foreign to me. What few experiences I did have were rushed and more or less fully clothed.

Edward's answer to my question thrusts all thoughts out of my mind.

"Because I know you're from Vulcan Village, Scarlett."

My heart stops.

I take a step back, but Edward follows me. The wet floor makes me slip, and I fall against the wall, banging my head hard enough for me to bite my tongue.

He catches me before I lose my balance, but now one of his hands is against the wall and his arm blocks me in. His other is looped around my waist, and one of his thighs is between my legs.

I stare up at him, stunned. The tang of blood is in my mouth from where I bit myself, and I lick my lips, waiting to see what he's going to do.

I've never heard the name of my home village before, but my soul seems to recognize it.

His stormy blue eyes appear dark in the frail light of my bath parlor. His gaze bores into me as I stare back at my own reflection in his blown pupils. "You're a prized selection, Scarlett," he says as he leans in, his breath hot on my lips. "But you were never meant for monsters. You were meant for *me*."

When he kisses me, I break.

Because no one has ever spoken my secret aloud. It's always been shoved into a box, contained, locked away.

Edward knows about it.

And he wants me *because* of it.

When his kiss goes to my throat, I suck in a breath. He

removes his thigh and I whimper, but I don't know what has me so pained.

He goes lower, and when his tongue flicks past the mark above my navel, desire shoots straight to my core.

I don't think. I act on instinct as I thread my fingers through his hair and guide him to where I want him.

Where I need him or else I'm going to implode.

When his tongue slides over my sex, I slam my head back against the wall again and close my eyes.

It feels wrong.

But right, too.

*I'm so confused,* I think as he thrusts his tongue over my entrance, making my hips buck with his movements.

"Tell me to stop, Scarlett," he says as his breath over my sensitive nub makes my core throb. "Because I... I want this too badly to stop on my own. You're not the only one affected by Cain's blood."

Right, the contract would go both ways. How callous of me not to realize that Edward is likely experiencing the same effects that I am.

*Why should we suffer like this?*

We're in a courtship, are we not? It isn't wrong to enjoy one another.

A little relief isn't scandalous or unexpected. In just a few weeks' time, I will accept him as my husband.

He will be inside me, so why can't we just have a taste of the life waiting for us?

"Don't stop," I say, which must be all the encouragement he needs.

Because he closes his mouth over my clit and he sucks, *hard.*

"Cain!" I cry out, the word meant as a curse. I must completely black out at that point because everything turns dark, and before I know it, I'm deep inside my nightmares.

Shadows unfurl around me as broken shards of glass flicker through the air.

I'm alone with the beast who wears Cain's face, and his nostrils flare. I'm not sure if he's scenting me, or angry.

"Hello, Scarlett," he says. It sounds almost exactly the same as when Cain said those words in the ballroom.

I distinctly remember his hands around my waist and how he made me feel.

*Like prey caught in a trap.*

His beautiful, monstrous face stretches into a grin, showing sharp teeth. "You called?"

# CHAPTER 24

# CAIN

I REALIZE my mistake when I detect the shame and panic in Scarlett's bright, mirrorlike eyes. She's even more beautiful in the Dream Realm than she is in the real one. And she's naked, which is new and delightful.

I want to play, but when I slip into her mind now that she opened the door, I see that she's not alone.

And she's confused. Aroused, yes, but something is off.

She'd frightened me when she had almost come to me in the Dream Realm moments earlier. I've never known a human to do that while awake. Walking between worlds can be dangerous if one doesn't know what they're doing. Scarlett's brush with the Dream Realm had sent a shock wave that had hit me square in the chest.

I had decided to anchor myself on a couch, then peer outside the windows at my dark city while I waited for her to call me so I could find her and make sure she was safe. Bernard was already on his way, but I doubted he would make it in time.

Then she said my name.

But she hadn't been really calling me, had she? My

name had slipped from her bloodied tongue as a natural expression of pleasure.

Pleasure I hadn't been giving her.

"I believe I've made an error," I say, my voice coming out gravelly and low while in my beast form.

He wants to stay, but he doesn't like the confusion in our mate's eyes.

*Not ours,* I remind myself.

Because she'd just been with Earl Rinhold. Not me.

She had let him touch her.

*Because my blood is inside her, confusing her,* I think, arguing with myself.

When Scarlett stares at me, the last few moments play out in her head, displaying them for me to see. Memories are like dreams, and I steel myself when I see her suitor kiss his way down her body.

And taste her.

"Are you him?" she asks, breaking off the growl I had been releasing, making the world around us tremble.

"What?" I ask, startled by the question.

"Cain," she says, taking a brave step forward. Her entire body is shivering. The Dream Realm can be a cold, desolate place, and she wraps her arms around herself. Bumps spread over her wet, naked skin, and I want nothing more than to warm her with my tongue.

I want to override this new memory she has with some of my own.

"Yes and no," I tell her honestly.

My Dream Eater half has become another entity entirely, and I'm not sure if I'll ever be whole again. Cain, King of the Elite City, is a different beast than the one who lives in nightmares.

She comes close enough to unfurl her arms, and she

grazes her fingers over my chest. She seems to be exploring me, and I let her.

Her body relaxes as if she found something she had been looking for. "You feel real... You feel *right.*"

Had Earl Rinhold not felt right to her? Most likely. I'm starting to suspect that he chose my blood because he knew of the compatibility I shared with her.

He must also have known that my blood would shield him. The blood contract impacts both parties, so whatever attraction Scarlett might feel for the male is likely fabricated from what she is actually feeling for me.

This is all my fault.

Clashing emotions squeeze my chest, and I wrap my arm around her and bring her in close. My other hand goes to her face, and I run my thumb over her lips.

Anger might have been my first choice, but I'm not angry with Scarlett. I'm mostly furious at myself for allowing a human to get the better of me.

It won't happen again.

I'll protect you, Scarlett. I'll fix this, somehow.

And I'll cut that male's tongue from his mouth for daring to taste you.

The thought of maiming Earl Rinhold satisfies the bloodlust in my soul. It's something to look forward to once I find what I'm looking for.

Which will require patience and creativity. I need to keep Earl Rinhold busy so that he can't intrude on Scarlett again.

I also need to reassure her that I'm going to save her from this.

But carefully. Any interference on my part might be misconstrued by the blood contract magically bound by my life force.

So I won't say anything.

I'll show her why this feels right. Sliding my thumb between her lips, I love that she parts them for me.

I can't help that my cock is hard as it presses against her abdomen and comes up nearly to her breasts. It feels natural to have her body conform to my size, and her tongue flicks out as she rolls it over my thumb. My cock flinches at her delicate invitation.

I'm massive compared to her petite, lickable form. But that's okay. If she chooses to stay, if she wants to see what she's capable of, I have the ability to force her body to accept me.

All of me.

"Would you like me to taste you again?" I ask her. I need her verbal agreement for anything I might do.

Earl Rinhold hadn't asked for permission. He'd tempted her and manipulated her.

That's the difference between me and him. I will make sure that Scarlett doesn't question what she enjoys with me.

She sucks on my thumb, and I'm nearly undone by her nonverbal rebuttal.

Perhaps she wants to taste me again instead, and I understand why. My essence would be addicting to her.

I'm a drug to humans. My blood has powerful properties, as does my cum.

But to a compatible mate? I could make her go insane.

She grabs my massive shaft with both hands, making me throb underneath her touch. "Tell me if this is real, Cain, not-Cain."

"It can't be real," I say.

Not yet.

"But it can feel real, little star," I offer. It's all I have for her right now.

She's safe in only this realm until I find what I'm looking for.

Her hands move up and down my shaft, stroking me and forcing silver liquid to drizzle from the top of my throbbing head. She licks her lips as she looks down at it.

But I don't want her drunk on me. I want her to feel what real pleasure is supposed to be, not a manipulated version of it.

"Lie down on the bed," I instruct. "If you want my tongue, I will give it to you."

"I want this," she says as she rolls her fingers over the head of my cock, taking the substance and slowly bringing it to her mouth.

I grab her wrist to stop her as I growl. Then I smear it across her cheek. She pants as I coat her face with the cum she's claimed.

"You'll have that after I fuck you with my tongue, little one," I promise. "I want you to be a good girl for me. Can you do that?"

She whimpers as she backs away and falls onto the bed, the same one that is re-created from the real one in her room.

Earl Rinhold had already tucked her body under the sheets. He hadn't taken the time to dress her, which is just as well. It leaves her naked for me.

My dream version of Scarlett slips into her body, merging them as I slide the sheets off her skin.

It's the closest I've ever come to interacting with the real world while I'm inside a dream. The sheer power and new capabilities that a potential mate offers me are dizzying.

I grab her by the ankles and spread her open for me. Glancing up at her, I ask her again, "Are you going to be a good girl, Scarlett? Tell me what you want."

Her chest heaves, making the moonlight glisten across her breasts. But my gaze is caught on the silvery spot smeared across her cheek.

*Mine,* I think, delighted by the sight of her.

"Fuck me with your tongue," she whispers, and I love that she repeated the dirty phrasing I had given her.

Wasting no time in rewarding her, I shove my tongue into her sweet entrance. My tongue is easily the size of a human's cock while I'm in this form.

Her blood dances across my taste buds, and I nearly explode on the spot. Even in the Dream Realm, I'm still able to physically interact with her body. Something changed to allow it.

Perhaps it had to do with her moment in the tub that I can now see in better clarity. She had slipped into the Dream Realm on her own. She has begun to awaken to her true nature. What makes her compatible with me is the fact of what she is.

She's a source of endless power, and she has just started to break the surface of the wall around the darkness she's kept hidden all her life.

I didn't mean to make this real, but I can taste her virginity shattering on my tongue.

Fuck, yes.

The world doesn't end. I don't die and neither does she. Whatever boundary the blood contract has in place when it comes to exclusivity doesn't seem to recognize what line I just crossed. For now, we're both still deep within the Dream Realm, camouflaging what's really happening.

It's a risk I wouldn't have taken had I been more lucid.

But now I'm crazed. I fuck her with my tongue, thrusting as I enjoy her whimpers and her scrambling fingers digging her nails into my forearms as I hold her hips down.

"More!" she cries as I close my mouth around her entire pussy and suck in obedience of her command. My tongue still moves in and out, lapping up every drop of blood her virginity has to offer as I force her to come for me.

Then the sweetness follows as she climaxes and screams.

Shadows swirl around us, and I command them to drag her under. Her body convulses on a final few shocks of pleasure as I ease out of her pussy and lick up the nectar dripping from my face. She blinks at me, struggling to stay awake, before she closes her eyes completely and succumbs to the peace I offer her.

"Sleep, little star," I whisper.

And she does.

I leave her—satisfied and slipping into a deep sleep—because I know if I stay, I'll do more than fuck her with my tongue.

I'll claim her. I'll devour her.

And neither of us is ready for that.

*Soon,* I promise her as I retreat. *Soon, little star.*

When the time is right... you will be mine.

# CHAPTER 25

# SABRE

"Why the fuck did you bring me all the way out here?" Cage asks as he kneels in front of one of the overgrown dark stalks and plucks at the vine.

"Careful," I say, not answering his question as the red moon rises on the horizon of the broken blood fields. It won't be much longer now. "If you touch one of those, it might grab you and drag you all the way to its nest."

Although, that's exactly what I intend. This particular vine leads to one of the largest nests in existence, and it's no coincidence the nest is located in a tunnel between kingdoms.

Cage leans back and frowns at the plant, then glares at me. "Sorry, I guess my Morpheus Kingdom botany lessons are lacking, given that none of my family has had access to the blood fields in generations."

"It wouldn't be in any botany books," I correct him. "It's a relatively new pestilence."

Cage rolls his eyes. "So you brought me out here to show me a new weed growing in your fields. Awesome, Sabre. I'm not a fucking gardener, if that's why we're here."

I chuckle at the imagery. "Hardly, Cage. But I think you'd find it doesn't need a gardener. It is a changed form of the preexisting stalks, and it feeds off of soil tainted by corpses, hence the name 'Rot.' It also serves to keep the scent of decay to a minimum," I add with a nod. "Which is a plus."

"There aren't supposed to *be* corpses here," Cage points out.

He's not wrong. The blood fields house sleeping humans kept in suspended animation underground, and the stalks that grow above offer fruit filled with their blood.

And their dreams.

Now, the Rot has taken over large patches, sprouting black stalks that only bear necrosis.

"You're correct," I admit. "It's probably what attracted the Corpse Fae who touched the stalks, creating the Rot in the first place."

Cage gives me a raised brow. "What's a Corpse Fae even doing out here long enough to infect the stalks with Rot?" He blows out a breath. "Your father is a shit King, you know that?"

I chuckle at the insult that would cost him his head if any other member of the Sanguinis line had heard it. "He is," I agree. "But at least now the Strigoi and Corpse Fae have something to bond over, hmm?"

He rolls his eyes. "I will never understand you having Corpse Fae friends. They're assholes."

"Perhaps," I concede as I slip a note from my pocket. "But not all of them are."

Cage's blue eyes flick to the item before he snatches it and unfurls the papyrus.

He reads the inscription, then pales. "Why am I looking at an invitation that has both our names on it?"

"It's from Maliki," I reassure him. Our relationship is a

well-guarded secret, and Maliki is one of the few friends I'd ever confide in.

And in this case, I'm glad I did, because Maliki gave me an opportunity I can't ignore.

Cage's bright blue eyes flash up to meet mine. He doesn't hide his emotions.

Surprise. Panic.

Trust.

They swirl together in a symphony of color that's all Cage. He doesn't have to practice hiding his feelings, mostly because he works in the shadows. Anyone who sees his face will soon be dead.

"What did you tell him?" Cage asks, mostly because I know he's trying to get on the same page.

He doesn't accuse me of keeping secrets, even though I have more than a few I've kept from Cage. I think he already knows that. He might even have discovered some of them by now, given how distant he's been with me lately.

But now that I have his full attention, he patiently waits for my answer. This invitation holds a promise that has him daring to hope for something more.

Like a future where we can be together. Neither of us has entertained that asinine possibility, mostly because our pairing will never be tolerated, not with centuries of bad blood between the Van Drakken and Sanguinis lines.

Not to mention the brutal truth he dragged out of me days ago—we aren't enough for one another. Or, specifically, he's not enough for me. Not with the kind of power drain that I have on my soul. Besides, as much as I love Cage, I need a female mate in my life. Preferably one whom Cage and I can share.

That would be impossible in this reality, but Maliki told me of another dimension, one where monsters openly hunt for their brides out on the streets.

The event is called Monsters Night.

An event I intend to join.

Maybe we'll simply play with a new toy. Fuck. *Bite*.

Or maybe we'll find what we're looking for.

It doesn't feel real.

It's like a dream, and as Strigoi, we know how fleeting dreams can be.

"You can ask him yourself," I say instead of giving him empty promises.

My expectations are low. All I can allow myself to hope for is a reprieve and a chance to recharge my strength before I take the Strigoi throne. The only way my father can stop draining me is if I leave this dimension entirely and find a clean source on which to feed.

And when I return, if I return, I will take his heart for all that he's done to me.

No matter what happens, the idea of hunting for fresh blood, new dreams, and a chance to rid myself of my father has me saying *yes*.

But I hope Cage comes with me. I need him to, or else I'm not sure I can go through with it. There will be reper-cussions to using an illegal portal.

But we won't be the only ones, at least.

"Do you think she'll be in that world?" he asks. I hate the hope in his voice.

"She who?" I ask, feigning ignorance.

He doesn't say her name.

Scarlett.

No matter what Cage believes, I'm not going for some fleeting hope of a dream. I'm going for a vacation from my asshole father before I rip out his heart and accept a shit destiny.

At least, that's what I'm telling myself.

"Is he waiting for you?" Cage asks, ignoring my question. "Maliki, I mean."

"Us," I confirm as I pocket the invitation and hold out my hand. "Will you come with me?"

Cage considers my hand for a moment. I'm a dreamwalker, but so is he, and he always has his walls up. I can't enter Cage's mind no matter how close we've become. I would trade anything to know what he's thinking.

To my relief, he slides his hand into mine. "Let's go see your new boyfriend, then."

Maliki is hardly my boyfriend, but I know he's just teasing.

Grinning, I delve us into the dream plane, and the world around us explodes in darkness and shadow. The Rot reacts to the invasive magic and bleeds death into the soil.

It makes the ground beneath our feet soft enough for us to sink. I don't react. Instead, I let it happen.

Cage watches me, and it says something about how much he must trust me that he follows my lead. His skin bleeds over with black shadows, and his eyes glow with a fiery red as I take us into the depths.

The blood fields swallow us up, the roots of the Rot dragging us down until we deftly land on the hard surface miles below.

A tunnel filled with Nightmare Fae spans out around us. The vines of the Rot nest take up the entire ceiling, but it has rooted this place securely enough to make it a hub between kingdoms.

The Morpheus Kingdom and Netherworld Kingdom exist on separate planes, but this is a place where they overlap.

All because of the rotted death stalks in our blood fields.

All because of my father's incompetence... I have the chance to destroy him.

"Where are we?" Cage asks as he backs into the darkness, but we can't hide. Not from the grouping of Nightmare Fae who have gathered in front of a massive void. I know it will soon turn into a portal, and my dark heart skips a beat.

*Excitement?* I ponder. It's a new sensation, one I haven't felt for a long time.

I like it.

"A communal tunnel between kingdoms," I briefly explain as I spot Maliki already approaching us.

I'm surprised there isn't a female, or a male, hanging off of him at all times, given how incredibly beautiful he is. Like most Hell Fae, he is a unique mix of species. In his case, I know that he's part Corpse Fae with some other powerful blood types mixed in. Even if I don't know the details, it's obvious by his striking appearance and aura of power that he's exactly the type of "abomination" the Hell Fae Realm was built for in the first place.

Strigoi are no less of an abomination deserving of Hell's protection. Any mixture of fae or supernatural bloodlines results in power that can't be checked or controlled. Pureblood fae don't like that, which is why Lucifer created this realm to keep us safe from their overwhelming numbers.

We might be stronger than the purebloods, but there are just more of them than there are of us.

We're supposed to be united in our focus under Lucifer's ultimate leadership. This is an unauthorized event. The King of our realm doesn't know about this little gathering, and the only Hell Fae who could get away with this sort of thing is Maliki.

He happens to be Azazel's half brother, and Azazel is one of Lucifer's bonded mates.

Talk about having a Get Out of Hell Free card.

I know Maliki isn't the one behind all this. He's being

used as a tool by one of the Gods; of that I'm sure. I don't know which one, and I don't need to know.

Strigoi stay out of Gods' games.

"Aren't you two adorable, already holding hands," Maliki says with a wry grin as he ventures within earshot. He runs his fingers through his dark hair, swiping it away from his uniquely gold eyes.

Cage doesn't drop my hand like I think he might. Instead, his claws scratch against my skin as he sizes up Maliki. "Call me adorable again and I'll hold your cock with this," he threatens as he flexes his clawed hand. The lengthy black talons extending from each finger might as well be blades. The tunnel is illuminated by magical orbs, providing a low, flickering light that makes Cage look particularly dangerous.

Maliki's grin widens. "I see why you like him, Sabre. He's hilarious."

"And serious," I add with a raised brow. "I wouldn't test him if I were you."

My old friend chuckles but clearly isn't threatened. As he probably shouldn't be, given that even Cage is no match for a Hell Fae like Maliki. He might rough him up and eat a couple of his favorite dreams, but in the end, Cage would lose without the element of surprise on his side.

Maliki is a mystery, which is precisely why I was drawn to him in the first place. He's one that I never solved, but that's fine by me. He's proved to be a good friend over the years.

But tonight, he's truly outdone himself.

"It's almost ready," he says, peering back at the dark void that seems to be breathing like a sleeping creature trapped in a cave. "It's only going to be open for a couple of hours, so keep that in mind, or else you'll be trapped there."

I frown. "A couple of hours?" That didn't sound like the reprieve I was promised. "I thought you said the portal would be open for at least the entire night?"

Maliki shrugs. "Lucifer is going to notice the second I open the portal. He'll find it and shut it down, and he usually works fast. In all reality, it'll likely only be open for an hour or two and then never be used again." Maliki glances up, his bright eyes glinting with nightmares that I'd find tasty if I noticed them within anyone else. "The Rot you told me about provides the perfect coverage, though. It'll take him some time to locate it between kingdoms. He won't expect the Netherworld Fae and Morpheus Fae to have common territory like this."

Maliki has clearly thought this out, but I don't ask why. Someone must be putting him up to it. I just hope his promised reward is worth the Hell Fae King's inevitable wrath.

"That sounds like a very big risk for opening a portal for an hour or two," Cage observes. His glowing red eyes flick to the groupings of Ghouls, Baku, and Corpse Fae. It's not common to see all those types of Nightmare Fae and Hell Fae working together, but they're surrounding the portal, eagerly waiting for it to open.

They're salivating for brides and willing to risk Lucifer's wrath. The Ghouls especially are hungry and starving, needing mates to survive. They're tired of waiting, and I don't blame them.

But I agree with Cage. It's not enough time to accomplish much of a hunt. At least, not the kind of hunt that a Strigoi requires.

When I feed, I take my time.

Maliki only grins. "In this case, it's worth the risk."

"Do you intend to find yourself a mate, Maliki?" I ask

honestly. It would explain why he's going through so much trouble.

"No," he answers. His eyes darken with ancient nightmares that pique my curiosity. "My time will come, Gods willing. But I need to stay on this side of the portal and keep it open." He jerks his chin toward the void. "Now join the others and slip in, blend with the crowd. You won't be noticed."

"Because everyone has pussy on their mind," Cage says, his fangs glinting with amusement. "I'm going to need a little more than a few hours, though, if we're going to play." He gives me a predatory look, one that says if we hunt, it'll be done right. He's no less of a Strigoi than I am.

"It's up to you," Maliki says as his fingertips turn black. The air turns cold as he dips into his Corpse Fae magic, and the hairs on the back of my neck stand on end. "But if you choose to stay beyond the portal's closure, you won't be able to return. Not unless the Gods bless you with a means to do so."

I doubt we'll run into any Gods, even in another dimension, but stranger things have happened.

"Let's go," I urge Cage and drag him toward the portal that has started to swirl.

Regardless, I intend to feed. I need my strength for the inevitable fight for when I return.

My father wants me to take the throne? Fine. I will.

But his head will be my crown.

The vortex opens, spinning with darkness and nightmares and *death*. I can't help the grin that stretches over my throbbing fangs.

The crowd is roaring with excitement now, sending mating cries beating against the stone walls. I haven't seen this sort of energy from the Nightmare Fae in years, if ever.

Excitement of my own builds in my chest, but I don't

cry out. Instead, I hold on to Cage and don't let go. He doesn't say anything as my claws dig into his skin.

The void yawns open, drowning us all in shadow.

Like walking nightmares, we step in.

And for the first time in my life, I don't know what I'm going to find on the other side of a dream.

# CHAPTER 26

## SCARLETT

Fᴜᴄᴋ.

That appears to be my new favorite curse lately, and it nestles into my mind, seeming to be the only singular word that can describe the gravity of my current situation.

One where I'm trapped behind a broken mirror, stuck as an onlooker to the world that passes by outside.

In this case, I found a mirror in an upscale viewing bar. Elites from the Magic Sector have gathered here for this year's annual Monsters Night, which gives me a good view of what my betrothed is up to.

*Do I even want him anymore?*

*What if I find a monster instead?*

My stomach tightens with anticipation, although I'm not sure why. I won't be anywhere near Monster City tonight. My real body is asleep in my bed in the Rinhold estate where Beatrix and Julie take turns caring for me.

I'm stuck in a strange in-between state when one of them disturbs me. My spirit might be behind a broken mirror far away, but my body still feels and senses everything back at the estate.

Julie presses a glass of water against my parched lips, and my tongue tingles. My body allows a few drops to move down my throat, working on a difficult swallow.

I'm lucid enough to perform basic tasks in the real world, such as eating and drinking, as well as performing assisted trips to the facilities.

But another part of me wanders the Elite City, and I'm fairly certain it's no dream.

I've been everywhere—except for the Immortal Sector, of course. Those walls seem to keep me out with a dense dark magic I don't understand. But it's clear that Cain understands his most precious sector needs to be protected from threats that aren't always physical.

That means I can't approach Cain unless he leaves his tower again, which he hasn't. His blood did this to me, so I suspect he'd be able to see my spirit if I found him.

Instead, I'm stuck here, hoping to hear word of where he might appear next, and spy on Edward in the meantime. It would be so much simpler if I could float on over to the glass he's drinking out of and demand answers, but I suppose it's good that I can't. When I talk to Edward again, it's going to be a serious conversation, one with answers, if I have my way.

Because he knows where I'm from. He knows the *name* of my birth village.

He doesn't seem very broken up about my state as he converses with another Earl. I can only watch from my perch inside the broken mirror that has a wide view of the bar I'm observing. It reminds me of when I was a child and I found secret passages in between walls. I would find a peephole and watch the comings and goings of my parents and other families for hours.

It's how I learned I was adopted.

It's also when I discovered that everyone wears a mask.

When someone thinks they aren't being watched, they're a different person entirely.

The past two days have certainly given me numerous observations to think about, including how I feel about my betrothed. The Earl he was talking with has left, and I watch Edward now as he perches on one of the stools. He seems pleased with himself as he hooks his boot into the rung. Blood diamonds glitter over his apparel tonight, the fashion having changed from blue and teal accents to something richer.

Other families are donning rubies, which is a more affordable gem than what my betrothed wears.

I had already witnessed him taking numerous bets on the Offerings for Monsters Night, and I suspect that's what his last-minute conversation was about. I'm not sure how he knows which selections will be the most successful, but I have a feeling the Rinholds will be filling their coffers tonight.

And, most disappointing of all, he isn't back at the estate caring for me after what he did. The trauma of our encounter and tempting the blood contract are what put me in this dream state in the first place.

At least, that's the only logical conclusion I can come to. I have Cain's blood dancing through my veins, and after experiencing Edward's desire, I was met with a figment of my own.

One who gave me exactly what I wanted.

*Did my figment really take my virginity with his tongue?*

A thrill runs up my spine with the memory, but I can't confirm it. Cain's blood might be powerful, but I'm not so sure if the Dream Eater can make a dream as vividly realistic as that.

*Was it some sort of test that I failed?*

*Maybe I* am *meant for monsters.*

*Or maybe it simply was just a dream.*

There was no blood on my body or on the sheets when Beatrix found me and dressed me, so I'm not sure of the truth of the matter.

She knows something happened, though, which is why either she or Julie has remained by my side since then.

No matter my efforts to speak, either in the real world or through a mirror, I can't tell them that I can see them.

I suspect only one can hear me.

Cain's blood did this, so I need to find him. I've been able to travel all across his city after that night, and I know it's because of some sort of foothold his blood has given me in a world he must know more intimately than I.

A dream world.

I don't know what to call it, and I desperately wish I could ask him, but I only seem to be able to travel through reflective surfaces. Broken ones work best, allowing me a peephole to peer through.

One which I utilize now as I observe the magical screens coming to life in the viewing bar, making the crowd gasp.

Edward glances up to watch the show.

I do the same.

Monster City comes into view, a place of impressive buildings and trees infused with iron. I've never been there, but my spirit longs for it as if my soul knows I was always destined to be an Offering wandering those streets.

An announcer counts off villages and their Offering numbers, and I perk up when they reach the Nightingale numbers. Our particular announcer will focus on the Magic Sector, but there are many families in this sector. It's unusual that the focus would be on the Nightingales.

*Perhaps my blood contract has caught the interest of the entire sector.*

That can't be good.

The screen zooms in on a male and female, a pair who seem to be close.

"And here we are on Nightingale's selections!" the male announcer declares, earning an abnormal cheer from the crowd.

As Edward beams, I realize they're trying to impress him now that a Nightingale Lady has become his future bride. No one questions why I'm not sitting with him, which disgruntles me further.

But I keep listening as I watch for any news of where Cain might be. I can only assume he's still in his tower. He never participates, as far as I'm aware, but I fully intend to take note of the most successful pairings, because Cain might visit those estates as a reward. That'll be my best chance to talk to him.

"The betting pool places these three at the top of our charts, so we're going to be following them for the majority of the night. If you placed bets on other Offerings, tune in on the alternate projections..."

The announcer drones on, advertising the other channels no doubt sponsored by various families hoping for more of a spotlight. The game is for selections to match to the most powerful monster categorized by rank, but it's no secret that the betting games highly contribute to family survival, too.

*Why doesn't Cain put a stop to the gambling?* I ponder as the announcer zooms in on the first two selections.

I already know the answer. It works. The gambling often features underdog families like mine, helping them elevate to the top. Competition is what drives Elite families and, ultimately, what helps the monsters find their compatible mates.

"Bartholomew and Miranda!" the announcer shouts.

"My, they seem cozy, don't they? And, oh, what about the third surprise Offering? Her chart says her name is... Alina! She has broken the record for entries in the Nightingale Village, so she's a watcher. Let's revisit their departure from the train before the night begins..."

I lean into the mirror as the screen flashes to a depiction of my father exiting a train car with a female on his arm who I can only assume is Alina.

She's gorgeous, but her expression suggests she's mightily pissed off. She is stiff in her corset as if she's not accustomed to wearing one, but it suits her nicely.

What stands out about her is a mask I've never seen before.

Because it's white. I can't even see her eyes beyond the veil of power that cloaks her from head to toe.

*Have they done something to her?*

*Or is there something otherworldly about her that makes her a perfect Offering?*

"Thank you for your sacrifice," my father tells them before the screen cuts back to the live feed.

Other selections are giggling and excited, as they should be. I recognize them from families in the Immortality Sector, so the announcer only briefly introduces them. We're supposed to be competing with each other, but I find it interesting how the immortal families have obviously trained their Offerings.

They seem excited.

They're boasting about what sort of creature they'll seduce, while others say it doesn't work that way. Offerings are formed to fit the monsters, not the other way around.

*At least they're well educated when it comes to Monsters Night.*

I know it's a beneficial pairing, and I'm reassured when

I hear that exact language from the Offerings themselves as they discuss it before the countdown.

The Nightingale selections don't seem so confident, though. It makes me question what our village is really like to make the first two so frightened while the third wears a veil of power so thick I can hardly see through it.

The coverage of the Nightingale Offerings has never been this detailed, so it's the first time I'm seeing their emotions and any genetic alterations firsthand.

I decide that there's just something different about Alina that the others don't seem to see, because the announcer doesn't comment on the white sheen of power. Instead, he seems more interested in Bartholomew and Miranda.

*She's the one who'll attract the most powerful monsters, you idiots.*

No matter their fate, the three Offerings freeze when the countdown begins. Another voice echoes through Monster City, the terminology and accent foreign to what I'm used to in my city.

"Fifteen!"

The one named Bartholomew turns into a dark alley-way, earning a gasp from the crowd. If they're trying to avoid monsters, that's a poor selection.

Then again, I notice right away he has avoided the camouflaged buildings where monsters watch through one-sided windows. To him, the empty alleyway might seem like a better choice.

*Meaning he can see them.*

It's a positive indicator that Bartholomew, at least, is suited to a powerful monster if he can see through magicked disguises.

"What's this?" the announcer excitedly asks as the trio enters one of the empty buildings. "They've walked onto a portal platform floor! Any bets on a mate pairing in the first ten seconds? Because we're about to see it, Dukes and Duchesses! Ladies and Earls!"

The female named Miranda starts to cry, twisting my heart.

It's not supposed to be like this.

This isn't how the Offerings who keep our families alive should be treated. They shouldn't be *afraid*.

"What do we have here?" the announcer asks as Bartholomew goes to Miranda, who has crumpled, and brushes his lips across her cheek to her mouth. "It seems we have a two-for-one pairing for a lucky monster!"

The crowd cheers because that means extra points for the Nightingale tally. It's rare that a monster will take more than one human mate.

But my eyes are on the female watching them. Alina seems frustrated, like she doesn't know what to do with herself.

And her power is fluctuating all over the place. She might as well be a beacon for the monster she's calling.

I grow weary of the announcer as he joins the count-down with Monster City's voice, echoing each number as the screen loses the female who has darted into a nearby hallway.

Three!

Two!

One!

Everything goes black, including the viewing bar as the crowd goes silent.

Then the air rips with screams.

After a moment, I realize the screams aren't coming from the Monsters Night feed.

They're coming from me.

# CHAPTER 27

# CAIN

*A few moments earlier...*

Two compatible monsters.

*They're here.*

I stare at the blood diamond that glows with a pattern of two steady pulses. It reminds me of a heartbeat.

"Helia," I whisper, immediately trying to summon her because I'm going to need her help with this. She doesn't answer, but I imagine she's busy since the portals just opened. I'm not the kind of monster who needs an appointment, but in retrospect, I should have warned her I might need her.

Because I actually fucking found them.

Every time I've ever performed this location spell, it has always broken the blood diamond and turned it black. Thousands of years of seeking have taught me that there aren't any monsters, or humans, compatible with me.

Yet now I've found not one but three beings who are.

I know it's no coincidence. Scarlett herself likely called them here. She's a beacon of light in the darkness.

As Earl Rinhold aptly said, she's the key to everything.

But these monsters... they are like me.

They are dangerous, depraved, and *hungry*.

Now, it bleeds with literal blood, sending the thick red liquid oozing over my fingers onto the table and dripping onto the floor.

My head shoots up when a scream rips through the dream plane, interrupting my stunned fascination.

*Scarlett.*

I know her screams well, even if they have usually been screams of pleasure in my presence. I've left her be since I crossed a line.

Since my beast took her with his tongue, nourished by the memory of what he did to her.

What *we* did to her.

Now, she's alone and afraid.

She's *hurting*.

Cursing, I shoot to my feet and wince when my head hits the ceiling and my horns drag through the coffered design.

I've transformed into my monster form.

And I'm chained to the floor, precisely because I predicted my beast would attempt to take control. The spell allows me to think for myself, but the second I leave this tower, *he* will be in charge.

Scarlett's screams make my chest tighten and my fangs extend. A low, threatening growl rumbles in my chest as my beast urges me to tend to our mate.

*Not ours yet,* I try to reason with him, but even I don't believe that anymore.

I flex against the dark chains made of shadow that are anchored into the tower itself. They wrap around my calves, my forearms, and strain against my neck. The prongs on each one dig into my skin, making me bleed.

This is the safest place for me to be. Not for my safety, but for the safety of my people *from* me. I knew if I found compatible monsters, I might lose control. I'm not the kind of beast who can prowl the streets for a mate. I'd wind up maiming anyone in my path and devouring any dream they have ever had until they're nothing but withered husks.

*But now Scarlett needs me, and I'm bound for the rest of the night.*

That's how long I made the spell last, and I do it every year. If compatible monsters ever did come through a portal, I knew it would set off my beast.

"I'm here, Cain," Bernard says from the doorway to my office.

He's either very brave or very stupid to try to speak to me when my beast has come out.

*Or stupidly loyal.*

"Helia isn't answering my summons," I growl, surprised I'm able to form words while in this form. My thick tongue makes it hard to speak, as do my massive canines, but I manage it.

It takes more of my strength than I care to admit to prepare the chains that can keep my beast restrained like this, but I work all year on it. A portion of my feed goes directly into this tower and into my city.

My protections line the Immortality Sector, especially, and connect me to my most dedicated worshippers. Their prayers ensure I stay in power.

And they keep my beast at bay.

I might be in control now, but I'm not going to let myself be deceived. The second I'm untangled from the suppressing magic of my tower that's protecting my sanity, my beast will take over my mind.

And then the bloodshed will begin.

Bernard clicks on one of the feeds to Monsters Night I

probably should have been watching instead of scrying. I immediately look for the compatible monsters I had sensed, but I'm confused when I see Helia slinking through a dark alley.

"It seems she's participating in this year's Monsters Night."

Helia is hunting a mate? Well, that explains why she's ignoring me. I fully expect her to be hunting for fun because it's just as likely that she's found a compatible mate as I have.

*And yet, here we are.*

Whatever the fates hold for Helia, I can't bring myself to care if she'll be successful or not. In fact, I'm irritated. Like a fool, I prioritized the safety of my people over a potential mate.

And now I'm the one paying for it.

"Get to Scarlett," I growl as my voice echoes through the Dream Realm. My world fluctuates, and my grip on reality slips as blood drizzles down the walls. I have no idea if it's real or just my fears coming to life as a living nightmare.

"You told me to stay away from her," Bernard reminds me. He doesn't like conflicting orders, so I know he's just trying to clarify what it is I actually want.

Snarling, my beast takes over for a second, but it's enough to have snapped one of the chains and left me growling in my Raven's face.

He doesn't move. He doesn't even flinch as my fangs linger just inches away from him. I could tear him to shreds, but he keeps to his post.

*My stupid, faithful Raven.*

"What would you have me do when I reach her?" he asks. His tone is calm, but his dark eyes are wide enough to reflect my fearsome image back at me.

I know the order is wrong. It's one I've never asked of anyone, but this is the only way I can get to Scarlett while chained to my tower. This is the only way to keep her safe.

I lean into my chains, ignoring the blood that trails down my chest at the movement. "I need her to let me in, Bernard. It's the only way to help her."

He goes stiff as I give the one command I said I'd never do.

"Make her pray to me."

# CHAPTER 28

# CAGE

Terror hits me like a wave, but it's not mine. I can sense those around me forming an ocean of dreams. My chest constricts as if I'm drowning in their fear, their excitement, and their rage. Digging deeper, I know I'm not feeling any of those things.

My emotion is a singular spike that hits me straight through the chest.

*Lust.*

I can hardly see straight as the world around me goes fuzzy, and the faint taste of peaches has my mouth watering. The dream plane is different in this dimension.

*More like a realm than a plane.*

This one still overlaps with the real world like I'm used to, but it's so much *larger*. It's like an entirely new place where creatures lurk and dreams are impossibly vibrant.

And filled with blood. Delicious blood in rivers that flow like some sort of Strigoi heaven.

*And the screams... dear Gods.*

There's a female's scream that is a mating call to my senses. Every fiber of my being aches to follow it.

*Is that our Sigil?*

*Is that Scarlett?*

*It has to be.*

My throat works on a swallow as I try to orient myself in the moment. If there is a heaven for my kind, I might have thought I found it had I not been in such excruciating pain.

My vision fluctuates with blacks, reds, and flashes of the city street under my cheek. Sabre is only a few feet away, but based on his body writhing in agony, he's not doing much better than I am.

*We're going to die before we even get a chance to find her.*

Traveling through the dimensional portal Maliki had created had a side effect, one that none of us could have predicted.

It drained us on the way here, and neither Sabre nor I had much in the way of reserves to begin with. This Dream Realm is different and requires walls to be put up around my mind before it shreds me into pieces.

Concentrating, I imagine forming bricks and cementing them around myself, one by one, until I'm inside a dark tower and can't see anything at all. It mutes the delicious screams and makes me feel even more disoriented, but at least I can breathe.

*One.*

*Two.*

*Three.*

I count each long, deep intake of air as I force my body to function. As much as I want to dreamwalk and find my Sigil calling out to me, my physical body needs to be in top shape to endure the drain that requires in this world. Right now, I can't do both. Not until I drink blood to replenish what the dimensional travel has cost me.

"Cage," Sabre grounds out, his voice gravelly and hoarse as he turns onto his stomach and crawls toward me. "Did you put up a wall?"

I nod. "I did, but we need blood if that's going to last more than a few minutes."

"Hmm," he agrees, then hisses when he tries to move. "I'm in no shape to hunt," he says, glancing up at the empty street. "Please tell me you heard those screams, Cage. I lied before. When you asked me if I had heard her, I said I didn't hear anything."

"I know," I say as I rest my head against the ground and stare up into the dotted sky. The constellations are all wrong.

*Or for the first time in my life, they're right.*

"Do you know what a Sigil is?" I ask him.

He goes quiet for a moment. "I suppose that's one of my family secrets you found." He blows out a breath. "My father has been trying to breed one for years. I always thought he was an idiot."

"He *is* an idiot," I agree, then flick my tongue over my lips, still unable to shake the taste of sweet peaches and cream. "But he might have been onto something. He was just looking in the wrong place."

Sabre's red eyes brightly flash a few times before they go black. "We'd have to let our walls down to find her, but I can hardly move like this." His nostrils flare at the same time I scent mortal blood. We both glance down the dark street.

He rakes his claws over the ground, leaving deep gouges in the stone. He remains in his humanoid form, but his body is on high alert, ready to strike.

Power fluctuates all around us, making me dizzy with the rush of so many powerful beings all in one place.

This must be Monsters Night.

We both struggle to our feet when a woman approaches us. It's the first person we've encountered in this new world, but she's not our Sigil. I can tell when she comes close enough for me to spot a brand on her neck.

And she doesn't smell at all like peaches.

She's human. I can taste her mortality, but she's still magically protected. There's an icy, dark power that wraps around her like a shroud, daring anyone to tempt the veil of death she carries.

"Hello," she says brightly as she rolls back her shoulders and clasps her hands in front of her pantsuit. She looks like she's dressed to go to an attorney's office, but her attitude matches that of a preppy college girl.

Odd combination.

She flashes white teeth as she grins and takes her time perusing Sabre and then me. "You two must be the monsters I'm looking for."

"Monsters," Sabre repeats dryly as he drags out the word with a snarl. "Why don't you just call us abominations while you're at it? We're used to it."

The female's perky demeanor doesn't change, but there's a tic in her jaw. "Oh, um. I didn't mean to offend..." She clears her throat, then pulls her purse around from her hip and digs out a letter. "I'm an official Emissary of Monster City, and Queen Helia would like me to extend this invitation—"

Sabre moves faster than I would have expected him capable of, given the drain we just experienced. He snatches the letter from the female's hand and rips it open with one claw. Unfurling it, he frowns as his eyes skim the contents, then he reads one of the lines aloud.

"Welcome to my city, and please make yourselves at home. After you enjoy the festivities of Monsters Night, you are invited to my main tower to stay in a guest suite, where you will be supplied with any sustenance you require. In exchange, you will meet with me in a week to review the terms of our alliance with you and your world."

"She sounds bossy," I complain.

"Hmm," he agrees, then reads one more line. "If Emissary Sheila has located you, then my instincts were right." He flicks his predatory gaze up to the female. "What does that mean?"

I'm impressed that the little mouse doesn't squeak and run when faced with a beast like Sabre. He's itching to find our Sigil just as badly as I am.

Funny how everything changed in the span of a few breaths.

I don't have to ask if he still intends to return to our dimension. We're going to be staying.

Our Sigil is here.

There is no going back.

The female flashes us another annoyingly perky smile. "All your questions will be answered when you meet with the Queen in a week's time. Until then, I assume you're hungry?" She pulls two vials from her purse, then holds them out to us.

Sabre eyes the female and her throat bobs, but he must share my own thoughts. We want *fresh* blood, but not hers.

Only our Sigil's will do.

He snatches up the vial and downs it, demonstrating his acceptance of this invitation into this realm.

I do the same.

"Let your walls down, Cage," Sabre instructs me as a flood of nourishment burns in my veins. Whatever blood this new Queen prepared for us is not only rich in vitality but also rich in *dreams*.

She knew exactly what we needed, which means I fully intend to talk to her in a week's time.

For now, I gladly do as Sabre commands.

"Lead the way," I growl as the world around me turns red.

And we both march away from the city and into the forest, our bodies looking for a place to nest for the night while our spirits dreamwalk.

I grin as I follow the screams.

*Hold on, Sigil.*

*We'll be with you soon.*

# CHAPTER 29

# SCARLETT

"Hold her down!" someone screams as forceful hands try to keep me from arching my back again.

*It hurts!*

I want to tell them that I'm dying.

They need to know that something is horribly wrong.

But all I can do is scream as the sensation of a thousand knives pierce my stomach, poking me full of holes until there's nothing left of me to bleed out.

I thrash against the bedsheets and fight the hands trying to pin me in place until something inside me breaks.

*Snap.*

Everything goes quiet.

The pain slips away like a bad dream, leaving me nauseous and disoriented as I try to open my eyes.

I regret it the moment I do, because now there are two new creatures staring at me from the darkness. At first, they seem like terrifying dark shadows, but when they venture closer, I realize they're actually quite beautiful.

When their tongues slither out, I shiver with interest.

*I've gone insane,* I decide as I adjust to an alternate

version of my room, one with blood dripping down the walls and black veins cracking through the wainscoting.

My physical body is still lying on the bed, but whoever had been holding me down has disappeared.

*Or I'm not in the real world anymore.*

I've spent enough time in an alternate plane of existence to understand that there's another place that rests beneath my own. One where I have been spying on the comings and goings of the Elites and searching for Cain, to no avail.

But it seems I've found two new figments in my dreams.

"Where's Cain?" I ask them.

The creatures watch me with glowing red eyes, and their long tongues flick out again as if to taste the air.

A shiver runs up my spine as I realize they probably don't know where Cain is, or don't care.

They likely aren't even real. I've gone so far off the deep end that Figment-Cain has abandoned me and now I have two new creatures here to torment me. Although, I quite enjoyed Cain's version of torment.

They both look as if they want to eat me. My stomach flips when the larger one stalks me in a wide circle. The other has massive fangs that should frighten me.

Strangely, my heart flutters with morbid excitement.

*I need help.*

"Cain's not here," Large Fangs says, venturing closer. He seems to have to concentrate to form words, given the nature of his tongue. It's not oversized like Cain's, but the length of it is certainly inhuman.

He's gorgeous, and my eyes go wide as he comes close enough for our noses to touch. As unnatural as he looks with shadows for skin and glowing, blood-colored eyes, there's an incredible beauty about him like a marble statue come to life.

*And he's naked.* My eyes drop, then widen even further as I try to understand the rounded bulbs around his member. There's one at the base and one on his swollen head.

A faint buzzing sound has me biting my lip. *Is... that vibrating?*

A barrage of inappropriate thoughts tumble through my mind as I try not to picture all the possibilities of a creature with a vibrating cock.

"Cain..." he repeats. "I remember," he says with a smirk, even though his words don't make sense to me. My heart stops as his claws skitter over my hip. "My name is Sabre. My friend is Cage. You called *us*, Sigil. We came."

*I called them? What does he mean?*

*And what's a Sigil?*

Glancing at the other creature, *Cage*, I find he has chosen to watch from the billowing shadows in the ever-changing structure of this dream version of my room. But from what I had glimpsed, everything about him was primal and *large*. Not as large as Cain, but larger than any human would be.

The unfathomable urge to drag Cage out of the shadows so I can get a better look at him makes my fingers itch. I wonder how much of this is real and how much is a result of my fractured mind.

*This happened when the portals opened.*

Perhaps I couldn't handle the fluctuation of power that came with new monsters entering our world. At least, not while I was in some sort of strange dream state caused by Cain's blood.

My eyelashes flutter closed as Sabre's claw drags a line up to my rib cage, managing to cut my nightdress without scratching my skin.

A new urge to slip the sleeves off my shoulders leaves me flustered and confused.

*This is just the effect of Cain's blood,* I try to assure myself.

When his claw continues its path over my left breast, my lips part on a soft gasp.

*Then why does it feel so real?*

"You hurt, Scarlett," the creature whispers, somehow knowing my name even though I never gave it to him. He's closer now, but I don't dare open my eyes to see his sharp fangs or red eyes. His breath brushes my ear as he makes an offer I can't refuse. "Let me and Cage take the pain away. Do you want us to do that? Do you want our comfort?"

A distant thunder gives me my first real burst of fear.

Figment-Cain might be a fabrication of my mind, but everything feels *real* in my dreams.

If he finds me like this, what will he do?

Will he hurt me?

Something deep within me knows that my figment would never hurt me, but I'm scared nonetheless.

I don't understand what's happening.

*I'm so confused.*

My chest flutters with panic. Hands gently cup my face, and my eyes fling open, only for me to stare at Sabre directly in his incredible eyes that glow with raw power.

My mirrorlike irises reflect back at me in his gaze. I have no doubt now why he has fangs. He's a type of vampire. Real or not, he will feed on me if I allow it.

But that doesn't frighten me. For some reason, it feels right, as if I have fractured under the weight of too many souls and he'll take that burden from me.

"Cain will be angry," I warn as Sabre's eyes bore into mine.

"Cain isn't here," Sabre repeats over my lips. His gaze drops to my mouth. "Answer the question, Sigil."

I can feel Cage watching me from the darkness. I somehow find his quiet stalking more unnerving than Sabre's threatening presence.

But I'm not afraid like I should be.

In fact, I feel safe. Safer than I ever have in my life.

Sabre seems to take my hesitation as a rejection, because he releases me and backs away. He blurs for a moment as if he's going to vanish.

Buckling over, I cry out as a slice of pain cuts through my chest. "Wait," I hiss on a pained breath. "Don't... don't go. Please."

Cage is the one who steadies me from behind. He pulls me against his chest as he wraps his hand around my throat. It's not a restraining gesture, but a claiming one. He palms my skin as his hard erection presses against my back, making a new ache throb between my legs.

They're not hiding their intentions. They want to comfort me in a very sexual way.

Sabre comes before me again and passes his thumb over my lower lip. My mouth parts for him out of instinct, making him grin and show off those impressive fangs once more. "We won't leave you, Sigil. But we can't stay here forever, either. Can you tell us where you are?"

I blink at him as the haze of lust makes it hard to breathe.

*Where I am?*

He means my body. The one still asleep in my bed.

*He wants to know where I am outside of this dream world.*

If these figments were real, I might imagine they were monsters and I'd found myself in their trap. It's certainly not possible that monsters have targeted me to be their mate on Monsters Night.

*Is it?*

*No,* I decide. I'm bound by a blood contract, and I'm

nowhere near Monster City. Whatever this is, it's a trick inside my mind.

But I've learned how real it can feel, so if I'm going to be subjected to powerful sensations, they might as well be pleasurable ones.

"It doesn't matter where I am," I say, earning a scowl from Sabre. But I know my next words will cheer him up. "Take the pain away. Show me what you can do. *Comfort me*, Sabre."

Red flashes in his gaze as his disappointment vanishes, just as I predicted. "Hmm, I like my name on your lips," he teases as his claws glide over my skin again, delicately slicing away fabric as he goes. "I can do so much more than comfort you, my sweet Sigil. My specialty lies in dreams. Would you like to see what I can do?"

I try not to laugh. Does my figment not even know we're already in a dream?

Cage continues to palm my throat as his cock pulses along my spine. He seems content to spectate whatever game Sabre wants to play while holding me in place.

"Show me," I taunt.

The second I utter the command, everything goes dark. Stiffening, I am strangely comforted that I still feel Cage behind me and his hand remains secured around my neck.

Maybe this is why he's holding me—so I don't run into the dark.

An invisible claw tickles over my skin, slicing away the last of my nightdress as cool air makes my nipples harden.

Then a tongue wraps around one of them, making me squeak. I know it's a tongue because the texture and sensation are undeniable, but now I realize that there are wicked things a creature like Sabre can really do.

"Talk to us, Sigil," Cage whispers in my ear. His voice is gruff and husky with need, making me whimper again. Just the rumble of his chest against my back is enough to make my core throb. "Tell us what you like, what you don't like. We want to learn everything about you. Every inch. Every gasp. Every desire. Everything." He enunciates the last word by exposing my neck, then tickles my skin with his tongue.

My breath comes in short gasps as I attempt to come up with words but fail. I'm too overwhelmed. My entire body feels like a string gone taut and ready to snap. I need something, but I'm not sure what it is.

Sabre's tongue moves to my other breast, and he wraps it around my nipple, then tugs.

"Words," Cage encourages.

I have no words, so I claw my fingers over his forearm and dig my nails in. He hisses as I draw blood. The sticky substance is like an aphrodisiac, making me feel drugged.

The light tugging on my nipple disappears, and then a hard body is against mine. I go still when Sabre presses against my front and his cock wedges between us.

That bulb I saw earlier is settled between my legs, and the base of it vibrates on my clit. Sabre palms my face, and his tongue brushes over my lip before dipping into my mouth. I moan as pleasure builds like a swollen knot in my stomach, threatening to burst. His tongue vanishes, but Sabre remains pressed against me, wedging me between him and Cage like their prey caught in a pleasure trap.

"Sensation can be more powerful in the darkness," Sabre says. "But I agree with Cage. We need more than agreement from your body. We need your verbal permission to continue. Tell us what you want."

"I-I..." I stammer, fighting for words when my body feels like an instrument only these two creatures know how to make sing. Red eyes glow, eliciting a shiver from me. "I want more," I manage to say in a breathless whisper.

Sabre's long fangs flash as he grins. Then he dips and

kisses my stomach. His words flutter over the blood-mark just above my navel as if taunting Cain's magic. "Hold her in place, Cage. I'm going to lick her sweet pussy until she comes in my mouth." He chuckles when I freeze. "Do you want that, Sigil?"

I know I'll regret it, but my eager agreement drips from my traitorous tongue. "Yes. I... I want that."

I nearly black out when he shoves his face between my legs, his tongue thrusting up into me as I scream. Cage does as ordered and holds me in place, but I asked for this.

In my dreams, I'm nothing but a wallowing ball of need.

No one has to know. I remind myself of that as I give in to the pleasure and slump against Cage, enjoying the throb of his cock against my back as he lightly thrusts, seeming to seek friction as I arch my back and let Sabre use his skilled tongue on me.

My dreams are so vivid, even if it is Cain's blood that's responsible for such dreams.

Just as the inevitable orgasm crests over my body like a lightning bolt ripping through the sky, I spot a strange raven in the distance. His black feathers should blend into the background of shadows and darkness, but he stands out to me all the same.

It's as if Cain himself is watching over me. The after-shocks of pleasure make my toes curl, and I breathe out a long sigh, feeling as if I've released a burden I'd been holding on to for too long.

Now that I'm spent, everything begins to dissolve, and I fall into the bad habit of whispering a prayer before my dream ends. The urge overwhelms me, demanding I say at least one benediction to my dark Lord.

"Praise you, Cain. Thank you for your mercy, for this small reprieve, before I have to go back again."

Because I know when I wake up, I'll have to face

Edward. After our last parting, and how he has seemed so utterly unconcerned for my well-being, I'm not so sure how I feel about him now.

I only know that I won't ever be able to look at him the same way again.

Because I've already started falling for figments in my dreams.

*They aren't even real, Scarlett.*

*But... what if I'm wrong?*

*What if... they are real, and it's Edward who is the dream?*

# CHAPTER 30

# CAIN

I EXPECTED to experience jealousy after witnessing two other creatures giving my mate pleasure.

But I'm proud.

She had whispered a prayer to me on the echo of aftershocks of her orgasm.

Praising me.

*Thanking* me.

She had called it a reprieve, though, before she had to go back. I didn't want her to think that this was all there would be.

*You have an eternity of pleasure awaiting you, my star,* I think as I watch her settle into her dreams. She'll be awake soon, and the two other creatures seem to know that. They solemnly tuck her into the bed as she closes her eyes. Her lips stretch into a smile as she sighs.

*She's happy.*

My beast rumbles with a purr. It's a sound I've never heard from him, but I echo it as he tastes the aroma of peaches and cream drifting through the Dream Realm. We both watch as Scarlett flickers in and out of the dream plane. She'll be gone soon, but the transition is taking longer than usual.

She doesn't want to wake up. I don't blame her.

I allow him to linger in the ecstasy of Scarlett's release while I settle against the wall and close my eyes. The heat of the morning blisters over my tower as the chains binding me start to dissolve.

Monsters Night is over.

And for the first time, I can experience the euphoria of finding a mate of my own.

Not just one, but three. I knew this would never work without other monsters to stabilize a union like this. And it seems two have miraculously appeared.

I don't believe in coincidences. Something has triggered this. Or someone has drawn us all together.

*Maybe there really are Gods after all.*

No matter if there are higher powers at play or not, I know what happens next.

I will go to her. There's no stopping it now. Blood contract or no, Scarlett Nightingale belongs with me.

*With us,* I think. The two dream creatures I sense are sated after feeding on her dreams. They did more than pleasure her. They *helped* her. Her screams had been ones of pain. I hadn't been able to go to her, and I reluctantly consider what might have happened had the two others not been there.

*She could have died.*

They look hungry, though. Their eyes glow red-hot as they seem to grudgingly back away from her. The one with large fangs exercises his jaw, and the other tastes the air. Feeding on her dreams isn't enough.

*They need her blood, too.* They'll get it, when they find her in the real world.

But I will go to her first. She doesn't understand what's happening, and she deserves to know.

I've allowed her to believe it was all a dream because that's all I thought it could ever be.

I was wrong.

Sunlight spills through the windows of my tower, and my eyes fling open. The chains fall, and I rise to my feet, only for my beast's purrs to turn into growls.

My chest tightens as his power swells over me, his eagerness to *feast* making my canines sharpen and my jaw ache.

"Helia," I say before my voice is completely gone. One night of imprisonment wasn't enough, not now that my beast has tasted the awakened dreams of a true mate.

She's lying in her bed like a decadent treat just waiting to be devoured. It's too much for him to resist.

His strength ripples through me, making me grow as new muscles wind over my arms, my torso, and my entire body. My cock swells and throbs, the massive appendage enough to split Scarlett in two without a little magical assistance. I can't hope that my beast would have enough finesse to think of that.

*He's going to kill her.*

*He's going to kill everyone in our path, and then he's going to take Scarlett no matter if she's ready for us or not.*

"Helia!" I roar.

The Monster City Queen should have responded to me by now, but she hasn't. I don't have time to wonder what the hell she's doing that she can't answer my summons, but I know I have precious seconds to decide what I'm going to do.

My reflection in the window overlooking the city grows as my beast takes control. My skin darkens with nightmares, and my eyes take on a fractured glow. My jaw unhinges as a wide maw yawns open, displaying sharpened teeth. My beast overcomes lucid thought, shoving one singular thought into my head.

*Feed.*

My beast will drain my city dry. He'll devour everyone in his path and destroy everything I have built.

Oh, the irony—I have become my own worst enemy.

"No, beast," I growl as my words lose form. My massive tongue isn't made for talking; it's made for tasting. For devouring and doing wicked things.

I won't let him be wicked, not when it means the mate I have searched so long for will suffer.

If she's better off without us, then so be it.

My beast can't stop me as I use the last of my strength to propel us forward. The windows rush at me like a glimmering barrier. When I break through them, I dive *inward*.

I go to a place in the Dream Realm I've never ventured before. I find the nearest river of blood and throw myself into it.

My beast thrashes and roars as we slip under. Then blood is all I know. It's not like real blood. It isn't sticky or wet.

But it's *consuming.*

It's a place I don't belong. But it'll keep Scarlett safe.

I can't speak anymore, but I think my last words as powerfully as if they were a prayer.

*Don't come looking for me, star. Stay safe. Stay... awake.*

# CHAPTER 31

# SCARLETT

Sunlight kisses my cheeks, and I sigh. The sound exhales out of me with utter and complete contentment.

"Did you sleep well?" a male voice asks me, making me fling my eyes open.

Edward is leaning over me with a charming smile on his face. Guilt washes over me, even though I don't feel like I have anything to feel guilty about.

*Right?*

My dreams have become stranger and more vivid as time has gone on. And it's not like Edward has been by my side the entire time.

"Have I slept well?" I reiterate, bewildered by the insensitive question. "I've been asleep for days, haven't I?"

His smile fades a fraction. "Yes. I'm afraid I, well." His stormy blue eyes flicker with an emotion I can't place. "I fucked up, Scarlett, and I apologize."

My eyes widen. "How crass," I mutter, even though I actually appreciate Edward showing me some genuine behavior for once. "Please, tell me how you fucked up," I say as I manage myself into a sitting position. My skin feels like it has tiny pieces of glass embedded into it, and every movement slices me with fresh pain.

He sighs as he reaches out as if to touch my hand, then seems to think better of it. He doesn't turn over his palm so I can see the mark that binds him to me. He makes a fist as if to hide it and bites his knuckle before replying. "You're irresistible, Scarlett. But I shouldn't have done what I did. You were scared. Pressed against me. *Wet...*" He says, then rakes his fingers through his hair as he looks at the ceiling. "I mean from the bath," he clarifies. Although, I think he meant I was a different sort of wet.

Memories flood back of Edward *tasting* me.

Only to be replaced by what Figment-Cain did with his tongue.

A shiver runs up my spine, and I suppress it by hugging my arms. "Do you regret it?" I ask. For some reason, this confession from him makes it feel like it's all my fault.

I was the one who nearly drowned myself in a tub for no reason.

I was the one who was naked.

I was the one who was *wet.*

A voice inside my head seems to chide my line of thought. I have nothing to be sorry for. Edward is the one who crossed a line, and even if I let him, I'd been vulnerable. And when I had fallen into a coma, he'd gone about his business without a care of what happened to me.

Remembering him placing bets in the bar on Monsters Night has me stiffening my lower lip in defiance.

"No, I don't regret it," he says with a low voice. "But I should. And that makes me even worse, doesn't it?"

"Hmm," I agree. "And my condition? What have the doctors said?" I ask. He stares at me, so I narrow my eyes. "You *did* have doctors check me, didn't you?"

His jaw clenches before he replies. "You're under a

blood contract, as am I, Scarlett. I can't have anyone touch you for an examination, not until the courtship is completed. We don't know how what happened impacted it."

"By 'what happened,' you mean fucking me with your tongue?" I snap.

He flinches at my crude choice of words but doesn't chide me for it. "I shouldn't have done that, Scarlett. For all we know, the premature bond between us caused your coma. For that, I apologize. But I had hoped that the flux of Monsters Night would bring you out of it. I'm glad to see that I was right."

"Is that why you didn't check on me, not even once?" I ask, unable to help myself. I know it makes me sound whiny and needy, but I need to know why he didn't care enough to stay by my side.

He narrows his eyes, and I realize my mistake.

I shouldn't know that.

"I'll be back to talk more in a few days' time, Lady Scarlett," he says, rising and keeping his fists clenched. He doesn't answer my question, and I notice he's gone formal on me. "Now that you are awake, I will send for your mother. We haven't informed her of your condition due to her fragile state. But I know she'll be delighted to see you." He dips his fingers into his pocket and produces an anti-aging vial, making my eyes widen. He quietly places it on my bedside table. "I'm sure she'll be needing this. Give her my regards."

While I stare after him, Edward moves to exit the room, then pauses. He marches to my vanity and pulls out a tray of standard tonics. He plucks one up and brings it to me.

He lets the vial drop into my palm. "I think you should use this for a little while, too. Just as a precaution."

I stare down at it, knowing he's right.

It's the tonic that prevents me from sleeping.

Prevents me from *dreaming*.

I won't see my figments again, not even the new ones who fascinate me in every way.

*They're not real.*

*They can't be.*

Slowly plucking the cork off the vial, I tip the contents into my mouth and shiver.

"Good girl," Edward says and turns on his heel and exits the room, leaving me alone with my spinning thoughts and a knot in my stomach I can't explain.

# CHAPTER 32

# SCARLETT

*A few days later...*

Julie's reflection blinks at me as she holds up a tray of tonics. She can't believe that I want to make amends with Edward.

I can't either, but after yesterday, I feel like an idiot.

"Are you really going to forgive him, Lady Scarlett?" she asks, her wide brown eyes a fixture I'm so used to on her face that I imagine they'll just stay that way from now on. "I watched you lie there, helpless, for days." The tears twinkling in her eyes touch me in ways I would never have expected.

Somehow, I've made a friend, even in a place like the Rinhold residence.

Sighing, I turn and select one of the blasted tonics. I had better get used to them, because this is the way of a family in the Magic Sector.

And soon, I'll be in the Immortal Sector. The stakes will be even higher, and expectations will be as high as the clouds.

"He explained everything," I say, knowing I don't really need to convince Julie, but it would help if I reiterated it for myself. After watching Edward make underhanded deals with various families in a gambling scheme, I imagined he didn't care about me at all. He hadn't come to visit me, but he had a reason for that.

"Did he?" Beatrix asks from the doorway. She's scowling, which is also a permanent fixture I imagine I should get used to. "The young master is no fool, my lady. He could talk his way out of a beheading in the middle of an execution just by charming the poor soul holding the axe."

"That might be so," I agree as I pop open the cork on the tonic I've selected. The aroma of peaches makes me relax. I'm not sure why it's my favorite lately. "But there is evidence I have to consider. My mother came to visit me just two days ago, and she is doing well." Better than I've seen in years—maybe ever. "That's why he did what he did," I say, more to myself than to anyone else. Edward had waited until after I had seen my mother to explain everything. It made it hard to be mad at him, so I see now why he'd waited.

The explanation, though, still boggled my mind.

He had a gambling scheme going, one that was rigged. He has a monster ally in the city, one who seems to know which Offering will make a strong match and which won't. Edward didn't tell me what he had on the monster, but I knew it must be something good.

Because Edward knew the best matches already before the night had even begun. That monster had given him his foresight and allowed Edward to make risky bets, ones that had earned him a lot of money.

*Enough to buy my trust?* I wonder as my dress changes color and form, courtesy of my peach-flavored tonic. I'm about to see Edward for lunch, but I'm feeling rather lethargic.

There's a pit inside my stomach that only seems to grow. I hunger for something I can't have. Something dark, depraved.

Something dangerous.

Sniffing, I grab another one of the tonics.

The one that keeps me awake.

I haven't slept in four days, and I don't intend to sleep tonight. Sleep is something I can't face, not until I'm satisfied that I won't encounter figments in my dreams.

Yet, my treacherous body yearns for what it can't have. The sensation of being poked full of holes until I want to scream makes me woozy, and I waver on my feet.

Beatrix scowls again as she steadies me. I know she doesn't approve, but she doesn't chastise me. Instead, she seems resigned.

Footsteps at the door make me glance up with a practiced smile.

"I was just finishing up, Edwa—" I begin, only to cut myself off when I see Duchess Rinhold, not my future husband.

And she seems furious. A pinch in her brow makes her look older, despite her plentiful use of anti-aging tonics. Her curls fray around her head as if she's been grasping at them.

A staff of cloaked figures stand around her, making my spine go stiff. Whatever she has in mind, it can't be good.

Her lips twist into a snarl when I try to smile at her. It's an odd reaction, and I certainly don't expect the foul word that drips from her mouth.

"*Whore.*"

My eyes fling open wide. "Duchess Rinhold," I begin,

not sure what to say against such an accusation. "If you presume I've been unfaithful, I assure you—"

"I *know*," she says, dipping her chin with finality as if I should know what that means.

"Know what?" I ask.

She sighs as if I'm being ridiculous. "Did you think there wouldn't be any evidence?"

"Evidence?" I parrot.

She actually growls at me. "Edward's courtship mark is gone!"

My jaw drops open.

*Why would it disappear?*

*Unless...*

"Check her," the Duchess says with a snap of her finger.

The blood drains from my face when I realize who the cloaked figures are. Reflective metal glints on their chest as they move, betraying stethoscopes hiding underneath the fabric. They're not servants.

They're medical doctors. All of them male, based on their physiques.

*Check her.*

What are they going to check?

I already know the horrible answer. "Beatrix!" I scream when a rough hand grabs my wrist and yanks me to the floor.

The Duchess rolls her eyes as Beatrix looks like she's going to break her jaw if she clenches it any harder. "She can't help you. Stay still for the examination, girl. It'll be easier for everyone without hysterics."

*I'll show you hysterics, you—*

Another man is on top of me, and all I can hear is the sound of my enraged screams paired with the tearing of fabric.

*Riiiip.*

What's left of my dress is yanked off of my chest, leaving me exposed as I try to use my teeth. I'm rewarded with a male's grunt as I snag a finger and chomp down until I taste blood.

They want to treat me like an animal? I'll behave like one.

It's unnecessary to completely strip me for the examination, but Duchess Rinhold has chosen to make this some sort of humiliation. My jaw is wrenched open by a strong grip, freeing the trapped finger, as the work is continued.

"Where is Edward?" I scream.

The Duchess straightens as another man grabs my knees, but I lock them closed.

*No.*

*They can't.*

Julie finally unlatches from her rooted position, and the tray of tonics shatters onto the floor. She screams as she rushes one of the men, but they easily pull her aside. Beatrix is crying as they drag both women out of the room.

*At least they won't have to see this.*

"Edward will hate you for this!" I bellow as the male fights with my legs that I refuse to open.

*I'm going to kill them.*

"Trust me, I already hate her," my betrothed's voice says from the doorway.

My strength wavers when I see him. His face is expressionless, but his eyes seem sad.

Yet, he does nothing. He stands there in the doorway with his hands folded and *watches*. I want to beg him to take off his gloves and show me his palm so I can see for myself.

*He was wearing gloves yesterday, too.*

Gloves are currently out of fashion, but now both Edward and his mother are wearing them. And Edward has been wearing them for days.

*He knew.*

My mouth bobs open in disbelief. "Why explain every-thing, why regain my trust, if you were just going to let her do this?" I ask. I need a reason for this sort of betrayal.

His jaw flexes. "She saw my hand, Scarlett. I'll fix this. Just don't fight her, please."

I've never heard Edward beg, but he seems to be begging me now to cooperate.

*I could never accept this!*

"Get on with it," Duchess Rinhold snaps at one of the men.

Hot, angry tears stream down my face when the last of my dignity is ripped away, and a single finger pushes inside of me.

"I've never been with a man," I weakly protest.

That might be true.

But...

*I've been with a monster.*

Figment-Cain's tongue had been real enough that I'm not sure what the result of this so-called examination will be.

"She is spoiled," the male working his finger around confirms, then pulls it out and wipes it on the tattered remnants of my dress. He dares to cast me a pitied look before his dark eyes drop.

I should be shocked by the verdict.

But I'm not.

*My dream... it was real.*

Duchess Rinhold whirls on her son, and her hand flies out so fast that I don't even see it strike his face. His always perfect hair flings over his forehead, and blood bursts in a pop of red over his chin. *"Spoiled,"* she repeats to him like an accusation. "Do you know what this means?"

The male who had been probing me has the decency to

hand me a blanket, and I wrap it around myself as I glare daggers at him. Adrenaline is pumping too hard for me to fight. It's over. My humiliation is sealed.

Edward palms his jaw, then drags his thumb over his bloodied lip. He dares to glance at me with those stormy blue eyes that I used to think were so deep and soulful.

Edward Rinhold has no soul.

"What if I was the one who spoiled her, Mother?" he asks, not looking away from me. "I couldn't wait. I took what I wanted. She's mine anyway."

I go still. I know he's lying, but no sign of a mask appears on his face.

There's no crack. No hint of his deception bleeding the truth underneath a disguise like I would normally see with anyone else.

*I can't see his truth.*

*Edward... has the perfect mask.*

I don't know how, but Earl Rinhold has prepared for everything. He must have known about my ability to see people for who they really are, just like he knew the name of my village.

*It's Cain's blood,* I realize as my fingers twist around the blanket.

*Cain's blood is his mask.*

My tongue goes dry as I wonder what that might mean and all of the implications.

Especially given the nature of my dreams.

Duchess Rinhold clicks her tongue as she fusses with her gloves, one of them now stained with her son's blood. "Then you are a fool, Edward. You couldn't wait until the courtship ended? Now you might have cost us everything. If word of this gets out, Cain himself could void the contract. You could *die*."

My eyes widen. If Edward had actually violated the contract, perhaps that was true.

But he wasn't the one who had taken my virginity.

Figment-Cain had.

*What if... that hadn't been a figment at all?*

The mark just above my navel throbs with a distinct reminder of how much I enjoyed Figment-Cain's company. My marks hadn't disappeared. Only Edward's.

*Because I'm still bound by blood to my potential mate, only it's not Edward who I'm destined for now.*

*But the other two figments... who are they?*

They'd saved me when I'd been dying. Now, I wonder how real that whole experience had been.

Why had I been dying?

More questions than answers flutter about in my head as Edward and his mother come to a conclusion about my fate.

"We speed up the timeline," Edward says, the finality in his tone making me wrench back to reality. His eyes seem to have gone dark as he glances at me again. "We make it a public ceremony. No one will question the legitimacy of our union if we marry in the old-tradition style."

*Old tradition?*

I have no clue what that means, but the numbness in his gaze only tells me that there's something wicked hiding beneath Edward's perfect mask.

I can't trust him.

I should never have trusted him in the first place.

*What have I done?*

"No one can see her until then," the Duchess declares, then snaps her fingers. "Throw her in the dungeon. She can rot in there and think about the misfortune she's cast on this family while arrangements are made."

"What?" I screech as hands haul me to my feet.

I'm biting again, thrashing like a wild animal, and my blanket is ripped from me. I'm making a scene, but damn if I'm going to go quietly.

Darkness engulfs me faster than I'd like, and I'm thrown into what can only be described as a cell.

The floor is wet.

The air is rancid.

And my breath rushes out of me as my back slams into the wall, and the door creaks closed, leaving me in utter darkness.

I hadn't taken the anti-sleep tonic for today.

Which is a good thing, but I'm going to have to calm myself enough to fall asleep.

*You had better be real, my figments,* I think as I shiver and curl into a corner. I don't know how I'm going to sleep like this, but I'll eventually pass out.

I pray it won't take long.

Although, when I start praying to Cain, it feels like he can't hear me.

He hadn't been there the night of Monsters Night.

And he's not here for me now.

I try not to let the darkness crush all my hopes.

*There were two others,* I remind myself.

*Sabre. Cage.*

I allow myself to remember their names from the fogginess of my dream. Resting my head against the wall, I close my eyes.

And I wait for sleep to find me.

# CHAPTER 33

## CAIN

*Four-and-twenty hours later...*

MY WORLD IS nothing but red hues and the sensation of suffocating. I can't breathe. I feel like I hardly even exist.

It's not unpleasant, once I got used to it.

And after a few days submerged in the blood rivers of the Dream Realm, my beast is worn down. My body has returned to a human shape, even within this place, and I trail my fingers through the liquid.

*I'm sorry, Scarlett,* I think as I lazily drift in an endless river. The current has carried me downward to places no soul should ever go.

But it's peaceful here, somehow. It feels like death, if death were an undertow of rushing sounds and a beat that echoes through my entire body.

*It's like a mother's womb.*

This is a place of rebirth, perhaps. If there is such a thing as a second chance with a new life, I doubt there's one in store for me. That leaves me in purgatory. After all the death I have caused, all the suffering, it's fitting to be trapped in a place with no future, no past, and no hope.

*This is where I belong.*

"Cain," a distant voice calls, making me glance upward where I know the surface must be.

That's where the voice had come from.

My first instinct is to move toward the sound, but even if Scarlett has finally chosen to reach out to me, it still isn't safe for her.

I'm grateful now for the two monsters who found her in the Dream Realm on Monsters Night. Perhaps they'll be enough to take care of her.

Scarlett is something special. She has unique needs, both in the real world and the one of dreams. Her soul draws everything around it in, and now that part of her has unlocked, she can't be expected to take on that burden alone.

She's like a well, one with no end, and it could drive her to the bottom just like the blood rivers in the Dream Realm. She could suffocate and be lost forever without mates to keep her afloat, to keep the tides low and help her manage her incredible gift.

She would have been the answer to my beast. A power like that could satisfy him for the first time in my very long life.

Thousands of years. That's how long I've starved and existed in a state of constant pain. Scarlett doesn't know what an answer to a prayer she really is for a so-called God such as me.

I don't deserve the hope she offers. But the creatures who came through that portal on Monsters Night, perhaps they don't have the same dark history I do. Perhaps I was nothing more than a medium to bring them together. Happiness is not in the cards for a beast like me.

"Cain, please. Don't leave me here..."

My fingers clench into fists as I try to resist her call. Why aren't her new mates going to her?

Maybe they can't find her again, not without my help. They're from another world, which means they might still be in Monster City.

Helia should guide them. There aren't any other dream creatures like me, so it wouldn't be such a stretch for her to know where they might belong. But if she's been as unavailable for them as she has been for me, they might be stuck.

Helpless.

*Like being trapped in Purgatory.*

Growling, I start to swim. The current has pushed me down, but Scarlett keeps praying to me, *calling* for me, and giving me a lifeline that draws me skyward.

*I'm coming, my star,* I say in my mind. I know the inevitable choice I must make.

Leaving her is not an option.

I can only hope my beast has been subdued enough to keep me in control while I seek her out. Scarlett needs me, and I'm powerless to ignore her plea.

When I break the blood barrier of the rivers, I rise into the real world and take my first breath of air in days. My lungs seize as I cough up the Dream Realm's lifeblood. I crash through broken glass, and I realize I've come through a glass window—one belonging to Helia's personal room.

It's not where I would intentionally choose a meeting, but she doesn't seem to mind. Her oversized bed is made, spanning behind her while she sits in a wide chair with raised armrests, one that is facing the now broken window.

*It's almost as if she knew I was coming.*

She's in her human form, wearing a tight-fitting dress as she crosses her legs. A smirk plays on the edge of her wicked mouth as she patiently watches me cough up blood onto her clean floor.

"Well, hello, Cain. Isn't this a nice surprise?" she says.

I have a feeling it's not a surprise at all.

A growl rumbles in my throat, but it's only an echo of my beast that lies within. He doesn't have the energy to come out, so for that, I'm grateful that my hypothesis was correct.

It means that Scarlett and my people are safe, for now. And if I had come into Helia's tower out of control, she would have dealt with the problem herself. In that situation, I would have become a threat.

And therefore, her enemy.

Now, though, I am her friend. One she has neglected.

"Where have you been?" I ask, my voice a low, dangerous threat of a whisper. It feels as if knives have scored my insides and every word creates a fresh dagger to slice through salted wounds. But I don't flinch; I don't show her what kind of discomfort I'm in.

This is what I deserve, after all. Once I'm done here, I'll be going back to the undercurrent of the Dream Realm.

For Scarlett's sake.

I can't pick up her prayer on the wind now that I've left the ethereal plane, but that makes sense if my beast is weak. There must be a reason I've surfaced here, though, in Helia's tower rather than closer to home.

Helia flicks her tongue and shifts the weight of her hips. She's sitting in a single sofa chair that could easily double as a throne. She has a talent of making everything around her a piece of her royalty, of her power, and to accent her complete and utter control.

Sometimes that's a façade. Sometimes it's real.

Today, I can't tell. I only know there's a new glow about her that certainly wasn't there before.

"I've been... busy," she says as she drags a long, manicured nail over her lower lip. I don't take her flirtatious behavior too seriously. Helia would flirt with a houseplant, given the chance. It's her nature.

Being so evasive, though, is unusual. At least when it comes to our relationship.

"I don't have time for your games," I growl as I turn toward the shattered window.

We're high up, higher than my own tower, given the way that Helia's city has developed. The skyscrapers here are characteristic of what this territory used to be. Once upon a time, it was called New York. Just as my Elite City was once named Chicago.

Those names are as ancient as dust. Only their memory lingers over the newly developed cities that have taken over the ruins. The buildings and towers were made in our image and carry little pieces of ourselves within them.

We've built our cities differently, but we've always ruled alongside one another.

It feels like everything is falling apart.

"I don't either, Cain," she says with a sigh. "So if you've come here for the dreamwalkers, then I suggest you go talk to them and stop wasting your time with me. They are your new mates, after all. It's rude how long you've kept them waiting."

Glancing at her from over my shoulder, I give her a raised brow.

She gives me another one of her characteristic smirks, then bounces to her feet. She pops her hips as she marches to her closet and emerges a few moments later with a tailored suit. One I know will fit me perfectly.

"They aren't my mates," I argue. She doesn't try to correct me. "Did you know they were coming?" I ask as I accept the clothes. I put them on while I wait for her reply.

She shrugs, sending her long, silky hair unfurling over her shoulder as she moves. "I suspected it based on the type of distortion I had been sensing closer to Monsters Night, but I didn't want to get your hopes up in case I was wrong."

"Distortion?" I ask.

"Do you recall the peekaboo portal that kept popping up? Someone from the other dimension had their eye on us, but there was more to it than that. Many of them came through, and a few decided to stay." She grins. I know there's more information, but she isn't going to share it with me right now. "Including your new mates," she continues in complete disregard of my protest about them being *mates*. "I had an Emissary ready to locate them once the portals opened. They accepted my invitation and have been staying here."

"Hmm," I say as I decide if it's worth it to argue with her or not. While I highly doubt these two monsters are also my mates, Helia likely can sense their connection to Scarlett. Explaining that to her would require explaining my connection to Scarlett and therefore risk her understanding that I'm going to have to leave this world. Permanently. I don't need anyone trying to convince me to stay when it's not the right thing to do. "Anything else I should know?"

Her smirk turns into a full-on grin, which is usually a horrible sign of misfortune on its way. "They aren't the only interesting monsters who traveled here from that dimension."

Any monsters worthy of Helia's attention are typically powerful, but I can't shake the feeling that she's hiding something. There's a refreshed energy about her.

*No, that's not just rejuvenated energy. She has* new *energy.*

"What aren't you telling me?" I ask her with a raised brow.

Her eyes glitter with delight. "Guess."

I blow out a breath. "Helia."

She rakes her fingers through her hair as she gives me a softer smile, one I haven't seen on her in a very long time.

One that comes from a place of happiness.

"Bernard didn't tell you?" she asks, but she knows he couldn't tell me whatever it is she chose to share with my Raven instead of me.

That's not his fault, though. I've been in the Dream Realm for days.

She finally chooses to end my torment and spits it out. "I found my mates, Cain. At least, I found two of them." She tilts her head to the doorway. "They're both enjoying the spa level. I sensed you'd be invading my space tonight." She eyes the broken glass on the floor with distaste. "They're human. I didn't want your brutish beast to break them."

I go silent. I take no offense to her concerns about my beast around fragile humans, but I can't ignore the impossibility of this coincidence.

*What are the odds that the Monster City Queen and the Elite City King both find mates after centuries of failure?*

"I wouldn't dream of allowing even a hair to be harmed on your mates' heads. I offer you my congratulations."

She hums in reply. "Congratulations to you as well."

That might be a little preemptive of her. As powerful as Helia is, I doubt she understands the depths of my predicament.

"Don't you find it unusual? Both of us finding mates, I mean. There could be foul play."

She shrugs. "Perhaps. Who do you suggest would be interfering with fate?"

"Have you met any Gods recently?" I ask. I mean it in jest, but she doesn't laugh.

"I'm about to meet with one named Orcus," she replies, surprising me. "But he seems as lost here as the rest of us were. If there is a deity meddling, I don't think it's him." She tilts her head as if she's pleased with herself. "He's... interesting, though. I think you'll like him." Her eyes glitter with delight as I try to keep a straight face, but it's as if the Monster City Queen can read my mind. After how many centuries we've known each other, she practically can. "Would you like to stay and discuss the circumstances of a budding new alliance? I promise it'll be interesting."

"I'm sure it will be," I say as I adjust my cuff links. "But I trust you to handle monster affairs."

I don't mention that I doubt I'll be remaining in this plane for very long. Helia might know me well enough, but I've never given up my city.

Not even when I lost control and my beast destroyed everyone and everything in Vulcan Village. That place is now a pit, nothing more than crumbled ruins at the edge of my city.

I remind myself of those ruins. Of what little memories I can pull up full of shredded dreams and splattered blood.

Because that can never happen again.

*I'll find these dreamwalkers. I'll help them get to Scarlett, and then I will leave.*

*For good.*

My city will run on its own for a time even without me. Bernard would let Helia know when a replacement needed to be found, once he was satisfied I wasn't returning.

I'll slip away like a lost nightmare, never to be seen again.

Taking Helia's hand, I brush her knuckles with my lips. She remains perfectly statuesque with inhuman stillness as she watches me.

"Farewell, Queen Helia," I say.

If she knows the permanence of my goodbye, she

doesn't comment on it. She smiles, showing a glint of white teeth. "Farewell, Cain."

DESCENDING THE TOWER, THE ELEVATOR DOORS OPEN, ONLY TO reveal the God that Helia had mentioned.

There's no question about what he is.

He matches my height at over six feet tall and boasts broad shoulders, and everything about him screams *Alpha.*

His aura is what gives him away as something divine. A shadow of wings spans from his back. A distinctly foreign power glimmers around him like gold specks that I suspect other creatures can't see. His impact on the Dream Realm is noticeable, only because this is a creature with nearly infinite power. Even his dreams are capable of changing the world around him, and that is a terrifying gift indeed.

"Who are you?" he demands. It doesn't surprise me in the least that a God would notice there's something different about me as well.

But I suspect he can't tell what I am. The answer to that question isn't a simple one. I don't have a species designation other than the one the Elites have given me, as I've never met anyone else like myself. He might be a God, but he's in a dimension entirely different from his own.

"Cain," I easily reply.

"*What* are you?" he adds, his words holding an accent similar to my own.

I smile, intrigued by this Alpha. "Are you always so demanding of those you just met?"

"Only potential threats," he counters.

Oh. I definitely like him. "I'll take that as a compliment."

"You shouldn't," he informs me with warning. "I don't like threats."

"Ah, well, then you and Helia are going to get on famously," I drawl. "I almost wish I would have stayed for the meeting now."

"Helia?" he repeats.

"The Monster City Queen," I explain, catching the elevator door before it can close. "She's ready for you, by the way."

He cocks a brow at me. "Are you here to escort me up?"

I laugh as I try to picture that. I respect Helia's power, but I'm not her lackey. "I'm not in the habit of escorting anyone anywhere, Orcus. But unless you want an Emissary to come find you, I recommend heading up to see Helia. The Emissaries around here are all about punctuality and rules." Which is precisely why I know Helia entrusted an Emissary with the task of locating my potential mates while I was tied up.

I let my arm fall then, and I start down the hallway. I can feel Orcus watching, and I brace myself for him to bark more orders at me.

Fortunately, he doesn't.

Because I wouldn't have stopped even if he had asked me to. Now that I'm closer to the dreamwalkers Helia had told me about, I can sense them.

I can *feel* them.

They're so much more than compatible mates. By playing with Scarlett, they have begun a link not only with her but also with *me*.

Perhaps that's what Helia had sensed about me and had made her so confident.

*Okay, Helia. You think I have not one mate but three?*
*We shall see...*

# CHAPTER 34

## SABRE

"Drink," Cage orders me as he shoves a glass of blood into my face.

My nose wrinkles at the unpleasant scent that's sour, wrong, and makes my stomach churn. I shove it away before hanging my head. I'm sitting on the floor, which is a waste of all the stupidly expensive furniture in our guest suite. It's nice to be in a place that isn't paid for in my blood. It's no doubt paid for in *someone's* blood, just not my own. But I can't enjoy anything when I feel like death.

Blood itself can't sustain me anymore. I came to this dimension in hopes of feeling rejuvenated, but then we found her.

Our Sigil.

*Where are you, little one?*

It's been days of silence, only to faintly hear our Sigil trying to call out for help.

For *Cain.*

Not for us.

*Who is this asshole, and why is our Sigil so intent on finding him?*

We've learned that Cain is the name of a King, one who rules a city of humans where Chicago used to be. This world is reminiscent of the Human Realm we are already familiar with. The landmark locations are similar, but not much else is.

Outside of common knowledge in this dimension, we've learned little else so far. Which makes me anxious to find our Sigil before something goes wrong. I can't shake the sensation that something big is coming.

And it's not good.

The problem is that she hasn't been in this dimension's dream plane since we met.

"No one stays awake for four days," I complain as Cage kneels at my side and places the glass of blood on the floor within reach. If he's hoping I'll change my mind, he's being far too optimistic.

"Our Sigil shouldn't be underestimated," he tells me. "She needed time, so she found a way to stay awake as long as she required." His voice is impossibly calm, and he's keeping it together much better than I am.

That's because he wasn't as weakened when we arrived here, nor is he the one most dependent on our Sigil. I was closest to the throne; therefore, the burden of a Sigil's energy falls hardest on me.

I fed on her nightmares and the power of all the dreams she had begun to absorb. I know the lore of how a Sigil's power works. They are like an endless well, one that is filled with the life force of others lingering around it. A Sigil is activated in the dream plane, and everyone and everything around her experiences the pull to be drawn into her. She is the medium.

But she is also human, which means Strigoi must take the excess before it tears her apart. That's exactly what we had been doing in the dream plane when we found her.

But this dimension is different. The dream plane is more like an entire realm here. It has territories, rivers, and a richness to it that makes it a place all on its own. I need time to learn it, to navigate it, to be able to find my Sigil now lost within it.

And without enough strength, I don't even seem to be able to enter it again. My vision flashes with red as I try and fail, again and again.

I know I need blood. The glass of red liquid taunts me from where Cage had set it, but that's not the kind of blood I need.

I need our Sigil's blood, which means I need to find her body, not just her spirit within a world of dreams.

My lengthy fangs ache, and my entire body screams to finish what we started days ago. The legend of the Sigil speaks of a perfect mate, one who fulfills every need and is just as dependent on her Strigoi as her Strigoi are on her.

Yet, she has avoided us.

Avoided *me*.

"We need to know if there are more Strigoi in this dimension," I say as I glance up at Cage. His blond hair hangs loosely around his shoulders and glimmers with health offered by the blood he forced down. But his eyes show hunger within. The soft red glow overtakes his quiet blue irises as he struggles with the perpetual sensation of hearing our Sigil's call.

It's too faint to make out much, but I know she's calling for the other entity again.

Cain.

My lover rests a hand on my shoulder, and his fingers are cold to the touch. "Our meeting with the Queen is set for tomorrow. We can ask her our questions about this *Cain* then."

It feels different to know that he's just as real as Scarlett is.

None of it had been a dream. She had really been calling us, and I suspect Cain had allowed it.

Maybe he'd had a hand in it.

"Or you can ask them now," says a voice with a British lilt that has me launching to my feet.

The glass of blood shatters and splashes its contents across the white marble floor. A tiny river glittering with shards flows toward a tall man leaning against the doorway.

I hadn't even heard him come in.

And hadn't the door been locked?

The air around him fluctuates and moves as if he's walking through water. It's the first time I've seen dreams literally cling to a living creature. He drips with them, his entire body obscured by splashes of red and sticky tendrils of shadow.

A larger beast lingers over him almost like a separate entity, but it moves when he moves and watches me with the same intensity.

The dark-haired stranger steps inside—uninvited—and the faint aroma of peaches makes my nostrils flare. It's the first pleasant scent I've tasted on the air since...

Since her.

Why does he smell like her?

"Who are you?" Cage asks. Claws extend from his fingertips, and the red in his eyes glows brighter. He's drawing on strength that he should be conserving, but I don't chide him for it in front of the stranger.

I already know who he is.

"Cain," I say, but I don't share the snarl and contempt dripping from Cage.

He's in his human form, but I can see the monster lurking beneath.

I understand why our Sigil was seeking out this beast now. He's a dream creature, like us.

But he's also something *more*. He's an anchor in a dimension that has a dream plane so massive that it is its own world entirely.

This is why we couldn't find our Sigil. This is why she needed him.

This is why *we* need him.

Cage's eyes widen as he glances at me and then back at the Elite City King. "Do you know where our Sigil is?" he asks.

Cain raises a dark brow. "Sigil? You mean Scarlett?" His tongue flicks out to wet his lip as he adjusts his cuff link. "I saw what you two did to her." He eyes me, then grins. "Especially you, with the large fangs. You could have at least learned her name before tasting what's mine."

I don't correct him that I did already know her name.

To anyone else, his words would sound like a threat, but there's a kinship in his eyes.

He's testing me.

"What's ours," I say.

Cain's grin grows. "Yes, ours." The air shifts as he moves again. He approaches me until he comes within reach. He doesn't seem to care that he's walking through the spilled blood as his shoes crunch over the broken glass.

With the kind of power and energy radiating from him, I imagine he's had his share of bloodshed on his feet.

"We can talk more about this mateship arrangement queen when we find her. Scarlett is in the Dream Realm, calling for me, but I can't go to her. Not without your help." He unfurls his palms and holds out his hands, one to me and one to Cage. "You clearly drink blood for your sustenance, so I suspect mine will top you off. And Helia tells me you are dreamwalkers. So... let's go for a *walk*."

Cage and I look at one another. We've been together long enough to have conversations without words.

Cage's chin dips in a light nod. He's willing to take a risk that this King can lead us to our Sigil.

To Scarlett.

Kneeling at Cain's side, I run my fingers over his palm and turn his hand to the side to expose his wrist. Thick veins throb in invitation, and my fangs ache.

I feed on mortals, but that's because mortals are the ones who are most connected to the world of dreams. Creativity and ambition are practically inscribed in their DNA.

This beast... he is a master of dreams.

When I sink my canines into his skin, the burst of power that burns my throat makes me groan. I latch on and take a long pull, drawing the life force into my mouth.

So fucking good.

Cage does the same, and I sense his presence in a trio of power.

Something snaps the moment we're all together. Cain throws his head back, and an inhuman growl rumbles through the room.

The shattered glass seems to duplicate and expand over the floor until we're standing on a broken mirror.

I look down at my bloodthirsty reflection, only to feel the world spin and change.

And then we're in the Dream Realm.

And falling into a place of blood, of tears, and of endless suffering.

This must not be how portal travel is supposed to work in the Dream Realm, because Cain growls a single word.

"Fuck."

# CHAPTER 35

# SABRE

THE EUPHORIC DRUG of power is gone in an instant. I feel like I'm falling, but my feet are securely on the ground. Familiar marble with silver veins stretches through a massive dais.

*What the fuck is this?* I wonder as I glance around my father's throne room.

I'm definitely not in Queen Helia's guest suite anymore.

Instead, I'm right back where I started. There's no audience or subjects in the area as my father sits by himself, making him look like a lonely specter with only his four guards standing sentry at the doorway.

What stands out to me is the beacon of power lying at my father's feet. It reminds me of a blood diamond, but it shines with energy that radiates from within. Gold flecks spark around it, promising a nectar of possibilities, should I pick it up.

But something is off about this place. The walls waver, and there's a hint of other places that occasionally overlay the walls and the floors. I spot a flicker of trees unique to the other world, as well as flashes of the Elite City.

My father, too, shifts and changes as if he's a...

Dream.

*Maybe this isn't real.*

I'm still in the Dream Realm, but everything is off. It's as if my memories have merged with Cain's power to show me what he wants me to see.

*Why would Cain show me this?*

Cain doesn't know me, but I can feel his power prodding me and searching for something.

If I'm worthy as a mate, perhaps?

*If so, that makes this a test.*

The beacon of power at my phantom-father's feet seems very real, though. I don't know if it's from Cain or something else, but I inherently know that if I touch it, I'll be given more power than I could possibly imagine. If I one day find my way back to my world, every problem I ever had in the Strigoi Kingdom would vanish.

I could do whatever the fuck I wanted.

*Maybe this is the power of our Sigil.*

Maybe she doesn't like this test that Cain is giving me, so she's offering me an out. If I want it.

*Or maybe she's testing me, too.*

As I lean in to get a better look at the dreamlike artifact, my father speaks, startling me.

"You can go," he says. At first, I think he's talking to me, but then I hear the Strigoi guards retreating, leaving us alone.

My father hangs his head when they leave. He sinks into his throne with his head in his hands, looking utterly defeated.

Not a look I'm accustomed to seeing on King Nos.

There's a beacon of power, right there, at his feet. Can he not see it?

"Father," I say as I approach the throne.

My father's head shoots up, his long, shaggy hair in

wild dark tufts that stick out from his crown. He looks like a Strigoi who has forgotten how to sleep.

How to dream.

"Sebastian," he says quietly, using my full name when he damn well knows I prefer "Sabre." I don't understand the disbelief in his tone. "Are you really here?"

"Are you?" I counter.

Ignoring my question, my father asks, "Are you a ghost?"

I have already decided that my father is the ghost here, but dreams can blend reality and memory. If this is a test, I need to play along.

"Don't insult me," I tell him. "This isn't the Netherworld Kingdom. If I die, my soul had better be recycled for our Sigil, not left to waste away as a bodiless corpse for a Death Fae to feed on."

My father chuckles, sending long tendrils of hair puffing over his lips. The wild red in his eyes flickers as a result of the dying light of a fading world.

A world I have already decided to leave behind. The gift at my father's feet won't fix the sickness that lies within its people, even if it is real. Even if I did somehow find a way back, there's no point.

This is my home now.

"As much as I wish it to be otherwise, our kind will never see a true Sigil again," he says with defeat. "I've tried, my son. I've tried and failed. That's why you left me, isn't it?"

A faint scream rends the air, making me stiffen. I walk to the nearest window and look outside. All I can see is the corrupted blood fields, but I know that scream. It's one I had once denied.

Never again will I deny my destiny.

My Sigil is calling for me. I can't stay here for long. I will return to her and embrace Cain because that's what my Sigil wants me to do.

I will respect every choice she makes at any cost. She isn't just a power source to me.

She's life itself.

"You can't *make* a Sigil, Father," I say as I slowly turn back to him. I wish he were real. I wish I could tell him a truth that he has always denied, so this little role-playing game will have to do. "You have to be worthy of one, and then she will appear."

That's the key we've been missing all this time. That's why my kingdom hasn't seen a Sigil in generations.

I can't hope to say that I'm worthy of my Sigil, but I will do my best to be. It might only be the circumstances of her existence that she called Cage and me to her side.

Cage and I are Strigoi royals. We're powerful enough in our own right to be Kings—but neither of us has ever wanted a throne.

If Cain wants to rule his world, I have no qualms about that. Scarlett is all I want.

"Why didn't you come home?" he asks.

It's a good question. I had a chance to return before the portal closed. I didn't.

"Because of her," I say simply.

His red eyes flash as they widen. "Her? Meaning... you found a Sigil?" He shoots to his feet as his fangs grow and sharp, twisted claws emerge from his fingertips. "I'm the King. You'll give her to me. You'll—"

Stepping onto the power source, I feel it shatter under my boot as I shove my claws into his chest.

Fuck power. Fuck my memories. Fuck *this*.

I wait for the sound of my father's death, but none comes.

Instead, I look down only to see my claws have harmlessly passed right through him. But the power source that had piqued my interest is now gone.

Backing away, I glower as I allow the dreamy fog to overtake my senses.

It seems the test is over.

King Nos stares at me, disbelief and rage burning in his eyes because his son tried to kill him. I imagine that's how he would respond, if this were real.

I have been *his* power source for so long that I know the wound would have been fatal. I had just been too much of a coward to do what needed to be done.

It doesn't matter. Now I know I don't need to kill King Nos. I can see the slow death in his eyes.

He'll never be worthy of a Sigil.

He'll die soon enough. And if the Strigoi don't get their shit together, they'll die with him.

My Sigil is life.

This place is death.

*I choose life.*

"Goodbye, Father," I say as he darkens and fades.

"Sebastian," he growls with pure venom dripping from his fangs. "You cannot leave me like this. You do not get to abandon your duty, your—Sebastian!"

I close my eyes, unable to hear him anymore as the sense of torment and dreams washes over me.

*Goodbye, Father.*

*May you die alone.*

## CHAPTER 36

## CAGE

*I KNEW NOT to trust that asshole,* I think as I glower at the training yard undoubtedly unique to the Van Drakken house.

My house.

My brother seems to teleport from one location to the next, using his phasing ability that makes him one of the best assassins in the kingdom as he practices tossing daggers.

It's cheating, of course. Strigoi can't teleport, but the very rare ability to briefly step into the dream plane and exit a few feet away is a skill that some do possess and has given him an edge.

He might be a skilled assassin, but he hasn't spotted me yet. A smirk lights my face. I've always been the better brother when it comes to the art of stealth.

I haven't seen Xan for a while, but a pang of worry hits my chest as I remember I can't stay.

My Sigil is waiting for me.

*Did Cain send Sabre and me back home?*

I frown as I wonder about that possibility. After tasting

361

Cain's blood, I recognize his power. It's immense, terrifying, and unparalleled in its strength and scope.

But I doubt even Cain has the ability to traverse realms. Plus, I can *feel* him.

He's with me. His soul is a kindred spirit, and he hungers for our Sigil. Our desires are equally matched in that regard.

I've taken so many lives, only to never know what it was like to live my own.

I thought Sabre had been an indulgence at first. But he was a purpose, one who led to our Sigil and a future where I could finally use my skills for a cause worth fighting for.

*I will make all of her enemies bleed.*

When my brother turns and looks directly through me, I expect him to frown or ask me where I've been.

He does neither of those things. He looks right past me.

Then he walks *through* me.

*I'm not actually here,* I realize.

My brother might not really be here, either.

Everything is a little off. The moonlight shines down with prisms and flickers. The shadows appear and disappear, only to change shape and distort the longer I look at them.

*I'm still in the Dream Realm,* I decide.

"Xan," I say, needing to talk to him. Maybe my brother is a piece of this dream world, or maybe he's really here. Regardless, I will take advantage of the ability to talk to him.

He ignores me as he moves to the next section of the training grounds, one designed to train for long-distance kills in crowded areas.

I stop in my tracks when I notice something very out of place.

A golden dagger rests on the table. It gleams with

intense power, promising abundance, and infinite energy to any who wields it.

*Not unlike a Sigil,* I realize.

Reaching out to claim it, I stop just before my fingers graze the hilt engraved with symbols.

*I've seen those before.*

They are also engraved on temples to Morpheus.

Retracting my fingers, I ponder what that might mean as I glance around for any other artifacts in the training yard.

There are various targets, some of them small, some of them behind obstacles, making them more difficult to hit from the established vantage points. There's nothing else out of the ordinary.

Still seemingly unaware of my presence—or, apparently, the powerful weapon on the table just a few feet away—my brother snatches up four throwing daggers and angles them between each finger.

He phases to the first vantage point and flicks a blade, sending it directly into the target.

"Xanthus," I try again, using his entire first name.

There's something terribly wrong here. I know that dagger could be the answer to all of the Van Drakken problems. Our clan would kill King Nos with ease, and any who opposed us, and rise as the rightful rulers of this kingdom.

I could be its King.

Lucifer would respect the power shift. We manage our own kingdoms our own way. This is how the Strigoi have always done things.

I never desired to become a King, but the flicker of a chance to fix this rotten kingdom interests me.

I like the idea of rooting out corruption and mending what has been broken.

But it won't mean much without Sabre. Without Scarlett. And Cain knows her and her world better than we ever will. We need him—and he needs us, too.

I feel a connection to all of them that seems insurmountable. Whatever problems need fixing, I can do that in my new world where the dreams are richer and the nightmares darker—the blood *thicker*.

And there is no replacing Scarlett. She is one of a kind.

She is a star that burns brighter than any I have ever seen, and I want to be near her just to bask in her brilliance.

I glance at the weapon again, knowing it would be strong enough to cut through anything—even mate-bonds. I could start over.

*Do I want to?*

Hell no.

"Xanthus!" I shout.

My brother still doesn't hear me. He phases between the next two locations and flicks two more blades, each one finding its home.

The last one is the most challenging. He swoops back his cowl, and messy blond hair gets into his eyes. His irises fill with blood as he draws on more power than he should. He readies his last blade that teeters on his pinkie. He needs to practice launching all four without changing hands if he wants to achieve his next mark.

One that will take out four of the top Sanguinis guards who protect King Nos.

Growling, I walk right in front of him and shout into his face. "Brother!"

He curses when he falters on his throw, nicking his finger as the blade clatters noisily to the ground.

"Fucking hell, Cage. Where did you come from?" he says as he takes a cloth from his coat and wraps it around his hand. His wound will take longer to heal than that of most

Strigoi, mainly because he is low on reserves. I'm no stranger to that issue.

But the wound flickers like a distorted image, then vanishes.

*Maybe Xan isn't really here.*

"I don't know," I admit, answering his question. "But I have an idea. Can you pick up that dagger over there?" I ask while pointing at the table.

He looks at the gleaming beacon of power and then back at me. "A training dagger?"

I frown. "What? No. The gold one that's all lit up. Don't you see it?"

He raises one brow at me. "Did you drink Siren blood again? Brother. I know they're pretty, but for Morpheus's sake—"

Shooting up a hand, I sigh. "Never mind. If you can't see it, then it's not meant for you." It's meant for me, but I know if I take it, something within me will break under the power it offers. There's an innate assurance beating against my chest that tells me this is a choice I have to make.

Scarlett, or ultimate power with no strings attached.

*I choose Scarlett.*

My brother stares at me for a moment, all the red leaving his eyes until only the striking blue irises remain. They're lighter than mine, giving him a startling effect when looking at him straight on. "Banshee blood?" he guesses with a wrinkled nose.

That earns a chuckle from me. "You're never going to let me live that one down, are you?" Kneeling, I swoop to pick up the dagger he dropped, but my fingers pass right through it.

No, not fingers.

Claws.

*I'm still in the Dream Realm.*

My brother's humor vanishes as he frowns down at me. "Did you have a run-in with a Death Fae or something? What's going on, Cage?" he asks as he picks up the blade and cleans it.

He starts to retrieve the other daggers that are buried in their targets when I don't answer right away. I'm not so convinced he's real anymore.

He wrenches a dagger free from the target, then gathers the rest until he reaches the weapons table and starts cleaning them. The glowing dagger is fading as if it knows I've made my choice.

I don't have much more time.

Sighing, I approach him and reach out to rest a hand on his shoulder, then think better of it, given that he's not even real.

My real brother is in another dimension, and he's the only soul on the other side I care about. "I might not see you again, Xan," I begin.

He turns and gives me a raised brow. "Are you trying to tell me you're dead? You could haunt much better entertainment than me." He whistles. "Like those Hell Fae Brides. They're vicious and have killer bodies. Go haunt one of them."

"I'm serious, Xan," I press. "Just... promise me you won't go after King Nos." Without Sabre, it's a matter of time for the old Strigoi anyway. "Live your life. Do something else, start a new clan, go mortal side and hunt pussy—I don't care. Just don't let the Van Drakken power struggle be your life."

My brother stops cleaning and points one of the daggers at me. "Are you asking me to disavow the one thing I've trained all my life to do? Fuck, Cage. I can't agree to that. I'll be disowned."

"At least you won't be dead," I counter.

He tilts his head in concession, sending blond tendrils over his eyes. He swipes them away. "True."

The world darkens as the dagger completely vanishes. "Promise me," I say. "Please."

He blinks at me a few times. He must hear the urgency in my voice, because he backs off when I know he would have argued with me. "I will if you answer one question honestly for me."

"Anything," I say.

"I knew you'd always run off with the Sanguinis Prince one day. Is it everything you had hoped it would be? Did you find whatever it is you were looking for?"

A wicked smile lifts my lips as I think of Scarlett between me and Sabre. With Cain in the mix, I have an interesting mate dynamic ahead of me. "Yes," I answer.

My brother nods, then begins to fade. "Then you protect that, Cage. You fight with everything you have to make sure no one takes it from you."

"I will," I vow as a roar enters my ears, giving me the sensation that I've been swept underwater.

I've made my choice.

Scarlett is mine.

And I'll burn the world to keep her safe.

# CHAPTER 37

# SCARLETT

"Cain!" I cry as I spot him finally appearing in the blood-red sky.

I've been stuck in this place for hours. It made no sense why I couldn't find him. It seemed like every time I closed my eyes, my figment was there waiting for me.

I should have known something was wrong.

My heart races, and I lift onto my toes as though I can reach him if I just try hard enough.

The first time I met him in the real word, he caught me when I lifted in a dance.

Now, I wish I could catch him.

He's not alone. Two others fall with him as they plummet through the clouds. Dark shadows streak above them as they twist and writhe, making me wonder if they are in pain.

The world cracks with Cain's roar, and the rivers of blood surge as if ready to gobble them up.

My chest tightens as they strike the surface of a river swollen with blood. The impact shatters the world as if everything has fractured into glass. Very real shards splinter out in all directions, and one of them drives right into me.

My reality splits into multiple possibilities. The shard engulfs me for a moment, showing me what my life could have been like had things been different.

In an alternate world, I'm still lying in my bed. Edward's mother never came to have me humiliated, and I wasn't found wanting.

My dream beasts aren't lost in this world. They aren't plummeting from the sky.

They're with me, revealing the truth to me in a much more pleasant way.

I watch from inside my own body like a spectator as this reality's emotions play out. Only a glimmer of broken glass informs me that it's simply a projection of what could have been.

*"Get off me!" I scream, not because it doesn't feel good what the one with an unnaturally long tongue is doing, but because this was supposed to be a dream.*

*"Not a chance, Sigil."*

*Why do they always call me that?*

*I move to push the one between my legs away, but I realize I can't. My muscles don't comply.*

*Red eyes glow at my right. Eyes that belong to a face crafted by a master sculptor, but his fangs dripping with my blood suggest he's anything but a benevolent being. "You're far too delicious to release now. Plus, you invited us into your mind. You told us to play."*

*Yes, but that had been when this was all a fanciful dream full of orgasms and forbidden desires.*

*I open my mouth to say as much, but the creature on my right groans at the sight. "Yes, open that mouth wide, our Sigil. We're starved for more of your screams."*

The shard that had broken from this place finally dissipates and leaves me wavering and dizzy. My vision blinks in and out of reflective realities, the one I had just experienced fading away like the dream it is.

*They were real,* I realize with certainty.

This reality might have played out differently, but the figments in my dreams aren't figments at all.

*They're dream monsters.*

Panic seizes my chest as I watch the river sheen without a single fracture.

"Cain! Sabre! Cage!" I cry all their names now, knowing there's only one reason the connection I felt with them could have been so powerful.

They're my mates.

Or at least, they were supposed to be. We didn't get to finish what was started.

I drive my hands into the river of blood and ignore the shards that drag up my fingers, protesting the disturbance that ripples out from where I broke through. My extremities go numb as pain jolts up to my elbows.

It feels right to insert my hands into the place where my mates fell. I don't know how it can help them, but it doesn't matter. I simply need them to know I'm here.

"Come back to me," I urge them. I don't think they can hear me, but I utter that prayer in my mind with such fervor that if Cain really is the God he pretends to be, he won't be able to ignore it.

I would have stayed there until I froze over, but light spills into my nightmare and drags me out by the ankles. I scream as I realize that I really am being yanked around as my eyes fling open. One of the Rinholds' manservants pulls me into the light as Duchess Rinhold scowls down at me.

"You're a lucky whore," she tells me as she peers down her perfect nose. Her eyes narrow as I try to fathom what about any of this could be lucky. "I've managed to arrange an old-style marriage to take place. Tonight. No one will challenge the validity of the union if they see it with their own eyes."

I stare at her as another servant pops open a vial and pours the contents onto me. The grime of the dungeon seems to evaporate as new layers of fancy silks snake over my cleansed skin. The layers are revealing and shift and move with me, leaving gaps of skin in view.

"See it with their own eyes?" I echo, not sure if I understand what she means by that. Wouldn't any marriage ceremony be an affair with Elite guests in attendance? I didn't imagine that the Earl would have a wedding with only private members invited. The Rinholds prefer to flaunt their wealth, and festive occasions are a wonderful place to do that.

Although, it doesn't really matter. "I won't agree to the union. If you choose to invite other families, you're only going to humiliate yourselves. The courtship is over. The deal is off."

I get a choice in this. A courtship is a mutual affair.

Or it's supposed to be.

"The contract is already dissolved," she says, nodding to my body.

I look down and realize what she means.

The mark I had cherished above my navel is now gone. The smooth skin is clearly visible through the tight strips of silk winding over my torso where there should be a jagged mark.

Panic seizes my lungs.

I don't know if that indicates my mates are dead or lost. I did just witness them crash into a river in my dreams, and that river sealed over.

*No,* I decide. *They can't be lost.*

One of the servants crowding the small cell offers

Duchess Rinhold a tray of vials, and she selects a number of them, acting as if the matter is closed.

The courtship might be over, but now the Rinholds are in control.

"You still want me to marry your son?" I ask, bewildered.

"You *will* marry my son," she clarifies. "The courtship was your chance to do this the easy way. You could have been one of us. Now, you'll be what we need you to be, and nothing more than that."

What could the Rinholds possibly need from me?

One of the servants produces a knife, and my eyes go wide.

"Do it," the Duchess barks when he hesitates.

The male kneels and positions the blade above my navel. "Apologies, my lady. Please, don't move," he says. I bite my lip as he carves a neat line.

Then he goes to my back, and I panic.

They're trying to re-create my marks to make it look as if the courtship is still active. "Stop it!" I screech as I use my nails, clawing and catching someone's arm. I'm rewarded with a grunt of pain before a shin comes down on my wrist, making me cry out.

A slash rakes over my spine, making spots glitter over my vision.

Then another.

Then more until I think I might pass out. I pant through the pain as the weight is finally lifted from my wrist.

After the servant uses the vials on me, I realize one is to remove the bruises and to clean the blood of the new wounds, making them heal just enough not to look so fresh. Another is to wind decorations through my hair with pins and chains, and the third doesn't seem to do anything. Maybe it's some sort of perfume I can't smell. A pheromone

one, perhaps. Those are popular at weddings. Although, I don't know what for, given that I have no intention of going through with it.

"You will *behave*," the Duchess declares with finality. "You will do as you're told, and you'll submit. That is your role now. You will only speak when you're spoken to, and in the old-style format of matrimony, your verbal agreement isn't required."

I open my mouth to tell her to fuck off.

But when my lips part, no sound comes out.

The third vial wasn't a perfume.

It was a silencing potion.

I'm dragged out of my cell, unable to make a single sound as I fight with every ounce of strength in my body.

*I'm going to be forced to marry Edward,* I realize with horror as they take me down the halls, and hot, angry tears stream down my face.

I have a feeling if the Rinholds win, my mates will be lost to me forever.

Fuck if I'm going to let that happen.

*I won't marry him.*

*I have three dream monsters trying to break through the surface. And when they do... they're going to kill all of you.*

# CHAPTER 38

# SCARLETT

My brows furrow as I'm brought to a more intimate setting than I had been anticipating. Open windows allow in a soft breeze. Sheer drapes surround a central area, billowing on the gentle wind, while chairs surround it on all sides.

I'm expecting for the soft barrier to hold a platform inside, given that it's big enough for two people.

Instead, there's a bed.

A knot forms in my stomach as I scan the Elite families who have already taken their seats.

Each row has another sheer drape. It might obscure their view, but they can clearly still see everything.

I have a sinking realization of what was intended with an "old style" wedding ceremony.

"*No,*" I try to say as I pull back against the two manservants escorting me in.

The Duchess pinches the back of my arm so hard that tears sting my eyes. I can't cry out, ask for help, or even make a sound, thanks to the magic vial that had been used on me.

Duchess Rinhold leans into my ear and snarls a threat

that makes me go still. "Your mother has all the anti-aging vials she needs. You didn't think I wouldn't find out, did you? Edward was trying to woo you, girl. Well, no need for that anymore. But we will maintain relations with your family, mostly because they are useful to us. However, if you choose to make a scene, we'll have no need for them. So behave, or your mother will die, and you can live with that for the rest of your unfortunately long life."

She releases me, and I stare at the bed in the middle of the room.

Edward is standing on the other side. He's wearing a handsome marriage suit, and his hands are clasped in front of him as he waits for them to bring me.

Even if I were willing to cooperate, I'm given little opportunity. My toes barely touch the ground as I'm lifted by my elbows and escorted through the rows.

Desperation clenches my stomach in an iron grip as I scan the rows of faces for anyone familiar. I spot a few I had met at the fête, but no one whom I could call a friend.

I don't know why my spirits lift with hope when I locate my brother. My father isn't here, nor is my mother. I'm not sure if that upsets me or if I'm glad they didn't get an invitation. It would have been more powerful to lord my mother over me if that was Duchess Rinhold's threat, but I realize why when my brother's gaze meets mine.

They wouldn't sit by and allow this.

My brother, though—he seems to have been preparing me for this day my whole life.

He doesn't have to wear a mask anymore. I can see exactly who and what he is, and he's not hiding it. There's cold calculation in his eyes, and the joyless smirk playing on his lips demonstrates his amusement by this situation.

I don't deserve this.

*"Sabre. Cage. Help Cain. Bring him to me. Stop this, please!"*

I would have preferred to say my prayer aloud, but a mental one will have to do.

Still, when I'm brought to the central circle of sheer drapes, servants tug on ropes to open them, revealing Edward to me without the visual barrier of the drapes in my way.

On the other side of a large bed that has no pillows or sheets.

I scan the area for a priest or some sort of authority figure who would dare to sanction this sort of "ceremony."

There's no one. Edward himself chooses to address the room, instead, as if he's the sole figure of authority required.

"Thank you, everyone, for coming here on such short notice," he says as he lifts his voice and takes his time acknowledging various families. His hands are still clasped in such a way that no one can see his palm, and he keeps them that way as he speaks.

*The coward couldn't even cut his hand to make it look real like they did to me.*

His tongue flicks out to wet his lips before he continues. "Lady Scarlett and I are as concerned as all of you are by recent events. Our Lord Cain has gone missing, and there have been monster violations through various territories, including areas in the Elite City."

I frown as I wonder what he could be talking about. While I have been indisposed, I know of no such violations.

Cain's absence, though, can be blamed on me.

"Because of this," Edward continues, turning his blue eyes on me, "we have chosen the old way to conclude our courtship. The contract was written in Cain's blood, after all. We don't know what would happen to the future mother of my child or the Rinhold heir should anything befall our great King."

My stomach turns sour at his words.

*I will never carry a child with your blood,* I vow.

But I've come to the sickening realization of what kind of marriage ceremony this is. Edward lowers his chin with finality. "You all bear witness to our union. May it be blessed by Cain."

My laughter at that statement would have echoed through the quiet of the room had I not been spelled into silence.

Every Elite member holds their breath as the silks around my body are undone. I know why the style was so revealing now. I wasn't meant to wear it for very long. I'm too numb to fight, not when I know that Duchess Rinhold will use my mother against me if I don't comply.

But I can't allow this to happen, either. Can I?

*Fuck. What do I do?*

The servant tugs the ropes again until the drapes close around us, leaving only Edward and me in the circle of sheer fabric.

He peels off his jacket as he watches me. "Come, my bride," he says as he indicates the bed.

A shiver of defiance runs up my spine. Edward seems to have prepared for this sort of reaction, because he doesn't appear perturbed. Instead, he pulls his shirt over his head, mussing up his hair before he works on the band of his pants.

His body is beautiful, but his soul is filthy, ugly, and wicked. His skin seems broken, as if he's made of shards of glass. I can now see through a disguise that I hadn't even realized was there.

Earl Rinhold's mask was the most perfect mask of all. I

might never have seen through it had I not met all three of my monster mates.

But I can see who he is now. He doesn't care about me. The truth in his eyes says horrible things. They roll through my mind even though I don't want to know. I don't want to hear what this man wants to do to me.

*Submit to me.*

*Break for me.*

*Bleed for me... my little plaything.*

He reaches me on the side of the bed, and he rests his fingers on my hips. I try not to flinch, but my body reacts to him with revulsion.

"I know you're nervous," he says in a hushed whisper, as if we're the only two people in the world. But the room is like an echo chamber. I know that everyone in the room can hear him. That's all part of his mask.

All part of the role he plays.

I shake my head and try to back away, but he has his proverbial claws in me now. He digs his fingers into my hips and holds me in place.

"I'm sorry your mother couldn't be here," he continues, making me freeze. There's a wicked gleam in his eyes that shows me the meaning he intends with those words. "There was an incident that required both the Duke and Duchess Nightingale to attend. When they return, I will personally make sure they're invited for a visit, and that they are *safe.*"

He says the last word with enough emphasis for me to understand the threat.

If I don't comply, they'll both be killed.

And I trust the Rinholds to be able to do it. It doesn't matter if I'm supposed to be Cain's mate or if I've found two other dream monsters to take my side.

They're trapped underneath a layer of glass in another

realm, and I don't know when or if they'll ever be able to find their way out.

*And even if they do... by then, my family will be dead.*

I have to play along. I don't have a choice, so I tremble as I allow Edward to guide me onto the bed.

There's a sigh from the spectators as Edward reclines me onto my back, as if this is some romantic gesture as he settles himself at my side. I press my legs together and try to cover myself with my arms.

I stare at what should be the ceiling, but it's a mirror instead. The reflection seems all wrong. The bed underneath me is black, not white.

And there are three distinct shadows lurking underneath the glass.

"I wanted you to be able to see our union for yourself," Edward explains as he drags my hair away from my neck, then presses his lips to my pulse.

My wide eyes stare back at me, full of fury and rage. Maybe I'm just seeing what I want to see. My mates aren't coming to save me, or else they would have appeared by now.

Turning my head away from Edward so I don't try to do something violent, like bite him until he bleeds, I find my brother in the crowd. We can easily see each other through the sheer drapes that offer no privacy at all.

He grins at me, then mouths the words I can already see behind his eyes.

*"Spread your legs, whore."*

My jaw aches from how hard I'm clenching it. Edward begins to kiss my neck, harder this time, as he runs his hand down to my elbow. He continues, then gathers my wrists in his grip and gently pulls my arms over my head.

"Don't look at them; look at us," he instructs, as if that's comforting advice.

I do it, only so I don't have to look at my brother while this happens.

*This... is happening, though.*

*It can't happen. Can it?*

Those three shadows are still there, waiting for me to speak them into existence.

My breath comes in short pants as Edward pushes his other hand between my thighs, then forces them open.

*No.*

His weight presses on my thigh, pinning it down as he settles between my legs.

I stare at the mirrored ceiling and will it to shatter. I will it to break into a thousand pieces and to fall onto us, to make Edward bleed for this.

To my shock, a fracture appears straight down the center, splitting the reflection of my face in two as red eyes peer behind it, staring back at me.

*I'm not imagining them,* I realize. *They can use the mirror.*

Yes, that makes sense. Broken mirrors were how I moved around in that alternate plane while my body had been trapped in sleep. Now I'm grateful for that practice, because I can use it to guide my beasts to do the same.

Mirrors are what Cain's eyes look like in the dream world.

*As do mine.*

I'm like him. Or maybe, I can *channel* his gifts, if I try hard enough.

Concentrating, I try to ignore as Edward palms my breast and presses his lips to my skin. His length nudges at my entrance, and I know he can't finish this. He can't unite our bodies when it would destroy my soul in the process.

*I'd rather die.*

Drawing in a lungful of air, I try to scream. Edward

chuckles against my mouth and whispers his cruel words, this time ones that no one can hear.

"Don't worry, Scarlett. There will be plenty of nights for you to scream for me."

I might not have made a sound in the real world, but my scream echoes through the dream plane. The mirror above us shatters, making Edward flinch to look up at it.

But he's too late.

Because three beasts come pouring out of it.

A manic grin stretches across my face as everything goes dark.

*My nightmares are here.*

## CHAPTER 39

## CAIN

I CAN'T REMEMBER the last time I allowed my beast full and complete control, not in hundreds of years. Whenever my beast had come out before, it had been against my wishes and a battle of souls between the rational and darker parts of myself.

But when I see my mate pinned and naked beneath Earl Rinhold, I throw off the shackles and let him rip free.

*Kill them all.*

He eagerly agrees as our power locks all the doors, ensuring that no one gets in.

Or out.

Our mate has brought us through the depths of the Dream Realm and revitalized us with her sweet, decadent prayers. I intend to answer them with bloodshed in her name.

Cage and Sabre are called Strigoi in their world. I learned more about them than would ever have been possible with words while we had fallen in the Dream Realm.

387

I will take time to learn both of them in the real one, too, when our mate is safe.

First, we have useless humans to kill, and my beast needs to feed.

Starting with Earl Rinhold.

He screams when I rip him off of her. His body tumbles through gauzy drapes that had parted him from a sizable crowd.

I'd been around during the early years when this sort of marital ceremony had been popular. It was distasteful then, and it's distasteful now.

Especially given that the bride in question was coerced. That's precisely why I abolished the practice in the first place. I don't like to interfere with my Elites, unless they stray too far and require correction.

This is one of those times, once again.

Sabre goes for the Earl, but I hold up a bloodied hand. My claws had dug into the mortal's side, and the graze might have been fatal had I not held back.

But my beast and I share our intentions. Neither of us wants the Earl's death to be a quick one.

He scrambles backward as I march toward him, towering over the insignificant human who dared to paint himself with my blood.

Now, I will return the favor.

"Cain, wait. You can't kill me," he says as screams rip through the air.

I know that the other two, the Strigoi, are feeding. They will take their fill before they comfort Scarlett. For now, they're killing everyone around her who dared to participate in this insanity.

The most efficient way to keep her safe is to make sure no one who was in compliance with this is left breathing.

"Why's that?" I ask as I grab him by his ankle and drag

him toward me. My claws sink into his flesh with the motion, making him grunt in pain.

I don't just want grunts, though. I want his screams.

"We control over half the Offerings in the Magic Sector," he babbles. I imagine it's a rehearsed defense should I ever decide the Rinholds aren't worth keeping alive. "If I die, you won't know how to continue the programs. You will be decades behind without us. Centuries!"

I've heard it all before. Elites tend to be arrogant, and they get ahead of themselves.

They think that monsters need them. We don't. It is a more efficient way of running things, and effective, at times, but this is all an experiment to see what'll reap the best rewards.

"Scarlett is a compatible mate," I growl.

It's difficult to talk in this form, but my beast wants me to make Edward fear us. He wants to watch the light bleed from his eyes when he knows he's lost.

I tilt my head as I drag my claw over my massive tongue, tasting Edward's blood. "But you knew that."

His chest rises and falls on his deep, panicked breaths. He knows he's going to die, but I'm waiting for him to give me what I want.

A confession.

I need to know how this happened so that Scarlett is never threatened again.

"It's because of the work at Vulcan Village," he sputters. "The Vulcan family stole magic tonics and genetic material from the Rinhold labs. It's the only reason their crop was so advanced."

I raise a brow as I lean in, casting a shadow over the human. "You allowed them to steal from you?"

His throat bobs on a swallow. "We needed the studies

to be tested. We couldn't risk..." When his words drift off, I snarl until he continues. "My father found a way to harness dreams inside a human soul."

I go silent as I digest what this pitiful human's line had discovered.

Glancing up, I find Duke Rinhold reduced to a maimed carcass seeping fresh blood onto the floor. His blank gaze stares at us, and I know I won't be pulling any truths from him.

So I turn back to his son. "Go on," I say.

He sits up as the carrot of hope is dangled in front of him. How quaint. He thinks I'm interested because I want to use what he's learned.

No. I want to hear how to destroy this research before it's used against me.

"The process required death on a large scale to successfully test. So... we set them up."

Anger stirs in my chest, but I settle my beast with a promise of bloodshed very soon.

I am angry, too. The destruction of Vulcan Village was my doing.

This went so much deeper than I could ever have realized. I had been manipulated from the very beginning.

"That's blasphemy," I snarl. "You sent thousands of people to their deaths, and an entire family, all for an experiment."

"One that worked," he says, growing bolder as he dares to lean in. My face is twice the size of his while I'm in this form. I quell the urge to bite his head clean off. "Scarlett is what she is today because of that loss of life. She sucked it all in, and it changed her. My family has been watching her for years, looking for the right opportunity to bring her into our fold. With her genetics, we were going to start the perfect breeding program. One with humans who can harness the power of dreams. Imagine the possibilities, Cain. Imagine if you find others like you out there because you have something that interests them. They could just be hiding. Don't you want more alliances? Isn't that why you do all this?"

I glance to find Sabre and Cage taking their time killing their prey. They're little more than a blur of shadows painting the room with blood.

Scarlett watches them with a sense of fascination. The blood that coats her looks like a red dress, one that makes me want to lick it off. She doesn't try to hide herself now. In fact, her spine is straight with pride as she finally slinks off the bed and picks up one of the shards of the broken mirror.

And heads toward her brother, who limps across the floor on a broken foot.

*Good girl,* I think.

"Now, everything I do is for her," I say, speaking to the pitiful excuse for a human being at my feet.

"There can be more like her," he promises. "That was always the plan, Lord Cain. It can still *be* the plan. If you give her to me, you will have our firstborn. You can even—"

I don't allow him to finish that sentence. I shove my hand into his mouth and wrap my claws around his tongue.

And yank.

A garbled scream rips from his throat as I tear it from his mouth. Blood gushes down his chin and chest as I toss his rendered tongue onto the floor.

"You won't be needing that any longer," I say dismissively as I watch him bleed.

He doubles over and screams again, but I really have no need of him anymore. He only has one more use to me now.

I clamp my claws around his head, and I allow my beast to feed.

His dark dreams pour into me and settle inside my soul.

I feast on them, devouring them as I tear them apart until they're nothing more than splintered fragments in bite-size pieces.

Edward blinks up at me, his eyes glassy with pained tears as I keep going. I take every dark dream, every subconscious thought, and everything that he hides in the deep recesses of his mind until nothing is left.

His skin pales until it turns gray. He withers before me, and finally, he's gone.

"Pleassse don't do that again," Sabre says from my side. He's covered in blood, and now he's in his Strigoi form, not his human one. His unnaturally long tongue seems to make it difficult for him to speak properly, but I can relate. Everything about me in this form is oversized, including my tongue as well.

He wrinkles his nose at the carcass as it falls over into a withered clump. Edward's bloodied mouth gapes open as his eyes stare into the distance.

"Why not? That was fun," I say.

Cage appears by my side, closer than I would have expected, given that I hadn't seen him coming. "Can't feed on the dead," he says, glancing up at me with a toothy smile full of fangs and danger, before he vanishes again.

Rolling my eyes, I turn from them and face a beautiful Scarlett now painted in her brother's blood. My massive cock instantly goes rock-hard.

"I'm done killing anyway," I say as I go to her.

My beast doesn't need bloodshed, not when our mate is naked and covered in nightmares and death.

She's the perfect depiction of an Offering.

One made just for me.

# CHAPTER 40

# SCARLETT

FEAR AND EXCITEMENT shoot through me as Figment-Cain stalks toward me.

Except, he's not a figment.

He's very, very real.

Just like in my dreams, my gaze drops to the massive cock that went hard the moment he saw me.

My fingers sting from the jagged piece of glass I had used to kill my brother. I was going to use it on Edward next, but I can see that my mates have already finished the job.

I only feel peace now that they're gone. I had expected to feel sick, or at least upset.

But seeing the way Cain looks at me... I'm only aroused. He's pleased with me. Very pleased.

Cain stops as his cock brushes my stomach and throbs against me with unrepentant need. "Give me your hand, Scarlett."

I flash my gaze up to him, mostly because I didn't expect him to be able to speak. His tongue is thick in his mouth, and my body shivers as I recall him using it on me.

Between my legs.

Now, I suspect he intends to do more than taste me. Even if my body doesn't seem to be compatible with his, I feel an innate trust in this beast that has saved me from ruin.

The glass clatters onto the ground when I unfurl my palm.

Cain has to bend down to reach me, but he lifts my hand with his massive claws, being impressively gentle. His long tongue drags over the wound caused by the jagged glass, making me shiver as he takes my blood into him.

A hum of rightness settles in my chest when he does that.

"Do you want to become my Queen, Scarlett?" he asks.

My eyes widen. "Queen?" I ask. My voice is a soft whisper after having broken through the silencing spell by whatever power I had unleashed, but Cain seems to have no problem hearing me.

He grins, showing off sharp teeth. "Yes. That's what it means to be my mate." His gaze drags over my body with appreciation. "And you will need to take as much of me as you can. Will you do that for me?"

I know that he's seeking my verbal agreement. The Strigoi had been the same way about making sure I approved of any intimacy before they engaged.

"Yes," I say without hesitation, even if I don't know how to achieve it.

Cain's cock is so large that I'm certain there's no way it'll fit.

He guides me to the bed now stained with blood. "It'll require some magic," he informs me as he waves a hand, his power over reflective surfaces dissolving any glass shards glinting on the bed so that it's safe for me.

I relax as I rest on my back. Cain seems like he wants to

drag his tongue over me and taste me everywhere, but that's how my dreams have always gone.

This time, it's real.

I spread my legs for him, sucking in a breath when he slides the head of his enormous cock over my pussy. It's so large that it stimulates every inch of me as he does it again, making my toes flinch and then curl.

I'm not sure what kind of magic I expected, but I watch with a sense of awe as he brings his wrist to his mouth and sinks his huge fangs into it. Blood drips from his arm, and he holds it out over me, coating me with it.

My skin tingles everywhere his blood touches. There's power in his blood. I have no doubt about that. My body drinks it up, and immediately I feel a change.

He wastes no time centering his massive cock at my entrance. It certainly doesn't fit.

But then, he pushes.

What didn't fit before now shoves an inch into me, making me suck in a breath as shock jolts through me.

Because it feels... good.

I had expected pain as he pushes in another inch, forcing my body to stretch around him and allow him in.

"Relax, little star. You're doing such a great job for me," he says, and each praise makes me give him a little more, just so I can hear it again.

My breath comes in short gasps as I curl my fingers into the bed, willing myself to take more of him.

Somehow, I do, and he groans as the ridge of his cock's head pushes inside. I feel like I'm going to burst at the seams.

But then he begins to move.

"Keep your eyes on me," he says when my eyelids start to flutter from the overwhelming sensation. He holds my ankles and spreads me for him, then continues to lightly thrust, each time going a little deeper.

"Cain," I say on a desperate breath when I feel like I'm going to explode. He's so big, so thick. It makes me feel so... so...

*So full.*

"Don't hold back," he says with a wicked glint to his eyes. They still represent shattered glass just like in my dreams. "If you're going to come for me, then come. And when you're ready, you're going to take Cage and Sabre next, should you desire." He thrusts a little deeper into me, making me squeak. "At the same time, preferably."

I can barely process my new mate-bond with Cain. Sabre and Cage seem like a duet of power and death. I know they're around us, feeding and able to see everything.

*Gods. Are they watching?*

"They're watching, yes," Cain confirms. His grin widens when I glance up at him with wonder. "Our bond is deepening now that we're connected, little star. I can hear your thoughts. At least, when you shout them like that."

I bite my lip as he drags one thumb over my clit, being careful to avoid nicking me with his long claw.

I lose track of sensations as he presses on the sensitive bundle of nerves.

"Cain, I'm going to..." My words drift off into euphoria as he continues pumping into me. "Can you come with me?" I ask, not sure why I'm asking it. I think I don't want to be vulnerable. I can feel Sabre and Cage watching me, waiting to see what I'll do.

"You can always have my cum," he says with a growl to his tone. "Now, come for us, little star. Don't hold back any longer."

My stomach bulges as he pushes deeper inside, forcing

his massive cock into me. I can almost see the outline of it on my abdomen as my orgasm slowly crests, then shatters.

I scream as he rolls his thumb over my clit, working me to the edge well after I had fallen off of it.

He keeps his word to not let me fall alone. His climax is soft, slow, and he pumps me full of his cum until I feel even fuller than before.

"So much," I say as I thrash my head from side to side. The aftershocks of my orgasm only grow stronger as wetness spills down my ass and soaks the bed.

"Mine," he practically purrs. The low rumble of sound is one of pleasure as he finally eases out of me, slowly, until the pressure is gone and his cum rushes out of me.

"Now," Cain says, his accent even thicker than before, "you're going to do that again on Sabre's cock while I watch him play with you. Would you like that, mate?"

A shiver runs up my spine when Cain calls me that. I thump my head onto the bed and stare up at the shattered mirror hanging above me, only to see the broken reflection of a dark creature made of nightmares stalking onto the bed.

I'm not afraid.

Excitement shoots through me as Sabre's long tongue begins to explore my skin, including my soaked entrance that is dripping with Cain's cum. He doesn't seem to care as he licks and tastes, making my body hum with pleasure.

I'm not sure how it's possible that I want more after a full-body orgasm like the one Cain's beast just gave me, but I don't even feel human anymore.

I feel... ravenous.

"I would like that... very much," I concede as Cain settles himself on the floor against one of the pillars. He's far too big for any of the chairs, even if he could find one that wasn't broken.

"Hmm," he says, the sound one of pleasure as he strokes his cock, which is still hard. His silver cum drips from the head, and he coats his shaft with it, making me shiver in response.

Sabre's voice in my ear reminds me that it's his turn now. "I might not be as large as Cain, my Sigil. But I do have a trick up my sleeve." When he eases me onto my stomach and slides his cock into me, I instantly remember what he means.

Because there's a bulb around his cock vibrating at my entrance, and one inside hits a sensitive place, the duality of pleasure almost making me come again on the spot.

"Look," he says, curling his fingers around my throat, then lifting my chin to glance up. He continues to pump into me while he directs my attention. He's rougher than Cain, which I now suspect is part of the reason Cain had taken me first. He has more control; he has to, given what he is.

Sabre thrusts in deep and makes me gasp as he holds me in place. "It looks like Cage is making a friend."

# CHAPTER 41

## CAGE

So much blood with wicked dreams in my system is making me delirious, but I'm locked in place when I see Sabre fucking our Sigil from behind.

And based on the look on her face, she's thoroughly enjoying it.

There are still threats in the room. I had been taking my time working through the wicked souls as I picked them off one by one, but now I want to make quick work of it so I can join in the proper ending to this "wedding."

In the traditional sense, it is still a wedding. Only, the bride is now being claimed by her three monster mates in front of an audience of the dead and dying.

A true Strigoi party, if I'm being honest.

I'm about to bite through a male's throat when the light leaves his eyes, confusing me.

Because I hadn't been the one to kill him. It was as if his soul had been sucked right out of his body.

Then I look up and see a familiar face. The Death Fae with silver-blue eyes and a myriad of tattoos wisping off of him as he feeds on the souls of the wicked isn't who I expected to attend the Rinhold massacre.

"What the fuck are you doing here?" I ask the Death Fae appropriately named Reaper.

He gives me a raised brow. "I could ask you the same thing. Shouldn't you be in the Morpheus Kingdom, dream-stalking?"

"It's dreamwalking," I correct him. "And no. I'm right where I need to be." I give my Sigil another glance, glad that Reaper can't see what Sabre is doing to her from this angle. He's fucking her harder, maybe too hard, but after taking Cain's massive cock, she seems to be warmed up enough for his pace.

"Ah, I see," he says, glancing down. I suspect he knows I'm referring to my Sigil, but he's being polite enough not to ogle her during an intimate moment. "This is a fascinating realm, isn't it?" he asks me, glancing up, only to match my gaze as his eyes glitter with darkness and death. The silver-blue fades in and out as I imagine he works his way through the soul he had just absorbed. "Compatible mates every-where, it seems."

I'm curious about what he means by that, but I know he won't elaborate.

He sighs, seemingly pleased. And I would think that he is. The number of wicked souls in this room is more than enough for a reaper who feeds on evil to feel a little giddy. "Well, happy massacre, then. If you don't mind, I think I'll stick around and feed a bit before I report back to Orcus."

I give him a raised brow and wonder if Orcus had met this dimension's God yet. Normally, I'd shudder upon hearing that name, but now I feel empowered and alive.

Maybe a little bit reckless.

*That's probably all the blood talking.*

Reaper must misunderstand my expression for something else, because he adds, "Don't worry, mate. Orcus won't interfere, not after I tell him you and Sabre came here willingly. Can't promise the same for Morpheus, though."

Morpheus is my God—or was—and he's the one I should worry about.

But after everything that has happened, I'm curious about whether he had something to do with how everything has played out.

With that, Reaper vanishes and reappears near a dying Elite across the room. His lips curl into a cruel smile as he bends to absorb the dark soul.

Since Reaper is getting back to his meal, I decide to return to mine.

I turn to Sabre and our Sigil, and my dick throbs at the new sight.

Cain watches with his cock in his hand, seemingly just as mesmerized as me.

It's a sight to behold.

Scarlett is riding Sabre. She's not letting us claim her.

She's going to claim us.

Sabre holds her hips and thrusts up into her sweet pussy, but our Sigil grinds down on him, panting as she seeks her pleasure and throws back her head. Sabre's tongue slides up her chest, giving her perfect nipples attention as she moans.

He notices me watching, because he grabs her ass and spreads her for me, showing me the beautiful sight of his dick deep inside her and her adorable little back hole just waiting for me.

I can't resist the invitation as Sabre holds her steady, and I settle against her back.

She goes completely still as I press a kiss against her neck. It's where that asshole had kissed her, and I fully intend to retrace every inch of her body that had been betrayed and retrain her in what pleasure is supposed to feel like.

"Cage?" she asks.

Gods. I love my name on her lips.

"I'm here," I tell her as I nudge my cock against her back entrance. I don't know how experienced she is, but everything about her seems too innocent to suggest she's taken two men at the same time.

If at all.

"I... I want both of you, but can you use your blood? Like Cain did?"

I blink at Sabre until I realize what she means. There are sensual qualities in our blood, especially when it comes to our mate.

I bite myself and drizzle my blood onto my cock, using it as lube.

"Ready, my Sigil?"

She seems to hold her breath before she answers.

"Yes."

# CHAPTER 42

## SCARLETT

MY VISION GOES black when Cage pushes inside me from the back. Thanks to the effects of his blood, my body accepts him as he fills me and forces me to stretch around him and Sabre at the same time.

It feels surreal that I have never had sex before, yet now my body has accepted not one but three cocks.

All of them of monster quality.

Cage is no different. His cock has ridges over it that make me suck in a breath as he moves inside.

"Do you like that, my Sigil?" Sabre asks as he holds on to my hips, keeping me in place while Cage thrusts inside.

I wonder if he can feel the ridges of Cage's cock through the thin barrier of my body.

*Can he feel that? Fuck. It's so good.*

I didn't think I'd enjoy this kind of sexual play, but I do.

"Yes, I can feel it," Sabre says, surprising me with the confirmation that he, too, can hear my thoughts. He groans as Cage thrusts into me again, then ups his pace. "He knows I like it, too." The vibration of the two separate glands seems to increase in intensity, making my entire body jolt with pleasure.

Cage pants in response, then curses. "Stop vibrating so hard, Sabre."

"Stop fucking her so hard, Cage," he easily replies.

Heat flushes over my face as I realize that they're stimulating each other through me.

"Make her come, or I'll make her come for you," Cain says from his position on the floor.

Blood and bodies are the backdrop to the sight of him stroking his cock while he watches me. My arousal rushes through my core as his broken irises rake over me, and I can practically feel his lust inside my chest.

I want more of it. I want him to lose control.

He seems pleased by my thoughts. I have no doubt that he can hear them.

And he enjoys watching me with Sabre and Cage.

They're new to me, newer than Cain is, but I feel no less connected to them. No less compatible.

I fit perfectly between them as I seek my pleasure. I had been riding Sabre, but now I'm pinned in place while he thrusts up into me. Every stroke sends his vibrating bulb rolling over my swollen clit, and the one deep inside hits a sensitive bundle of nerves. I'm trapped in a triangle of pleasure as Cage fucks me from behind. The power of his blood soaks into me as each thrust drives it deeper.

It's overwhelming, and when I fall forward, Sabre goes still. His massive fangs graze my neck, and he pants with a new rush of need washing through our connection.

"I'm going to bite you, Scarlett, if you are this close to me," he warns me. "I... I can't resist it. You smell like peaches and cream. Fuck."

New excitement rushes through me at the realization that my mates are vampires.

All of them. They might be of a dream variety, but they need blood.

And it seems they need mine, specifically.

Arching my neck, I offer myself freely to him. "I want you to bite me. Both of you."

Cage makes a pained sound from behind me when Sabre hesitates, then drives his fangs into me.

The shock of the puncture makes me wince, then his tongue laps up the blood the wound created. He gently feeds, making me moan when Cage does the same to the other side. His fangs aren't nearly as large, but I can't keep my control in check as they both feed on me.

And begin to fuck me.

Hard.

"Oh, yes. You're taking such good care of them, Scarlett," Cain praises at the perfect moment, securing my push over the edge into another powerful climax.

I scream, and the sound ripples through this world, as well as the one of dreams. Something in me clicks into place as Sabre and Cage follow me into bliss, filling me with their cum as I ride the wave of orgasmic euphoria.

They pump into me, thrusting again and again until every last drop is emptied and we all slump into a useless heap together.

Cain is patient while I remember how to breathe again. He gently untangles me from the two Strigoi, who seem drunk on my blood.

He coddles me against his massive chest, then sets me on the bed. "Sleep, little star. And when you do, I'm going to make you come all over again in your dreams."

I shiver, knowing this is my reality now. In my waking hours, my mates will fuck me into oblivion.

And then when I fall asleep, they're going to do it all over again.

I'm Scarlett Nightingale, destined to be an Offering for vampiric monsters who feed on my flesh and my dreams.
I was always destined to be their blood Queen.

# CHAPTER 43

## SCARLETT

*Three days later...*

I NEVER THOUGHT I'd actually see the Immortality Sector, but it's exactly as I imagined it would be.

Perfect.

"Isn't it lovely?" my mother asks as she joins me at the two-story window. We have a view of a massive garden with fountains and birds. There's *life* here. Butterflies that look like they're made of glass flitter around similarly crystalline roses. Life looks different here, but that's to be expected.

Sunsets are my favorite. Everything looks as if it's on fire and glimmers with reds and golds. The roses are the most spectacular displays at this hour, and they cast gleaming reflections across the ponds and the trees. I imagine it's a great way for Cain to keep his watchful eye on this sector, given what I've learned about how his power works. He needs reflective surfaces to peer through, as well as a prayer to be let in.

If everything is as wonderful as it seems here, I imagine

the Immortal inhabitants are regularly sending their gratitude to the Elite City King.

I haven't met the other families in the Immortality Sector yet, but I look forward to it. Cain has told me that there are many monster-human pairings in the Immortality Sector as well, which I didn't know. But it makes sense when this place is so serene and peaceful.

Lovely, just like my mother expressed.

When I turn to her, I can see the fruit of the immortality elixir that has erased the dark circles under her eyes. I hadn't realized how the anti-aging tonic had simply been a bandage, something that masked an illness deep within but made it seem like she was doing better.

Now, her brown curls are silky and bouncy around her rosy cheeks. She looks more like my age, if only slightly older, which is going to take some getting used to. Her bright eyes are silvery, like mine, as a result of the immortality elixir, but it suits her.

"Lovely," I agree, but I'm talking more about her than the sector we now call home.

I won't be living here in the new Nightingale Manor. I'll be residing in Cain's tower, and that's something I'm going to have to wrap my mind around.

My evil brother is gone.

So are Edward and most of the Rinholds and their allies.

Flashes of the massacre spark through my mind. I know I'll be having recurring dreams, but Cain promises he's going to help with that.

*"I'll eat them for you, if you'd like. Nightmares taste the sweetest."*

I'm not sure how I feel about that, but if it makes Cain look at me like he wants to eat me, I'm happy to offer him a meal.

Because he rewards me with praise after.

And other things.

I didn't realize my train of thought had brought the sting of tears to my eyes until my mother is gently swiping them away.

"Oh, Scarlett. I'm so sorry. You've been through so much because of me." She cups my face as her eyes turn glassy, and a tear rolls down her round face.

It's strange to be comforted by a woman who now more resembles my sister than my mother. In a strange way, I feel like I've lost the woman who raised me, only to have a new friend named Eveline replace her.

"Because of you, I am alive," I remind her as I rest my hand over hers. I curl my fingers over her palm and lean into her touch. When I close my eyes, it still feels like my mother. So I keep them closed as she talks.

"I don't know if I should get any credit, sweetheart. Duchess Rinhold is the one who poisoned me years and years ago, making me barren and inflicting me with a disease that ultimately put me into a coma."

My eyes fling open as I drop her hand and fall back a step. "What?"

She takes a deep breath and steadies herself on the windowsill as she looks outside. Her gaze is distant as she pieces together the whole story. "Bernard, that Raven monster who seems to be close with the King, he dug up the intel and shared it with me yesterday. He wanted me to be the one to tell you." Her lower lip quivers, making my heart break. "I sent you right into the viper's den and played into their plans. You're only alive because you found a way to save yourself. You had to do what I could not. Your brother died a long time ago. A monster wearing his skin was walking around in his place." I know she doesn't mean a literal monster. Humans have a propensity for wickedness, especially when power is on the line. It's a choice to be good or evil. My brother made his choice.

And he paid the price.

My mother seems to force herself to face me as she straightens her spine. Her skin has a light glitter to it now that she's immortal. There seems to be an effect of broken glass on everyone who has taken the elixir, leaving me to believe it's something that Cain himself had created. "You have always dealt better with monsters than I. That's why you saved yourself. You aren't weak."

"You aren't weak, Mother," I say with a sigh. "And don't put me up on such a pedestal. My nightmares saved me," I add, meaning Cain, Sabre, and Cage, but I lovingly refer to them as my nightmares. That's what they are, and that's what they'll always be. "I was a victim just as much as you were, Mother. Please don't be so hard on yourself." I take a step toward her again.

She huffs a humorless laugh as she rests a hand on her stomach. "I was naïve. You, my sweet daughter, questioned everything. You called your nightmares to you, as you call them. You saved yourself. Don't let anyone tell you differently. You're a light in the darkness."

Her fierce gaze gives me pause. I recall that Cain's power only works when he is prayed to, and my Strigoi can more easily find me with their dreamwalking gifts, but they still need me to open the door for them. This world is different than the one they come from, or so they tell me.

"Don't let Cage or Sabre hear you say that," I add with a smirk. "They hate light." I've come to learn that they can't handle sunlight very well. It damages their skin and their eyes, and it also drains their power. The sun is setting, so I expect to see them soon.

"I'll brave anything for you, Sigil," a husky voice says as

an arm loops around my middle. I squeak as I'm yanked against a hard chest.

Sabre is behind me, and his dangerous air gives me a thrill every time. He presses a kiss to the top of my head, allowing me to feel the large fangs that are persistent even in his human form.

My mother isn't afraid. In fact, her smile stretches across her face as she looks up at Sabre. "Your Majesty, I didn't know you could come out at sunset. Is it painful?"

The fiery reds of the dying sun filter into the room. Sabre is wearing a suit and gloves, so I imagine that's protecting him from the worst of the light. "A little pain never hurt anyone," he says with a growl to his words.

He's incredibly possessive of me, and I give my mother an apologetic look as a blush creeps over my cheeks. "I think Sabre is trying to tell me it's time for our date."

She only giggles, which makes me blush harder. "Yes, you lovebirds are in your honeymoon phase. Where will you be going, again?"

Sabre rolls his thumb over my stomach as he speaks. The gesture is subtle, but it sends heat throbbing through my body without fail. "Cage says he's found a place in this world's Dream Realm that'll make a lovely outing. We'll retire our bodies in the guest room for the evening, if that's all right with you, Duchess Nightingale."

She beams, and I know it's because she loves that Sabre —now a Prince of the Elite City—gives her complete control and respect in her home. My father is off doing Nightingale business, which leaves my mother in control.

I know that in all reality, he's processing Laurence's death. My brother doesn't deserve to be mourned, and my father knows that. There is the complication of a Nightingale heir, given that there are no males left. But now that my mother has taken the immortality elixir, I suspect it's possible for her to become pregnant again. There will be plenty of time to talk about that whenever they are ready. Immortality definitely has its perks.

For the time being, I have a new family to focus on and new mates to learn. When I glance at the doorway, I spot Cage in his monster form lingering in the shadows.

Upside down.

On the ceiling.

I'm glad my mother doesn't seem to notice him when she cordially says, "Please, enjoy any suite in the manor you'd like. You are always welcome here, Prince Sabre." She gives him a curtsy, one that is full of grace and skilled movements befitting a Duchess. She takes her leave, and I'm alone with two hungry vampires. A chill goes up my spine when Sabre's hand snakes between my legs. "Let's get this date started, shall we?"

# CHAPTER 44

## SABRE

"Do you like it?" I ask as I carefully watch Scarlett's reaction.

A smile glimmers on her perfect lips. "Like it? I love it. How did you find this place?"

"Cage found it," I say, rewarded with his mischievous smile.

"It's linked to the Immortality Sector," Cage explains. "It wasn't difficult to find when I had the energy to dreamwalk again. But I wouldn't have thought to look inside Cain's mind when he suggested that we take our Sigil on a date," he says, giving her a flick of his long tongue.

She giggles in delight. We're maintaining our human forms for now, mostly because when we're in our monster ones, we're going to want to feast on our new mate.

Cage visibly restrains himself as he curls his tongue back in, and his eyes pulse with red light. He's hungry, just as I am, but we aren't in a rush.

Time doesn't always pass differently in the Dream Realm, but it can, if one goes deep enough. This place is nearly at a standstill, making it an ideal location to take our time getting to know one another.

Cage explains the nuances of this territory in the Dream Realm while Scarlett glimmers like a walking sculpture with silks trailing behind her. She wanders through the garden and kneels to pick a rose. The smile on her face has my heart leaping for joy and my body eager to please hers.

We'll have sex. Plenty of it, but first I want to learn more about my new mate and what makes her tick. I want to know what delights her. What keeps putting a smile like that on her face so I can make sure that happens every day for the rest of eternity.

Cage is uncharacteristically open as he joins her and plants a kiss on her cheek. He adores our Sigil, and I've gotten to see an entirely different side of the skilled assassin.

He's not even that sweet with me. Scarlett has carved out a special place in his heart—as well as mine.

We belong here, with her.

Forever.

I join her on the other side and take the rose from her fingertips. Under my touch, it turns black, mostly because I'm turned on as fuck and I can't seem to control my power. Nightmares bleed out of me, darkening the beautiful garden around us.

"Sorry," I murmur as I move to set the rose down.

Scarlett stops me and curls her fingers around mine before pulling it to her chest. "Don't be sorry for being yourself," she says. Her words are kind and genuine, just like she is. She glances down and takes the rose, then twirls it around by the stem. She's careful of the jagged thorns that could easily draw blood, but she isn't scared of dangerous things.

Our Sigil is never afraid.

"I want to learn more about you, Sabre. And you, too, Cage. Can you tell me more about your world? Where you come from? Why you're here?"

"You're why we're here," I say easily. "You called us."

She tilts her head, sending her wavy red hair unfurling over her shoulder. "Yes, you mentioned that. But why did you answer? Why would you leave everyone and everything you know for me before you even knew me?"

I lean back and make myself comfortable. I'm wearing a simple pair of pants and an open vest that displays my abdomen and chest. Scarlett drags her gaze over me with appreciation that makes my cock vibrate. A little smirk on the side of her mouth suggests she's aware of what she's doing to me, but she patiently waits for my answer.

"Because we were living a nightmare, love. You are our Sigil."

I don't know how else to explain it. The life I abandoned is a bad memory now. I no longer care about overthrowing my father or the kingdom I left behind.

It'll be someone else's problem. I have no loyalty to my birthplace and no need to return.

Everything I could ever want or need is right here.

"And what is a Sigil, exactly?" she asks as she leans back into Cage's embrace. His hands roam over her body, exploring her with gentle touches.

The term has such innate meaning to me that I'm speechless at first. Cage surprises me by being able to articulate what's in my heart, because I know it's also in his.

"The word for what you are doesn't really matter. We call you a Sigil because you are a symbol of everything, a symbol of the beginning, of the end, and of all that exists in between. You are a medium of power, one who exists in the Dream Realm and the real world at the same time." His fingers trail across her arms, sending goose bumps over her skin. "You are endless."

"Endless?" she asks, glancing at me. There's arousal burning like low embers in her eyes, but I want her to understand how special she is.

I lick my lips before I add to Cage's description. "Every dream, every darkness, every shadow, every thought, you are capable of holding on to all of it, Scarlett. You've protected yourself all these years, finding outlets for all the horror you've already absorbed. You're stronger than you can possibly know."

She blinks at me with understanding. "My nightmares have always been real."

I nod. "Cain activated you. I don't think he understood what you were or why you were compatible with all of us. But you knew, on some level, and you called us so that the true power you contain wouldn't destroy you. You need us to drain you, to divert your power and help you manage it."

She tilts her head while Cage caresses her shoulder. "Where does it go? All this power."

I hum in thought. "Well, if we had been in my kingdom, you would power the blood fields and help me maintain my people with sustenance and the peace you offer. Now, it channels through Cain and helps him control his beast. For the first time in his very long life, he's healing. And for us, well, we're happy to give it to him. We only want you."

A shadow passes over her gaze. "Are you sad? That you can't return to your people?"

Cage chuckles behind her as he answers for me. "You're all that matters to him now, Scarlett. His people never accepted him. He owes them nothing." The ferocity in Cage's gaze warms my cold heart. "He is more of a King than the Strigoi will ever know. Even here, he accepts his role as a Prince because he doesn't want Cain's throne. He doesn't want the power you offer. He only wants *you*."

She smiles at me, the sight making my cock vibrate again. "Are you both saying I'm your dream?"

I grin, enjoying the sight. "You're everything, Scarlett. Now, spread your legs and let Cage please you while you tell me what it is you like. What it is you dream, because we're going to make every fucking one come true."

# CHAPTER 45

## SCARLETT

I FIND my legs falling open in immediate compliance with Sabre's orders.

This was supposed to be a date where we learned one another, but my body is screaming for more than just teasing touches.

Cage peels away the wedding silks wrapped around my body, exposing me inch by inch.

In this dream, I wear Cain's marks, but my marriage vow is to my mates.

There are two new slashes, each consisting of four claw marks on either side of my rib cage.

One for Sabre, and one for Cage.

Cage's fingers explore his mark, and my skin tingles under his touch. When his fingers move down between my legs and rub me over the soft layer of silk pressed against my clit, I moan.

"Do you like me watching Cage please you?" Sabre asks.

He's been pushing me to answer many questions about my preferences.

"I like it when you're pleased," I answer honestly.

He smiles at me and slowly lowers the zipper on his pants, then pulls out his beautiful cock. It's long and thick. The head vibrates when he strokes his fingers over it, and the other bulb at his base is hidden by the fabric.

My pussy throbs at the sight as Cage grazes his fingers over me again. My lips part on a gasp when he uses his claw to snap the fabric, giving him full access to my sex.

"Do you like this better?" Sabre asks while he pleasures himself, his gaze on me before dropping to my pussy as Cage spreads my legs wider, giving Sabre an unimpeded view.

"Yes," I whisper as I try to close my legs, but Cage keeps them open. "But..."

Sabre's eyebrow jolts upward. "But you want my tongue?"

I bite my lip before nodding.

His eyes flash with red as his features change, and his long tongue darts out. "You'll get my tongue soon enough. First, I want to watch Cage feast on you. Would you like that?"

Sabre apparently has a thing for watching, and that drives me insane in all the right ways.

"Yes," I whisper helplessly as my body aches for everything he just said.

I expect Cage to lay me down. Instead, he lifts me up by my hips until I'm kneeling. He walks around me, then lies down and rolls onto his back. "Come sit on my face, Sigil," he says, making me whimper.

His legs are facing Sabre, and I know what's going to happen when Sabre starts to peel Cage's pants down.

He wants me to watch, too.

*Holy Cain.*

I hadn't intentionally been calling for Cain, but the

instant the thought crossed my mind, the Elite City King was inside my head.

*"Hmm, you called, little star?"*

"Sit on his face, Scarlett," Sabre says, overriding Cain's words in my mind with his that are spoken aloud.

I move forward and Cage grabs my thighs, then drags me over him. His long tongue thrusts into me, making me cry out.

Sabre grins before he takes his equally long tongue and rakes it over Cage's bulging cock.

*"Cain,"* I whisper in my mind, only to hear him chuckle.

*"What are our Strigoi doing, little star? I can practically hear your fluttering heartbeat from here."*

*"They're..."* My mental words cut off when Cage swirls his tongue around my clit and does something I didn't even know he could do.

He tugs.

Then squeezes around the sensitive bundle of nerves while he thrusts his hips, forcing Sabre to take his cock into his mouth. It's a trusting gesture, given the danger of Sabre's fangs.

And it's hot as fuck.

*"They're learning you,"* Cain finishes with a purr to his words. *"Hmm, well, enjoy them as long as you like, little star. When you are ready, I will place a crown on your head and name you my Queen for the entire world to see."*

*"A crown?"* I ask as Cage moves his tongue from my clit to fill my pussy, making me suck in a breath. Sabre grabs Cage's dick and strokes it while he leans over him to give my clit attention with his tongue. The dual stimulation has my legs shaking.

When I'm about to come, Sabre looks up at me. "Do you want Cage inside you, Sigil?" he asks me.

I'm incapable of speech, so I nod. Sabre picks me up and settles me on Cage's cock, making me cry out.

*"A coronation,"* Cain continues in my mind, mentally stroking me as his presence sends a dark shadow over the glass garden.

We are in his mind, after all. It only makes sense that he can watch if he wants to.

Sabre kisses me in a way that only a monster could. His long tongue grazes my tongue, and he closes his mouth over mine, swallowing my screams as Cage pumps into me.

*"Enjoy your Princes, little star,"* Cain says as his voice grows distant. *"And explode for them, again and again. When you're done, you're going to explode for me."*

My climax surges and I cry out, Sabre still swallowing up the sounds as he wraps his arms around me. He lets me ride out my orgasm on Cage, allowing me to feel him pulse and spill his cum into me.

"Do you want me?" Sabre asks against my mouth.

Black spots of desire sprinkle my vision, but I'm all in now. I don't hide what I really want. "I want you to feel the same pleasure I do," I say.

"What does that mean, Sigil?" he asks. His red eyes glitter with promise. He knows what I mean, but he wants me to say it.

"Bite me while you fuck me," I say. "Both of you." Cage is already behind me and still hard, ready for more. He's not human. They're going to fuck me until I fall into oblivion.

Cage leans in to whisper in my ear as Sabre lifts me up so that we're standing. "Wrap your legs around his hips," Cage instructs as he effortlessly holds my weight when I obey.

Sabre lifts me, then slowly moves me onto his cock. Cage's cum slides down his shaft, but he doesn't seem to care. In fact, he probably likes it, if the glitter in his eyes is any indicator. "Scream for us again, Sigil," he demands as he fully sheathes himself in me.

His cock vibrates inside me, and the bulb that's pressed at my entrance, paired with the one inside, nearly pushes me over the cliff again.

But then Sabre bites his wrist and offers it to Cage. "Prepare her," he instructs.

"I don't need that," I say. We're in a Dream Realm, so I'm not bound by my physical limitations here.

Cage ignores me as he gathers the blood in his palm, then coats my back entrance. He slips a finger inside, and my entire body relaxes.

"Dreams might not be in the same realm as your physical body, but it's still real to us," Cage explains as he takes his finger out, only to position his cock while Sabre holds still. The vibration is still making my body throb, even though he isn't moving. "This world is for your pleasure," he says as he slides his cock into me, making me stretch around both him and Sabre as I cry out.

Then they begin to softly thrust. I hang on to Sabre, but I don't need to hold myself up. Both Strigoi Princes do the work for me, guiding me to a place of ultimate pleasure that has me deliriously begging for more.

"Bite me," I say, knowing they need my blood to thrive.

I sense them move in the real world. Ever so slowly, Sabre sinks his fangs into my neck, then draws out a long pull of blood.

Cage goes for the other side until I'm wedged between them, in both the real world and the world of dreams.

I feel so complete. So perfectly fit for my two Princes as they feed on me and provide me with incredible pleasure that my body can't even recognize.

When Sabre ups his pace, thrusting harder, I'm panting in time with his approaching orgasm.

I want his cum. I want his pleasure. My Princes might think this is about me, but it's also about them.

"Give me everything," I demand of him. I reach behind me and feel for Cage, encouraging him to do the same. "Fuck me until you both fill me with your cum."

"Such a filthy Sigil," Sabre says against my mouth, but it's a praise. He kisses me, allowing me to taste the peach flavor of my blood in this realm. It's a heady sensation, and when he groans and fills me up, the vibration of his cock increases until I fall over the edge, and Cage comes tumbling with me.

We're a mess of limbs and ecstasy as I soar, as I cry out and thrive in the knowledge that this is heaven.

This is my dream.

This is a nightmare of beautiful darkness, one that will never end.

# EPILOGUE : CAIN

"I CAN'T DO THIS," Scarlett says as she heavily leans on Cage's offered arm.

I can tell that Scarlett had enjoyed more time than might be natural with the Strigoi Princes in the Dream Realm, but it has brought her closer to them just like it had for me. Time had passed differently underneath the glass river before Scarlett called us out of it. Enough time for me to have learned the Strigoi better than I even know some of my closest friends.

I crave to learn Scarlett, and a part of me is jealous of her "date" with the Strigoi Princes, but I'm glad for it. It has made her more comfortable, and they fully understand the complexities of what she is. I am the feed on her power source that keeps her stable, but they are her guides in ways I could never be.

I'm looking forward to my time with her, when she's ready. I haven't yet decided if I'll be sharing her with the Princes or keeping her to myself. Either scenario gives me pleasure.

*I'll let her decide.*

In the meantime, I need to help her accept her place as my Queen of the Elite City. Our work here is now more important than ever, and the plans I have for her will shift much of the power regime to her control, as far as my territory goes.

"Scarlett, darling," I say as my beast purrs in adoration. "Everyone loves you. You have no need to be afraid."

She glances up at me, her wide eyes glittering with silver. Sabre and Cage call her a Sigil. Apparently, there's a word for what she is in their dimension.

Here, she's something entirely new, which makes sense to me. A compatible mate has never existed in thousands of years in any of the worlds I've been to. That makes Scarlett unique.

"How do you know that?" she asks. "I'm no one. I killed my own brother and the man I was supposed to marry."

I dislike the mention of those who wronged her on such a sacred day. A snarl lingers on my lips, but she doesn't shrink away from me. All her fear is reserved for the judgment of those outside. I want to take that from her, but this is her war she must wage.

I've never seen her so terrified. Not even when she faced me for the first time in the Dream Realm, or when death shattered all around her on her wedding night.

Of all things, this is what petrifies my beautiful bride.

Suppressing my beast's anger, I cup her face in my hands and angle her how I want her. I take her mouth with mine in a brutal kiss, and she seems to hold on to Cage even harder.

Sabre watches from a chair he's sprawled out on like a King. He has accepted his role as my Prince, but I know what he really is. In any other world, he would be a King of his own.

But he doesn't care about power. He only cares about

Scarlett. His eyes glitter as he watches me calm our mate with my tongue.

She prefers tongues.

And she likes us to guide her, so that's what I choose to do now.

"You are already my Queen," I tell her before running my tongue over her lower lip. "This is a formality. Everyone will see you for what you already are."

"It's barely been over a week for everyone else," she says as she presses her hand against my chest. If she's trying to push me away, I don't obey at first. I nip her tongue in reprimand, and I am pleased by her yip of pain. But I won't be cruel to my Queen. I immediately bite my own tongue, then lave my blood over her wound. She sighs into me, calmed by the aphrodisiac.

"Are you going to crown her as Queen or fuck her in lieu of her coronation?" Cage asks, earning a smile from me.

He's usually quiet, but I'm pleased he feels confident enough to challenge me.

"We will fuck later," I promise without specifying who will be doing the fucking. I'll let him wonder. "It's time to begin."

Clapping my hands, Bernard in his Raven form caws and takes flight. We're in my tower on one of the balcony platforms reserved for public events and speeches.

Today, a throne is centered on the balcony, and shadows curtain the area, hiding it in darkness. When Bernard passes through, he claws it open and reveals the moonlight.

I would normally make a coronation during the day, but my Strigoi fare better at night.

It makes the evening particularly spectacular when I gaze out over the Immortal Sector. Each member is holding up a glowing crystal or a candle, creating a sea of glittering light.

Multiple screens spark to life on the peripheral walls, displaying the other sectors also watching.

Every eye is turned up, and breaths are held as they wait for the introduction of the first Elite City Queen.

It's a monumental moment for me to take not only one mate but three. I will rule with them and use Scarlett's power to better this city and all the villages connected to it.

Especially after what happened to her family's village, I have realized I need more help. It does me a service that Duke Nightingale has earned enough points to naturally ascend to the Immortal Sector, bringing her entire family closer to the tower without showing favoritism. No one can deny it was an earned achievement by the mere fact that Alina, one of his Offerings, mated a literal God.

Orcus. The very one I had run into in Helia's tower.

And two others mated Helia, the Monster City Queen.

Now, his very own daughter will rule at my side.

There will be envy and gossip when it comes to the Nightingale family, but I will protect Scarlett from all of it. I make a mental sweep through every mortal and monster mind in all the sectors and wait for them to open their minds.

Bernard's crow form flutters to the long extension of the platform, and he swirls in an impressive show of shadows and sparkle as he transforms into a man. He's fully clothed, thanks to a tonic he had taken earlier, to prevent trans-forming naked in front of the entire city. That would have certainly dampened the effect of his introduction.

"Elite citizens!" he says, loud enough for everyone to hear. His voice magically broadcasts and echoes through every sector. Eyes flicker upward in reaction on the screens.

"This Monsters Night has been an eventful one. Before we begin, let us pray."

He holds up his hands and bows his head. Every citizen does the same. When he utters the prayer, I feel the Dream Realm shift and move as if an entire landmass has cracked open and given me access to a new stream of fresh water underneath.

"In Cain's name, we pray," Bernard says. "Praise our Lord Cain for his mercy, his strength, and his guidance as we enter the Nightingale Era."

A gasp goes through the crowd, but it was an intentional decision to name this reign with my Queen after her family. I want her to understand how important she is and what she means to me.

She might have been born in a village, but she is one of us. She is an Elite.

He ends the prayer with a flourish, then snaps his head up. "Elites! We celebrate tonight with this unprecedented coronation. For the first time in our city's history, our King has found his mates!" The crowd roars in approval as Bernard smiles.

Scarlett shivers at my side, but I'm proud of her when she straightens her spine. I can taste her thoughts that are swirling with reminders of how important she is to me, and how hard her new Princes have fallen for her. They gave up their world, their kingdom, their family and friends, and everything they've ever known to be with her. Nothing else matters.

So why should she worry about what a few Elites think of her now?

She's no coward. She's the strongest creature I have ever seen.

"I introduce to you your new Princes, Cage Van Drakken

and Sebastian Sanguinis. As well as Scarlett Nightingale, your new Queen!"

The crowd cheers as my beast practically purrs at the sight. Cage and Sabre stand on either side of Scarlett and take her hands.

She's beautiful. Her tight-fitting dress cups her curves, and dainty silver chains glitter with moonlight every time she moves. Her red hair seems to be made of fire under the soft light, delicately pinned back in a simple style that suits her.

She holds her head high as she marches forward until she's at the end of the perilous platform. Any other mortal would tremble and be at risk of falling, but not my Scarlett.

I walk up from behind her and hold up my hands to quell the roar of the crowd until utter silence fills the city.

"Elites, humans and monsters, inhabitants of this great city, I ask you, do you accept Scarlett Nightingale as your Queen?"

Silence meets my question, but I don't let worry gnaw at me like I know it must be for my mate.

My fingers work with all the power I had been absorbing from the prayer. Every member of my city had partaken, giving me access to their minds and their dreams.

I fashion a crown with it, making a spectacular piece of jewelry that is a mixture of fractured glass, diamonds, white gold, and the pure form of a city's dream.

One of a new era of peace and prosperity unlike any we have ever seen.

"Queen Scarlett!" a voice cries from the Immortality Sector. I recognize it as Duke Nightingale's from the crowd.

I smirk. Given everything he's been through in the past few days, I wasn't sure if he was going to be supportive.

For that, I will bless his village with a boon none of my Elites have ever seen before.

"Queen Scarlett!" another voice echoes.

Then another.

And another until the entire city across every sector is chanting my mate's name.

I can't see her face, but she's holding on to Cage and Sabre for dear life.

She knows what comes next after I have crowned her.

I lower the crown and nestle it onto her head. It's a perfect fit, and there's a hum of energy between the three of us, priming us for a connection unlike one we've ever been able to achieve.

The three of us having sex is one thing, but this is the culmination of all our power concentrated into one place with one goal, one purpose, one *need*.

"I present to you, your blood Queen," I say before I lean in.

And bite.

Scarlett's lips part on a silent gasp as she endures my teeth puncturing her flesh. The intoxicating taste of her blood makes my beast purr in contentment. He heels completely under control with this final claiming.

She is not just a Queen in name. She will be the final factor in all decisions. The city will irrevocably change in beautiful ways under her leadership.

She will grow into her role, starting with today. Starting with this.

Cage and Sabre gently take up her arms and pierce her skin with their fangs. I know Sabre's hurts more than mine, but Scarlett doesn't cry out. She doesn't make any sound of complaint.

To my surprise, her eyes flutter closed, and she smiles as she leans back into me.

*That's my good girl.*

*Delicious,* Sabre agrees, surprising me with his thoughts in my mind.

*Like peaches and cream and sex,* Cage adds with his crass tone.

The crowd roars in approval, and I know nothing will ever be the same. All because of Scarlett.

She's everything.

She's perfect.

She's our blood Queen.

**The End**

Turn the page to enjoy additional bonus chapters from Cain's and Sabre's points of view for a peek into other Monsters Night standalone novels. Enjoy!

# BONUS SCENE 1: CAIN

*A few weeks later...*

I'm eager to get back to my new Queen. The last thing I want to deal with is another city's mess.

"I hope this is important," I grumble at Helia as I take my favorite sofa facing the window. I'm wearing a dark velvet robe for Helia's sake. I had vowed to remain naked for at least a week—while adoring my new mate in the real world. As much as I enjoy pleasing her in her dreams, I'm taking advantage of my ability to please her during her waking hours, too.

Not to mention there's been a strange disturbance in the Dream Realm that makes me wary. Until I know what's going on, I've ordered my Princes and our Queen to stay in the real world as much as possible, for now.

My Princes have no trouble obeying that command. Scarlett's quiet pleasure hums through a strengthening bond that has been established between the three of us as they take care of her. I would never have imagined that sharing a mate could be so... enjoyable.

Helia gives me a knowing grin as she twirls a little silver necklace around her finger. The new piece of jewelry seems simple, but she won't stop touching it as if it has great value to her. My suspicion is that one of her new mates gave it to her.

"The Monster Isle King has been compromised. That impacts both of us," she says. She brings the charm on the necklace to her mouth and runs it over her lower lip. "I expected you knew already."

I give her a raised brow. "Why would I know already? I've been entertaining my new mates." A smile lifts the side of my lips as I watch her dote on her little necklace. "And I imagine you have been equally occupied."

She drops the necklace as if she hadn't realized she'd been toying with it. Leaning back, she curls her fingers over the armrests of her chair as she crosses her legs. Her dress rides up her thighs, but my attention is entirely on what she's going to say next. "I'm serious, Cain."

"I can see that."

She frowns. "So you don't know what's going on?"

"No, enlighten me."

She analyzes me for a moment more before she seems to believe me. "Monster Isle is experiencing a coup."

"A coup?" I ask, curious as to how that would even be possible. "I don't see King Njord tolerating that. He's too much of an asshole."

She smirks. "I know you and King Njord don't get along, but his role is an important one to what we do here. Without King Njord managing the monsters who don't qualify for Monster City, we could have a war on our hands. I won't tolerate them damaging the structure we have established. And those are dangerous monsters, Cain. They're insane and greedy and *will* come for Monster City —then your Elites—if we aren't careful. Only Monster Isle is secure enough to handle them with King Njord at the helm."

"You don't have to lecture me, Helia," I growl. "I understand the problem, but I don't understand your concern. We all signed a blood contract not to interfere with the happenings in other cities—including power exchanges. They are bound by the same rules not to invade us and take what is ours."

Unfortunately, I'm well versed in the limitations a blood contract puts into place, but it protects my city from the threat Helia is worried about. So I still don't fully understand why she's bringing this to my atten—

"The coup is from new monsters not bound by any contract," she says, interrupting my thoughts. "Monsters of a *dream variety*."

My eyes widen. "You know as well as I do that I have never come across a monster with the capability of entering or manipulating the Dream Realm, until recently." It's why I've never been able to find a mate. Cage and Sabre are from an entirely different dimension. There's something about mine that seems to have prevented monsters from entering the Dream Realm, making my situation of managing my monster side particularly dire.

She waves her hand as if she had expected my disbelief. Helia doesn't try to argue with me, though. Instead, a projection appears on my window.

One of the latest Monsters Night, but this time from the perspective of Monster Isle based on what had once been called the Isle of Man. I don't typically watch Monsters Night feeds of the other portal locations, mostly because I'll grow irritated at how the annual event is managed by other Kings.

Particularly this one.

A silver moon hangs in the sky and shines down on the

unforgiving terrain of Monster Isle. The poor humans sent there to die or to be bred with insane monsters are running for their lives, but at least they are trained warriors.

*"Thirty minutes!"* one shouts, then takes off down a dirt path.

A female with wide eyes full of terror stares after him. *"Jackson! Wait!"*

He doesn't seem keen on waiting, so the female curses as she withdraws a knife from her boot and starts running. She seems fully capable of taking care of herself, but it's clear the male had betrayed their plan.

As interesting as the warrior variety of humans is, it's the flicker of dark magic that catches my eye.

Steepling my fingers, I try to understand what I'm seeing. The portals don't open for another thirty minutes, but there are shadows stretching over the ground.

Ones that originate from dreams.

I recognize the dark veins that bleed through the weeds and sand, seeking to claim their victims. It's how I used to feed before I learned I could live on prayers.

Helia waves her hand again, skipping to when the portals open.

Sirens sound, making the ambience so much more terrifying than it is in Monster City, where Helia lives. At least in old New York, humans are going to be cherished mates guaranteed to be pampered for the rest of their lives. It is a competition of what type of monster they will match with, more so than a game of survival.

But survival is the game on Monster Isle.

Screams rend the air as monsters of a darker variety make their choice of whether they are going to feed.

Or breed.

Sometimes there are successful mate bonds, but it's not as common as I would like. If I were King Njord, I would have abolished the practice altogether and shoved the irredeemable monsters into a pit in the Dream Realm so deep they'd never claw their way out.

Which, admittedly, wouldn't leave him much of a city to rule.

As distasteful as I find the whole thing, I'm curious about the dark tendrils that don't go for the humans. Some of the Offerings are impressively winning, including the female who uses her knife to carve out a monster's eye.

The dark streaks avoid her and go for a monster watching her. They climb up his legs and make the veins in his neck swell until they turn black, and then that darkness reaches his eyes.

He grins, then turns around and walks away, leaving the female covered in blood confused but relieved.

"This nightmare disease has been selective," Helia explains as she cuts the feed. "It has targeted King Njord's highest-ranking monsters until eventually it infected the King himself."

"That's the coup," I clarify. When she nods, I lean back. "If another entity is controlling King Njord from the Dream Realm, they might be able to bypass the blood contract."

"Precisely," she confirms.

I understand the problem now.

"What do you propose we do?" No matter what a possessed King Njord can do, we'd still have our hands tied behind our backs because the contract would remain active on our end.

A menacing smile stretches her glossed lips. "We just so happen to have one of your Elites on a boat there right now. We let her do our dirty work for us."

I straighten immediately. "Her?" My citizens are everything to me, second only to my mates.

If one of them has been taken—

"Edward Rinhold—" she begins, earning a vicious snarl from me as I shoot to my feet.

"Do not utter that creature's name," I growl as black claws spear through my fingers. My beast had been listening to the Strigoi pleasuring Scarlett, but now Helia has his attention.

She bows her head in apology. "It is the last time you will ever hear me say his name. The tongueless corpse performed one last act before his most-deserved death."

"And what act would that be?" I ask. I don't sit back down.

Helia remains in a submissive position, which is entirely unlike her. But she knows this conversation is hard for my beast, and hard for me. She is showing respect for my situation. "He sold his sister to King Njord, securing a new body for his soul." Her gaze flicks up to meet mine as ice scores through my veins. "He knew you were going to kill him. Maybe not at his wedding, but eventually. He already had a plan in place."

My robe stretches as my beast threatens to consume me. I have better control over him, but in this case, I share his anger. "The vile creature still lives?"

She shakes her head. "No, he is very much dead, but King Njord has his soul. He is an Undertaker Monster, as you know. He can place souls into new bodies, if a contract had been previously signed. He seems to understand the value of that particular soul, so he's holding on to it for leverage, for now."

I knew about King Njord's gift, but it's a useless one. No one would trust an insane King with their soul like that.

He often uses them as power sources, thanks to loopholes in the contracts he typically places in the fine print.

Unfortunately, Scarlett's former betrothed had ample practice with monster contracts.

"What does he want for the soul?" I ask. A tiny thrill runs through me as I fantasize about recalling Reaper, a Death Fae from Sabre's dimension who is particularly skilled in tormenting a vile soul before destroying it.

Helia is toying with her necklace again, which tells me King Njord wants something we can't give. "He wants eighty percent of our breeders."

A dark laugh rumbles out of me as I finally sit down. "He really has gone insane."

The humans reserved for Monster Isle are trained for the kind of monsters they'll be pitted against. Not only is it insane to give such a large share of our fertile humans carefully curated over centuries for monster pairings, but it's also unjust.

They're soft humans often trained in culture and education, not in the ways of warfare.

"Which is why Liliana is going to have to play her role. We can't rescue her anyway. Not now that she has passed the boundary of our territory. King Njord owns her, so she's going to have to get to the bottom of this for us."

I shake my head. "A Lady of an Elite house? She has no training for that sort of thing. What is she going to do? Curtsy him to death?"

Helia's eyes sparkle as she smiles wide enough to show her white teeth. I know that's never a good sign. "You're going to train her, Cain. The Dream Realm has no boundary. Your mates are dreamwalkers, yes? Have them locate her, then guide her. You have a year to prepare her for surviving Monsters Night. And once she does, she can kill King Njord herself. That'll give you a chance to pounce on the invading force when it doesn't have a host to hide in."

"That's insane," I say.

"Maybe," she admits. "But when dealing with the insane, it seems this is a case where fire must fight fire."

A growl rumbles in my throat, because I don't like this plan.

But I also know that Helia is right.

It's the only way.

*And when she kills King Njord, the soul he's holding hostage will be mine to do with as I please.*

That's motivation enough.

I just hope that Lady Liliana is up for the task. She might surprise me.

Scarlett was a Lady, too, after all.

And now she's a Queen.

"Consider it done," I murmur as I rise to my feet.

"King Njord must die."

***Read Next in Monsters Night...***
**Their Broken Queen**

***Their Broken Queen***

Offerings are chosen every year and given a thirty-minute
head start to *run*.
Monster Isle is a prison for the damned. Only evil souls find
themselves here, deserving to be a sacrifice to dark
monsters hunting their mates.
Or their next meal.
**They might feast or they might breed.**

Either way, the three monsters on my tail want my screams.
Ze'ev.
Godric.
Arwan.

They're monsters of darkness and dreams.

They feast on nightmares, and I have plenty of those.
Horror lives in my mind, such as the memory of the night I
was sold into this trade. My brother knew I didn't belong
here. He didn't care.

It doesn't matter now. The countdown has begun.

And it's time to run.

Into the darkness.
Into the Void.

To be a sacrifice.
Or to be a *bride*.

# BONUS SCENE 2: SABRE

*Damn, please say we don't have to stay here much longer,* I think as I watch Scarlett lick some frosting off of a cupcake.

Cage shifts his weight and mentally adds, *If she uses her sweet little tongue on one more thing like that, I'm going to blow my pants.*

We're in one of the confectionary shops in the Immortal Sector, and we're discovering all the new ways our mate enjoys tormenting us.

*It's not torment if it's fun,* she counters, giving us a smile before running her tongue over her lips.

Cage and I groan.

It's been a handful of days since Cain told me about the problems brewing in the Dream Realm. That's why we're here, attempting to pass the time in the real world instead of giving our Sigil as many dream orgasms as we can force out of her perfect body. The mate connections between the three of us all drive us to pleasure our mate.

It's not just because we enjoy it. There's a practical use, which has been my excuse for keeping her in the Dream Realm for so long.

The more pleasure she experiences, the more power she can absorb.

And the more power she can absorb, the more stabilized Cain becomes. Cage and I have grown to learn what a vital role Cain plays in this realm.

We already knew something was wrong in the Dream Realm when parts of it seemed to be closing off. There's a reason we've kept Scarlett out of the Dream Realm except for the safest territory—that being Cain's direct mind where he is in complete control.

Still, it's refreshing to be out and about with my Queen. I watch her with interest as she peruses the shop's selections for her latest creation. She's a creative spirit, which is something I'm starting to learn about her.

And I love everything about my mate, especially that she can create something unique I would never have thought of. Perhaps that's the human element in her, or maybe that's just one of the things that make my Sigil special.

Cage watches with interest as he remains by Scarlett's side as she follows the owner of the shop around.

"This is from a farming village with the most excellent peaches," says the female as she selects a fuzzy fruit and holds it up on display.

Scarlett offers a knowing smile. "I suspect it's from Nightingale Village?"

The owner's eyes widen. "Why, yes, Your Majesty." A blush warms her cheeks. "I suppose you would know, given that was your family's village and is renowned for its farming land. My apologies."

Scarlett waves a hand adorned with rings. All of them are blood diamonds, courtesy of Cain's intense need to spoil our mate. I'm not complaining, but I plan on one-upping him if I ever see one of those golden gems again.

"No need to apologize," Scarlett says to the woman with practiced ease. "I'm new to many of you. That's why I'm making a point to personally visit every shop in every sector." She gives Cage a slanted gaze. "Assuming my protective Princes allow me out of the Immortal Sector."

Cage flexes his fingers. I know he's uncomfortable without a shadow to hide in. The shop itself is annoyingly bright and cheery, but we'd do anything for our mate. "Just following Cain's orders, Sigil."

She chuckles but doesn't argue.

Cain is King. He doesn't tell her what to do, of course, but she respects his desire to keep her safe. Plus, she seems to be plenty entertained in the Immortal Sector by running errands and getting to know her people.

It's nice to see her thrive.

Even if I'd prefer to have her all to myself, and therefore to remain between her legs indefinitely, her smile makes the loss of her screams temporarily worth it.

She shoves a fluted drink into my hand. "Stop looking at me like that," she whispers.

I grin, showing off my large fangs. The shop owner doesn't even flinch, impressing me. "Like what?" I ask.

She gives me a smirk. *Like you want to eat me.*

My long tongue flicks out as my eyes flash with red. The shop owner does jolt this time, making me chuckle when an oven dings in the distance. "The, ah, Mini Monster Muffins are ready!" she declares with unnecessary vigor before running into the back.

"That was rude," Scarlett chides. "You scared her off."

"I'll get the muffins," Cage says with a chuckle as he follows the poor human.

"Sorry," I concede as I continue to eye Scarlett like I want to eat her. Although, I'm definitely not sorry for *that*.

"Please, try it," Scarlett requests, no doubt referring to

the fluted drink in my hand. "I call it a Peaches and Dreams Elixir." Her silver irises glitter with broken mirrors, reflecting my amused expression as I sniff the concoction. The strong aroma of peaches and fizzy wine are pleasant enough.

Sipping the contents, I note the definite absence of any dreams, but I appreciate what my mate is trying to re-create.

The cool temperature of the sorbet mimics the Dream Realm, while the sparkling wine adds an Elite flair of cele-bration.

The peaches are my favorite, of course. I know she's aware of what she tastes like to me.

"It's missing one ingredient," I say as I pull my mate onto my lap. I thoroughly enjoy her squirming as her hip presses against my growing erection. "Would you so care to offer your wrist?" I lean into her throat and breathe her in. "I'll make it a true Strigoi delicacy."

Having reappeared from the back, Cage growls at me, which hardly seems threatening when he's holding a plate of the Mini Monster Muffins.

"Stop trying to fuck her in a confectionary," Cage dead-pans before he plucks up one of the muffins and stuffs it into his mouth.

He groans in approval, then he grabs my elixir to wash it down even though Scarlett made him his own that's waiting on the table.

When that's gone, he grins at Scarlett as though he isn't behaving like an uncultured pig. "It's delicious, Sigil. You said this was for your mother?"

Scarlett beams. She always lights up now when we bring up her mother, which is refreshing and foreign to me at the same time. My own mother's idea of a celebration is planting new living corpses in the blood fields.

"This is a sampling for my mother's housewarming party," she says. "Do you realize we couldn't even afford a housewarming party in the Magic Sector?"

Cage and Scarlett strike up a conversation about her past, which I find just as riveting as he does, except something familiar catches my eye.

A glint of gold, and then a whiff of power that doesn't belong.

"Sabre?" Scarlett asks. "What's wrong?"

My stomach drops as the cheery light of the confectionary vanishes. Once floral wallpaper now drips with blood. Black veins skitter through fresh cracks, and shadows curl around the chandelier, blocking out the light.

Scarlett is frozen in time. So is Cage. I stare at them as they resemble mirrored statues that reflect what little light glints over them.

"Hello, Sabre," an accented voice murmurs, one that sends a chill down my spine.

I turn toward the sound, knowing exactly who has decided to pay me a visit. The presence is too powerful, too rich in the energy that radiates from within my soul.

"Morpheus," I breathe with a sense of disbelief.

The God of Dreams smiles at me. His vibrant blue-green eyes don't look at all like a Strigoi's.

None of him does, in fact. He has pointed ears, long silver hair, and a face of dreams—too perfect to be real.

"I came to thank you for the amusement," he says casually as if he hasn't frozen the entire world around us.

Or maybe we're the ones who are frozen.

He tilts his head, sending tendrils of silver hair flowing over his shoulder. There seems to be a weightless quality about him, making me wonder if he's even really in front of me. "And to take back what's mine, now that my little problem is resolved."

That sounds ominous, but I'm too speechless to react. I can't believe that this is actually Morpheus.

Actually my God. Standing before me. Having a conversation.

Morpheus *never* visits with his fae. He's a recluse, a living *myth*, just like all the others of his kind.

"You can have whatever you want, my lord," I say reverently, then flick my gaze to Scarlett's frozen form. "I only ask that you spare Scarlett and Cage. If I have offended you, take whatever you need from me."

He chuckles. "You've far from offended me, Sabre. As I said, I came to thank you for the passing amusement. You've been most useful to me." He comes up to me and I stiffen, then I relax as he places his hand on my head.

A weight lifts from me, making me realize that there was a power stirring inside of me that had never been mine to begin with.

*"Take back what's mine..."*

I glance up as he curls his fingers and pulls away. Light flashes through his veins as a shiver runs through his form. The air bows around him until it settles again.

"Do you like it here, Sabre?" he asks. He dances his fingers over the countertop until he reaches the Mini Monster Muffins. Tilting his head, he plucks one up and examines it.

"She's here, so yes, I do," I answer easily. Scarlett is my everything now.

He gives me a raised brow. "Is she your only reason?"

I tilt my head. "Well, there's Cain. He's my mate, too." He completes a part of me that I didn't know I needed.

Someone else to lead.

Someone else to take the spotlight so I can devote my entire being to Scarlett and our mate-circle.

Cain serves a purpose, but I respect him as well. He has

given all of his power to Scarlett without a second thought. I will stand by him as the four of us navigate everything that comes next.

Together.

"Cain," Morpheus says as he sniffs the muffin, then places it down without tasting it. He moves to the fluted glass that had been poured for Cage next and lifts it up. He swirls it and holds it up to catch the light. "Now, he's a fascinating creature."

"You've been watching him?" I ask.

"Watching him?" he repeats with a soft laugh, one that sounds more ominous than humorous. "I do enjoy watching, yes. And Cain's Dream Realm is an intriguing creation. I actually thought he might be my equal—another God. Alas..."

"Cain's Dream Realm?" I ask, curious as to why he'd word it that way.

He takes a sip of the drink, then licks his lips. "You haven't figured it out yet? Cain *is* the Dream Realm in this dimension, Sabre."

My eyes widen. "That explains a few things."

"It does, doesn't it?" He grins. "Cain has searched all his life for a monster who could enter his realm, but he never let one in. And thus, he thought none like him existed. Quite the existential crisis, if you ask me."

"So how did I get in? And Cage?" I ask.

Morpheus sets his glass down and approaches Scarlett's mirrorlike statue that has begun to glow from within.

She's fighting this.

*That's a good girl, but don't fret. Morpheus won't hurt us.*

Probably.

Either way, it's best not to anger him.

"I felt my cousin poking around this dimension, so, out of curiosity, I opened a window of my own. Color me surprised when a redheaded Sigil's scream reached for you through my creation." He studies Scarlett while he speaks, his gaze more shrewd than lingering. Like he's examining a research subject, not a female of interest.

He shrugs then, turning back to me. "In summary, she called for you. So I suppose you could say the Fates intervened. Or perhaps I did." His lips curl again. "What do you think happened?"

Something tells me that question isn't one I'm meant to answer.

In the next instant, he proves it by adding, "Because I think you just happened to be in the right place at the right time. A proper anchor meant to help aid me in a very personal quest."

I'm not sure what he means by *anchor*, but I suspect it has something to do with that weight he just removed from my being.

A shiver runs up my spine as I realize we've been under the scrutiny of a God this entire time, which puts my Sigil in danger. One never knows how a God will react out of the desire to find more *amusement*.

"Is your personal quest complete?" I hedge, concerned for my mates.

Morpheus's gaze goes distant. "Mmm, my personal quest has only just begun. But that's for me to worry about. Your role is complete. Hence..." He spreads out his arms in a gesture I don't quite understand.

"Hence..." I prompt him.

"Hence, I am here to repay you for your part. It was one you didn't mean to play, but mate-bonds can be such finicky things."

"The visions," I guess. "The *tests*, those were you?"

Morpheus's eyes sparkle as he unfurls his fingers and a peach appears in his palm. He takes a bite of the fruit, then tosses the peach into the air and it puffs out of existence. He swallows before speaking. "Part of it was me, part of it was Cain, as well as Scarlett, and your connection to them. Regardless, it created a mess for me to fix." His powerful gaze lands on me, making me stiffen. "I fix my messes. And I pay my debts as well. For being a puppet in this quest, I will offer you a boon."

"A boon?" I echo. That's a lot better than the wrath I had expected for causing him an inconvenience.

He nods. "Would you like to return to your people, or do you choose to remain here?"

I frown at the idea of returning to the Strigoi Kingdom. "My people don't care about me. My father has drained my power and driven the kingdom into ruin. I would kill him with my own hands if I ever saw him again." The vision I'd seen of my father had likely been Cain's doing, not Morpheus's, to test my worthiness as a mate. Either way, it proved to me what I would do if the scenario played out.

"I could give you power to remedy that," Morpheus offers.

It's a tempting offer. I had played out this scenario once before in the Dream Realm, but now that it's really happening, I find that my choice remains the same.

This is my home now.

This is Scarlett's home. This is where Cain has built a functioning society where he can survive, and with our help, he can thrive.

He couldn't join us in the Strigoi Kingdom. There aren't enough resources to go around, and never mind the fact that his needs are different from those of the Strigoi.

He wouldn't belong.

"I wouldn't be able to bring Cain with us," I say.

"No," Morpheus agrees. "He belongs here. Scarlett, though, can adapt."

"She would hate me if I took her from Cain." And if Scarlett hated me, I'd hate myself.

He shrugs. "That depends on your opinion of Cain, then. Is he worthy of her?"

"Yes," I answer immediately.

He glances at Cage. "And your assassin mate, he is worthy, too?"

"Absolutely," I nod. Then I remember what Cage told me about his dream vision with his brother. He realized the same that I did, that none of it had been real. It had been a test, and Morpheus just confirmed that for me. "If you wish to give me a boon, then, may I ask for a message for Cage?"

He hums with interest. "I offer you a boon, and you wish to bestow it upon someone else?" He takes my measure once more, the scrutiny giving me pause.

*Have I just offended a God?*

*Fuck.*

"That's the mark of a true King," Morpheus says, a note of respect in his tone. "Perhaps I should force you to return. Realms know your kingdom could use a capable leader."

"The best Kings are those who never wanted a throne," I say.

Morpheus grins. "You're making me want to take you home, Sabre."

"This is my home," I reply without hesitation.

He cocks his head to the side, evaluating me once more. "Perhaps it is. A shame for the Strigoi." His gaze turns distant once more. "But one can't fight fate, hmm?" He shakes his head then and sighs. "What's the message?"

*He's agreeing,* I realize.

Not wanting to waste time—or risk Morpheus changing his mind—I nod to Cage. "Could you unfreeze him so he can tell you?"

Morpheus narrows his eyes. "I'm expending enough energy to talk to you. Don't bore me, Sabre."

The warning sends a chill down my spine, so I reiterate the message as best as I can remember. "Cage has a brother, Xanthus. Xan has been training all his life to assassinate my father and his four guards. Cage doesn't want him to play the royal game and get himself killed. His message is to not go after King Nos."

The God's brow inches upward. "You don't wish for your father's death? Even after all that he's done?"

I ponder that. "My father will wither and die just like the blood fields he's neglected. He'll get the death he deserves."

Morpheus hums as he places his hand on Cage, and light flashes through him. He flicks his fingers as if to return feeling into his hand.

"Consider it done."

He rolls his wrist as the flashing light disappears, then turns like he intends to leave.

"Oh." He pauses, his silver hair billowing in an invisible breeze when he glances back at me. "As for the Strigoi royals you've left behind, they'll have to solve their own problems. My presence is required elsewhere." He smiles. "There's a pretty little blonde Omega calling for me in her dreams, and I fully intend to make those dreams come true."

I bow my head and open my palms in reverence. "Of course, my lord. Thank you."

When I look up, I'm startled to see that the world has returned to exactly how it was before.

Except now Scarlett is staring at me with wide eyes.

No, she's not staring at *me*; she's staring at the other-worldly golden gem bound to a silver necklace in my hands.

A massive grin makes my fangs throb.

It seems that Morpheus left me with an additional boon, one that'll put Cain's blood diamonds to shame.
Now... all of my dreams have officially come true.

Get your Morpheus fix in *Bride of Death*
Book 1 in the Netherworld Fae trilogy.

**A Persephone & Hades Retelling with a "Why Choose" Twist**

The God of Death says I'm his long-lost bride.
His soul mate.
An Omega who betrayed him two thousand years ago.

He believes my memories are the key to our survival.

Only, they're memories I no longer possess. Because I'm not who he thinks I am.

I'm Serapina, not Persephone.
A human, not an Omega.
And that knot he keeps talking about? Yeah, that's not coming *anywhere* near me.

Except Hades isn't the only one threatening to claim me with his knot. Morpheus, the God of Dreams, says I belong to him, too.

And don't even get me started on Maliki, the sexy fae guard in charge of my captivity. That deadly fae has a body crafted in sin and a smirk that makes me question my sanity.

All three men want access to my nest. To my heart. To my *mind*.

It's that last part that scares me most. Because if I truly am the Omega that betrayed my own kind, then I'm not worthy of being a Goddess. Let alone *their* Goddess. And what happens then?

# BONUS SCENE 3: CAIN

*Fuck, she's perfect,* I think as I watch Scarlett dip her chin in recognition of one of her subjects.

She looks like the Queen she is.

Her crown glitters atop her silky red hair that frames her porcelain face. Her eyes have slightly changed into their Sigil form, holding a fractured, glassy texture to the silver irises that certainly hadn't been there before. Even her skin has a broken-diamond effect when she moves, making her look like a masterpiece come to life.

She's taken on three dream monster mates—one of them being me. That has irrevocably changed her, but she's taken those changes in stride.

Not only that, but she has thrived.

The Duke of one of the Immortal Sector families sweeps into a low bow of respect as he addresses his new Queen. The immortals have been visiting daily, wishing to pay their respects to Scarlett Nightingale. I know they all hope they will gain favor with the new Queen, but Scarlett has a talent they don't know about.

She can see right through the masks they wear.

She glances at me in the window's reflection and gives me a faint smile.

*This one wishes to donate a village in my honor, but what he isn't saying is that there's a plague rampaging through it that he hopes you'll be able to heal.*

I chuckle. Scarlett's abilities have fully awakened to the point where she can practically read the thoughts of those around her. It's a stab to my heart that the only reason she hadn't been able to uncover Edward Rinhold's vile intentions is because of my blood he used to hide behind.

But that is in the past now. I ripped his tongue from his filthy, lying mouth before I devoured him from the inside.

Leaving nothing behind.

That's what happens to those who wrong my mate. And if any of the Elites in this city try to take advantage of her, they'll meet the same fate.

*I suggest that you tell him you'll accept the village,* I say in her mind, quietly adding, *if he lives there himself for a week to prove its quality.*

Scarlett's eyes sparkle with delight at my suggestion. Being immortal, he'll likely be immune to whatever illness has befallen the village, but it'll be a lesson for him to think twice before trying to manipulate her.

Killian raises a brow. "What'd you tell her to say to that one?" he asks.

I'm at a table with Killian near a window—one with ample reflection, given the strategic lighting—as I watch the mirror image while pretending to gaze at the city under the night sky. I chuckle when the Duke goes pale.

"That he needs to live in his own village for a week."

Killian smothers a laugh with his mug of ale. When he composes himself, he sinks into his seat and sighs. "I don't think it would be so bad to live in one of the villages."

I give him a raised brow. "What makes you say that?"

He makes a face as his eyes refocus on the city below us. "Elites just get on my nerves after a while. I wouldn't mind a place where the people focus on things other than the latest gossip, fashion, or who fucked who."

It's rare that I laugh, but Killian earns a chuckle from me. "Then you need to become the new Viscount for Nightingale Village," I jest. "The custom set by Scarlett's grandfather has made that community a fanatical mess. Sexual activity outside of the approved arrangements are too severely punished to be entertained by the women. And the men... Let's just say I don't mind that the prior Viscount died. Brutally." I had been there, in fact, but Killian didn't need to hear the details right now where other ears might be listening.

His gaze flicks to me with interest. "Does that mean there's an opening?"

What had been a jest now feels very serious. "Technically, yes. I was going to review the replacement personally, given the situation. Normally, I don't interfere, but Queen Helia agrees that it's time for healing. A new Viscount of my choosing needs to be placed, at least temporarily, until we have undone all the damage that the prior Viscount had inflicted."

Killian sets down his mug and leans his forearms onto his thighs. His eyes are brighter than I've ever seen them when he speaks. "I've never asked anything of you, Cain. But I'm asking you now—let me be that temporary placement. I'll fix it for you."

I find myself wishing I had Scarlett's ability to see behind the mask, because I know Killian is hiding something.

But I trust him. That's the difference between him and a nameless Elite citizen I would likely have to interview, so I tilt my head and nod. "Then you have the job, my friend."

I smile knowingly. "I hope you find what you're looking for."

Read Killian's tale as the new Viscount of Nightingale Village and join his quest to find his fated mate...

**Their Pretty Little Monster**

**In their arms, danger becomes desire.**
Every year, monsters demand their Offerings—women like me. This year, I thought I escaped. I thought I was safe.
Then he arrived.

The Viscount.

Dangerous and ruthless, he declares me a late Offering. Swept into the deadly realm of the Shadowfen, I realize I'm not here by chance.

They want to rule, and I'm their key. My reality crumbles, and as much as we act like enemies, they refuse to let me go. Their touch ignites a fire I can't resist, fueling desires I never expected.

They call me their little monster.

Maybe they're right.

Because when everything is stripped away, a fiercer side of me no one expected—not even me—emerges.

You see, in the shadows, temptation and peril collide. So, ready or not, the monster within is about to be unleashed... and these three Shadowfen are eager to claim their prize in the Monster Bride Trials.

Me...

**Run. Hide. *Fight*.**

It's Monsters Night, the annual event where the portals to other realms and realities open, and monsters flood the streets to search for their potential mates.

And I'm one of the candidates.

Why?

Because I broke all the rules. I fought back against the elitist system hellbent on enslaving humankind. And f-ck if I'm going to let one of these monsters claim me. Let alone three of them

Orcus.
Reaper.
Flame.

477

They saved me from a compromising situation. But that doesn't mean I *like* them. I don't care how gorgeous they are or how well-endowed they seem to be—I kneel for no one. And I have no interest in becoming their lethal little pet.

"Try to tame me," I dare them.

"We have no interest in taming you, sweet pet," they say. "We want to make you ours."

"Ours to worship."
"Ours to love."
*"Ours to keep."*

**Author's Note:** *Their Lethal Pet* is a standalone dark paranormal romance featuring three Nightmare Fae and their chosen female mate.

# MINI MINI MONSTER MUFFINS

## THEIR BLOOD QUEEN
### BY J.R. THORN

### MUFFIN INGREDIENTS:

2 EGGS

1 CUP ALMOND MILK

1/2 CUP APPLE SAUCE

3 CUPS AP FLOUR

1/2 CUP SUGAR

1/4 CUP PACKED BROWN SUGAR

4 TSP BAKING POWDER

1/8 TSP SALT

2-3 LARGE FRESH PEACHES (DICED)

### STREUSEL TOPPING INGREDIENTS:

1 1/4 CUP AP FLOUR

1/2 CUP SUGAR

1/2 CUP BROWN SUGAR

1/2 CUP BUTTER (VEGAN)

### GLAZE INGREDIENTS:

2/3 CUP POWDERED SUGAR

TSP 2 TSP WATER

# MINI MONSTER MUFFINS

## THEIR BLOOD QUEEN
### BY J.R. THORN

### MUFFIN DIRECTIONS:

PREHEAT OVEN TO 400°F (200°C)

MIX WET INGREDIENTS TOGETHER THEN ADD IN DRY INGREDIENTS.

NEXT FOLD IN YOUR DICED PEACHES.

SPOON INTO LINED OR GREASED MUFFIN TINS, ABOUT 3/4 FULL.

SPRINKLE ON THE STREUSEL MIXTURE TO EACH MUFFIN.

BAKE 15-20 MINUTES (DEPENDING ON YOUR OVEN)

LET COOL ALMOST COMPLETELY BEFORE TOPPING WITH GLAZE.

### STREUSEL DIRECTIONS:

IN A BOWL ADD IN YOUR STREUSEL INGREDIENTS.
USING A FORK, PASTRY CUTTER, OR HANDS,
COMBINE THE INGREDIENTS UNTIL FULLY COMBINED.

### GLAZE INGREDIENTS:

IN A SMALL BOWL COMBINE POWDERED SUGAR AND
WATER. MIX UNTIL COMBINED. IF IT'S TOO RUNNY
ADD MORE POWDERED SUGAR. IF TOO THICK ADD A
LITTLE MORE WATER.

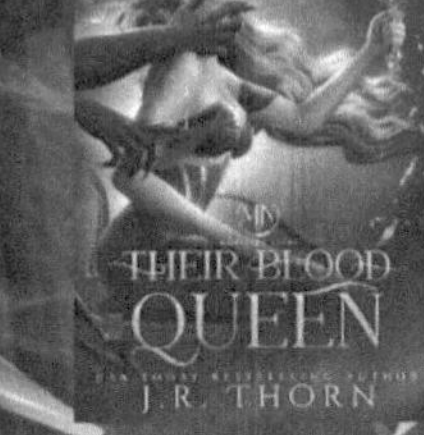

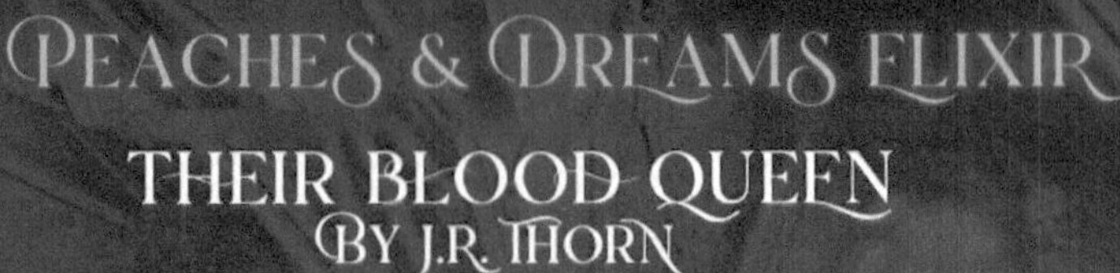

# Peaches & Dreams Elixir

## THEIR BLOOD QUEEN
### By J.R. Thorn

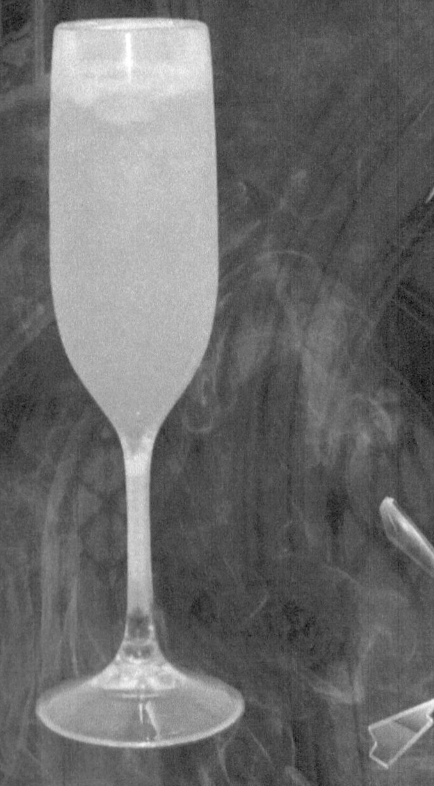

<u>SORBET INGREDIENTS:</u>

3 SLICED AND PEELED PEACHES

1/4 CUP GRANULATED SUGAR

1 TSP LEMON JUICE

# Peaches & Dreams Elixir

## THEIR BLOOD QUEEN
### By J.R. Thorn

### SORBET DIRECTIONS:

- START BY PEELING AND SLICING UP YOUR PEACHES. IF YOU ARE USING FROZEN PEACHES, GUESSTIMATE ROUGHLY WHAT 3 SLICED PEACHES WOULD BE.
- ADD INTO A BLENDER OR FOOD PROCESSOR ALONG WITH THE SUGAR AND LEMON JUICE. BLEND UNTIL COMPLETELY SMOOTH.
- POUR INTO A FREEZER SAFE DISH AND FREEZE 4-6 HOURS. OPTIONAL POUR THROUGH A MESH STRAINER TO ENSURE NO CLUMPS SNEAK IN.
- WHEN ASSEMBLING YOUR "PEACHES & DREAMS ELIXIR" USE A SMALL COOKIE OR ICE CREAM SCOOP AND SCOOP ABOUT 3-4 SCOOPS IN YOUR CHAMPAGNE GLASS.
- TOP WITH YOUR FAVORITE SPARKLING WINE, CHAMPAGNE, OR SPARKLING JUICE FOR A MOCKTAIL VERSION.
- TO MAKE IT EXTRA FANCY TRY ADDING LUSTER DUST TO YOUR GLASS BEFORE ADDING IN LIQUIDS!

# Author's Note

The journey to write this book has been an unexpected adventure that has resulted in one of my favorite worlds, with some of my most cherished characters. *Their Blood Queen* is written by me, J.R. Thorn, but the world of Monsters Night has been a group collaboration between Lexi C. Foss, Mila Young, and yours truly!

The idea began way back when Lexi and I were writing Hell Fae—a series we co-write together in our fae universe—and as part of that world, Nightmare Fae were created. We quickly realized the large span of creatures hidden under the surface and the lore that was full of kingdoms, exciting worlds, and even new dimensions.

We knew we couldn't do this alone, so when the concept came up of an annual Monsters Night where monsters "hunt down" their new mates, we approached Mila Young to join us. Mila is a powerful author with vibrant stories, and it feels like this world wouldn't have been complete without her.

Each story is written as a standalone with a new heroine and her mates. Sometimes you'll encounter a member of a village intended to find her monster mates. Or perhaps you'll find yourself in one of the Elite Cities where political games are afoot. Regardless, I hope you're enjoying this world as much as I am, because we have a lot more for you!

Reverse Harem Paranormal Romance - Never Choose.

J.R. Thorn is a Reverse Harem Paranormal Romance Author who loves coffee, stormy weather, and heated discussions with her inner muse. She can often be found scribing her steamy stories in her writing cave far away from the prying eyes of her toddler, husband, two vocal cats, and canine pack.

www.AuthorJRThorn.com

facebook.com/BloodStoneSeries

amazon.com/stores/J.R.-Thorn/author/B01LYC5DM9

tiktok.com/@authorj.r.thorn

# RECOMMENDED READING ORDER

All Books are Standalone Series listed by their sequential order of events

**Standalone Stories**

Taste Me

Their Blood Queen

Dragonrider Academy

**Elemental Fae Universe Reading List**

Elemental Fae Academy: Books 1-3

Midnight Fae Academy

Fortune Fae Academy

Fortune Fae M/M Steamy Episodes

Candela

Winter Fae Queen

Hell Fae

**Blood Stone Series Universe Reading List**

**Recommended Reading Order is Below**

**Seven Sins (Books 1-3)**

*Book 1: Succubus Sins*

*Book 2: Siren Sins*

*Book 3: Vampire Sins*

**The Vampire Curse: Royal Covens (Books 1-3)**

*Book 1: Her Vampire Mentors*

*Book 2: Her Vampire Mentors*

*Book 3: Her Vampire Mentors*

**Fortune Academy (Part I)**

*Year One*

*Year Two*

*Year Three*

**Fortune Academy Underworld (Part II)**

*Book 3.5: Burn in Hell*

*Book Four*

*Book 4.5: Burn in Rage*

*Book Five*

*Book Six*

*Book 6.5: Burn in Brilliance*

**Fortune Academy Underworld (Part III)**

*Book Seven*

*Book Eight*

*Book 8.5: Burn in Ruin*

*Book 8.666: Burn in Darkness*

*Book Nine*

*Book Ten*

**Crescent Five**

*(Rejected Mate Wolf Shifter RH)*

*Book One: Moon Guardian*

*Book Two: Moon Cursed*

*Book Three: Moon Queen*

*Book Four: Moon Kissed*

**Dark Arts Academy (Vella)**

*Ongoing serial*

*Book One (KU)*

*Book Two (KU)*

**Unicorn Shifter Academy**

- *Book One*

- *Book Two*

- *Book Three*

Non-RH Books (J.R. Thorn writing as Jennifer Thorn)

**Noir Reformatory Universe Reading List**

Noir Reformatory: The Beginning (Standalone)

Noir Reformatory: First Offense

Noir Reformatory: Second Offense

***Noir Reformatory Turns RH from this point with the addition of a third mate***

Noir Reformatory: Third Offense

**Sins of the Fae King Universe Reading List**

(Book 1) Captured by the Fae King

(Book 2) Betrayed by the Fae King

Learn More at www.AuthorJRThorn.com

MAY YOUR
NIGHTMARES
BE BLOODY...
AND WET.